THE SACRIFICE STONE

By the same author

THE HERB GATHERERS
THE EGYPTIAN YEARS
THE SUN WORSHIPPERS
TIME OF THE WOLF
THE QUIET EARTH

ELIZABETH HARRIS

The Sacrifice Stone

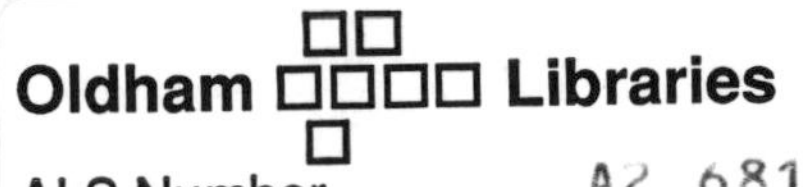

HarperCollins*Publishers*

HarperCollins*Publishers*
77–85 Fulham Palace Road,
Hammersmith, London W6 8JB

Published by HarperCollins*Publishers* 1996
1 3 5 7 9 8 6 4 2

A catalogue record for this book
is available from the British Library

ISBN 0 00 225461 1

Set in Palatino by Rowland Phototypesetting Limited
Bury St Edmunds, Suffolk

Printed and bound in Great Britain by
Caledonian International Book Manufacturing Ltd, Glasgow

For Win Skipper,
an armchair traveller, First Class,

with much love.

Author's Note

Almost all the locations described exist,
but some have yet to be discovered.

Prelude

GLANUM, AD 175

The moon was almost full, its brilliant light dimming the stars in the clear sky. On the lower slopes, the tall juniper trees cast long black shadows on the scrub-covered ground; higher up, where only the thorn bushes grew, the rocks lay bare beneath the night.

The warm earth, remembering the heat of day, gave off scents of dust and of herbs. The noise of the town had ceased, now that midnight was near and its good citizens all abed; no loudly stated opinions echoed from the forum, no sudden female laughter burst from the steps leading down to the sacred well. The small sounds of a dog's bark, a slamming door, were too distant to make more than a momentary impact.

Deep silence covered the hillside: the land was asleep.

A soft breeze breathed down the narrow valley; the long shadows of the conifers wavered against the moonlit hillside.

As the movement ceased, a patch of shade detached itself and began to creep up the slope above the town. Behind it came another, and one more that flanked a shadow of a different shape.

The man, who had waited so patiently in the cramped space under the overhanging rock, watched. He could hear them, despite their efforts to be silent. One of the men was big and ungainly, and the exertion was making him pant. And the young bull, resentful at being led, perhaps in pain from the newly inserted ring through its nose, was giving snorts of anger.

He settled back against the rock. He would be there for a long time yet, he might as well . . .

Suddenly he shot to his feet.

No!

He swallowed the oath before he had made any sound, but the sight of the slim figure darting from tree to tree, tracking the leading group so skilfully that none of them would know it, made his heart race with fury.

For once in his life indecisive, he stood in front of the rock shelter, his thoughts racing.

Then, mind made up, he set off after the others.

High in the hills behind the town lay a fallen monolith, its ancient stone pitted and worn by the harsh sun and the strong winds of Provincia. The moonlight struck the long pale shape as if deliberately illuminating it; it looked like an altar.

Behind, in a shallow dell sheltered by the rocks into which it was built, was a small temple.

From the doorway the temple's interior was dark, apart from the dim and steady light of a candle. The men emerging into the moonlight blinked as their eyes adjusted to the brightness.

The bull bellowed, once, twice, the furious sound so loud in the silence that the very rocks rang. Then anger changed to fear, and the bellow became a squeal which rapidly rose to a high note of pure hysteria.

Abruptly it stopped.

Another cry began, but one not made by any bull.

It was human.

The voice, made shrill by terror, grew louder and more piercing as panic rose. It was a sound to make the skin creep.

Then the nature of the scream changed, and the

sharp tone fuzzed as it trailed off into a bubbling choke.

And the bright, moonlit stone of the monolith gradually darkened as the blood flowed across it.

PART ONE

ARLES

THE PRESENT DAY

1

'You used to do that when you were a kid,' Joe said.

'What?'

'Chew your hair when you were anxious.'

She didn't care for the vaguely patronizing tone. 'Well, you make me nervous.' Damn! Instantly she regretted admitting to it.

'Beth, I'm only asking you to map-read, for goodness's sake. It's me who's having to cope with all this traffic, and driving on the wrong side of the road.'

He was right about the road – although since it was a motorway she couldn't see that it made a lot of difference – but not about the traffic. Since coming off the boat at Calais a couple of hours ago, they'd probably seen scarcely more than a hundred vehicles. It was, after all, the small hours of the morning.

Once upon a time, Beth reflected, glancing down surreptitiously to check that it really was Reims they wanted and she hadn't made a very early boob, Joe would have said 'For God's sake', just like everyone else did. But now he was a theology student – a mature one to boot, and doing an MA – he'd ironed even minor blasphemies out of his speech. Since *The Rector's Wife*, theologians were getting a better press – 'They're human, aren't they, just like you and me?' people would remark, often with slight amazement – but still, it was surprising how many of her girlfriends suddenly cancelled foursome dates in favour of prior engagements when she told them what Joe was studying.

Looking at it honestly, she had to admit that actually

quite a few of the girlfriends lost interest after meeting Joe, not after finding out about the theology; it wasn't what he did but what he was that seemed to put them off.

My brother, she thought, glancing across at him. Staring intently ahead, as if still trying to impress on her how noble he was being in taking on the perilous task of driving, he didn't notice. I've known him all my life, we were pretty close when we were young, and even now, when we don't get together all that often, I'm always glad to see him when we do. Only . . . Only what?

She hesitated over answering the silent question. We're at the very start of a three-week trip together, she thought ruefully, and maybe this isn't the moment for me to be asking myself why my brother irritates me so much.

She decided to think positive. Three weeks in the South of France! Arles, the Camargue, and it won't all be work, Joe's absolutely promised we'll have the occasional day off to find a lovely beach to lie on, with a picnic of bread, local cheese and wine, a jar of black olives and a couple of peaches. And it'll be gorgeous down there now – late enough for all the holidaymakers to be long gone, but not so late that the weather's turned unreliable.

When Joe had proposed that she accompany him on his research trip, she had given the matter only token consideration before saying yes. It wasn't just the attractions of Provence that outweighed any doubts she had over spending three weeks with her brother, it was also what he was planning to research. He was writing the first major thesis of his course, and he had chosen to concentrate on early Christian martyrs, taking a contemporary view of the question of martyrdom and comparing it with the faith of the first centuries AD: the purpose of going to Arles was to investigate the legend of an obscure child saint who had apparently been killed by a Roman officer for refusing to make a sacrifice to the state gods of Rome.

Little Saint Theodore wasn't going to be obscure for

much longer: not only was Joe going to write his thesis – Beth smiled to herself at the thought that one insignificant paper presented in a small-town university was going to rock academia to its foundations – but, far more importantly, it was rumoured that a thirteen-year-old girl had seen a vision. She'd gone to pray in her village church, just outside Arles, taking Madonna lilies to lay before a statue of the Virgin. Stripped of all its trappings of religious mania – Beth reflected ruefully that she was probably more ruthless than most when it came to such stripping – the bones of the story seemed to be that the girl had seen the Virgin point to a plaster effigy of St Theodore, suggesting that the little boy was a worthier recipient of the flowers. The girl had prostrated herself before the boy's statue, and he had smiled down on her, so touched at her gift that real tears had flowed down his cheeks, mingling with the blood issuing from the wounds of his martyrdom.

Beth had been almost sorry to read of the lurid details; until she was asked to believe the impossible, she had kept an open mind on the subject of the Roman officer and the child saint. Against her will – for she was imbued with twentieth-century cynicism – she had found herself touched at the idea of a small boy whose faith was so strong that, pathetically, death was preferable to betrayal of the gentle God he loved. And what a death – Joe had told her, not without a certain relish, that a common method of execution among the Romans was to cut the victim's throat.

'That's what they did to St Theodore,' he had explained, 'and a miracle happened because, even though his head was almost severed from his body, he went on singing Ave Marias till someone found his remains.'

'Like in "The Prioress's Tale",' she had responded eagerly – she'd done *The Canterbury Tales* for O level, and it was always nice to be able to match Joe's sagacity with a bull's-eye of her own.

Joe sniffed. 'That's just a story,' he said dismissively.

'And your Little Saint Theodore isn't?'

He seemed to be taking his time about preparing the clincher, and she smiled to herself. 'No, it isn't. St Theodore really lived – you forget we're talking of an era when history was recorded, so the details of his life can be proved. We know when he died, we can make an educated guess as to how. And there was certainly something miraculous concerning his death, because St Theodore was able to cure throat infections. There are heaps of well-documented cases, up till the early Middle Ages. And now this girl's had her vision!'

He nodded as if to say, so there! But somewhere in his speech for the defence he had shifted his ground, moved from the written records of the administration-minded Romans to the gullible superstition of the medieval religious fanatic. Not to mention that of all the twentieth-century ones busy hurling themselves out of the woodwork. She was sorely tempted to probe, to ask exactly what he meant by well-documented, but she was only too aware what it would lead to: she would become more forceful as she edged him on to the ropes, he'd respond by getting lofty and sanctimonious – he'd once terminated a heated argument about abortion by stating that it was wrong because it wasn't God's will, slamming the door on her furious comment that it was typical of a male to resort to a higher authority when he was cornered – and she'd lose her temper. This time, assuming he hadn't got as far as slamming the door, he'd greet her outburst by smiling condescendingly and remarking that women shouldn't get involved in philosophical discussions, their emotional make-up was too fragile.

Joe, she reflected as the sign for 'Reims Sud' flashed by, had absorbed the doctrine of male supremacy that had ruled in the family home. In spades.

Her thoughts were interrupted: Joe said, 'Do you mind

if I put a tape on? If you're not going to talk, I'd like some music.'

'Carry on.'

She wondered if he'd consult her over what to play. He won't, she thought, it's a major concession that he's asked if I mind in the first place.

She was right: he didn't. Soon the car was filled with the calm, controlled sounds of a choir of monks singing plainsong. She almost laughed out loud; it's not the music, she thought, controlling the impulse – that's enchanting. It's just – oh, God, it's just Joe!

'Hmmm, hmmm, hum,' Joe chanted, singing along with the monks, slightly off-key. 'This is the choir of St Nicetus's monastery. It's in a remote part of Hungary, they have nothing at all to do with modern civilization. Hum, hmmm.'

They're canny enough to make a recording and sell it, she thought, amused at his determination not to see the proof of worldliness staring him in the face. Still, no doubt they give the proceeds to charity.

Joe's humming soon ran out of steam, and, gratefully, she returned to her analysis of his character. Of course, he's just like his father. *Our* father, she corrected herself. Our Father which aren't in heaven, and, if there really is a heaven and any justice in the world, probably won't ever get there. In fact, considering what the old sod is like, Joe's really remarkably well balanced – it must be dear old Mum's influence.

Her mother's face shimmered in her mind's eye, and she was filled with love. Is life any better for her now, with Joe and me away from home and the cause of all those rows no longer there? She doesn't have to try to defend me any more – poor darling, not that she was ever very effective, you could tell her heart wasn't really in it – and she can revert to being the dutiful wife who keeps house and keeps her views, if she has the temerity to possess any, to herself.

A scene from years ago filled her memory. Her mother had just dished up Sunday lunch, the beef slightly burnt because the vicar's sermon had gone on ten minutes longer than it normally did. Joe – a sixteen-year-old Joe, all pimples, testosterone surges and dogmatic opinions – was holding forth about what he was planning to study in the sixth form, and how his long-term career prospects were shaping up. Waiting patiently until he'd finished – they'd eaten the first course by then and were starting on the cabinet pudding, also burnt – Beth ventured to say that her science teacher had recommended she seriously consider going on to do science A levels, as her work was outstanding.

Several unexpected things followed her apparently innocuous remark. Joe gave a disparaging snort and declared, despite the evidence he'd just been given to the contrary, that girls couldn't do science. Her mother, pouring oil on the waters before they were any more than slightly rippled, said timidly, wouldn't it be nicer for Beth to do something useful such as domestic science – and she knows I hate cooking! – or English, which would help towards being a secretary, or . . .

Across the gentle voice came her father's autocratic boom.

'Your brother is quite right, Elizabeth. Science is unsuitable for a girl. Especially biology,' he added enigmatically. He fixed her with a glare. 'I would have thought' – Beth's heart sank as she recognized her father's way of introducing some dictum which immediately became law – 'that education to O level will suffice. Despite the opinions of your science teacher, whom I am sure is a conscientious enough woman in her way,' – he sniffed to express his disapproval, and Beth didn't dare point out that her science teacher was actually a man – 'I see neither the need nor the wisdom of your continuing your scientific studies when you could be employed in some little job.'

She thought he'd finished. God, it was enough! But, after taking another mouthful of cabinet pudding and chewing it a thoughtful twenty times, he said, 'And go to your room for your boastfulness in announcing that your work is outstanding.'

'But –'

There wasn't a but. In Beth's father's book, the man of the house made the rules and everyone else abided by them. Out of touch with modern ways, a man who had married too late, begotten children too late – even been born too late, for he was surely some forgotten relic of the Victorian days of his grandfather – he saw nothing amiss in sending a fourteen-year-old girl to her room for boastfulness.

And I wasn't boasting, Beth thought, furiously punching her pillow, I was only repeating what Mr Thomas said.

I thought that was the end of it, that day. I hadn't made my dream then, the only progress I'd made towards it was to recognize there was something I could do well and promise myself I'd work as hard as I could at it. Then along came good old Father, crushing out the flame when it was only just starting to flicker.

She had done what she was told for ten more years, leaving school after O levels to take a year's shorthand and typing course. Mr Thomas had been quite right: although her grades for five of the eight subjects were only average, for physics, chemistry and biology she got 'A's. Mr Thomas had made a last-ditch attempt to persuade her to stay on; for the final time she'd explained she couldn't – 'for family reasons', she'd said, and Mr Thomas, who had met her father on a parents' evening, seemed to understand. Nevertheless, when he'd turned away, he'd looked as sad as if she'd been his own daughter.

The shorthand and typing course had been okay, and as soon as she'd got her certificate she started work; her first job was in an estate agent's office, where, in addition to polishing her secretarial skills, she picked up quite a lot of information that was to stand her in good stead later, when she bought her first flat. After several years there, she'd worked for a firm selling folding bicycles, and when the short-lived craze died down found herself out of a job. The remarks over the Sunday lunch table became acerbic within a fortnight – her father left her in no doubt as to what he thought of offspring who expected to sponge off their parents when they were perfectly capable of earning their keep, which was somewhat hypocritical in view of the fact that Joe was then doing his first degree and wrote home repeatedly for extra funds, which were always dispatched immediately. Unable to find a permanent post – there was just nothing being advertised – Beth joined a temping agency.

Her father, predictably, disapproved. He'd seen something on TV about temps, and had got it into his head that they were universally flighty. For some inexplicable reason, he also thought they were all on the look-out for husbands. Beth, who couldn't begin to see why a temp should be more desperate for marriage than the next woman, kept her peace and maintained a low profile.

She almost didn't take up the second post which the agency offered her. It sounded excruciatingly dull, the journey was inconvenient, and throughout the weekend before she was due to start work she'd had an appalling cold.

But she went. Family conditioning – you went to work unless you were on your deathbed – made sure of that.

For the first time, she was grateful for that family conditioning. The dull, inconvenient job had turned out to be the next step on the way to her all-but-forgotten dream: she had never looked back.

And now, she thought, turning the map over to see how far it was from the intersection of the motorways at Beaune to the next service area where they might stop for a coffee, now I'm on the very brink. The way has opened up, all the years of effort seem to be paying off, and I'm –

A large blue sign by the roadside said *Aire de Meursault*; under the writing were the symbols for petrol, lavatories, food and drink.

Joe said, 'I'm dying for a pee. We'll stop, shall we?'

'I'm dying for a coffee and something to eat. Yes, let's.'

The combination of her recent thoughts and the imminent prospect of hot strong coffee made her suddenly very happy: she reached out for Joe's hand and gave it a squeeze. Smiling, he squeezed back.

They had two large cups of coffee each and a hot croissant, and went back to the car revitalized.

'Nearly midday,' Joe remarked.

'Nearly one o'clock,' she corrected. 'You've forgotten to put your watch forward an hour.'

'So I have.'

While he did so, she considered the idea she'd just had. Looked at from every angle, it still seemed sensible, especially as Joe was stifling a yawn.

'You've been driving for hours,' she said before she could change her mind. 'You must be tired, even after two coffees. Why don't I do a stint?'

'You?' Looking up from adjusting his watch, his expression was a mixture of amusement and incredulity.

'Yes. Me.'

'You've never driven on the continent!'

'No, but it doesn't look too demanding.' Was that a mistake? she wondered. Perhaps I should have pandered to male vanity and said, Gosh, it's clearly hugely difficult and you've done marvellously, Joe, I can only hope to do half as well.

Joe was frowning. 'How long have you been driving?'

'Twelve years.' Two years longer than you, she could have pointed out; she'd passed her test a month after her seventeenth birthday, overtaking Joe, who had taken two unsuccessful attempts and then given up for six months.

'You'd be insured,' he muttered, 'that'd be okay.' He was still frowning, but she thought he might be about to give in.

'Shall I drive for a few miles and see how I get on?' she suggested. 'There seem to be plenty of these "*Aire*" places, I can pull into one and we can change back if I can't manage it.' She had to grind out the words – Of course I'll manage! she wanted to shout.

'All right, then.' Joe handed her the keys. 'You'll need to put the seat forward.'

I'll need to put it *back*, she thought, doing so quickly while he was still making his way round to the passenger seat, I've got longer legs than you. And not all women drive with their chins pressed anxiously to the top of the steering wheel, some of us are quite relaxed about it.

It wasn't easy, accelerating down the slip road into the now-heavy traffic when she wasn't used to joining a motorway from the right and having to look over the other shoulder. Especially as Joe's car seemed to have a particularly large blind spot exactly where she was trying to look.

'Yes – no – go on – STOP!' Joe shouted contradictorily.

Ignoring him, serenely she pulled out into the inside lane in her own time and at her own pace. For a few hundred yards she tucked in behind a Renault truck then, when the middle lane was clear, signalled, accelerated and moved out. She glanced down at the speedometer – 75 mph – and decided to settle for staying behind a Mercedes doing about the same.

'Aren't you going a bit fast?' Joe said after a few minutes.

'No, I don't think so.' She realized she'd sounded snappy. 'But it's your car. If you think I'm pushing it too hard, I'll slow down.'

'She can cruise at a good eighty!'

Wisely, Beth opted to stay at seventy-five.

'Watch that Merc! What's he doing?' Joe said after a while, making her jump.

'He's driving steadily along in front of us minding his own business.'

'Supposing he stops suddenly?'

'I'm leaving a big enough gap to stop too. Anyway, it's hardly likely, is it? People don't just stop in the middle of a motorway.'

'There's the Chalon turn!' he shouted.

Almost thrown into panic, she remembered in time they didn't have to take it. 'So it is.' She wondered if he was doing it on purpose.

In case he had any more little surprises, she said, 'Would you have a look at the map and see if you can work out how far it is to Lyons?'

'Why?'

To give you something to do to get you off my back, was the honest answer. 'Oh, someone told me the traffic could get very thick round Lyons, and I was wondering if we might aim to get the other side before we stop for our picnic lunch.'

For some time she heard him muttering as he totted up the distances between the markers. 'Two hundred and sixteen miles.'

'*What*? I think you've made a mistake.' Actually she knew he had: while he'd been bent over the map she'd seen a sign by the road saying Lyons was seventy-nine kilometres, which according to her maths was about fifty miles. She said, laughing, 'You've probably added in a couple of road numbers.'

He'd gone huffy, she could tell by the way he suddenly seemed fascinated by something out of the passenger side window.

She was about to make some placatory remark, then decided not to. Damn it, why should I placate him because his maths is lousy and his map-reading so rudimentary that he can't *see* it couldn't possibly still be over two hundred miles to Lyons?

'If you're not going to talk,' she said levelly, 'I suggest we have some more of your Hungarian monks.'

It was well into the afternoon before they were the other side of Lyons – the traffic had indeed thickened – and after they'd eaten the sandwiches she'd brought from home, they spread Joe's car-rug out on the grass and both had a sleep.

She woke to find him kneeling down beside her with a steaming cup of coffee. 'I got us both one, from the shop,' he said, grinning at her obvious pleasure. 'A man has to keep his research assistant happy!'

'Thanks, Joe. Just what I needed.' She took a few sips, feeling the caffeine bump her into alertness. In the general bonhomie engendered by a good lunch and a snooze in the sun, she added, 'And I'm looking forward very much to the research.'

'You'll be a wizz at taking notes.' He glanced at her. 'Dad was right, that shorthand course does come in useful.'

He winked at her, and she realized he was joking. Steady, Joe, she thought, it's best not to joke about things like that.

Don't be so touchy, she told herself as he took their empty cups over to a rubbish bin. Even if he'd been serious, it shouldn't matter to me if my brother and my father still think a woman's place is as a permanent assistant, that she must never aspire to the top slot. I knew Father was wrong, even then, and I've always been able to shrug off Joe's disparaging remarks.

Her thoughts flew back to home, to the post she'd just left and to what awaited her when she got back.

Smiling, folding up the rug and getting back into the driver's seat, she thought, if every man in the world agreed with Father, it wouldn't matter *now*.

2

They reached Arles in the early evening. Both worn out – they had been driving hour-on, hour-off since the late lunch stop – it was, Beth felt, a tribute to both of them that they didn't start yelling at each other when they couldn't find the house.

One of Joe's fellow students had an aunt with a house in Arles, and she had taken pity on her nephew's friend and let it at a reduced rent. So reduced that, on enquiring how much Joe had paid in order to give him her share, Beth decided the house must be a bit of a tip. Driving round the narrow and confusing streets of the old part of Arles, trying to read French street names, she prepared herself for the worst.

Finally they saw a newsagent's shop that was fortunately still open, and bought a street map.

'*There* it is!' Beth shouted after they had pored over it for several minutes. 'Place de la Redoute. Oh.'

'What's up?'

'Nothing,' she said brightly. It would be too depressing to tell him how disappointed she was that the Place de la Redoute, far from being tucked away intriguingly inside the old town, appeared to be right on one of the two huge modern boulevards to the south and east of it. Directing him through the light traffic, she wondered idly what a *redoute* was.

'Boulevard des Lices . . . that's right . . . Now, we have to turn left in a minute, it's another big road called Boulevard Emile Combes . . . *there*!'

Joe swung the car across the road, smiling with triumph. She didn't like to tell him he'd just cut up a man on a bicycle; apart from being furiously angry, the man seemed to be perfectly all right. 'Now it's just up here on the left . . . oh, dear.'

On the left was a forbidding city wall, unbroken except for a narrow flight of steps.

'What now?' Joe asked through gritted teeth.

She stared frantically at the map. 'Go on,' she said, hurriedly deciding. 'There's a way through the walls further up the road. Yes, that's it – now go left . . . keep on . . . and it should be at the end.'

It was. A blue sign on the ancient wall said Place de la Redoute, and, answering another worry that had been growing in her mind, there was even a small car park. Joe backed into a space, and, switching off the engine, looked across at her, smiling broadly.

'Now we just have to find the house,' she said, smiling back.

'It's called La Maison Jaune,' he said. 'Not very original – Martin's aunt must be a Van Gogh fan.'

'Perhaps we'll find his ear,' she remarked.

'That one, do you think? It's certainly yellow.'

She looked where he was pointing. On the level above them, a spur of the old city wall apparently forming part of its boundary, was a low tile-roofed house made of yellow stone. On the end facing them was a colonnaded terrace, healthy-looking greenery rambling over and between the graceful arches.

She recalled how much rent they were paying. 'It can't be. It's far too lovely.'

'I bet it is.' He was getting out of the car. 'There aren't any other yellow houses in the square.'

She followed him to the flight of steps leading up to the terrace. On the gate at the top it said, 'La Maison Jaune'.

He had a set of keys in his hand. Swiftly he took the

padlock off the gate, then ran up the remaining steps and unlocked the door. Turning on lights, she saw they were in a terracotta-tiled hall; on the telephone table was a note addressed to Joe.

'It's the right place, no doubt about it.' She didn't think there had been any need to tell her. 'Martin's aunt says welcome, linen's in the cupboard on the landing, and there's a restaurant round the corner if we arrive too late to shop.'

Suddenly hot food was what she wanted more than anything. Preferably accompanied by a bottle of wine. 'What are we waiting for?'

'Don't you want to unpack?'

'No. I want to eat.'

He laughed suddenly. 'So do I. Come on!'

They unpacked no more than overnight necessities on arriving back: Beth had got her bottle of wine, and, when they'd finished a wonderfully filling meal of fish soup followed by an unidentified but delicious white sea fish with a mussel sauce, Joe threw caution to the winds and ordered a couple of brandies.

Trying to make up the beds, Beth decided that smooth sheets and nice hospital corners were beyond her: I'm too tired, she thought, and not entirely sober. I'll do it properly in the morning.

Her room looked out to the back of the house; the old city wall ran along beneath her window. Joe called out, 'Better close your shutters – I've just swatted a mozzie.'

She did so, although it seemed a shame to shut out all that beauty and atmosphere. We'll get some of those electric things tomorrow, she thought as she lay down. And we could get a . . .

Her mind was wandering. Almost asleep, she saw again the long miles of motorway, cars flashing by. The hills of Provence rose up ahead, and a brilliant sun beat down on a rocky hillside. Junipers cast deep shadow on the pale land.

The dream had begun.

The sunshine of her dreams greeted her in the morning. As she went through into the kitchen – also tiled with terracotta, bright blue crockery against pale yellow walls making a satisfying contrast – she noticed that the tiles under her bare feet felt warm where the sun fell on them.

There was coffee in the larder, but no milk except for a jar of creamer. She made herself a cup, taking it out on to the terrace.

The quiet peace of the house and the garden – which was informal, and sightly overgrown – seemed to settle round her: this, she thought as she sank into an old-fashioned wooden steamer chair, is going to be heaven. And to think I was expecting it to be a tip! Sorry, Martin's auntie.

Half an hour later there was still no sign of Joe. She had a shower, finished unpacking her bag, made her bed with corners her mother would have approved, and brought in from the car Joe's box of books, leaflets and notes; she couldn't see his laptop computer, and decided he must have taken it into his room.

The next thing's shopping, she thought. I'll tell Joe I'm going out.

She knocked on his door, then banged, then went in. He seemed to be fast asleep, but, watching, she saw his eyelids twitch.

'Aren't you going to get up? It's gone eleven.'

'I'm so tired!'

She stifled the urge to say she was too, but it hadn't stopped her doing the unpacking. 'We need to go shopping.'

'Money's in my wallet.'

'I've got money! I just wondered if you wanted to come too.'

He opened his eyes and gave her a winning smile. 'Not much. Can't you go?'

'I suppose so, if I can find the shops.'

He muttered, 'Great girl, my sister.'

'But do get up, Joe! While I'm out, you could see to your books and things – I've brought the box in, but I just dumped it in the hall, and we'll keep falling over it.'

'Yes, fine. I'll do it.' He turned his back and pulled the sheet up over his head.

'Okay, then. See you later.'

He grunted a reply.

She took the map with her, and asked the first passer-by to show her the way to *les magasins*. The passer-by – an elderly man full of Gallic charm – took her by the arm and walked her the few hundred yards to a small supermarket, bowing in farewell and wishing her *bonne journée*.

She spent some time wandering up and down the aisles, filling her trolley with bread, cheese, pâté, eggs, tins of cassoulet, and the odd necessity such as washing powder, a couple of anti-mosquito gadgets and a pack of tablets to burn in them. Then, coming to the drinks section, she had to move everything to one end of the trolley to make room for wine, beers and a bottle of pastis.

Packing the lot into five incredibly heavy plastic bags, she wished she hadn't been so profligate. Or, a better alternative, that she'd made Joe go with her.

By the time she had struggled back to La Maison Jaune, she was wishing it even more fervently. Pushing the door open, she called out, 'Joe? Can you come and give me a hand, I'm –' and fell over the box of books.

He was still asleep when she burst into his room, but not for long. 'You lazy bugger!' she said furiously. 'You *said* you'd move that bloody box!'

'I will, I will,' he muttered.

'It's too late! I've just fallen over it, carrying all the shopping!'

'Oh, dear.' He sat up, rubbing his eyes. 'Anything broken?'

'No,' she admitted.

'That's all right, then.'

'Look at my knee!' She bent her leg and pushed her knee under his nose. 'It'll be swollen as hell later!'

'Beth, your language!' he said mildly.

She'd had enough.

Moving away from his tousled bed, she stood in the doorway. 'I'm going out,' she said quietly. 'I've done my share of work for today. You can unpack your books and put the shopping away while I'm out.'

'What about lunch?'

She glared at him.

'There's plenty of food in the five bags spilling their contents all over the hall.' She hesitated, knowing he really didn't like swearing, but decided that at that moment she didn't care. 'Get your own sodding lunch.'

Outside in the square, she realized she'd forgotten the map. Since going back inside when she'd just stormed out would undoubtedly undermine the grand gesture, she decided she'd manage without it. If I get lost, she fumed, it'll just serve him right.

She didn't bother to work out the logic of that.

She turned left, and marched off parallel to the wall. I'm inside it here, she thought, if I go and look down – she went over and climbed up on to a step in the wall that made a viewpoint – I'll see that road we turned off last night.

There it was, just below her.

So the old town must be behind me. I wonder if these ramparts go all the way round?

Ramparts, redoubts. Suddenly she realized what had

evaded her the previous evening: Place de la Redoute must be Redoubt Square, and a redoubt, of course, was a fortification.

If I'd remembered that at the time, I'd have known the house was in the old town.

She wandered on, seeing few people, only an occasional car pushing past her in the narrow street. Up to her left, she spotted what looked like the rear of a church; in the absence of any better plan, she thought she might make her way round to the front and have a look inside.

She lost sight of it behind the jumbled buildings of the old town but, by bearing left and left again, soon found herself in a square, at the end of which was the church.

The door was closed, but opened when she lifted the latch. A young woman was arranging flowers, and she looked up and nodded to Beth. Nodding back, Beth moved across to the far wall and inspected the first of a series of little shrines set into it.

St Joseph, holding Jesus in his arms. Several worshippers had lit candles to him. She wondered irreverently if they were people who'd come adrift with DIY-ing the new bookshelves.

Stop it, she told herself. Just because I'm cross with Joe, there's no need to take against the whole Christian world.

She walked slowly on. The church had a serene atmosphere, and she was calming down with every step. In front of the next shrine, someone had placed an arrangement of vine leaves and ripe corn; admiring its artistry, at first she didn't take in the statue.

Then she looked up. The boy was young, only a child, with fair hair and, considering they were in southern France, improbably blue eyes. He had an expression of piety, somewhat marred by a crack in the stone across his throat that made him look like a cartoon Frankenstein's monster, head sewn on to neck with ludicrously clumsy stitches . . .

It wasn't Frankenstein's monster. And it wasn't a crack across the neck, it was a deliberately painted gash.

The child had had his throat cut.

Although the statue was crude, with chocolate-box details and insipid pastel colours, the cut throat had a power to shock which made her knees shake and the sweat break out across her back.

There was a handwritten notice at the boy's feet. Leaning forward, fighting the dizziness, she read it.

St Theodore d'Arles.

Joe, Joe, she cried silently, I've found your boy!

Eyes returning to the child, she noticed he was pointing to the wound in his neck; remembering Joe's story that the little saint could cure sore throats, she realized why. There were several ceramic plaques fixed to the wall behind the shrine, most bearing a simple 'Merci', sometimes with a date. The latest date was 1955: for a medieval superstition, the reputation of St Theodore's legendary abilities had endured pretty well.

Still feeling slightly sick – and cross with herself for being so susceptible – she went to sit down in one of the pews. The young woman, who was now placing fresh votive candles in front of the shrines, glanced at her. I wonder if she wants me to go? Beth thought. Then: why on earth should she? I'm not doing her any harm – my scepticism can't possibly show.

For a moment, forgetting she was angry with Joe, she thought she would rush straight home and tell him what she'd found. Then, getting up and walking out of the church, she changed her mind and set off to continue her exploration.

She crossed the square into a narrow street sloping steeply downhill, lined with tall houses. Some of them had washing hanging on poles outside. A man watering his potted plants smiled at her.

The street curved round in a tight bend, then opened out on to a wider road.

Staring at what stood immediately in front of her, she thought she must be imagining it.

Vast and solid at the top of a wide flight of steps, its double tier of arched walls soared up into the blue sky and curved away to either side in perfect symmetry. It was huge, dominating the scene and crowding out all the little houses, shops and bars that huddled around it as if flexing its great muscles and shouldering them away.

At first she just stood and stared. Then, coming back to herself, she wondered what it could be, answering her own question instantly: it's an amphitheatre.

She felt illogical tears start in her eyes. I didn't *know*, she thought, angrily brushing them away. I'm so ignorant that I had to actually stand here looking at it before I realized there was a Roman amphitheatre in Arles!

Ashamed, she had the fleeting feeling that everyone must be jeering at her, pointing accusing fingers and saying, *she* didn't know! She's stupid!

Stop being ridiculous, she told herself. It's not down to me, it's my family's fault, them and their dreadful, archaic attitude that you only need educate your sons, it doesn't matter about your daughters, all they're going to aspire to is to be someone's secretary or someone's cook. It's certainly not necessary to tell them about the Roman occupation of Provence.

'Damn you, Father,' she muttered.

The emotion ebbing, she was surprised at how much it could still hurt. Here, I'm miles from home and it's years since I used to be so in awe of him, so spineless that I couldn't summon the guts to rebel, yet the resentment is as strong as if he'd only just this minute put my school report in the drawer without even glancing at it.

'You can't get at me any more,' she said softly. 'Not now.'

She crossed the road to the steps, walking slowly up them, the amphitheatre rising up above her till it blotted out the bright sky. There was an entry booth under one of the deep archways into the arena, beside it a notice informing her of the opening times and how much it cost to go in. She was reaching in her bag for money when the thought came: not yet.

No, she thought, rationalizing, now probably isn't the moment. In all fairness, I ought to wait for Joe. And besides, it's very hot – it's the middle of the day, and there's not a cloud in the sky.

She moved away from the entrance; observing that it was possible to walk round the arcaded walls on the outside, she set off, keeping close to the massive stones where there was some shade.

Peering through the arches into the shadowy galleries inside, she wished she were better informed. On a building opposite she noticed a poster advertised bullfights; the Romans used their amphitheatre for something fairly similar, didn't they? They had gladiators, she thought, fighting each other with peculiar weapons – nets that they flung over their opponents, long ropes with hooks on – and they also fought wild beasts. The crowd could vote for whether a beaten gladiator should be executed or not – they shut their thumbs inside their fists if they wanted him to live, or put their thumbs out if he was to die. Then sometimes the beasts would be set to fight each other – they used to bring back exotic wild animals from all over the Empire, to satisfy the crowd's perpetual desire for something new. And they threw Christians to the lions, when they weren't cutting their throats.

An echo of the dizziness came back: she made herself stride on.

What a feat of architecture! She stared up at the walls, deliberately turning her thoughts away from Christian martyrs. Here it's stood since – since – oh, for a couple of thousand years, roughly, and it looks as if it will last for ever.

A group of people were walking round inside the gallery, being addressed by a guide. I'd like to do that, Beth thought, I'd like someone telling me about it, filling in the enormous gaps in my knowledge.

The group moved on round the structure's curve and out of sight. She stood looking after them into the deserted arcade, where patches of brilliant light alternated with deep shade. On the far side of the gallery, she could see steps leading down into deeper darkness, and she seemed to feel the chill, clammy air rise up from underground to disperse in the sunlight.

She started to shiver.

This is crazy! Here I am, standing in the full sunshine in a temperature that must be well up in the eighties, and I'm shivering!

She swayed slightly, and, stepping forward, leaned against the wall for support. Perhaps it's something I ate – perhaps one of last night's mosquito bites has infected me with something – God, but I feel awful!

Staring into the gallery, she saw something move. Something dark, a deeper black against the dense shade, it seemed to be issuing from the steps on the far side like some foul miasma that welled up from the underworld.

There was despair in the air, and she was overcome with a hopeless sorrow. Here we sit, awaiting our turn, and nothing can save us. We must renounce our God or die; since we will not abandon our faith, there is only death.

She pulled away from the wall, wrenching her head round so that she was no longer gazing into the dark.

Daylight, people, that's what I need. I'm letting my imagination run away with me, and I didn't even know I had one!

On woolly legs, she broke into a staggering run, away,

away from the amphitheatre and its ancient miseries. Down the long flight of shallow steps, past a crowd of cheerful tourists laughing as they listened to their guide cracking a joke, and suddenly there in front of her was a bar. A wonderful, sunlit bar, where nice ordinary people sat drinking coffee and cold glasses of beer.

She collapsed into a seat, putting her elbows on the table and dropping her head into her hands. A voice said, 'Madame?' and she looked up to see a concerned waiter beside her.

'Oh – *une pression, s'il vous plaît. Une demie.*'

'*Une pression. D'accord.*'

He was back within moments, and gratefully she drank a few sips of beer. The faintness receded, and she drank some more. By the time she had finished it, she was feeling so much better that she wished she'd ordered *une grande*.

She paid her modest bill, then, ready for anything and more than prepared to make Joe's life hell if he hadn't done his unpacking, she swung her bag over her shoulder and headed back towards the Place de la Redoute.

3

She got home to find that Joe had unpacked all the shopping and put it tidily away. He had also, she observed from the hall, turned the living-room table into a desk, with laptop, books, papers and stationery arrayed as if he was going to start work at any moment.

He'd also cooked supper: she could smell onions and garlic as she came in the door.

'I'm sorry about earlier,' he said as she entered the kitchen, where he was washing pans. 'Supper's ready when we want it.'

'What have you made?'

'A sort of ratatouille thing – I found a market down on the main road, and the veggies looked so good I couldn't resist them.'

'I didn't know you could cook.' It was an aspect of her brother she'd never suspected. Where had he learned? Not from their mother – Father would never have allowed anything as exotic as ratatouille on *his* dinner table.

'I shared a flat with a chap who was dead keen.' He opened the oven and peered at his casserole. 'I got fresh fruit for pud – okay?'

'Lovely. Let's have a drink out on the terrace. I've got something to tell you.'

He was so excited about her discovery that he wanted them to go and look there and then.

'The church is bound to be closed up now, it's well after six,' she said.

'I suppose so.' He sat back in his chair. 'It's all but unbelievable – the very first church you come across, there he is!'

'Surely it must be mentioned in one of those books?'

He shook his head. 'If it is, I haven't seen it.'

'Well, maybe the majority of Arles churches have a statue of St Theodore.'

It seemed likely to her, but he was apparently determined to look on it as a minor miracle. 'No, I'm sure they haven't. It really is amazing, I can't get over it.'

'Have another drink,' she said, reaching out to top up his wine. 'I always find that alcohol helps me keep my feet on the ground.'

He smiled. 'It has the reverse effect on most people.'

'Let's look it up after supper,' she suggested.

He looked at her gratefully. 'I was going to propose we got down to work later, only I was afraid you'd think I'd done supper and everything just to soften you up.'

She laughed. 'I might well have done. Don't worry, I'm getting as eager as you.' She glanced at him. 'Well, nearly.'

The evening was bringing about a steep increase in mosquito activity, so they went into the kitchen to eat. Joe's ratatouille was delicious, and afterwards he did the washing-up. By the time they were sitting at Joe's improvised desk, she was sufficiently grateful to work for as long as he liked.

'Right,' he said decisively. 'I suggest I give you a brief précis of what I've done so far, and perhaps find you something to read by way of background. Then we'll list what I need to look at here, and tomorrow we can get on with visiting the sites and trying to find sources in libraries. And we'll get out to the village where the girl had her vision.'

The light in his eyes made her think he was probably hoping for a similar experience. To bring him back to earth she said, 'How did you come across Little Saint Theodore?'

'In a huge tome in the university library on early Christian martyrs.'

'I hadn't realized there were enough of them to fill a huge tome.'

'Well, the authors admit that some of the stories are probably apocryphal. You get the same details being mentioned in several cases, so it's possible that the martyrdom aspect sometimes got grafted on afterwards.'

'Why?'

'Because it would bring visitors to a place if they could claim a canonized martyr, particularly if the saint had a few miracles accredited to him. Or her.'

'Like St Theodore and the sore throats.'

'Exactly. You often get a link between the method of martyrdom and the ailment the saint can cure. Or else it becomes the saint's emblem – St Lawrence, for example, was roasted on a gridiron, which appears as his. And St Agatha had her breasts cut off, and she's often depicted carrying them on a plate. Funnily enough, she's the patron saint of bell-founders, because of the resemblance of breasts to bells.'

Beth didn't think it was funny. 'God. I'm not sure I'm going to enjoy this after all.'

'You haven't heard anything yet.' He was reaching out for one of the books. 'I'm just about to tell you what Nero did for illumination in his gardens.'

'I don't think I want to hear.'

'Oh, but it's important.' He put down the book and stared at her. 'Are you serious?'

'No, go on.' I said I'd help him, she thought. I can't back out just because I'm squeamish about two-thousand-year-old atrocities.

'Well, the Christians were a high-profile target for popular hatred from early times, although the ancient writers don't specify exactly why. Perhaps it was just because they thought differently, and didn't try to hide it. Anyway, when a fire started in Nero's new palace which destroyed half of Rome, he diverted suspicion from himself by accusing the Christians of arson. Just to fuel public anger a bit more, he also said they were cannibals and practised black magic and incest. The Romans always enjoyed savage spectacles, the bloodier the better, and Nero obliged them by crucifying a few Christians in his garden and setting light to them.'

She swallowed. 'But Nero was potty. They didn't all carry on like that, did they?'

'No. In the main, the Roman administration tolerated worship of any god, although of course there were the officially approved state gods that had to be recognized. They were pragmatists – provided you paid your taxes and your private worship didn't threaten the security of the state, then what you believed was between you and your conscience.'

'So how did all those people in your tome get to be martyrs?'

'Because Christianity grew so fast, and the faith of its adherents was so strong, that it threatened to wipe out all other religions.' His voice became more powerful as he spoke: she thought, I must bear in mind he's not exactly an objective witness in all this.

'The Christians became scapegoats,' he went on. 'In the second century AD, the general view seems to have been that everything dreadful that happened, from plague to earthquakes, was down to the Christians, as punishment for not worshipping the Roman gods. And, to whip up the hatred, the Christians got accused of the same old things Nero had thrown at them a century earlier.'

'You told me before that your St Theodore was killed for refusing to worship the Roman gods.'

'Well, bearing in mind what the Romans believed refusal led to, it's not surprising it made people like Theodore public enemy number one.' He leaned forward eagerly, riffling through a slim book. 'Listen to what Tertullian had to say – he was a Christian convert – "If the Tiber reaches the walls, if the Nile does not rise to the fields, if the sky doesn't move or the earth does, if there is famine, if there is plague, the cry is at once, Christians to the lion."'

He passed the book to her. She read where he was pointing. 'He went on to say, "What, all of them to one lion?"' She hadn't expected to find an early Christian with a sense of humour.

He appeared not to have heard. 'Matters went from bad to worse around the middle of the second century,' he said, 'culminating in persecutions in Smyrna, Rome and in Lyons.'

'What, Lyons that we drove past yesterday?'

'Yes.' He sounded slightly impatient. 'Of course. They held an annual festival of games there, and it was cheaper to use Christians as wild-beast fodder than trained gladiators. They rounded up all the Christians in the town, subjected them to a mockery of a trial, and tortured their slaves to make them confess to witnessing all sorts of unlikely acts carried out by their masters and mistresses. If the Christians didn't recant – and they didn't – they were chucked into prison, from where the only exit was out into the arena to face the animals.'

The sense of despair she'd felt earlier, outside the amphitheatre, came back fleetingly. 'Did they do that here, too? Make the Christians face the animals?'

'They did it everywhere.' He waved his hand expansively. 'Round about that time – it was during the reign of Marcus Aurelius – the entire Christian church was under attack. God was too important to the Christians,' – he wagged his finger at her – 'and their utter devotion to Him meant, in the Romans' eyes, that they must be failing in their loyalty to the emperor and the state. So there you have it – their lack of civic duty cast them in the one role the Romans wouldn't tolerate.'

'Their worship was threatening the security of the state,' she said, remembering his exact words.

He looked gratified. 'Excellent! You've got the picture.'

'I find it hard to believe that a child would die for its faith,' she said. 'Adults, yes, especially if they were convinced they were going on to a better world. But surely it goes against any concept of self-preservation for a child to accept death rather than worship an alien god? After all, how much does religion matter to your average child?'

'You're looking at it from a twentieth-century viewpoint. But children are capable of such actions, if they believe strongly enough they're doing the right thing. Look at Jude's son in *Jude the Obscure*, who killed his brothers and sisters and then himself "because we are too menny".'

'That, as you said in another context, is just a story!' she protested. 'And anyway, I've always felt it's a very weak bit of plotting by Hardy – like your Little Saint Theodore offering his teeny throat to be cut, it's just not likely.'

'St Theodore's martyrdom happened,' he said stubbornly, frowning at her levity.

'How do you know? Go on, give me chapter and verse, and win me over to your view.'

'Right!' He opened his notebook, so eagerly that she found herself hoping she was going to be convinced. 'He died in AD 175 in a town called Glanum – that's not far from here, it's in the foothills of the Alpilles near St-Rémy-de-Provence, we'll go there. He was tied to a Roman altar in the hills behind the town, and his throat was cut. A man called Lucius Sextus wrote about it, recording how they found the body in the morning, and, although there were wolves scavenging on the hills, by a miracle they hadn't touched him. Not only the wolves – they found the prints of a bull, which seems to have gone right up to the altar yet not touched the child.'

'But bulls are herbivores,' she protested. 'And they

normally leave you alone if you don't move or flap red capes at them.'

He ignored her. 'Here,' – he was showing her his notes – 'there's the reference. I'd have brought the book out with me, only it's so old and valuable it's confined to the library.'

She read the pages of closely written notes. Joe had added some conclusions of his own to what he'd copied from the ancient writings: 'Later references to breath still in body, despite wound; testimonies given that child was heard singing as body prepared for burial. Story that child killed on his way home from choir practice, because he annoyed Roman officer by singing Ave Marias, possibly a later embellishment,' – what a concession! she thought – 'cf. Little Saint Hugh of Lincoln, *c.* 1250. Ave Maria unlikely – of thirteenth-century origin. Poss. another Christian hymn. Check for early forms of worship.'

'Was this Lucius Sextus a Christian?' she asked, looking up.

He wouldn't meet her eyes. 'Yes.'

'I thought he might be,' she muttered.

'Turn the page,' he said neutrally.

She did so. Pasted in the notebook was a photocopied paragraph; above it, in Joe's handwriting, were the words, 'From the magistrate's records, Forum Julii (Fréjus), AD 176.'

The paragraph, fortunately, had been translated from Latin into English, and the magistrate had a fairly readable style:

> In the matter of Theodore of Arles, outbursts of reaction against the punitive measures taken at Glanum have been contained. The determination of the Christian community in the area of Arles, who claim the child as one of their own, contrary to received intelligence, has been countered by application of firm control. Those of the

> community who persisted in the spread of sedition, based on the gossip of women and the garrulity of the credulous, have been removed.

The paragraph concluded with a series of letters, of which she could make no sense.

'What's this?'

'It's abbreviations for the Latin – they did that when the phrases they wanted to write were a well-known and frequently used form of words. Like Fid. Def. on our coins for *Fidei Defensor*, defender of the faith. Here, it's saying that a group of Christian prisoners were tried, condemned, and sent to the amphitheatre at Arles.'

Again, a memory of that ancient despair. When it had subsided, she said, 'I agree that this magistrate's report verifies Theodore's death, if that's what he means by "punitive measures", although there's nothing about him having his throat cut. But, God, the rest of it's pretty vague! What does he mean by the Christian community's determination? To do what? Revere Theodore as a martyr? And what's this about claiming him as their own contrary to received intelligence? That it was said he came from Arles but he didn't really? And here, look, where it says –'

'I'm not saying that these details support the Church's version of St Theodore's martyrdom,' he interrupted, 'I'm merely pointing out that there *was* a child called Theodore, that he was reputed to be from Arles, and that he was killed at Glanum some time before AD 175.' He tapped his hand against the notebook. 'There's the proof.'

Inside her head a voice spoke. Vehemently someone said, *It's not true*. She was about to repeat the words out loud, and it was only with an effort that she did not.

Where, she wondered, did *that* come from?

She shook her head, as if to clear a buzzing in the ears. Then said calmly, 'Okay, I accept that.'

'Thanks,' he said ironically.

She looked up and smiled, relieved to feel so firmly back in the here and now. 'Come on, this is doing you good. You've got to write a convincing thesis about this kid, –'

'Not solely about him. I'm planning to cite several other examples of martyrs.'

'Yes, but the same doubts may well apply to them.'

'I don't have any doubts.'

'Well, you should have! If you'll just let me finish, I was trying to point out that having to argue your case to someone as unconvinced as me is the best thing that could happen. Prove it to me, and you'll prove it to anyone.'

'Typical scientist,' Joe said. 'You don't believe anything till you've proved it in the laboratory.'

'The good old empirical system.' She closed his notebook and handed it back to him. 'Joe, please don't think I'm irrevocably sceptical, because I'm not.' Or at least, she added silently, I don't *think* I am. 'I'm more than willing to traipse all round Arles and the surrounding area with you, and I'll take notes, photographs, anything you want, if it'll help. Will that do?'

She went to stand beside his chair, and he reached up and briefly touched her hand.

'It'll do,' he said.

'Right. I'm off to bed, then. Goodnight.'

'Don't you want a book to read before you go to sleep?' He had selected one, and was holding it out to her.

She looked back over her shoulder. 'If it's about human torches, cutting women's breasts off and other bizarre forms of mutilation and death, no I don't.' She blew him a kiss. 'I'll stick to my nice unviolent *Blue Guide to Provence*, thanks all the same.'

As she shut the door behind her, she thought she heard him mutter, 'Philistine!'

4

Joe kept his impatience more or less in check while Beth drank her second cup of breakfast tea, which he whisked away as soon as she'd finished. Then they set out for the church.

The little saint was still simpering from his plinth; someone had lit a candle, and its soft glow highlighted his pink cheeks. Beth thought he looked remarkably healthy for someone with a slit throat.

She waited at the back of the church for several minutes while Joe stood and gazed. Coming eventually to join her, he said, 'Funny sort of flower arrangement.'

'The vines and corn? Yes, I noticed that yesterday.'

'It's wheat,' he said. 'I wouldn't have thought they grew wheat here, although they did in Roman times. They got a huge cereal harvest from the northern Camargue, and a lot of it was shipped back to Rome.'

'What do they grow there now?'

'Rice, among other things. It's a lot wetter nowadays – they've been operating an irrigation programme since the war.' He turned to look back at St Theodore. 'I'm a bit disappointed, actually.'

'Why? It's got to be your bloke, there can't be two Theodores of Arles.'

'No, I'm sure it's him. It's just that – ' He broke off, frowning. 'Oh, I don't know. I expected to be more affected by him, I suppose. The statue's too . . . too . . .'

'Sentimental.'

'Exactly! It's as if the artist's trying to engage our

sympathy, whereas in fact there's no need because the story itself has already done so.'

She thought that probably applied to the majority of popular religious art, but it didn't seem the moment to say so.

'Have you seen enough?'

'Yes. Let's go.' He held the door open for her.

'What next?' she asked as they crossed the square.

'The Arles guide book says we can buy tickets giving admission to most of the main sights, Roman and otherwise. I thought we might head for one of the sights, get the tickets and make a start.'

She wondered how many main sights there were; perhaps it was better not to know. 'Fine!' she said. 'Where shall we begin?'

'There's a graveyard which was used first by the Romans, and later in medieval times. It's on the map . . .' He stopped to look. 'Yes. Les Alyscamps. Down across our Place de la Redoute, and it's there.' He pointed.

'It doesn't look far.'

He put his map away. 'Nothing's far. The advantage of an ancient city – very compact!'

The graveyard was far enough outside the walls for them to have to cross two busy roads; French drivers, Beth noticed, had no respect whatsoever for pedestrian crossings. It was a relief to walk through the iron gates and into the shade of the thick trees in the cemetery.

A small group of tourists had finished their visit and were just leaving; emerging from the ticket booth, Joe and Beth had the place to themselves.

'It's like a road,' Beth said softly; she was reluctant to break the silence.

'It is a road, or it was. It's the Via Aurelia, the Romans' main route from Italy to Provincia and Spain.'

She digested that. Then: 'Why are there stone coffins all along it?'

'It was strictly against Roman law to bury the dead where people lived, so cemeteries were always well outside the city walls. They often situated them along main roads.'

'How practical to get the populus to stick their sarcophagi along the roadside, and save yourself the cost of kerbstones.'

'Nothing if not practical, the Romans.' He walked over to one of the great coffins. 'Here lies Marcus Ulpius Cerialis.'

'Is that what it says?'

'Not in so many words. It says he was an official of the town, and that his wife Claudia caused this monument to be made. Roman names are fascinating – in their full, formal version they had six elements, and told you the origins of a man's family, where he came from, his voting district, and . . .'

She stopped listening. Somehow Joe's voice was distracting; the ancient graveyard clamoured for her full attention.

She strolled on up the dead-straight road, glancing at the stone sarcophagi on either side. After a hundred yards or so the road opened out, passing either side of a hollow in which were several more coffins. I wonder if there's anything in them? Unlikely, lots of them are damaged – the bones would have been removed and disposed of long ago, I should think.

There were buildings beyond the hollow, an arched entrance and a small chapel; it looked as though the hollow might once have formed the crypt of an older, larger church.

She wandered under the arch, emerging into an overgrown courtyard. A sign on the chapel door said: *Chapel de St Honoré. Fermé.*

On her left, another door led into a small side-chapel. She stepped over the raised threshold.

The high walls were unadorned, but a shaft of sunlight picked out the plain stone altar. Walking forward to examine it more closely, she heard a movement behind her.

For a split second she was terrified. The sound, breaking the utter stillness, was so unexpected that, nerving herself to turn and look, she was imagining unnamed horrors . . .

In the relative darkness of the far corner stood a young man. Although he didn't speak, she sensed he was reassuring her. Don't worry, I won't hurt you. He was tall, fair-haired, and dressed in jeans and a khaki shirt.

Wondering quite what she'd expected, she gave a nervous smile. 'You made me jump,' she said, instantly thinking she should have tried to say it in French: '*Vous m'avez fait sauter*'? She wanted to laugh.

But he replied in English. 'I'm very sorry. I didn't hear you approach, and by the time you were inside, there was no way of letting you know I was here *without* making you jump.'

He *was* English; with relief, she said, 'It's all right. I wouldn't have reacted, only it's so quiet here, you can almost hear the ghosts breathing.'

He stared at her, an intent expression on his face. Then, smiling, he said, 'Can't you just. Which is patently absurd.'

She had the distinct feeling he was making light of something he usually took seriously. 'All those Romans,' she said. 'My brother was telling me just now how they had to be buried out of town.' It seemed a good idea to mention the presence of Joe; you never know, she thought, even the nicest-looking men can turn out to be muggers and rapists. Although probably not simultaneously.

She wished she could stop the urge to break into nervous laughter.

'A sensible precaution, when disease caused the majority of deaths.' She realized he was referring to the out-of-town burials.

'Quite.' She racked her brains for something intelligent to say, but drew a blank.

'Shall we go back into the sunshine?' he suggested. 'There's not much to see in here.'

'Yes, let's. Joe will be wondering where I am.'

Right on cue, Joe's voice calling out, 'Beth?' greeted them as they left the chapel.

'Here. I found another visitor taking advantage of the lack of tour buses.'

'Adam Gilbert,' the man said, holding out his hand to Joe.

'Joe Leighton. My sister, Beth.'

'Have you found what you wanted?' Beth asked him.

'I'm not sure what I did want,' Joe said. 'I've noted down a few of the inscriptions, but there's nothing particularly interesting.'

'What were you looking for?' Adam asked.

Joe glanced at Beth, then said, 'I'm researching various events that happened under the Romans.'

She wondered why he wasn't more specific. He probably has his reasons, she thought, maybe students writing theses get paranoid and imagine other people are going to steal their ideas.

'What about you?' she asked Adam. 'Just having a look?'

'That's about it.' She noticed he was buttoning the flap of his shirt pocket over what appeared to be a small notebook; perhaps he'd been jotting down inscriptions too.

'Where do you want to go now?' She looked at Joe.

'Back into the old town for . . .' He flipped through the guide book. 'The Roman theatre, perhaps, or the Arlaten Museum.'

'Or a cold beer,' she suggested.

'After the theatre,' he said firmly.

'That's my next stop,' Adam said. She'd been rather hoping he might.

'We may as well go together.' Joe set off back towards the road between the coffins. She was unable to tell from his tone whether he was pleased or annoyed to have someone else accompany them; she thought it was more likely to be the latter.

The Roman Theatre was being visited by a large party of Japanese, all of whom seemed to want at least five photographs from every vantage point, so they gave it a miss and went on to the Museon Arlaten. Beth could happily have spent the rest of the morning studying the costumes and the old photographs of citizens of Arles, but there was less to interest Joe; catching up with him by a mock-up of a turn-of-the-century bedroom where a woman had apparently just given birth to a rather pallid infant – better pump some oxygen into *him*, she thought – she asked where Adam was.

'No idea,' Joe said tersely.

'I'll go and look for him.' She wasn't going to ask what was the matter.

'If you must, although I did think we might get through our three weeks without you picking someone up.'

He made it sound as if she picked people up every other day: the sheer absurdity of it made her laugh, once the initial anger faded.

'I didn't pick him up,' she said mildly. 'And if you don't want him with us, that's fine by me.'

It wasn't, since she had decided she definitely liked the look of him, but long experience had taught her that the best thing to do with Joe was imply you wanted the opposite of your real desire, which usually ensured you got your own way.

'It's all the same to me,' he said dismissively.

Taking a deep breath and letting it slowly out again, she said pleasantly, '*That*'s all right, then.'

And went off to find Adam.

They went to the Place du Forum for the cold beer; Van Gogh's Café de Nuit was closed, presumably saving itself for later, and they found a table in the middle of the square, in the shade of trees.

She was aware of feeling tense, and was cross that, even though she should surely have grown out of it, she still allowed herself to be affected by Joe's moods. He was glaring down at his innocuous glass of beer as if analysing it for the presence of hemlock.

'Isn't this jolly?' Adam remarked. She looked up and caught his eye: he seemed to be amused about something.

'It's wonderful,' she said firmly. Lifting her glass, she touched it to his. 'Cheers.'

'Cheers.'

Joe didn't say anything.

'Are you here on holiday, Adam?' Okay, she thought, it's as hackneyed an opening as asking him if he comes here often, but it's the best I can do.

'Not entirely – I'm working too.'

'What at?'

'I've been commissioned by the Beeb to make a film about the great gipsy routes from central Europe down to the Mediterranean. About the whole *gitan* culture, in fact, and how their folklore, music and dances spread down into the south.'

'They came here? To Provence?' It seemed an unlikely journey for middle European gipsies.

'They still do. I was down at Aigues Mortes yesterday, and the plain between the town and the sea was covered in gipsy caravans. There were campfires going, and a gorgeous smell of cooking, and a black-haired girl in a long flounced skirt read my palm for a few pieces of silver – well, for fifty francs. The caravans were great flash ones pulled by cars, admittedly, but the people are the descendants of those who made the trip centuries ago. Or so they claim.'

'You could have stayed in England and studied gipsies,' Joe said. 'A group of them were turfed out of some woods near us last winter, and the filth they left is still there, rotting into the ground.'

'You may be confusing true gipsies with diddicoys,' Adam replied. 'The sort of caravan-dwellers who muck up perfectly good woodland and leave a trail of old prams and bits of Morris Minor chassis are as much an object of disdain to the true Romanies as they are to you. Probably more so, as nobody keeps saying that you and the diddicoys belong to the same group of people.'

Thirty-fifteen, Beth thought, suppressing a smile. Joe made a sound like a snort, but, to his credit, said, 'How do you define a true Romany, then?'

'Romanies are one of a small group of principal families, the others being the Spanish gipsies – the name *gitan* really applies to them – Bohemians and Tziganes, to which we should add the English gipsies. "Romany" has come to be a blanket term for all of them – it was actually first coined by George Borrow to apply to the gipsies who arrived in England in the sixteenth century, and it derived from their own name for themselves, which was Rom, or Romni in the feminine. They themselves called their language Romani.'

'And they all came from central Europe?' Beth asked.

'It's believed they were originally low-caste Indians who spread via Persia to Turkey, Greece, Hungary, the Balkans, and eventually right across to Germany, France and Spain. Because they were dark, it was thought at one time they came from Egypt, hence Gypcians, or gipsies.'

Beth thought how bizarre it was, to be sitting in a café in Arles listening to a pocket lecture on the culture of the gipsies. Her imagination stimulated, she asked, 'Why did they leave India in the first place?'

Adam shrugged. 'Why does any people leave their homeland? Persecution, famine, overcrowding? It's too long ago to say with any certainty.'

'What I was really wondering was why did they leave and not settle somewhere else.'

'Why did they become travellers, you mean?'

'Yes. If persecution or whatever drives you away, you usually find somewhere else that becomes your new homeland. Like that religious sect who ended up in Salt Lake City – who were they, Joe?'

'The Mormons. They had to travel from New York State to Utah to find their new home, with several stops along the way before Brigham Young decided that Salt Lake City was the place.'

'Yes, but their travels were only because they weren't allowed to settle in all the intermediary places, were they?'

'No. They –'

'The combination of extreme religious devotion and outstanding financial success tended to make them unpopular, or so I understood,' Adam put in. 'Isn't that right, Joe?'

She glanced at him, again seeing on his face the look of suppressed laughter. She wondered if it was Joe's air of intensity that was amusing him. 'Joe's a theology student,' she said. Then, noticing Joe's sudden scowl, wished she hadn't.

'Really? Are you at theological college?'

'I'm not training for the clergy, if that's what you mean, no. I'm reading theology for an advanced degree.' He fixed Beth with a fierce glare, and, without knowing quite what she was apologizing for, she mouthed, 'I'm sorry.'

'You were asking why the gipsies went on travelling instead of settling in a new homeland,' Adam reminded Beth.

What a diplomat, she thought. 'I was,' she said gratefully.

'I would guess, from talking to scores of them – some of them claiming to be well over a hundred, with very long memories – the primary reason is that they simply got to love the roaming life. Being travellers, they soon developed skills that suited the way they lived – some of the present-day people speak proudly of ancestors who were acrobats or conjurers, and who would entertain the villagers in the places they passed through. There'd be a dearth of entertainment in an Anatolian village miles from anywhere – you'd probably have sold your grandmother for a troupe of tumblers. And many of them were merchants or craftsmen.'

'Like tinkers, or chair-menders,' Beth suggested. As a child, she'd learned a poem about a chair-mender.

'Yes. And they seem to have had a regular round, if you like, so that on their migrations to and fro across the continent, the same places were visited again and again.'

'You mentioned folklore,' she said. 'Did you mean stories and legends and things?'

'I did indeed. Plus music and songs – in Avignon I watched a group of little girls dancing round an upturned barrel, one of them standing on it and conducting, the rest circling her with linked arms. They were singing a song – singing it beautifully, harmonizing with each other – and when I got closer, I recognized the tune – Dvořák used it for one of his Slavonic Dances. Number seven, in C minor – you know it?' He looked from one to the other of them eagerly. 'Dum, dum da-de dum, dum, dum da-de dum, da de dum-dum da de dum . . .' He broke off. 'Obviously you don't.'

Beth said politely, 'It's vaguely familiar.'

Adam smiled at her. 'I'll take you back to Avignon and we'll see if we can find my little girls. They sing it far better than I do.'

Fine by me, she thought. But she didn't say so.

Joe said suddenly, 'What were you doing in the Alyscamps cemetery? There weren't any ancient gipsies buried there, surely?'

'Joe!' Beth exclaimed. I'm used to him being abrupt, she thought, but really he's too old to act like a suspicious child in front of strangers. And *why* is he suspicious, for God's sake?

'No, there aren't,' Adam said mildly. 'But I did say I was

only partly here in order to work – this morning I was just acting like a tourist.' He smiled at Joe. Then, unexpectedly, said: 'What were *you* doing there?'

'*I* was researching,' Joe said; Beth waited, but just what they'd been researching he didn't seem about to reveal.

This is ridiculous, she thought. 'Joe's writing a thesis about early Christian martyrs,' she said firmly. 'Aren't you, Joe?' He grunted. 'And we're going to spend the next few days immersing ourselves in Roman Arles, so that Joe can find out as many facts as exist about who believed in what, and who killed who because they wouldn't worship this or that god, and –'

'You're making it sound fatuous,' Joe said warningly.

'Joe, I'm not, honestly.' She reached out to pat his arm. 'It's just that I don't see –' I don't see why you're making such a mystery about it, she wanted to say. But it's his business, she thought, I suppose it's up to him who he tells and who he doesn't. 'Never mind.' She gave him what she hoped was a reassuring smile.

She realized, belatedly, that Adam had made no comment: turning to him, she saw he was sitting blank-faced, as if he had deliberately removed himself from the argument that had threatened to develop.

He went on staring straight in front of him. His lips moved, but he made no sound. It was, she thought, almost as if he was listening to a voice she couldn't hear, and, as silently, replying.

'Adam?' she said softly. She touched her fingers to his hand: it was icy cold. 'Are you all right?'

Slowly he turned his head and looked at her. His wide pupils slowly contracting, he said, 'Fine, thanks. Anyone join me in another beer?'

She watched him as he beckoned the waiter and ordered the drinks. He seemed all right, smiling, exchanging a few remarks in French. And yet, she thought, yet . . .

She didn't know what was bothering her.

Shaking off her misgivings, she took a sip of the new glass of beer the waiter had just put in front of her.

I'm being over-sensitive – it must be the effect of this sudden rush of culture. I've just met a very presentable, interesting man – which is more than I've done in months at home – and, with any luck, I'll be seeing quite a lot more of him over the next few days; as Joe pointed out earlier, this is a compact town.

Why don't I just sit back and enjoy it?

When she became aware of Joe and Adam's conversation, and realized they were planning a visit later in the day to the amphitheatre, the prospect of relaxing and enjoying herself suddenly became much more seductive.

And the memory of how his presence in the side chapel had seemed to bring with it unimaginable things, of how he'd sat in this very café, chilled, hearing some interior voice, faded away to nothing.

Almost.

5

They invited Adam to go back to the house with them for lunch – it seemed a waste of money to eat out when they were so close to the Place de la Redoute – but he said he had some notes to write up and would see them later.

Joe said as they got home, 'I ought to jot down a few points, too. Can you get lunch ready?'

I can, she thought, but whether I will is another matter; she almost asked what the hell he had to jot down when they'd scarcely seen anything yet. On the other hand – she restrained her irritation – he seems to have mellowed over having Adam with us, so maybe it's not the moment to make difficulties.

'Yes, I don't mind,' she said equably. It was, after all, only bread, cheese and a green salad. 'Tell you what – if you make some rough notes, I'll type them up for you after we've eaten.' She added: 'While you're doing the washing-up.'

She was quite surprised later, organizing Joe's notes under various files on his laptop while he clattered about in the kitchen, to discover just how much he seemed to have absorbed in the course of a morning. He had interspersed his impressions with facts he must have already known: when she'd finished, she felt she was beginning to catch him up on the whole subject of Christo-Roman Arles.

Adam was waiting for them, sitting on one of the wide steps leading up to the amphitheatre's entrance. Standing up as they approached, he fell into step beside them and they went in.

The entry tunnel emerged into the arena, and, the brightness affecting her eyes after the shade, she got the fleeting impression that the stone seats were thronging with people. Then, blinking and putting on her sunglasses, she realized she was mistaken; three small boys were racing around an upper tier shrieking, a group of elderly people were sitting fanning themselves halfway down the left-hand side, and a large party of tourists were standing in the middle of the arena listening to their guide.

Otherwise, the vast place was empty.

She noticed that rows of wooden seating had been constructed on top of the ancient stone tiers; it had the effect of making the arena smaller. Following the direction of her eyes, Joe nudged her.

'The vertical stone slabs show where the original perimeter was,' he said. 'You can see how high the wall surrounding the ring had to be,' – she could, it was at least twenty feet of sheer stone – 'much higher than they need nowadays for the bullfight.'

She tried to imagine the arena without the modern seating: into her mind flew an image of a lion at the foot of the stone wall, poised to leap, blood on the fur round its mouth. A surge of atavistic fear shot through her, as if it were she who sat at the top of the wall, leaning forward, trembling with the perilous thrill of danger that came nearly too close. Is it safe? Should I have sat further back? Oh, but then I shouldn't have had such a good view, should not have been able to see the very expressions on those terrified people's faces as the great gates slam behind them and they cower, waiting for whatever wild beasts are to dispatch them . . .

A great scream cracked through the whispering echoes: sweat broke out on her shivering body.

But it was only one of the boys.

She brought her attention back to Joe and Adam. Joe was providing a relentless running commentary – who needs a guide, she thought resignedly. 'They built the amphitheatres with great ingenuity,' he said. 'As an engineering feat, they were remarkable – you're talking about crowds of maybe 25,000 people, double that in the Colosseum in Rome – and they had to be got in and out without mishap. To stop mass sunstroke, they had retractable awnings – Caligula once punished the crowd for daring to protest about taxes by ordering the awnings pushed back and the people locked in to broil to death. And they had to have foolproof arrangements for the delivery of the animals – they were driven into cells underneath the arena, and brought up in lifts. They didn't want to run the risk of any beast having its ferocity or its appetite blunted by attacking an attendant before it got to the Christians.'

She heard the sarcasm enter his voice: that's why he's telling us this, she thought. He's going to make his point, with a vengeance.

'Thousands of Christians died here,' he went on, 'in unimaginably brutal ways. And all to satisfy the Roman bloodlust – why go to the expense of training gladiators when you had prisons full of Christians? And when they –'

'Christian martyrdoms formed only a small part of the entertainments,' Adam put in mildly. 'You're giving a false picture by implying that, throughout the years of the Roman presence here, the only victims were the Christians. It's just not so.'

'Do the actual numbers matter?' Joe countered. 'If only one man is butchered for refusing to give up his faith, that's one too many.'

'Perhaps, but the killing of Christians must be seen in the right context. Yes, the spectators wouldn't be too bothered whose blood was spilled, except that gladiators were much better fighters and so made a far more entertaining contest. And some historians bang on as if the whole purpose of the amphitheatres was for the elimination of Christians, whereas –'

'You sound as if you're defending the Romans!' Joe burst out. 'Are you?'

Adam hesitated. 'I'm – No. Of course not. I just feel that it's important to be objective, and to accept that sometimes the facts don't quite support the scenario that we want them to.'

'The facts speak for themselves! Here we have a . . .'

Beth walked away. Neither of them will notice, she thought, and anyway why should I be a silent audience to their arguing? It's just as well I didn't want to contribute, they weren't going to let me get a word in.

She was, she discovered, pleased to have the chance to circle the arena on her own. Okay, they both know more about it than I ever will, but that doesn't mean I particularly want to listen to them holding forth the whole time. By myself, I can pick up the atmosphere, listen to the memories . . .

She pulled up the thought: it was absurd to imagine any sort of impression of the past could be absorbed from inanimate material, and her scientific self told her not to be so stupid. It's not like me to be fanciful!

Yet as she moved on round the shadowy gallery, following it slowly as it circled the arena, the impressions she had received the previous afternoon came back. Only now that she was right inside the amphitheatre, they came more strongly.

Far more strongly.

To her right, the wall of the gallery was broken at intervals; sometimes the arches gave on to steps that went up into the sunlit arena. But sometimes the steps went down into the darkness.

What's down there? Dare I look?

It seemed her courage wasn't going to be put to the test; the downward flights of steps were blocked off after the first couple of worn treads.

Then she came to one that was open.

I don't want to go down, she thought as her feet took her from step to step. Four, five, six. It's dark. I might fall.

Ten, eleven, twelve.

The air tastes old, as if it's been shut away too long. And there's a smell – oh, God, a smell of leather. And of sweat.

Fifteen, sixteen, seventeen.

People were shut in down here, there's no doubt – I can smell urine, but it's not animal, it's human.

Eighteen, nineteen, twenty.

And she was face to face with a heavy wooden door, latched and bolted with iron, an iron grille let into it at eye level.

She peered through it.

The cell was roughly ten foot square, and the only light came through the grille. But she could still see, or she thought she could: then she rubbed her eyes and looked again, and the cell was empty.

What might have been there, if I'd looked two thousand years ago?

Leaning against the door, she closed her eyes and imagined. On the floor of the cell sat men clad in short leather tunics, silent, still men whose heads drooped and who exuded palpable despair. From somewhere above came the tolling of a bell, and the sound of some sort of machinery clanking into action – it could have been a hoist being wheeled down.

The cell breathed with a low collective sigh; for an instant the men appeared to shrink into themselves, then, one by one, they got to their feet.

Released from the trance, she turned and fled back up the steps.

I'm a scientist, she reminded herself. I'm not meant to have an imagination, it goes against the popular image.

She walked on round the gallery. Reaching a wider arch that led up to an area of seats above the arena, she went to sit in the sunshine. The boys had got fed up with careering round the upper tiers and had gone down into the arena, where they were pretending to be bullfighters, one waving an imaginary cape, one being the bull, fists with pointing forefingers to the sides of his head. The third – the littlest – had been excluded from the game and was sitting glumly watching.

'*Plus vite*!' the small matador shrieked. His companion obligingly speeded up, tripped, and fell on his face in the dust. Oblivious, his friend adopted a pose, then, to pass the time while the other one got up and dusted himself off, began to pick his nose.

Catch a matador doing *that*, Beth thought.

The elderly people had moved round the arena to seats in the shade. One of them seemed to have fallen asleep.

'. . . and down there are the cells where the gladiators would be waiting for their turn in the ring,' said a loud female voice in heavily accented English. 'Below, in cages under the arena, were kept the beasts. They would be safely locked away, but the gladiators would have been able to hear them and smell them. Now we will go and sit, and I will explain about the contests between gladiators and wild beasts.'

Turning, Beth saw the guide and her party coming up the steps. Smiling a brief greeting as she stood up, she eased past them and went back down into the gallery.

It was cool in the shadows. She glanced about her as she walked, noticing how the darkness seemed more intense after every passage across a patch of sunlight. You can make yourself see things that aren't there, see movements in the corners where really there's nothing.

And this gently curving gallery goes on and on, what may or may not be around the next bend always just out of sight, elusive, beckoning you forward . . .

She wasn't sure if the thought had been prompted by the sound: it seemed too much of a coincidence if it hadn't because, just as she was thinking it, she heard the footstep.

A footstep. Then, softly, two more.

So? What's so extraordinary about footsteps? There are plenty of people around, why shouldn't one of them be walking along ahead of me?

Come on! There's nothing to be afraid of!

She made herself go on.

The footsteps went on in front of her, but whoever it was remained out of sight round the bend.

She speeded up slightly, curiosity driving out the vague apprehension, and caught a brief glimpse of a man. Then he disappeared.

He must be hurrying, too. Perhaps he's like me, enjoying exploring on his own, and doesn't want me to catch him up.

She broke into a trot, and this time managed to get a good look at the man before he, too, started to run.

It's Joe! It must be, and he's playing a trick on me! Great – she was running quite hard now – if he's larking around it must mean he and Adam have finished bickering and are going to start being good company again.

The man wasn't Joe. She could see him quite clearly now, a dark shape silhouetted against the dim light, and he was taller and broader than Joe.

Adam! It's Adam! Joe's probably behind me, they're going to catch me between them. She stopped, spinning round to look. The gallery was empty.

She had come to a halt by an arched entry into the arena: peering along it, she realized she'd gone almost all the way round the amphitheatre and was approaching the entry booth.

In front of it, standing exactly where she'd left them, still arguing, were Adam and Joe.

She leaned against the wall, panting, shivering despite the heat. For an instant Adam turned his head and looked at her. She seemed to pick up his unspoken thought: I'm with you, but I can't help you. Then he turned back to Joe, and the moment of contact was gone as if it had never been.

If Joe and Adam are out there, she thought shakily, who's been leading me on?

I don't care who it was, I'm not going to find out! I'm going back down into the sunlight, I'll stand patiently listening till they've argued themselves to a standstill, however long it takes!

She pushed herself away from the cold stones, determinedly stepping out into the very middle of the gallery and briskly walking a few paces.

Then, momentarily confused, she stopped. Which way should I go? On, and turn into the arena through the entry tunnel? Or back, and in through the one I've just passed?

Go back, she answered herself. Go back, because *he*'s ahead.

She turned, hurriedly retracing her steps along the passage.

He was just in front of her, the folds of some garment he was wearing or carrying – a jacket? a raincoat? surely not! – flapping as he rounded the bend and moved out of sight.

She whimpered, instantly putting her hand to her mouth to suppress the sound. For God's sake, stop being such a fool! It's nothing sinister, probably just some innocent visitor who came in via another entrance, and –

There isn't another entrance. And if he came in through the one down there, he'd have had to walk past me.

And he didn't.

Go on? Go back?

She couldn't decide – the man seemed to be both ahead and behind, tantalizingly keeping himself just too distant for her to get a fix on him, to bring him into the safe realms of the normal, the everyday . . .

'Damn you,' she muttered, angry suddenly, 'you're not going to spook *me*!'

Walking fast, speeding up until she was all but running,

she followed him. *Chased* him. On round the never-ending corner, on, on –

He was standing in the middle of the gallery right in front of her. Turned towards her, hands by his sides, relaxed as if he had nothing better to do than wait for her.

She skidded to a halt.

'You – What do you want?'

She had intended to sound aggressive, but her words came out as a dry croak. She tried again.

'You can't . . .'

He took a half-pace towards her, raising one hand slightly – in greeting? threatening her? – and she recoiled. His dark shape loomed before her, broader than he'd looked at a distance. He took another step. Then, for the small movement had brought him out of the deep shadow and into the failing daylight, she gasped.

And, spinning away from him, started running as hard as she could towards the entry booth and the blessed company of Joe and Adam.

For the man was dressed in a toga.

INTERLUDE

ARLES

AD 175

6

My name is Sergius Cornelius Aurelius, son of Marcus, of the tribe of Aniensis. I was born in the town of Aesis, on the east side of Italia, in the tenth year of the reign of the Emperor Hadrian.

My father came from a long line of worthy administrators – his elder brother, according to his own account, managed all by himself to keep cereal export from Gallia Narbonensis running smoothly. However, such a life was not to my father's taste: he enlisted in the legions. After a career which was the usual army mixture of rare moments of dangerous excitement amid months of hard work and boredom, he retired and came home to Italia where he married my mother and begat me.

My father came out of the army with the rank of senior centurion. While it's true that getting on in the legions depends to an extent on having friends in high places prepared to put in a good word for you, no man ever made *primus pilus* unless he deserved it. My mother loved being married to an important man; in the small town where we lived, a retired officer of such seniority was a rarity. My father used to joke that she wouldn't have given him a second glance if he'd been less than a centurion, and everyone except him knew quite well it was no joke.

There was no question of my having been forced into an army career: from the time I was old enough to wave a toy sword, it was the only thing I wanted to do. My father's brother came to visit us when I was fifteen, and he spent one entire evening listing the delights of life as a senior administrator in Arelate.

'We always need youngsters to train up,' he said, picking a fig seed from between his front teeth. He glanced at me. 'You could come and be my assistant, in a year or so. Your old uncle Titus would see you right, my boy.' Phat! He spat the seed on to the floor.

I looked at my father to see if he was going to reply or wanted me to speak for myself. He smiled and nodded.

'Thank you for your kind offer,' I said politely. 'But I'm going to join the army.'

He didn't seem to have heard. We were treated to a further lecture on how wonderful it was to be him, until my little sister came in with a fresh jug of wine and diverted his attention.

As far as I can recall, that was the only time anyone suggested I should consider any other career.

I went into the Sixth, or Legio VI Victrix, to give the official title. It had been my father's legion, but don't go thinking that made life easy for me. Quite the opposite: the son of a senior centurion who turns up as a raw recruit in his father's old legion has to go through a special sort of hell. Even now, aspects of what I experienced still make me wince. Suffice to say that I endured, and probably emerged the stronger. As they say, what doesn't break me makes me.

Legionary recruits sign on for twenty-five years, which I can tell you is an eternity when you're eighteen. To take our minds off the awful thought of the years stretching ahead, they kept us in a permanent state of exhaustion throughout our basic training. Four months of route marches, running and cross-country exercises with a sixty-pound pack on your back certainly makes you realize how unfit you are. And when they'd finished yelling at us to hurry up, we were letting the others down by being such sluggards, they started on weapons drill and taught us the hand-to-hand fighting that remains the legions' most effective tactic. They yelled at us over that, too. And they taught us to swim. And how to march six abreast without anyone getting out of step. For the first few weeks with the unit, I can't even remember crawling into my bed at night.

The Sixth was based in Britannia, in a fort to the north of that legendary land at a place called Eboracum. Not that I spent much time there – during my advanced training I'd learned camp construction, and I was sent up to work on renovating Hadrian's Wall.

Have you ever been to Britannia? The south is quite pleasant – you get some sunshine, although nothing to compare with the Mediterranean – but the north is different. It rains. Sometimes it rains hard, great chill drops that sweep along on the wind and find every niche in your garments. And sometimes it's a soft rain, more like a fine mist, so gentle that at first you hardly notice it. Then, three hours later, you wonder why your cloak feels so heavy and you realize it's totally sodden with water. Mind you, a session in the bathhouse is all the more welcome when you're soaked to the skin, cold and thoroughly miserable – the British may mock us for turning our forts into little Romes, as they say, but we make sure we don't miss *all* our home comforts when we're far away.

By the time I was up on the wall, any sense that we were pushing the frontiers of the Empire back into wild, unknown territory had all but gone. With one exception – and what an exception it was – my years up there were spent on the reconstruction work going on in the fort at Coriosopitum, which lies a few miles south of the wall. When Hadrian's great project first got under way, they'd moved the army up from the old forts such as Coriosopitum into new accommodation right on the wall – you can see the sense of that – but later, when they got going on the Antonine Wall, suddenly Coriosopitum was right on the great route north, so we had to restore it. Believe me, sometimes it didn't feel so much like restoring it as starting all over again.

My father had been on the wall before me. It was his last posting; he and the Sixth went fresh to Britannia with the Emperor himself, and didn't my old father love to remind you. When I was little I'd badger him for tales of fighting, of days on the march and nights under the stars, but he'd just go on and on about how wonderful Hadrian had been, how he'd had this wide imaginative plan and brought it off, how nothing daunted him, how he'd improvise and surmount every crisis, etc., etc. Then he'd get going on the personal gossip – gods, he was worse than my mother and her friends when they got their heads together and started running down the neighbours. Father would repeat the old tales about Hadrian's love for his Greek boy Antinous, and the tears would appear in his own eyes when he recalled the Emperor's vast grief when the youth drowned in the river Nilus. Some grief it was, too; only an emperor has the wherewithal to build a city in memory of his beloved, and that's what Hadrian did. There would be no point in trying to distract Father at this stage in his monologue: I'd resign myself and listen patiently while he described how the poor old Emperor's life degenerated into illness and various unspecified diseases, and he'd drag up the soldiers' speculation that Hadrian had grown his beard not to cover his scars but to conceal the ravages of sickness that were eating into his face.

So there I was twenty-three years later on the wall my father had helped to build – well, I don't suppose he ever got his hands dirty, being rather too senior for that by then – and, instead of being able to draw on stirring tales of Father's exploits, I'd stand up there in that dramatic landscape and picture a grieving old man scratching at his beard. Such is life – I suppose it was quite funny, really.

My father ended his military career up on the wall, I began mine. A man is, I suppose, most susceptible to impressions in his late teens and early twenties, which is perhaps why the things that happened to me there remain so vivid in my mind. I don't know, though – they'd surely have been indelible whenever they happened. I learned to stand up for myself, to labour all day without complaint, to do my appointed tasks with such thoroughness that I could take a real pride in them. And all of this in a country-side so different from any I'd known before, one so wild, so desolately beautiful that, once I'd stopped moaning about the rain and the cold, I grew to love it as much as the small sun-bathed fields and vineyards of childhood.

I made my first true friends, and I met my first love. I was initiated into a new religion – Mithras the Unconquered was universally beloved throughout the army, and, once he had accepted my allegiance, I began to see why. I made my one bitter enemy – the only one I know about, anyway – and understood what it is to be hated and cursed. Or I thought I did: as it turned out, I hadn't experienced the half of it. Then.

But enough of that. I was speaking of my friends and my first love, and in fact the one led to the other – in the greater freedom earned by advancing in my career, I started going out with my friends to the small settlement that had grown up around the fort, and we would spend our nights of leave in the ways you'd expect of soldiers far from home and starved of female company. Yes, of course I visited the whores – most of us did. If you were lucky, you could get a girl who made you laugh as well as satisfying your lust. If you were really lucky, you'd get one who fleetingly made you think she was enjoying it as much as you were.

But I didn't meet Carmandua in a brothel; I'm quite sure her father and her brothers would have cut her throat if they'd even found her lurking in the street outside. Not that she ever would, she had better things to do with her time, as she used to say. I met her when I was in my mid twenties, when promotion had shot me up to the dizzy heights of a senior post on the commander's staff and I no longer went out carousing on my rare leaves. She came from an important local family, and every last one of them let me know from the start that I was barely good enough for her. Gods, they were a touchy lot, those Brigantes, we needed all the diplomatic skills drilled into us to cope with them.

Roman legionaries weren't allowed to marry until discharge, but since that was still thirteen years off when Carmandua decided she wanted to be a bride, we went through the form of ceremony used by her own people. I found that I was just as firmly married as if the Emperor Antoninus Pius himself had ordained it.

It was a year or so after we were married that I had my trouble. Perhaps that was why the marriage failed, I don't know. But it seems likely; it was difficult enough to be the sort of husband she obviously wanted with my legionary duties to perform – and perform well at that, I wasn't finished with promotion yet – without that other business. It gave me a guilty conscience, I suppose; although my logical mind accepted I'd done the right thing, a more emotional, susceptible part of me kept seeing that man die because I'd told the truth.

I think Carmandua found me distracted, and I imagine I appeared unloving. If I did, it was unintentional. I thought I did love her, although I'm not sure now that I knew the meaning of love then.

Anyway, lack of love or not, we had a son. He was the sort of boy I'd have ordered, if that were possible: gutsy, funny, sunny-natured yet with a stubborn, independent streak so broad that he and I came often to blows during his turbulent childhood. We called him Marcus, after my father – the old man would have appreciated his grandson. Carmandua and Marcus lived in a house in the settlement – a pretty decent house, too, I saw to that – and I spent what little time with them I could.

Marcus was twelve when I finally came out of the Legion. By then, he was the only good thing left in my marriage, and, although I went through the official Roman ceremony that made Carmandua my wife in the Empire's eyes, it was really only for Marcus's sake. She and I were at loggerheads as to what we should do next: I wanted to take my family back to Italia, where my money grant on quitting the army would enable me to build up my father's farm into something even more prosperous. Carmandua, predictably, said she had been a wife and a mother for enough years in her own homeland to have got used to it and she didn't want to go anywhere else.

It was stalemate. She didn't want to leave, I couldn't bear to stay on. It was partly my pride, I admit it – how would you feel if you had to go on living in a place where you'd been a senior officer, a man of importance, when now you'd been reduced to the status of just another citizen? Well, maybe you're more tolerant than I am, but I had to go.

To her credit, Carmandua agreed to give Italia a try. It was a brave decision, to travel right across the Empire when to date she'd been no further than a score of miles from home, and I did my best to make the journey as smooth and as comfortable as I could. Still, she hated the sea trip – if it's true that both Caesar's and Claudius's troops baulked at crossing the water from Gaul to Britannia, my poor wife was equally terrified at leaving her homeland and sailing into the unknown. Not so my son: his excitement conquered his seasickness, and he'd have sailed the ship himself if they'd let him.

I don't want to dwell on our time in Italia. I'll just say that, although the farm reached new heights within the first year and I could have been as happy there as it's possible for a man to be, Carmandua didn't settle. Never mind why – it's too complicated anyway, and I, a mere man, can't hope to understand how friction with her mother-in-law, lack of a common language with the local people and constant, unmitigating homesickness can make a woman so miserable. That's what Carmandua said, anyway, although I think I did understand. Even though I didn't love her, I felt very sorry for her.

I don't know what we'd have done, for in the event no decision had to be taken. One bright day, when Marcus and I had gone walking in the hills, he climbed one tree too many – 'I'm stuck, Dad!', he shouted from the top of its slender trunk, laughing at his predicament.

'Idiot! And just what would you have done if your father were not here to help, hmm?' I replied, heaving myself up from lazing in the sun to get him down.

He made some daft joke about landing in trouble again for more ripped clothes, and we were still laughing when he missed his footing and fell. He broke his neck: he was dead before I got to him.

Carmandua went back to Britannia. For the first awful weeks our grief united us, but then its effect changed and it drove us apart. Bless her, she never blamed me – she knew Marcus as well as I did, perhaps better, and she was well aware of his adventurous nature that had never once paid any attention to 'Be careful!' I took her home to her own people, then I left; Britannia was too full of memories.

But then so was the farm.

Uncle Titus rescued me. Remember him, the one who tried to make me go and work for him in his one-man administration of the entire city of Arelate? I don't want to go into details – I'm not proud of the wreck I'd become when he found me. Those who have not lost a child could never understand, those who have won't want reminding. Enough to say that Uncle Titus's compassion probably saved my life.

Good old Uncle Titus. From my brief acquaintance of him, I'd thought he was a big-headed, self-important, self-indulgent old fart. He may have been all those things – he was, in fact – but he also had a kind heart. Informed on the family grapevine of the state I'd fallen into, he came to Aesis and took me away.

If, as some of my well-meaning friends back home said, I needed a complete contrast, Arelate provided it. On the farm, I'd spent long days out of doors, alone unless Marcus was with me, in intimate communion with the land and its generously given bounty. I'd watch the weather, observe the smallest change in the condition of the soil, and I became as keen an omen-watcher as any soothsayer. The little town of Aesis I'd visit only when I couldn't help it, and even then its modest population would send me hurrying back for the peace of my fields.

Now suddenly I was slap in the middle of what seemed the biggest concentration of people and buildings I'd ever seen. Arelate was a thoroughly Roman town and had been for decades, quite long enough for its every institution to be a faithful replica of the best model the Empire could produce. The people were fun-loving and bright, eager for the entertainments put on regularly in theatre and amphitheatre (especially the amphitheatre); it was an affluent community, with many thriving businesses based on the wealth of the great alluvial marshes to the south of the town, where the Rhodanus flows into the sea. The vines of the delta yielded wonderful amber-coloured wine, the olive trees faithfully produced bumper crops, and the cereal output was so vast that the enormous storage cellars under the forum were always full: even when another cargo was dispatched to Rome, carts would be standing by to fill the crypt up again.

Titus had found me a post in the Procurator's Office. I was a sort of financial secretary – that was my official title – and the duties were well within my capability. I suspect that Titus had called in a favour in obtaining the job, since the Procurator could have managed perfectly well without me. But that's Roman life for you – without a recommendation you don't stand a chance, whereas with it anything's possible. I did my best to show willing, and did what work I was given as diligently as I could, and nobody complained. After a couple of years I'd saved enough money to build myself a modest villa in the hills outside the town and, with such a light workload, I found I could spend quite a lot of my time away from my desk. I got a couple of small fields under cultivation, and I decorated my new house; I even got in some specialists to lay a mosaic floor and paint inspiring scenes on the walls.

All things considered, life wasn't bad.

And then Theo came along.

7

I was finishing a long and tedious list of facts and figures for the Procurator to dispatch to Rome when a commotion outside my office made me lose count at the penultimate item.

I swore and threw down my stylus.

'Keep the noise down!' I shouted, striding out into the vaulted passage. 'What's going on?'

A fat sweaty man in a toga had hold of a young boy, twisting his arm up behind his back. The boy was clearly in pain, biting his lip to stop himself crying out.

'Ease off,' I said to the man. 'No need to hurt him.'

'No need?' the man bellowed, purple with rage. 'This little shit's just broken into my warehouse! He had his hands full of amber beads – my very best, too, a special consignment from the Mare Suebicum! He knew just where to look, I watched him. Not the first time you've dipped your thieving hands into what doesn't belong to you, is it, you filthy bastard?' He gave the boy's wrist a twist, and this time the cry burst out of him.

'I told you not to do that,' I said. 'You'll break his arm.'

'I should break his neck, never mind his arm!' The man, yanking the boy with him, came closer, putting his pasty, large-pored face right up to mine. 'Thieving's a capital offence. I demand you lock him up till the next games day, then throw him to the wild beasts!'

The boy made a sound, quickly curtailed. Glancing at him, I saw the fleeting terror before he resumed his attempt at disdain.

The eyes in the dirty, tanned face were grey-blue. They met mine. It could have been my imagination – probably it was – but I felt he was reaching out for me.

'We don't throw even boys to the beasts without at least a minimal trial,' I said lightly, trying to defuse the situation. 'Why don't we all sit down calmly and I'll listen to both sides of the story?'

'You fool!' the fat man spluttered. 'I tell you, I've just caught him red-handed! Ask him anything you like, he'll lie through his teeth! Stands to reason, he's not going to say "Yes, I did it," is he?'

I had to admit, it seemed unlikely. 'Perhaps not. But nevertheless, I doubt whether we can justify a capital sentence for one theft. One attempted theft – you have recovered your property.'

'This time, yes.' Once again the man wrenched at the boy's arm. 'But the good Jove alone knows how much of my stock he's had away before – half a warehouse, I shouldn't wonder, and enough amber to bedeck a hundred empresses!'

Suddenly the boy broke his silence. Defiantly, he cried, '*No!*'

I looked down at him. 'You deny it?'

'Yes! I never took his rotten amber, not till this time. I –' He clamped his lips together as if to stop what he was about to say.

I don't know why, but I believed him. Yes, he'd been in the fat man's warehouse, he wasn't denying it, but he hadn't got away with anything. And the accusation that he'd regularly been stealing could easily be a product of the fat man's over-heated imagination.

'You keep records, I presume?' I asked the man. 'You can prove you've lost goods before?'

'Yes!' He hesitated. 'Sort of.' He paused again. 'No.'

Suddenly he looked wary. I wondered if he had some scam going that wouldn't bear close scrutiny by one of the Procurator's financial secretaries.

'Well, what is it?' I put a tinge of impatience into my voice. 'Are you going to –'

Abruptly he changed tack. 'I demand to see someone in authority!' he said loudly. That put me in my place. 'This boy must be thrown into prison, then executed! I'm a hard-working citizen, I've got my rights, I don't have to see my goods trot out of my own stores in the hands of the likes of him!' He lifted the boy's arm violently, and the boy screamed. Twisting round – maybe he was hurting so much that he no longer feared worse pain – the boy wriggled his wrist out of the man's grip. Then, so fast that his movements seemed to blur, he bent down and, fisting his other hand, swung forward and punched a short stabbing blow right into the fat man's testicles.

The man's eyes rolled up. Moaning, he slumped against me. Grabbing at the boy with one hand, I tried to support the dead weight of the man with the other arm.

Something had to give: I let the fat man slide to the floor.

'Ulpius! Lucullus!' I shouted, wondering for the first time why none of my colleagues had come to see what was happening. But the two of them arrived so swiftly that I guessed they'd been peering out from behind one of the columns along the passage.

The fat man was opening his eyes. His hands going to his crotch, he moaned again.

'This man wishes to register a complaint against this lad,' I explained briefly. 'Will you see to him – give him a glass of wine from your special bottle, Lucullus – then, when he's recovered, take him along to the magistrate.' I fixed the lad with a glare. 'I'll see to this young man.'

He wriggled again, and I tightened my grip on the collar of his tunic. The material was rotten, and the collar ripped off; I grasped his shoulder instead.

I felt him tense, so I squeezed harder. He winced. 'None of your tricks,' I muttered, bending down to speak right in his ear. 'I'm not like Fatso over there,' – I nodded towards the fat man, half-walking, half being dragged off along the passage – 'I've been in the Legion for twenty-five years, fighting hairy-arsed Britons who stiffen their hair with bird-shit, and I'm more than a match for you.'

He subsided. Still holding him, I led him into my office, where I pushed him down on a bench and sat myself down next to him.

He said after a moment, 'What are you going to do with me?'

His voice was just breaking: I guessed he was about thirteen. 'For the moment, I'm going to talk to you.'

The light eyes widened. 'Talk?'

I smiled. 'Yes. You know, you say something, I make a reply, and you say something else.'

Briefly he grinned. His teeth were white and even – he didn't look like a child who'd always lived the life of an urchin.

'What do you want me to say?'

'Your name would be a good start.'

'Theodore.'

I waited, but he didn't add anything else. Still, it was better than nothing.

'I'm Sergius Cornelius Aurelius.'

'Oh.'

We weren't getting very far. 'Why were you in the fat slob's warehouse?'

He looked at me in surprise. 'Don't you like him?'

'I hardly know him, but on first acquaintance he doesn't impress.'

'I thought you'd be on his side,' Theodore muttered. 'Thought you'd take his word and –' He shivered briefly. 'And do what he told you to.'

'Wrong on two counts,' I said quickly; I could feel the sudden horror in him, and wanted to dispel it. 'For one thing, I resent being told what to do by some sweaty merchant with too much money for his own good.' The fat man's toga had been of finest linen, and he'd worn a heavy gold brooch on his shoulder. What with his well-fed obesity and his rich clothes, he'd made a startling contrast to the boy. 'For another, I don't approve of chucking human beings into the amphitheatre so that the crowd can get off on watching them being torn to bits.'

Slowly he shook his head. 'You're not like the rest, are you?'

I smiled, understanding all too clearly what he meant by the rest. 'No, I don't suppose I am.' I sincerely hoped not, anyway.

He was staring around my room. 'Is this where you live?'

'No, it's where I work. I'm a secretary to the Procurator.' He looked blank. 'I help the man who reports to the Emperor on money matters here in the province.'

He frowned. 'I thought you said you were a soldier.' Quite clearly, a soldier ranked far higher in his estimation than a secretary.

'I used to be a soldier, but I did my time and now I do something else.'

'Are you old?'

I wondered what a boy of his age would consider old, and decided probably anything over twenty. 'Terribly.'

He grinned. 'You don't look it. Old men have white hair, and yours is dark. What did you mean about them putting birdshit in their hair? Why?'

I remembered what I'd said. 'The Celts of Gaul and Britannia like to present a frightening spectacle, so they paint their bodies with blue dye and put lime in their hair so it stands up in spikes.'

'Why?'

'To help them alarm the opposition. They usually need all the help they can get, since they fight naked with just a shield and a long sword and don't prove much of a threat to a fully armed, disciplined troop of legionaries.' I leaned towards him, warming to my theme. 'They're brave enough, and they don't lack skills, but they're wild. They act too much as hot-headed individuals, instead of banding together and fighting as a unit.' I pictured again his swipe at the fat man's balls. 'You'd make a fine Celt.'

He looked pleased. 'Would I?'

'Yes. You swing a fierce punch.'

'It *was* a goodie, wasn't it?' He smiled smugly, and belatedly I realized I wasn't behaving very responsibly for the Procurator's financial secretary.

'Look, Theodore,' I began firmly, 'we said at the outset that we'd both talk, but so far you've done all the asking and I've provided the answers. It's your turn now. Agreed?' He scowled, and his open expression seemed to close in. 'Come on, fair's fair.'

Fairness was obviously something that mattered to him. 'S'pose so.'

'We'll start with where you live. Here in Arelate?' He nodded. 'In a house?' He nodded again. 'Where? In the centre? By the river?' Once again he nodded, and a smile spread over his face. 'Well, which?'

'I live all over,' he said, a hint of pride in his tone. 'I spot houses where the people aren't there, and I climb the wall or the fence and sleep in their courtyards. Or in their outbuildings. If I can't find a house, or if they come back unexpectedly, there's a place down by the river where I've made a shelter.'

'What do you live on?' I'd noticed he was thin, beyond the normal slimness of a boy beginning to shoot up: he looked half-starved.

'I know where to find scraps,' he said. 'There's an eating house by the forum where they throw out oysters more than two days old, even when they're still good, and there's a baker down by the Baths who gives me yesterday's bread. Then in the market they always leave a few bits of fruit that's going soft.'

Gods. No wonder he was thin. 'When did you last have a hot meal?'

He shrugged. 'Don't know.' Again, his face closed up.

Perhaps he was thinking of home. 'Theodore,' I said gently, 'where are your parents? Are they dead?'

He said quickly, 'Yes,' and I knew he was lying. But there didn't seem much purpose in pressing the point: if he wasn't prepared to tell me the truth, he'd simply go on lying.

I got up and went to look out of the window. It was late afternoon: we'd be packing up for the day soon, and I wasn't due to go into the office for the next two or three days. Maybe I could . . .

I thought it through. It was irresponsible, and if I got found out it could mean trouble. Still, I'd had worse trouble. And I didn't think my conscience would lie easy if I turned the boy over to the magistrate – if they were short of animal fodder for the next spectacle, or if Fatso had made a convincing case, Theodore might well end today in a dark, dank cell, where he'd stay till he next saw the light of day in the amphitheatre.

No.

I'd seen death in many ways, but, with the exception of my son – and one other, one that haunted me as much as Marcus's fall from the tree – death had been in battle, where, even if the odds were usually stacked in our favour, our enemies had at least stood a chance. That was acceptable, and the Britons I'd fought had inevitably been the aggressors. But this business of the games – games! that was a misnomer if ever there was one! – was something else. I don't believe a man deserves to die purely in order to entertain the crowd, especially in the ways they liked best in the arena.

I wasn't going to let that happen to Theodore for a crime I wasn't even sure he'd committed.

Making up my mind, I turned back to him. Until I saw

him still sitting there waiting to see what would happen next, it hadn't occurred to me that he might have slipped away.

I felt unreasonably glad he hadn't, and it wasn't just because it would have been embarrassing for me if he'd been picked up outside. 'Sergius is losing his touch,' they'd have said, 'the great soldier can't even keep a kid in custody any more!'

His expression was questioning, but he didn't speak. I found it touching – it was as if he knew it was no good appealing to adults, they never listened anyway.

'I'm going to take you out of the town,' I said. 'I've got a house in the foothills – nobody ever goes there except my servant, who lives in the nearby village, and the man who comes to attend me in the bath.'

His face was impassive. Expecting relief, even a little gratitude, I was about to protest when suddenly I understood. Even if he hadn't lived all his life on the streets, he'd surely have come across men offering to help him in exchange for his favours.

There was only one way to meet this, and that was head-on.

'I know what you're thinking,' I said. 'You're quite wrong. I don't sleep with boys or men, I prefer women. I lost my virginity with a very cheerful whore in Coriosopitum – that's in the north of Britannia – and I've never looked back. I was married, but my wife went back to her own people.'

Predictably, he said, 'Why?'

I could have told him about Marcus, but at that time I tried not to think about him if I could help it. It was enough that he was always in my dreams. 'We no longer loved each other enough to overcome her longing for her homeland and her family.' It was true, as far as it went.

He seemed satisfied; the sympathetic understanding in

his face made me the more certain that he had a home and a family he was missing, too.

He said suddenly, 'I'm sorry I ask so many questions. Is it all right?'

I almost laughed. 'It's all right. If you don't ask questions, you don't learn. Now,' I sat down beside him again, 'what do you like best to eat?'

He paused, obviously thinking, then said, 'Mussels. And those little honey cakes with nuts on them. And ewe's milk cheese, and olives. Oh, and fresh-baked bread. And –'

I interrupted him. 'I want you to crouch down in the corner behind this table,' I said. 'Nobody ever comes in here, especially at this time of day when they're all getting ready to go home, but if anyone looks in, just keep still and don't breathe.'

He grinned. 'I hope they won't stay too long.'

'Me too. I'll go and do some shopping, then, when we've finished eating and the coast's clear, we'll slip away. Is that a good plan?'

Moving silently behind my desk, he said softly, 'It's great.'

When I came back with the food – I'd bought a jug of cool white wine, too, which I certainly needed even if Theodore didn't – I looked into the other rooms along the passage. They were all empty. Outside, there'd been the usual few people around the forum, but it was a dull evening and there weren't many of them. There'd be even fewer by the time we left, and anyway nobody would be on the lookout for a man and a boy. With any luck.

I spread the food out on my desk, and Theodore fell on it. Cramming bread and cheese into his mouth with both hands, he choked and had to suffer me pounding him on the back before he could resume his meal. I'd brought a clay pot of cooked mussels, and had to elbow him off to get any at all.

My small hunger quickly satisfied, I sat back with my

wine and watched him eat every morsel. When he'd finished, he gave a tremendous burp then, as if hearing some distant reproving voice, said, 'Sorry.'

'Don't mention it. Like some wine?'

He seemed reluctant. 'I don't drink wine.'

'Fine. There's a jug of water on the window sill.'

'Wine makes people angry, doesn't it?' He sounded nervous, and I wondered if he was expecting my modest half-jug to turn me into a furious fiend.

'Some people, yes. Especially those who don't know how much they can drink and remain in control of themselves.' I toyed with my glass, wanting to reassure him but without making it obvious. 'Me, now, I used to take a pride in drinking other men under the table when I was a young man, but now I'm happy with rather less.'

'I don't like it when people get angry,' he said, returning to his theme. 'It's . . . it's . . .'

'Scary?' I suggested. 'I don't like it either, particularly when the people getting angry are bigger than me.'

He looked at me gratefully, then said, 'Not many men are bigger than you, are they? You're tall.'

I wasn't the tallest in my century, but there hadn't been a lot in it. 'Not much fun in a tent when you're tall,' I remarked. 'When you stretch out, your feet get cold.'

He smiled. 'I made a tent out of branches and a blanket when I was little. I stayed in it all day, and my –' He stopped, turning away.

My mother, had he been about to say? My father? I almost asked, but it wasn't the moment.

'You've finished all the food,' I said instead. 'We may as well be on our way.'

He stood up. 'Ready,' he said.

I was going to tell him to pack up his belongings, then remembered he hadn't had any. That tunic – whose collar was now hanging by a thread, thanks to me – and a scruffy pair of sandals seemed to be his only possessions.

'We may be away some time,' I said delicately. 'Is there anything you'll need, anything you want to fetch from – anywhere?'

He seemed to sense my awkwardness. 'I haven't anything to fetch.' He hesitated then, as if deciding that he should be as open with me as I'd been with him, said, 'I've already sold the last of the things I stole. I spent the money on my sandals.'

I looked at him for a long moment. I was slightly disappointed at his admission – I'd convinced myself the break-in at the warehouse was truly his first foray into crime – but then, I asked myself, what did you expect? Here's this kid all alone, sleeping rough, eating off scraps – he's had to steal to survive.

I said in my senior officer's voice, the one I used to use when I really meant business, 'You must not steal again.'

Meekly Theodore said, 'Very well.'

We took the journey at a slow but steady pace. Theodore was far too skinny to have much stamina, despite the food he'd just stuffed away, and I didn't want to show him up by making him have to ask for rest stops. For the same reason I didn't let him ride my old horse all the time, sharing the riding with him turn and turn about.

It was fully dark by the time we reached my villa. Theodore was dead on his feet, but still noticed enough to comment that it was a big house for one man. Since I agreed with him, I didn't reply.

The builders had been working on the bathhouse, and they'd left a mess in the courtyard. Cursing, I kicked some rubble out of the way, meaning to leave it till the morning. Theodore got down on his hands and knees and started to help.

Again, I wondered what sort of home he'd come from, what sort of a person had made him afraid of men's drunken anger, had made him a boy who instantly started working for his board and lodging, even when he'd scarcely had any yet.

What sort of a person had made him run away to the precarious existence of a street child.

I touched his shoulder. 'Leave it, Theo,' – the abbreviation came quite naturally, and sounded somehow right – 'I'll see to it in daylight.'

He got up, looking sheepish. 'Sorry.'

'Don't be – you were trying to help.' The next thing I had to say was rather delicate, but it had to be said. 'Look, I usually have a bath before I go to bed, but it's too late tonight, I'd have to light the furnace and it'd be ages before the water's hot enough. But I'm going to warm a pan of water on the kitchen hearth, and I suggest that – that –'

His laughter rang out, happy and unrestricted in that sterile house that hadn't heard the sound before. 'That I have a good wash before I climb between clean sheets? I'd like that, I'm not this way by choice, honestly.'

I believed him. Relieved, I said, 'I'll find you some clean clothes. The least I can do, since it was I who tore your tunic.'

I heard him singing as he washed – I'd put a bowl and the jug of hot water in the corner of the yard, and I stayed in the house till he'd finished.

It gave me a funny turn to see him in Marcus's clothes, for all that I thought I'd steeled myself for the sight.

'Your room's here, off the courtyard,' I said, my voice horribly over-cheery. I wondered if he'd notice, if so, what he'd make of it. I was past caring – the funny turn had grown into something I could only just handle, and all I wanted was to get away to the privacy of my own room. 'Here,' – I opened the door – 'just blow out the lamp when you're ready for sleep.'

He looked quickly round the room, nodding in appreciation. 'It's great. Thank you.'

'See you in the morning,' I said, closing the door. 'Sleep well.'

He muttered a reply, but I scarcely heard. Turning away, I ran across the courtyard and into my room, where I shuttered myself tightly away so that nobody would hear.

PART TWO

ARLES

THE PRESENT DAY

8

Beth didn't mention the figure in the toga to Joe or Adam. Very soon she was feeling bashful about the whole thing – within minutes of the man turning and striding away, in fact: having made an embarrassing noise like a sheep being throttled, she'd run backwards for half a dozen paces, then forwards for rather more till she came to an archway that led through into the arena. There she'd stumbled across to lean against the wall, where Adam and Joe had found her.

What would they say, anyway? she asked herself as she listened to Adam describing the present-day bullfights held in the amphitheatre. Adam might have some sensible explanation – someone in fancy dress, or an actor in costume rehearsing for some pageant – and Joe would dismiss it as my imagination.

She had to admit that both explanations were entirely feasible. She wondered why they failed totally to convince her.

She fell into step beside Adam as Joe led them off round the perimeter of the arena. Predictably, he was still ranting on about Christians being martyred. When they were almost back at the entrance Adam interrupted, pointing out the towers which had been added to the top of the outermost walls in medieval times. She wondered if he was as sick of Christian martyrs as she was.

'Let's go up,' she said, determinedly leading the way.

The view from the top of the tower was spectacular. Immediately below, the terracotta-tiled roofs of old Arles huddled tightly together, the narrow roads winding between them so deep in shade that they looked like black ribbons. Beyond the last houses was a thin band of greenery, and beyond that the river.

It was wide here, the Rhône, and it had carved itself out such a deep bed that the huge volume of water seemed to pass slowly, as if it were weary and could only just summon the energy for the last few miles to the sea. Beth leaned against a wide window embrasure and watched a small boat chugging upstream, its laborious progress an indication of how powerful a current was sweeping down against it.

'That way lies the Camargue,' Adam said, coming to stand beside her. 'Do you know it?'

She shook her head. 'Never been there. It's where the white horses and the black bulls come from, isn't it?'

'Yes. And it's the home of the gipsies, too – Aigues Mortes, that I was telling you about?' – she nodded, remembering – 'is on the edge of the Camargue, where the Rhône delta meets the sea. Well, strictly speaking it's no longer on the sea, since all the silt brought down by the river has built out the shore.'

She gazed downstream where he had pointed. 'Wild horses, bulls and gipsies. It all sounds improbably romantic – I expect it's just one big tourist attraction now.'

'It isn't. There's a clutch of new businesses offering horse rides to see the wildlife, but most of the area's quite unspoiled. The middle bit – round the Étang de Vaccarès – is a nature reserve.'

She had the feeling he was about to say something more, but he didn't. 'I read somewhere you can see flamingoes,' she said. 'I went to see the ones at Slimbridge once.'

He said, 'Mm,' but she wasn't sure he'd heard. Then he began: 'I'm going to –' and stopped.

She waited, but he didn't go on.

After a moment she turned away from the window and the stupendous view. 'I'm tired,' she said. 'And I can't take in any more.' She looked round for Joe, and saw him staring out of the next window. 'Joe, let's go home.'

Without waiting to see if he'd follow, she walked back to the steps and slowly climbed down.

It must be the heat, and all this tramping round, she thought later as she lay in bed: Adam had suggested a drink as they left the amphitheatre, but she'd said no thanks, she wanted to go back and put her feet up, and Joe had said he had notes to write up. After a light supper, she'd left him to it.

Comfortable under the crisp sheet, very soon she felt herself growing drowsy. Sights and sounds of the day flashed through her mind, faithfully reproducing the atmosphere of the place, and she smiled. An image of the Alyscamps took on momentum of its own: she was dreaming, fast asleep.

Some time later, the sound of a telephone woke her. It only rang once then stopped, almost as if someone had been waiting for the call and had pounced on it as soon as the ringing began. Must be next door, she thought vaguely, turning over, but then softly her door opened and Joe peeped in.

'Just going out to get some fresh air,' he whispered. 'Sorry if I disturbed you, but I didn't want you to wake and find me not here.'

'Thanks, Joe.' How nice of him, she thought. 'Night.'

'Good night, Beth.'

She was too sleepy to dwell on the coincidence of the ringing telephone and Joe's sudden need for fresh air: it was only later that it struck her as odd.

They were having breakfast out on the terrace in the morning when a white Peugeot drew up in the car park below. Just as she was registering that it had British number plates, Adam got out of it.

She went to the edge of the balcony, waving. 'Adam! Up here!'

He looked up, smiling. 'Good morning.'

'Come and have a coffee?'

'Thanks.'

'Over there – up the steps.' She watched him walk to the foot of the stairs, then turned to Joe. 'It's Adam.'

'So I gathered,' Joe said drily.

'Isn't that a coincidence, him parking right below our house?'

'Not really.' Joe went back to his notebook – he'd been engrossed throughout breakfast, and had hardly said a word. 'I told him where we were staying.'

'Oh.' She tried to work out why he'd have done that, if he wasn't keen on their spending too much time with Adam. 'Why?'

He didn't bother to look up, so she couldn't read his expression. 'He asked.'

'How – ?' But just then the front door opened and Adam came striding down the hall. She shrugged. I don't care, she thought.

'What's on your agenda today?' Adam asked. 'Lovely cup of coffee, Beth.'

'Plodding on through the list of sights, I expect.' She realized she could have been more diplomatic, thought briefly of ways she might mitigate her remark, decided not to bother since anything else would probably make it worse.

'I want to go back to the Alyscamps,' Joe said. 'There are a couple of things I want to check.'

She felt mildly disappointed: she'd have preferred to look at something new. He can go on his own, she thought, I'll take the morning off from being a research assistant and be a tourist instead.

'Will you need anyone with you?' Adam asked, catching

her eye as if he'd been thinking along similar lines. 'I only ask because, if not, Beth might like to come out with me – I'm going back to Avignon to try to record an ancient toothless gipsy woman singing what I fervently hope will turn out to be a Russian love song. I was going to ask both of you,' he added earnestly, 'only if Joe has to retrace his steps and revisit one of yesterday's places . . .' He left the sentence unfinished. Beth suppressed a smile – he'd virtually made it impossible for Joe to ask her to go with him without sounding unreasonable.

'No, I'll go on my own.' His tone was neutral.

'In that case I'll go with Adam.' She got up, collecting the mugs and plates. 'Strictly speaking it's your turn to wash up, Joe, but I suppose if you're engrossed I could do it for you.'

'I'll help.' Adam collected the remaining crockery. 'The sooner we get going, the sooner the work'll be finished and we can break for lunch.'

You sound, she thought as she ran hot water into the bowl, like my kind of man.

They reached Avignon after what seemed a very short time, but then, Beth thought, journeys do pass quickly when you're talking. Adam, she'd learned, came from Northumberland, where, having travelled extensively after university, he was once more living, within sight of Hadrian's Wall 'on a clear day'. He had a cat called Barty, whom a neighbour took care of when Adam was away. He didn't mention a wife or any other sort of permanent companion, and Beth didn't like to ask. In return, she told him about selling folding bicycles and being a temp: there will, she thought, be a time to tell him the rest. I hope.

He appeared to know his way around the town, and drove confidently through narrow traffic-choked streets to an underground car park.

'Well done!' she exclaimed as he nipped into a small space, effectively stopping the queue-jumping ambitions of a pushy Frenchman in a rusty Renault.

'It was nothing,' he said modestly. 'Getting into the Palais des Papes car park is the easy bit – getting out again can be tricky, even assuming you've managed to locate your car in the first place.'

'We'll manage,' she said confidently.

They went up some steps that led into the great square in front of the ancient Popes' Palace. She'd have liked to stop and look and, as if realizing, he said, 'We can have a wander round now, if you like, or you can if you don't want to come with me. Only I'm due to see this old Romany woman at midday, so I ought to go.'

'I'll come with you,' she said. 'If you don't think my presence will inhibit her.'

'From what I saw the other day, she wouldn't be inhibited by a company of marines.' He grinned at her. 'It's only fair to warn you.'

The gipsy woman lived with someone who seemed to be her daughter in a poky flat in the back streets, its small amount of space crowded by huge displays of plastic flowers and a large doll under a glass dome. The doll had bulbous blue eyes and an expression so vacuous that it was almost sinister: Beth sat down with her back to it.

The daughter, herself at least seventy, blundered about putting glasses and a bottle of something dark red and syrupy-looking on a tray, until her mother bellowed at her to stop. Adam said something in French, at which the old woman composed herself, sitting up straight and folding her hands in her lap. Adam produced a small tape recorder from his bag, put the microphone in front of her and started the tape running.

The old woman opened her mouth widely and began

to sing. In the tiny, cluttered room, the noise level was incredible. Beth, appreciating that it would have been impossibly rude to put her hands over her ears, was amazed that so much sound could come from one human throat. If this is a love song, she thought as the loud soaring notes galloped towards a climax – unfortunately the first of many – I'd hate to hear her when she's singing a battle hymn.

She hoped Adam was enjoying it. She didn't dare catch his eye to see.

Some seventeen verses later, the old woman paused to pour some of the red liquid into her glass. Whatever it was – she forgot to offer any to Adam and Beth – it galvanized her for another eight verses. Or it might have been a different song: Beth wasn't sure, since the tune seemed to have wavered into what sounded like a set of variations.

There was a click, and Adam said, '*Ah! Elle est fini, la bande*.' The old woman leaned forwards, and Adam quickly put the tape recorder back in its case. '*Quel dommage*!'

The daughter came back into the room and, with smiles and nods and a great many '*merci*'s, Adam and Beth were ushered out.

'Dear God,' Beth said as they reached the bottom of the stairs and emerged on to the street, 'I thought she was never going to stop.'

'So did I.' Adam was laughing.

'What was that click?'

'Me switching the machine off. I told her the tape had run out, but actually we had at least twenty minutes left.'

'Did you get enough?'

'More than enough,' he said forcefully. 'Beth, I'm so sorry, did you hate it?'

'Yes, it was absolutely ghastly.' She reached out to touch his arm. 'But don't apologize, I wouldn't have missed it for anything.'

'Liar.'

'Is that all you have to do?'

'Yes. Fancy some lunch?'

'I thought you'd never ask.'

They went to an open-air restaurant in a wide, traffic-free area which he said was la Place de l'Horloge. At the top end of the square was a carousel, where excited children were being treated to five-minute rides to the accompaniment of cheerful music.

'If they play a gipsy love song, I'm off,' Beth said as they were handed menus.

'If they play a gipsy love song, I'm going to nuke the carousel. The red mullet's lovely – shall we have that?'

She noticed it was far from the cheapest item. Still it was his idea, and she had just sat through twenty-five excruciating verses. 'Yes, let's.'

'And what about wine – ah! They've got Vin de Pays des Sables. I think you'll like it – it's a Camargue rosé from grapes grown in the sandy soil, and it's got a sort of honey taste. It's amber-coloured, it doesn't look like rosé at all.'

'Go for it.' She closed her menu, looking up and smiling at him. She thought, I'm going to enjoy this.

She did. The food and the wine were excellent, the waiter friendly, and the carousel didn't play anything remotely like a gipsy love song. And she discovered that Adam was the sort of person you could talk to all day without getting bored or the conversation flagging.

By the time they had finished coffee, it was the middle of the afternoon; she suggested that perhaps they should set off for home.

'Of course.' Immediately he beckoned to the waiter, reaching for his wallet.

On an impulse she said, 'Next time, I'll pay.'

Predictably, the inevitable protests rang through her mind: Why assume there's going to be a next time, that he'll want to see you again? She scotched them.

He looked across at her, his smile deepening the lines round his grey eyes. 'I look forward to that.'

He had been right about the car park; they spent some time searching for the car, and the exit took them up into a street he didn't know.

'Can you see Jesus?' he asked.

She wondered if she'd heard right. 'Where might he be?'

'Try and look up,' – he broke off to swerve round a truck backing out of a doorway – 'if you can spot the statue of Christ that stands above the cathedral, I can navigate by it.'

She saw what he meant. 'There!' she said suddenly. 'Up on our left and slightly ahead.'

'Great!' Confidently he turned left, then right, and very soon they were driving out through the thick city walls on to the ring road around the town.

They were both quiet on the journey back to Arles. She imagined he was thinking about his Russian love song, and didn't want to interrupt; anyway, she thought, I have quite a lot to dwell on myself.

Gazing out of the window as they drove through the outskirts of Arles, she noticed a garish poster advertising pony rides across the Camargue. There was an illustration of grinning people on docile-looking white horses, pointing ecstatically towards a distant view of a little house screened by tall cypress trees. 'Look,' she remarked idly, 'there's an ad for one of those horse-riding places you mentioned.'

He glanced briefly across. She heard him gasp, and, turning to look at him, saw he'd gone white. It seemed as if he couldn't take his eyes off the tawdry painting: in horror, she felt a bump as the car's nearside front wheel mounted the pavement. A very sturdy lamp-post loomed straight ahead.

She screamed, '*Adam*!' and, just in time, he turned his

head and saw what was happening. Wrenching the steering wheel, he lurched back on to the road, into the path of a bus which hooted long, loud and angrily.

I don't suppose he's the only one who's pale now, she thought, feeling sweat break out across her body as she began to tremble. Christ!

He drove on without speaking, then, as they drew level with a little square where a few tables indicated a café, suddenly pulled in to the right.

Not again! she almost shouted.

He stopped the car and, without looking at her, reached for her hand. 'I think I could do with a drink,' he said quietly. 'What about you?'

Several, she thought. 'Yes.'

They went over to the café and he ordered coffee and brandy. She put two sugars in her coffee. Sugar was good for shock.

After some time sitting in silence she said, 'What happened? Was it my fault for distracting you?'

His eyes shot to hers. '*Your* fault? Good God, no. I've been sitting here trying to think what I can possibly say to stop you deciding I'm such a headless chicken behind the wheel that you're never going to risk your lovely self out with me again.' He sighed. 'I wouldn't blame you in the least if you did.'

He looked away, dropping his head like a guilty child, then, as if he had to see her reaction, glanced sideways at her. She burst out laughing. 'Cretin,' she said. 'If you promise on your great-grannie's grave that was a one-off and you won't do it again, I might risk it.'

'I promise,' he said. Then, becoming serious, 'Beth, I . . . That poster was . . . Oh, hell.' And stopped.

She put it down to embarrassment. I'd be embarrassed, she thought, if someone had innocently pointed out some innocuous poster by the road and I'd gone catatonic and almost driven them into a lamp-post.

'Never mind,' she said kindly. She picked up her glass. 'Here's to a lucky escape.'

He touched his glass against hers. 'While you're cheerful,' he said carefully, 'can I make a suggestion?'

'Go on.' She found herself smiling again.

'I'm planning a trip down into the Camargue tomorrow. I was going to stay away a night or two, but that can be changed. Will you come with me?'

She thought back over the day. Managing to blot out the accident that had almost happened, she remembered laughter, good food, and endless conversation. Without thinking any more, she said, 'Yes. I'd love to.'

9

She got home to La Maison Jaune to discover Joe in a state of high excitement.

'Mithras!' he shouted out to her from his desk as she came in through the front door.

'I beg your pardon?'

He was waving a book over his head. 'Come and look at this – I can't think why I didn't think of it before, it's been staring me in the face all the time!'

It was impossible not to respond to such enthusiasm. She went into the room and stood beside him, hand on his shoulder. 'What has?'

'The fact that the Roman officer who murdered St Theodore was in all likelihood a worshipper of Mithras.'

'And who's Mithras?'

'He was originally a Persian god of light. The Romans encountered him in the course of their empire-building in the Middle East, and for various reasons I won't bore you with he became the favourite deity of Roman officers and merchants. Basically the legend goes that he slaughtered a bull – by sticking a knife in its throat, incidentally, the significance of which I'm sure won't escape you – and the bull's blood spilling on the ground gave the gift of life to mankind. Some people think that the bull symbolized Mithras himself, and that its death and rebirth represented Mithras's own self-sacrifice.'

'Like Christ dying for mankind.'

His face stiffened. 'No, not at all.'

'Yes it is, it's –'

'You don't know the first thing about it!' he interrupted.

'Yes I do, you've just told me.'

He ignored her. 'Mithraism was a mockery of Christianity. They even had some blasphemous ceremony that mimicked the Eucharist, and –'

'Hold on.' She'd spoken so firmly that, surprised, he stopped. Briefly she wondered why she should be defending so doggedly an ancient pagan religion she'd only just heard about. 'You just said the Romans brought Mithraism from Persia. Well, surely they conquered the lands around there before Christ was born, so how can you say Mithraism copied Christianity if it existed first?'

'It was a blasphemous mockery,' he repeated stubbornly. 'And I'm convinced this Roman officer slit St Theodore's throat in some twisted variation of the bull-slaying ceremony that he practised in his own faith.'

Thrown on the defensive, he sounded hurt. She felt sorry for him, that her innocent questions – intended only to find out, she thought, not to put him and his theory down! – had dampened his enthusiasm. 'Look, never mind the theological arguments,' she said pacifically. 'I think your idea's fascinating, and I quite see what you mean about the throat-cutting. It could very well be some sort of adaptation of slaying the sacrificial bull.'

'It could, couldn't it?' he said eagerly. 'That's not all – we already know that the child was killed because he refused to abandon his Christian God and worship the Roman gods, so wouldn't it be likely it was Mithras he was refusing to bow down to?'

She thought it was assuming rather a lot, but, not wanting to antagonize him again, said, 'I don't see why not. So, what new lines of research is this going to lead to?'

He was thumbing through a thick guide book. 'We could begin by looking at some temples of Mithras. There must be some in the area – they've been found wherever the

Roman army went, even in Britain – there's one in London, another up on Hadrian's Wall at Carrawburgh.'

Coincidence, she thought. That's the second time today someone's mentioned Hadrian's Wall. 'Were they great big buildings?'

'No, very small. They were built to look like caves. And they had to be near running water.' He picked up another book. 'There's a photo of the Carrawburgh one in there, or the site where it stood at any rate. And there's a mock-up of what they thought it looked like.'

She found the page. The site wasn't much to look at – a few stones marking out a rectangle – but the reconstruction was more interesting. In a dark, windowless little temple with a vaulted roof, a central aisle and two narrow flanking aisles led to the focal point of the altar. It was made of a tall stone slab upended, and a design of the sun's rays had been punched in it so that, lit from behind, it seemed as if fire was coming out of the rock.

Behind it was a relief of a youthful figure in a cloak and a cap kneeling on the back of a bull, one hand holding back its head while the other dug a knife into its exposed throat.

She whispered, 'Mithras.'

'Found it?' She hardly registered Joe's voice. 'Beth? Have you found it? Here, give me the book – oh, you've got it.' Her hands suddenly feeble, his gesture knocked the book to the floor.

She jumped. 'Sorry!'

'What's the matter?' He was looking at her anxiously. 'You'd better sit down, you've gone quite pale!' He pulled up a chair for her, and she sank into it.

'I'm fine.' I am! 'I didn't damage the book, did I?' She bent over and picked it up, giving herself a brief moment away from his worried stare. I can't tell him what just happened, it's too daft. Anyway, it's gone now, and it was probably only coincidence.

She didn't know how else to explain away the fact that

the picture of Mithras had brought vividly into her head the image of the man in the toga. He'd been closer than when he'd stood before her in the amphitheatre, so close that she could see the grey in his dark hair, look right into the deep-set brown eyes. He'd looked so sad.

Briefly she pressed her hand to her head, then, straightening, leaned back in her chair.

Apparently reassured, Joe had gone back to his books. 'There are a couple of possible sites of Mithraea,' he said. 'That's what the temples are called. One's down at a little town by the sea called Les-Saintes-Maries-de-la-Mer, only another source claims the temple was to Artemis, and anyway there's a church on the site now so there wouldn't be anything to see. I've seen another one mentioned, but I can't remember where it was and I can't find the reference . . .'

She wasn't really listening. She still felt slightly odd, as if she were getting over a bad shock. Pushing back her chair, she got up. 'I'm going to have a shower, then I think I'll lie down for half an hour. I've got a bit of a headache.'

'Oh, dear,' he said automatically. 'Anything I can get you?'

She smiled: he was poring over his books, and she wondered what he'd say if she replied, Oh, yes, could you just rush along to the pharmacy and see if they've got any tablets with codeine in them because they're the only ones I find any good?

Still, it was kind of him to offer.

'No, I'll be fine,' she said. 'See you later.'

'Oh, Beth?' He looked up.

'Yes?'

'Er – I was going to suggest we went out later and had a beer or two at that bar by the amphitheatre, but you're obviously not going to feel like it so I'll go on my own.'

She had the distinct feeling he was lying. Perhaps not exactly lying, she amended, but certainly handling the truth carelessly, as Mother would say.

But why?

It didn't really matter – she didn't want to go out, he was quite right. 'Fine,' she said. 'What about supper?'

'I'll fix myself something. You just rest.'

His very solicitousness made her suspicious.

'Okay,' she said easily, and left the room.

The shower was hot and relaxing, and, lying on her bed afterwards, she slipped into a light sleep.

Once again, she was awakened by the telephone.

Sitting up, she strained to listen. This time, there was no question of it being next door's phone – the ringing went on for long enough for her to locate the sound, and it was at the end of the hall. She heard Joe hurry to answer it, but there was only a brief, quiet murmur too indistinct to make out, which told her nothing.

Wrong number, probably.

She slept again. Waking an hour later and feeling hungry, she got up and went through to the kitchen. Joe, she noticed, had gone out.

She finished her bread and cheese, then decided she would like a drink after all. The bar by the amphitheatre, Joe had said. I'll go and find him.

The evening was warm, and there were still quite a lot of people strolling round the old town. There were also festoons of mosquitoes: she wished she'd brought some repellent.

The amphitheatre was floodlit, which somehow took away some of its aura. She glanced at it, but tonight felt no unease.

There were groups of people, most of them young, sitting at several of the bar's tables. None of the groups contained Joe.

Surprised, she stood and stared. He *said* this was where he was going! Why isn't he here? Unless there's another bar by the amphitheatre.

She looked about her. There were one or two other bars, and she walked round the perimeter to see if Joe was in any of them.

He wasn't.

I've probably missed him, she thought. I'll go back – I can have a beer at home.

With a vague sense of anticlimax, she turned and headed back for the Place de la Redoute.

He was still out when she got home. She had a solitary bottle of beer, then, as he hadn't returned, decided to go to bed.

I really wanted to tell him about tomorrow, she thought worriedly as she lay in the darkness. He's got every right to expect me to help him, since that's what I'm here for, and now tomorrow morning I'm going to have to dump in his lap the fact that I'm going out for the day, with no opportunity for leading up to it gently.

Damn!

She was too tense to sleep. Half an hour later, she heard voices on the steps leading up to the front door: one of them sounded like Joe's. Curious as to who he was talking to – there were at least two others, a girl and a man – she got out of bed.

'Joe?' she called. 'Is that you?'

He came in, swiftly closing the door behind him and leaning against it.

'Oh, hi, Beth!' He grinned at her, and she thought perhaps he might have had quite a few beers. 'How's your head?'

'It's fine, thanks. I came along to the bar, in fact, but couldn't find you.'

'Oh, I went on to the Place du Forum. I wanted to sit in Van Gogh's café.'

The explanation came out so quickly that either it was the truth or a prepared lie. But why, she asked herself, do I keep thinking he's lying?

'Like a coffee?' he asked, heading for the kitchen. 'I'm going to have one.'

'No thanks. But I'll come and keep you company – I wasn't asleep.'

'Good. I was about to apologize for waking you up. Again!' He glanced at her over his shoulder.

'Who was that with you?' She tried not to make it sound like an accusation, more a friendly enquiry.

'With me? No one.'

Now that, she thought, is definitely a lie.

But there seemed little point in saying so.

'I've been thinking about tomorrow,' he went on – changing the subject very efficiently, she thought – 'and the best thing we can do is pack up food and drink for the day and head off to this place I mentioned, where there was a temple of Mithras. I found the reference I was looking for, it's –'

Now or never. 'I've made other plans, I'm afraid.'

There was silence in the kitchen.

Then: 'What other plans?'

'Adam asked if I'd like to go down into the Camargue with him tomorrow, and I said yes.'

'Well, you'll have to cancel it.'

If you'd asked nicely, she thought, left some room for negotiation or compromise, I might have been prepared to change my arrangements. Perhaps ask Adam if we could go a day later.

But just to assume I'll do what you say!

A hundred childhood altercations flooded back into her mind. And how many did I ever win?

She breathed in and out a couple of times, slowly and deeply. Then she said calmly, 'No, Joe, I won't. I'm sorry, you have every right to expect my help, but why does our trip have to be tomorrow? I'll come with you when we get back. I'll only be away a day or two.'

Instantly she wished she hadn't said it. Two days meant

a night away, and Joe would jump to the conclusion that –

'What do you mean, a day or two? You mean you're going off overnight with this man, don't you?'

Yes, he'd jumped to exactly that conclusion. 'Don't be silly,' she said. 'We'll probably be away overnight, but you assume too much if you automatically think that means we're going to sleep together.' Suddenly she was furious, the benefits of the deep breaths flown out of the window. 'Joe, you're a crude sod, you've no *right* to imply such things!'

He said infuriatingly, '*I* didn't say anything about you sleeping with him, that's your guilty conscience!'

'It's not! I haven't got a guilty conscience, I've done absolutely nothing to feel guilty about, and even if I had, it's none of your bloody business!'

'Don't swear, Beth. I've told you before.'

'Bloody, bugger, sod, bastard, fuck!'

'*Beth*!'

For one absurd moment she thought he was going to say, Go to your room!

But even he drew the line at that.

She had another try with the deep breathing, then said quietly, 'This is stupid. We're both cross, and –'

'*I'm* not cross.'

She ignored that. '– and there's no point in going on with this discussion. I'm not available tomorrow or the next day. I'm sorry if that inconveniences you, and I suggest you either go off on your own or else occupy yourself with some more research in Arles till I can come with you.'

How's that for calm and reasonable? she thought proudly.

'You leave me little choice,' he said pompously. God, you sound like Father! 'Now you'd better go to bed – you're obviously overwrought.'

It wasn't quite 'Go to your room', but it wasn't far off.

She said gently, 'Joe, if you don't stop and take a good

hard look at yourself, you're going to end up just like Father.'

Before he could retaliate with something on the lines of 'And what's wrong with that?', she walked out of the kitchen and went back to bed.

Her heart was pounding with the aftermath of her anger as she lay down, and she almost gave up the idea of sleep and reached for her book.

Then she thought, I've got my own way! I've just had a fairly major difference of opinion with my elder brother, and I've won!

It was exhilarating, as much so as the thought of the new job that was waiting for her when she went home at the end of the summer, something that, even if she didn't often consciously dwell on it, lay quietly at the back of her mind all the time. The confidence it gave her was extraordinary.

Perhaps that's why I stood up to Joe, she reflected. Because I don't have to let him put me down any more.

Of course – she was getting drowsy – he doesn't actually *know* yet that I'm no longer the pathetic kid sister, the one he was always better than, at virtually anything you cared to name.

None of them know, not Mum, Father or Joe.

Ha!

The prospect of the delicious moment when she finally told them was all she needed to send her over the brink into the soundest night's sleep she'd had in a long time.

10

Breakfast would have been a miserable meal with Joe, but fortunately he didn't put in an appearance until Beth had finished. She wished him a courteous good morning as he came out on to the terrace, to which he grunted a response, then she collected up her plate and mug and retreated into the kitchen.

She filled in the hour until Adam was due to collect her having a long shower – she took a perverse satisfaction in keeping Joe out of the bathroom which, although she told herself it was childish and unworthy, she still enjoyed – and packing a shoulder-bag in case a toothbrush and nightshirt proved necessary.

It would be better, she decided, to speak to Joe before Adam arrives. It might just make him behave like a human being when we leave.

'You're really going through with this escapade, then?' he greeted her as she went into his workroom.

'I am.'

'You're acting very irresponsibly, going off with some man you hardly know. When it all comes to grief, don't say I didn't warn you.'

'No, Joe, I won't say that.' She wanted to laugh: her determination not to let him rile her seemed to be working. 'Don't work too hard while I'm gone.'

'I –'

Whatever he was going to say was interrupted by a knock at the front door. 'That'll be Adam. I'm off, then, Joe – I'll see you tomorrow, I expect.'

She wasn't quite sure what she'd do if Adam had rearranged the trip so that they returned that night, but as soon as she opened the door to him he said, 'Morning, Beth. Look, I think it'd save time if we did stay down somewhere in the Camargue tonight, so, if that's all right with you, perhaps it might be an idea to tell Joe we won't be back.'

'She already has.' Joe had followed her to the door.

Don't! she cried silently. Don't you *dare* say anything about trusting Adam will behave properly and not compromise your sister! God, I'm not some Victorian miss going off without her chaperone!

'You should –' Joe began.

She hissed, 'Joe, shut up. I don't need a keeper, and even if I did it wouldn't be you.' Then, ushering Adam down the steps, she pulled the door closed behind her.

As they reached the bottom of the steps Joe opened it again. He shouted, 'Don't expect any sympathy from me!' then banged the door.

Adam didn't say a word as they drove through the morning traffic out of Arles, reinforcing her opinion that he was a considerate man. When they had left the urban areas behind and were heading down a dead-straight road, lined with ditches and tall rushes and running far away into the distance across the flat, wide spaces of the Camargue, at last he spoke.

'I'm sorry if I interrupted something back at the house. Or perhaps you don't want to talk about it.'

Do I? She wasn't sure. 'It was nothing. Joe can be unreasonable sometimes. He tends to take over from our father as the dominant male.'

'Oh dear.' He glanced across at her. 'I wouldn't have thought you took kindly to domination.'

'No more than the next woman.' She realized she'd sounded angry, and added, 'Or man.'

He smiled. 'Do I guess right that Joe wasn't best pleased about you coming out on this trip?'

'You do.' There seemed nothing more to add.

He waited, then said, 'I'm glad you decided to come anyway.'

'Me too.'

They drove on in a companionable silence. Gazing out at the endless landscape, she said, 'What's that crop?'

He looked where she was pointing, slowing the car. 'Maize. And on the other side of the road, rice. It's very fertile up in the northern parts of the Camargue, but down towards the sea, where the water gets more brackish, the land's not so good.'

'They grow vines down there on the sand. We had some of their wine yesterday.'

'We might have some more today, if we play our cards right.'

'What are those bushes?' They had feathery foliage which was dancing and bowing in the breeze.

'Tamarisks.'

'Has it always been as wild and beautiful as this? And what about the bulls and the horses, have they always been here?'

'The horses are said to have been here since prehistoric times, relics of the great herds that Palaeolithic man used to hunt, driving them off that precipice at Solutré you can see from the motorway north of Lyons.' She didn't like to say she hadn't actually noticed it. 'The bulls, too – the Camargue was their final refuge when civilization encroached across Gaul. The Camargue's been quite thinly populated for centuries, I believe, although in Roman times the northern areas were a favourite place for the citizens of Arles to build their posh villas. It was more heavily forested then – there's a place not far from here called Sylvereal, whose name comes from the Latin for forest.'

'As in sylvan. Have they excavated any villas?'

'No, I don't think so. There's probably a fair weight of

river silt covering them by now, they're probably several miles down.'

'Several *miles*! Surely – ' She looked at him and saw he was joking. 'Joe's interested in – ' She stopped. I don't want to think about Joe. 'Is this trip to interview more gipsies?' she asked instead. 'Because if you've got any more prima donnas lined up, I'll stay in the car – I've brought my book.'

He laughed. 'No more like her, honestly. No, today's for something else. It's all a bit vague, I'm afraid – just a couple of places I want to have a look at.'

'What, for possible locations for your film?'

'My film?' He recovered himself quickly. 'Well, they could be, I suppose.'

'Is that what you've always done, make films?'

'I worked in journalism when I left university, then it was a sort of natural next step to go from writing about places and events to wanting to film them.'

'So you got started, just like that?'

He smiled again. 'God, no. I went to great trouble and expense filming stories I found fascinating, only to discover when I tried to sell them that few people shared my zeal. So I offered my services to a friend already in the business, and went with him to do a piece for Channel Four about American Indians in Arizona. With him I learned to do it properly. After that it became easier, and a year later I got my first commission.'

'What made you want to do something on gipsies?'

He hesitated, then said lamely, 'I don't know, really.'

Surprised that he shouldn't have an answer when he must surely be talking about his latest enthusiasm, she pressed him. 'You mentioned the music and the folk tales – I could well believe they'd be sufficient to set someone off on the gipsy trail.'

'Yes, that was it,' he agreed. Then: 'This is the turning for the Étang de Vaccarès – let's go and have a look.'

She had the distinct impression that, just like Joe the

previous night, Adam too had just neatly changed the subject.

The roads round the Étang de Vaccarès were narrower and even less populated than the main road; other than a few cars pulled up in lay-bys while their drivers and passengers stared earnestly out across the water through binoculars, they saw no one.

The rushes were higher and thicker: she couldn't see through them, and Adam obligingly opened the sunshine roof and let her stand up on the seat. It was wonderful – the wind in her hair and the salt smell were so exhilarating that she could have sung, except that Adam had probably had enough of singing.

They saw their full quota of every type of wildlife; in one waterlogged pasture bulls, ponies, and egrets all together and, in a nearby pond, a group of flamingoes.

'Seen enough?' he asked as they got back in the car after ten minutes' flamingo watching.

'Yes, I have. I'm satiated with the splendours of nature. What about you?'

'I've seen it before. This little detour was for your benefit.'

'But your film? I thought –' She stopped. If he didn't want to go charging about making notes and sizing up camera angles, or whatever film producers did, that was up to him. And if he wasn't doing all that, it was especially nice of him to have brought her to have a look.

'Thank you,' she said. 'What now? Back to work?'

'You might map-read, if you feel the need to work,' he said lightly. Opening the Michelin of the Camargue, he pointed. 'That's the place – I don't think there's actually a name marked, it's just that collection of buildings at the place where the thin road crosses the water.'

'Got it. Okay, I'll navigate.'

They went gingerly down increasingly narrow and waterlogged roads – towards the end they were more like tracks – until she began to hope whatever they were aiming for was going to be worth it.

Staring anxiously ahead – they'd just narrowly averted skidding off the track when the right-hand edge had disintegrated into a vast muddy puddle – gradually she began to feel a strange sense of *déjà vu*. It's familiar, this prospect of trees round a clutch of thatched buildings, she thought, yet I know I've never been here before.

Then, rounding a corner, they came to a sign advertising riding stables, with pony rides to the distant sea and back. Behind it, incongruous in this desolate setting, was the poster they'd seen in Arles.

'*That's* why the view's familiar!' she burst out, glad to have found a rational answer. 'Because I've seen it before!' She didn't understand. 'Adam, why have we come here? Did you know about it – have you been before, so that when you saw it again on that poster you recognized it?' Was that what made him almost kill me, she wondered wildly. God, why?

He didn't answer. The car had slowed to a stop and, still clutching the wheel, he was staring out at the trees and the buildings.

Suddenly she was very afraid.

Then, as if coming out of a trance, he turned, smiled, and said, 'Not much to see after all, I'm afraid. Sorry to have dragged you out here – let's go back to that last junction and make our way back towards the main road. We'll see if we can find somewhere for lunch.'

Perhaps it hadn't been the right place after all. Yet he'd been affected by it, she'd seen that clearly enough. 'If you like,' she said guardedly. He sounds normal enough now, she thought. But still . . .

She didn't know what to do. In the absence of any better idea, she opened the map again and worked out the most direct route back to the main road.

* * *

They got lost. She felt it must be her fault, she was the one with the map, yet she was so anxious to get back to something resembling civilization that she'd been terribly careful with her directions. Maybe I said left when I meant right once or twice. It has been known.

A village materialized out of the wilderness before them. Scarcely a village, she thought, but it's quite a relief to see human habitations again. Even – she was looking nervously around – if there doesn't seem to be one solitary human within sight.

The houses were shuttered, closed up behind thick hedges or high fences with locked gates. On a wall topped with rolls of barbed wire a notice said *Defense d'Entrer*. Another warned of a *Chien Méchant*, with an illustration of a fierce, slavering Alsatian with long fangs.

Friendly little place, Beth thought.

Adam had stopped the car. 'There's a bar across the road. I'll go and ask for directions.'

'I'll come with you.' It's stupid, but I don't want to be left in the car on my own. I keep thinking eyes are watching me from behind barred doors, that savage dogs are going to leap up and slobber down the car window.

She noticed that he locked the car. Perhaps he feels uneasy too. On the other hand, perhaps he always locks it.

Stop being such a wimp!

There was no one in the bar. Adam coughed a couple of times, and a man in a stained apron came out through a doorway hung with a tatty plastic anti-fly curtain. He jerked his head questioningly at them.

She said, suddenly quite desperate for alcohol, 'Shall we have a drink?'

'What a good idea. Beer?'

She'd had something stronger in mind, but maybe it would be a mistake. 'Lovely.'

He ordered a couple of *pressions*, and she listened as he

spoke to the barman in French. She thought he was probably asking for directions.

'We missed a left,' he said, turning to her. 'It'll be a right now, of course, as we'll be going back in the opposite direction.'

'Sorry.'

'Please, don't be. I didn't spot it either.'

They stood drinking their beer. There was utter silence in the little village. The barman had disappeared, and there were no sounds of barking dogs or slamming doors.

She whispered, 'Quiet round here, isn't it?'

'It is. I wonder where everyone is?'

'Perhaps they're holiday homes, those houses, and only occupied in summer. It's probably overrun with jolly laughing people in August.'

But somehow she couldn't picture it.

'Come on.' He touched her hand briefly. 'Let's get out of here.'

He left two ten-franc coins on the bar, called out *'Au revoir'* – nobody answered – and they went back to the car.

'Now,' she said, spreading out the map, 'I'm looking for a right turn, yes?'

'Yes.' He was turning round, preoccupied with avoiding a litter bin.

'I can't see one. Unless – No, that can't be it, it'll take us back the way we came.'

'Well, that's what the man said.' He sounded distant.

'What shall we do?' Even to herself, her voice sounded forlorn.

'We'd better take the turn,' he said firmly. 'Otherwise we might get even more lost.'

'Perhaps it's like Looking Glass Land,' she said, trying to lighten the atmosphere, 'and you have to set off in the opposite direction in order to get where you want to go.'

He didn't respond.

After a mile or so she said, 'Right turn coming up.'

He took it.

They came to a junction: trying to locate on the map the places signposted to right and left, she spotted one that lay between them and the main road. 'Go left!' she shouted.

He turned right.

'Adam, this is the wrong way – we have to go left, towards that place St something, then just a bit beyond that we'll come out on the main road!'

He didn't answer.

'Adam!'

He turned to her briefly. 'Don't worry, Beth, this is a short cut.'

But it isn't, she cried silently, it can't be, unless this map's got a really appalling misprint.

They were driving in completely the wrong direction.

She felt fear creeping up her backbone, cold and sinister.

They were returning to the place on the poster. She could see the trees now, and there were the buildings. They looked neglected, crouched low to the ground, hunching in on themselves as if trying not to be seen. As if – she couldn't prevent the thought – they had something to hide.

In her head came a sudden scream, and she heard a child sobbing.

Then it stopped.

She spun round, looking wildly in all directions. 'Adam! Stop, I heard –'

Did I? Or did I imagine it?

She couldn't see a soul.

They were almost at the buildings now. There was a long, low house, mud-walled and thatched with reed. Among the sheltering tamarisk bushes she could see a stout chimney. No smoke came from it.

Behind it were two smaller buildings, little more than cabins. One of them had its door hanging by the hinges.

She thought she heard a boy's voice. I hate you! Leave us alone!

She pulled at Adam's sleeve. 'We've got to go! Please, turn round, let's get away from here!'

But slowly he opened the door and got out of the car. Stiff with fear she watched him walk up to the house, peer in at a small window.

Then, very deliberately, he moved on to the cabin with the broken door.

He disappeared inside.

The cry that cracked the still air was a man's, not a child's.

She flung open her door and raced after him. Past the house, leaping over tussocky grass, she sped across to the cabin.

He wasn't there.

She screamed, '*Adam*!'

There was no answer.

A narrow doorway led out of the back of the cabin, and she squeezed through it. Beyond, a track ran along beside a water-filled ditch. Adam was hurrying down it, and she ran after him.

Then, abruptly, he stopped.

Catching up with him, she skidded to a halt. He was standing stock-still, eyes tightly closed, muttering under his breath.

She edged closer.

What's he saying? What's the matter with him?

Now she could hear the words he was whispering. But it didn't do her any good, because he was speaking in Latin.

11

Now she was as still as him, both of them standing as if they'd been turned into marble statues.

She became aware of a high-pitched whining: a cloud of mosquitoes floated in the air around her head. Looking down at her bare arms, she saw three of them already settled and sucking her blood.

She wanted to scream: from somewhere came the courage to speak calmly.

'Adam, we should go back to the car. There are rather a lot of mosquitoes – they're probably coming from the ditches – and we're being bitten to death.'

He opened his eyes. At first he didn't seem to recognize her. Then, to her vast relief, he was himself again.

'God, Beth, I'm sorry!' Grabbing her arm, he hustled her back along the path. 'I've got some stuff in the car, come on.'

They ran past the cabin, past the house. She thought she heard mocking laughter.

It's all right, we're going, we're going!

They got into the car and banged the doors closed: in her haste she'd left hers open, and the interior of the car was full of mosquitoes.

'I'll get us moving,' he said, starting the engine. 'If we open the windows, the mozzies will be blown out.' He turned round then, reaching into the side pocket of his door, got out a tube of ointment. 'Sting relief.' He handed it to her. 'If you bung it on your bites, it'll stop them itching and swelling up.'

'Thanks.' She squeezed huge blobs on to both arms, rubbing furiously.

'There's a mirror behind the sun visor. You've got a bite coming up on your cheek.'

Pulling down the visor, she looked in the mirror.

As well as showing her a big red lump on her right cheek, it also provided a clear picture of the scene they were swiftly leaving behind them. Standing outside the cabin was the man in the toga, only now he was barelegged, dressed in a tunic and heavy-soled sandals with elaborate leather straps.

Gasping, she twisted round. 'Adam, look! I can see –'

But the man had gone.

Hunching down in her seat, she covered her face with her hands and began to weep.

'I really am sorry about that, I hate women who cry.'

They were sitting in a restaurant on the square at Aigues Mortes, in the deep shade of an awning and with glasses of chilled kir in front of them. Beth was feeling much better, and deeply ashamed of herself.

'It's I who should apologize,' Adam said. 'That was an awful place, and I should never have taken you with me.'

Emboldened by the kir – she had drunk most of it and it seemed to have gone straight to what was left of her brain – she said quietly, 'Why did you have to go there? It's nothing to do with your film on the gipsies, is it?'

He didn't meet her eyes at first but sat staring into his glass, swirling the dark drink gently round and round. Then, looking up, he said, 'Very perceptive of you. No, it isn't.'

'Why, then?'

He hesitated, then said, 'Beth, I owe you an explanation, I appreciate that. But can it possibly wait?'

She stared at him. He still looked pale, and his grey eyes were dark with whatever was troubling him.

What do I do? Decide he's a nut, wish him *au revoir* and get myself a taxi back to Arles? Or stick with him and wait till he feels like providing a few answers?

There wasn't really any question. Stretching across the table to hold his cold fingers in hers, she said, 'It can.'

She didn't feel very hungry and doubted if he did, either, but it seemed a good idea to eat, if only to counteract the alcohol. They had pasta with a shellfish sauce, accompanied by another bottle of the amber-coloured rosé, then hot, strong coffee.

They'd eaten in silence, but the coffee stimulated her and she managed to dredge up something to say.

'Joe's got a fresh line of research he wants to follow up,' she began. 'That's partly why he was peeved about us going off today, he wanted me to do the following-up with him.'

'Oh, really?' Adam said politely.

'Yes. He says the Romans worshipped some Eastern deity called Mithras who miraculously killed a bull and gave life to mankind. He thinks one of his Christian martyrs may have had his throat cut in some sort of parody of the bull-slaying ceremony, and he's convinced himself that the person who did the deed was a follower of Mithras, and that he killed the saint for refusing to sacrifice to his god.'

Adam made no response; he was sitting gazing out into the square as if he hadn't been listening. Well, *I* thought it was quite interesting, she reflected.

She had another sip of coffee, then drained her wine. She was feeling light-headed. 'I suppose he could be right,' she mused, mainly to herself. 'If you believe you have to make sacrifices to your god to keep him sweet, then if someone wouldn't, it might mean the god got angry and everyone suffered. Plagues and earthquakes, famine and fire.' She leaned her elbows on the table. 'It wouldn't have been much fun living with a tetchy god you had to keep propitiating, would it?' She picked up an unused knife from the table, weighing the handle in her palm. Then, taking a grip, she made a firm slicing movement as if cutting some animal's throat. 'Slurp. There goes the blood.'

Adam's fingers were round her wrist, grasping so tightly that the knife fell out of her hand and clattered to the floor. 'Don't do that,' he said quietly.

She snatched back her hand, both angry and hurt. 'What's the matter? Delicate stomach? It's all right, Adam, I was only pretending. As it happens I don't even eat meat, let alone slaughter it myself.' She rubbed at her wrist, turning away from him.

But he pulled his chair closer to hers so that he could speak into her ear. 'You're wrong – Joe's wrong. Quite wrong. What you don't understand is that the Mithraists didn't make a habit of slaughtering bulls. Oh, yes, they made occasional sacrifices, but purely as a part of their special rituals. And they certainly didn't sacrifice human beings, no Roman religion tolerated that. This idea of the followers of Mithras being bloodthirsty killers is pure propaganda, put about by the Christians who had to either discredit them or lose out to them. And you know *that* didn't happen.'

She turned to face him, spurred by his tone into hotter anger. 'We've done a film on the religions of ancient Rome, have we? And that's why we're such a little know-all? Well, you can stuff your bloody Mithraists, I'm fed up with hearing about them! I've been lost in the back of beyond, scared witless and bitten to bits, and I've had enough.' She stood up. 'You can either drive me back into Arles right now or I'll get a taxi, which on the whole I think I might prefer.' Picking up her bag, she strode out of the restaurant.

He caught up with her outside the town walls; she'd been unsuccessfully trying to find something remotely resembling a taxi rank.

'I'd have been here sooner only I had to pay the bill,' he panted. 'Beth, please come back with me. I shouldn't have got cross with you, it's not your fault, nothing to do with you. It's . . . oh, Jesus, it's . . .'

'Another of those things that you're going to explain if I can only bear to wait?' she said scathingly.

He nodded.

She sighed. 'I must be off my trolley, but for some ridiculous reason I feel sorry for you.'

'That's something,' he murmured.

'I *will* let you drive me home, but just don't talk to me, all right?'

A faint smile crossed his face. 'Whatever you say.'

And he led the way back to the car.

They got back to Arles in the late afternoon, and spent some time sitting in slow-moving homegoing traffic. Letting them into La Maison Jaune, she called out, 'Joe? It's me.'

There was no reply, and, when she looked into Joe's study and his bedroom, no sign of him.

'Perhaps he's out researching,' Adam suggested. He'd followed her down the hall.

'Who invited you in?' But she was smiling as she said it.

'I'll go if you like.' He was standing right in front of her, so close that she could have stretched up and kissed him.

Whatever, she wondered, made me think of that?

'No need,' she said briskly. 'I'll make some tea – do you drink tea?'

'Yes, please.'

She led the way into the kitchen. 'You'd think he'd have left a note,' she said. 'Now I've no idea where he's gone or when he's likely to be back.'

'Does that matter?'

'No, I suppose not.'

'He wouldn't have been expecting you home this evening,' Adam pointed out, 'so he wouldn't have thought it necessary to tell you where he'd gone.'

'True.' She put tea-bags in cups and went to the fridge

for milk. 'Shame the French can't produce a decent pint of milk, isn't it? The taste of this stuff taints your cuppa something rotten.'

'Welcome, though.' He reached for his cup and stirred in sugar. 'Thanks.'

She stood drumming her fingers on the worktop, biting her lip. She noticed he was watching her. 'I wonder if he's coming back for supper. Joe, I mean.'

'I thought so.' There was a hint of amusement in his voice.

'I'll have a look on his desk.' She headed off for Joe's workroom. 'He might have left out some papers or a book that could give us a clue where he's gone.'

Adam followed her, and together they stared down at Joe's tidy desk. Not a book was out of its place in the neat row across the back, not a file had been left lying open.

'Damn!'

Adam said, 'I know it's none of my business, but why are you so worried? He's big enough to look after himself, surely, and, knowing you were going to be out, isn't it likely he's decided to spend the afternoon strolling about, then gone straight on to find himself a quiet drink and a nice supper somewhere?'

'Highly likely.' She smiled ruefully. 'The thing is – ' She stopped. Do I want to tell Adam? She glanced at him. He was perched on the edge of Joe's desk, looking at her with a kind expression. 'I've got a feeling he's up to something, and I'm worried about him.'

'What sort of something?'

'I've no idea, that's the problem. It's just that he had a couple of mysterious phone calls, and yesterday he pretended he'd come back here on his own when I distinctly heard him talking to other people outside.'

Adam thought for a few moments, then said, 'It doesn't add up to much.'

'I *know*! Oh, I wish I hadn't said anything, I knew you wouldn't understand.'

'It doesn't matter if I do or not. But I can see you're rather upset, so if you like I'll stay with you till he gets back. Although,' – now he sounded amused again – 'bearing in mind your embargo on my talking to you, perhaps you'd prefer that I went.'

'I only said you weren't to talk to me on the way home,' she pointed out. 'It doesn't apply here.' She met his eyes. 'And I'd love you to stay. Thank you.'

There was enough in the fridge and the larder for her to make supper for them both; the frozen coquilles from Monoprix were surprisingly good, and it was a novelty to make a salad with all the local vegetables. In case Adam was still hungry she cut up some bread and put out a goat's cheese.

'Have you tried this hot?' he asked.

'No. Is it nice?'

'Lovely. I'll do it for you, one day.'

The idea that there might be a day when he would cook for her somehow failed to surprise her; comment didn't seem appropriate, however, and she didn't make one.

'Is Joe older than you?' He shared the last of the Côtes du Rhône between their two glasses.

'Yes. By two years.'

'And he's doing a degree?'

'His MA.'

There was a pause. Then: 'And what about you? Did you go to university?'

'Not – no. Girls don't need to, according to my father.'

'So Joe gets to do two degrees and you left school at sixteen.' It was a statement, not a question, as if he knew.

She waited for the old resentment to build up and boil over into the usual invective, but surprisingly it didn't. Instead she found herself saying calmly, 'I was good at science at school, but my family didn't encourage me so when I left I became a secretary, and went on being one for the best part of ten years. But then I got a temporary job in a science lab, and all the ambitions I'd had at fifteen came rushing back.'

'So what did you do?'

'I enrolled at night school and did chemistry, physics and biology A levels, which of course led on to a much better lab job.' She smiled. '*And* a permanent one.'

'Good for you. What did your father say to that?'

She tried to remember his exact words. 'He said, "It is certainly not the career I should have chosen for a daughter of mine." Oh, and he said I was stopping some "decent man" from having the post.' Suddenly she laughed out loud. 'Honestly, my father's incorrigible – he truly believes all women should be wives and mothers and remain firmly in the home at all times. I once tried to tell him that was as silly as saying all men should be engine-drivers, but he didn't begin to see the point. He can't bear female newsreaders – he gets up and leaves the room when Anna Ford or Moira Stuart are on.'

'*I* don't,' Adam murmured.

'No, I'm sure most other men don't either.' She smiled indulgently. 'Poor old Father. It's sad, really.'

'Sad for you, that you've had to suffer his extreme chauvinism.'

She looked at him, considering. 'I did suffer,' she said quietly. 'I hated him, couldn't see that he had any love for me whatsoever. But now – oh, I don't know. Perhaps I'm getting wiser as I get older, but I can see that, in his way, he was trying to do what he thought was best for me. Even if he was wrong!'

'What's this job in the laboratory? What sort of lab is it?'

She was grateful to have something else to think about. 'Pathology. I was a secretary first – I went there as a temp – and all I did was filing, a bit of typing and a lot of teamaking. You wouldn't think people would come from analysing cervical smears and mucus samples and instantly down a cup of tea and a couple of biscuits – well, I didn't when I started – but they do.'

'Then you decided what was going on in the lab was more interesting than filing?'

'Exactly. I was lucky, the head of the lab encouraged me – I thought it was a hopeless dream, wanting to be a professional scientist, but gradually I began to believe I could do it.'

'You must be very grateful to him.' Just like Father all those years ago, she protested silently, assuming my science teacher had to be a man! But, unlike her father, Adam added, 'Or her.'

'It was her. I'm sure that was why she never let me get discouraged, because she too was a woman battling in what's seen as a man's world.'

'There you were, then, with your A levels and your permanent post, and –'

'I got a degree, too,' she said diffidently: it still went against the grain to make any remark that could sound as if you were patting yourself on the back. 'With the Open University.'

He stared at her. 'This is going to sound like a patronizing male remark, but I have to say you don't look old enough to have left school at, what, sixteen, spent ten years as a secretary, then done A levels and a degree.'

'I've only just got my degree,' she said. Let him work it out, she thought, I'm not going to tell him!

'I really admire determination,' he said. 'Not to mention hard work. So, what's the next step? What does having a degree mean?'

'Dr Amery's a specialist in forensic science, and she's been training me in –'

There was the sound of a key in the front door.

She looked at Adam. 'There's Joe!'

He seemed to be having a problem getting his key in the

lock, and she jumped up to go and open the door. 'Hello, Joe, we came back and –'

It wasn't Joe. On the step, pushing back long, tangled brown hair to get a better look at the lock, was a girl in jeans and a T-shirt that said 'Red Hot Chili Peppers'.

Beth said lamely, 'Are you sure you've got the right house?'

Then she saw Joe's key-ring in the girl's hand.

The girl pushed past her into the hall. Past Adam, too, who was standing in the workroom doorway.

'Hi,' she said laconically. 'Joe sent me to get a bottle – he said it's in the cupboard behind his desk. This his desk?' Beth nodded. 'Must be in here, then.' She opened the front of the low dresser standing against the wall.

'Make yourself at home,' Beth said, too amazed to try to work out what was happening. The girl didn't respond.

'I'll only take the brandy,' the girl said, 'he didn't say to fetch anything else.'

'The other bottles don't belong to us,' Beth said severely. 'You mustn't take them.'

'I said I wasn't going to, didn't I?' She sounded surly.

'Where *is* Joe?' Beth burst out. 'What does he think he's doing, sending some stranger round to raid the drinks cabinet?' She went up to the girl. 'And who the hell are you?'

Maddeningly the girl nodded, as if a long-held suspicion had just been proved correct. 'He said you was touchy. But he said you wouldn't be here so it'd be okay to come. Never mind, eh? Nice meeting you. And your mate.' She smiled at Adam, edging her way towards the front door.

'Just a minute! When's he coming back? What about –'

'He's not coming back, not tonight.' The girl was at the top of the steps, poised to leap off down them. 'It's an all-night party, and if him and me get tired, we'll kip on the floor. I've got my sleeping bag.' She grinned, looking suddenly lovely. 'Plenty of room for both of us, it's a double! Cheerio!'

Slowly closing the door, Beth leaned against it. Catching Adam's eyes on her, his expression suggesting he didn't know whether to sympathize or burst out laughing, she couldn't think of one single thing to say.

After a moment Adam said, perfectly mimicking the girl's diction, '"If he gets tired, he can get in my sleeping bag and get his leg over."'

The shock receding, she started to laugh. As the ups and downs of the whole long day caught up with her, her knees went weak and, still leaning against the door, she sank down to sit on the floor.

'Sorry,' Adam said, 'that was uncalled for.' He went back into the workroom. 'I'm going to have a look in your drinks cupboard. If there's anything as decent as that brandy she's just walked off with, I think we'll both have a drink.'

12

As Adam ushered her to the sofa next to Joe's desk, she said, 'I didn't know he had a girlfriend! I didn't think he'd *ever* had one!'

Adam, still clearly struggling with laughter, said, 'Are we using "had" in its colloquial sense?'

'You're not helping!'

'No, sorry.'

'I can't get over it! Just can't believe it.' She took a large mouthful of whatever it was Adam had found in the cupboard – it was quite nice, tasting vaguely of apples – to see if it would aid credibility.

'She seemed all right,' Adam remarked. 'Pretty, in a gamine way. Nice hair, and long legs.'

'Quite.' She wasn't sure she wanted him to go on. 'Do you think they know each other at home? Why didn't he tell me she'd be here? I wouldn't have minded, she could have done his note-making for him.'

'He's probably well aware you'd do it better.'

She looked at him. 'Thank you.'

'He might have picked her up here in Arles,' Adam suggested. 'Why are you laughing?'

She had some more of the apple-tasting drink. 'Because that's exactly what he accused me of. When you and I met at the Alyscamps cemetery, he said I couldn't be away for five minutes without picking someone up.'

'Rather hypocritical of him, under the circumstances.'

'That's my brother for you.'

They lapsed into silence. Adam topped up her glass – it

was only a small one – and absently she sipped from it.

After a while he said, 'This previously unsuspected side of Joe's nature might have its advantages for you, you know.'

'Yes? How come?'

'Well, for one thing, once he knows you know about his girlfriend and her double sleeping bag, he can't go on lecturing you from his position on the moral high ground.'

You don't know Joe, she thought.

'For another, that pretty little girl may well make him more human. She would me,' he added.

'Hmm. It's always possible, I suppose.' The concept of a new, laid-back Joe who laughed a bit more and wasn't constantly carping at other people for having jobs unsuitable for girls, swearing, and simply having fun, was something she was having trouble with. 'She's not what I'd have thought of as the type he'd choose,' she reflected.

'No pebble glasses and tweed skirt? Now you're stereotyping people, too.'

'Too?'

'Like your dad. "Girls can't be scientists".'

He was right. She giggled. 'I'm the scientist. I ought to wear tweed and glasses.'

She drained her glass and looked round to see if the bottle was handy. 'I've put it away,' he said.

'Why? I was enjoying it.'

'I imagine you were, it was thirty-year-old Calvados. But it's also about 40 per cent proof, which is why it's back in the cupboard. Even if you only have to crawl off to bed, I shall have to drive home, eventually.'

'Not to Northumberland?'

'No, only across town for now.'

'I could have had some more,' she said wistfully.

'It's bad for you, drinking alone. Shall we have some coffee?'

'All right.' She got up, wobbled a bit, then went with him into the kitchen. 'Shall I do it?'

'No need. Just show me where things are.'

She waved vaguely at the cupboard above the fridge, then propped herself against the worktop. 'Suddenly I feel very tired.'

'I'm not surprised. It's been a long day.'

The great British gift for understatement, she thought. Perhaps it gets more pronounced the further north you go. Northumberland. I remembered about him living by Hadrian's Wall when I read about – what was it? Yes, the temple.

'There's a temple of Mithras on Hadrian's Wall.'

He dropped a cup.

'Oh, dear, there goes one of whatsit's auntie's mugs.' She bent to help him pick up the pieces.

'Don't cut yourself,' he said. 'Sorry about that.'

'Don't worry, we'll replace it when we replace her thirty-year-old Calvados.' I was saying something – what was it? Yes, Mithras. 'Do you know it? The temple? I saw a picture of it in Joe's book – actually there's nothing much to see but there's an artist's impression of what it looked like in its heyday. Shall I show you?'

He had his back to her, stirring boiling water into the coffee cups. 'No need. I know it.'

'I expect there are lots of Roman bits along Hadrian's Wall,' she said as they took their coffee back to the sofa. 'Old forts, swords, coins. That sort of thing.'

'Yes. There are some fine exhibits in the museums.'

'I wasn't thinking of them.' Eyes closed, she was seeing a long wall winding away over hill and dale into the misty distance. A man was striding along the top, his heavy cloak billowing in the fierce wind. 'I was thinking of all the things there must be buried deep in the ground that nobody will ever find.'

The silence extended for so long that she thought he must

have dropped off – she was nearly asleep herself. Opening her eyes, she turned to see. He was awake, staring at the opposite wall as if some fascinating film were being projected on to it.

'Adam? All right?'

He didn't speak at first but reached to take her hand. Holding it tightly, she heard him sigh. 'Adam?'

'I've got a confession to make.'

'Good grief! Whatever is it?' She spoke lightly, but the shiver that his words sent through her had been unmistakable.

'I really don't know where to start.' He sighed again, withdrawing his hand. 'I've misled you – I'm not here to research a film.'

'No? You're not a film-maker?'

'Yes, that bit was true, as was the claim to be doing one on the gipsy routes. I *am* going to, but something's got in the way.'

'Go on.'

'Researching into the *gitans* and their songs and legends is, as it happens, a very convenient cover – I very much needed to come down to Arles, to the Camargue, and to say I was coming to research a film – one I'd already announced I was going to work on – provided me with an excuse. I have actually done some work, as you well know.' He glanced at her.

'Thank God those twenty-five verses weren't all for nothing,' she said fervently.

'No, they weren't. It's funny, really – I'd had the idea for the gipsy film before – before this other thing. Sometimes I think it was all meant to be, that Fate, as they say, has been taking a hand. I just can't turn my back on it, and I've tried, believe me – it's illogical and probably a complete waste of time, but I think I'm hooked.'

'You're not explaining very well. Could you try a bit harder?'

'I can, but I may not succeed.' He stopped, clearly thinking. 'Beth, do you know anything about spiritualism?'

'Not much. Séances, do you mean?'

'Yes, in that séances are one way in which people in this world try to get in touch with the spirit world.'

'You believe in all that?' Somehow she was surprised.

'I do and I don't. I don't because my logical mind finds it hard, if not impossible, to accept that we in this life have a mental pathway through which we can contact the dead. Or, more accurately perhaps, through which they can contact us. I do because . . .' he hesitated, then said, 'because I think someone has got in touch with me.'

The man in the toga hovered in her mind's eye, wavered, disappeared. 'Oh, yes?' Her voice was barely audible.

'I went with a friend to sit in a spiritualist circle.' He spoke firmly, as if, having at last made up his mind to tell her, he wanted her to get an accurate picture. 'I enjoyed it – I found it most stimulating. Somehow the deeply relaxed state you get into makes access to the unconscious much easier, at least it did for me, and I started going regularly. I'd been seeing the same two images again and again, almost since I began going – a lion, and something that looked like a thunderbolt symbol – and then one day I experienced what some of the others had said happened to them. I'd been hoping it would, and it did.'

'What was it?' She almost prayed he wouldn't tell her: she had a strange urge to get up and put all the lights on.

'I saw someone. I was sitting there with my eyes shut, involved in some long and fascinating thought process to do with my mother's rose garden, and suddenly someone was beside me. I always sat at one end of a long couch – we met in a member of the group's living room – and this figure was standing on my right.'

'Someone could have walked into the room.'

'Beth, it's not like that. You'd know if they did, and anyway we usually sat with the door locked. No, this man just appeared.'

'I thought you said you had your eyes shut.'

'Yes. Which is why I believe it must have been an apparition: I could see him with my eyes open or closed.'

She tried to imagine what it would have been like, and failed. 'What – what sort of a man was he? Was he – did he frighten you?'

'Not in the least. He was just a presence at first – I could hear him breathing. He gave out reassurance – it was almost as if he wanted to make quite sure I *wasn't* afraid, probably because if I had been, I'd have panicked and the channel would have closed.'

'What did you do?'

'I just sat there, experiencing him – I can't think of a better word. Gradually I started seeing pictures – Hadrian's Wall, the legionary fort at York, a legion marching, the eagle standard flying above their heads. And, just as before, the lion and the thunderbolt symbol.'

'Was it like in the films, the marching and the fort?'

'Nothing like that, if you're thinking of some Hollywood epic. This was Roman Britain without the glamour – you could almost feel the chilblains prickling.'

'Was he making you see those things?'

'Who can say? Yes, I think so, but, although I'd never seen them quite in that way before, they were all scenes and places I knew.'

'The legionary fort in York doesn't exist any more.'

'No, but I've seen diagrams. Reconstructions. I wouldn't put it past my imagination to make a reasonably convincing image.'

'I'm not pouring scorn on what you're saying,' she said quietly.

'I know. Believe me, you're not making any objections I haven't already made myself.'

'What did he do next, this man?'

'I started to notice that the same figure appeared in all the scenes. He was a soldier – sometimes he looked young, as if he'd only just been recruited, and sometimes he was more mature. Once I saw him with a child, a boy, and a bored-looking woman in a long gown. And in all the visions, wherever they were, this man was there, so I guessed it must be him. The apparition. And, for some reason, he was linked to those two recurrent symbols.'

'I don't see what he has to do with you coming to Provence.'

'You will. Over successive meetings, he widened the range of what he showed me. It was almost as if the early pictures had been to establish a link between us – one of the places he showed me on the wall, for example, has been a favourite spot of mine since childhood.'

'Perhaps he saw you there. Perhaps he'd been waiting all that time to get through to you.'

He turned to her, eyes alight. 'That's just how it seemed to me! I tested it out – one winter evening I went to the place and stood on the wall in the rain to see what would happen. He came. Stood beside me so that we looked out over the rolling moors side by side, like two centurions planning an advance. Then he went away.'

'All right then, bona fides established, what did he do next?'

'I started to see other places, and again, he was there. I saw Provençal scenes – the amphitheatre here in Arles, what looked like the old Roman forum, a country house with cypress trees round it and a mosaic of a dolphin on the floor. And the Camargue.' He broke off.

'You saw that place on the poster,' she supplied for him. 'That's why it spooked you so much – your man had put it into your head, hadn't he?'

Adam nodded. 'Yes. It was one of the images he gave me at the last meeting before I came away. He kept showing it – if my mind stopped concentrating on it, he brought me back. Those three reed-thatched buildings, the tamarisks and the ditch are etched on my brain as if they'd been tattooed.'

'Why are they so important?'

'I've no idea. But I always associated them with suffering, with pain and deep unhappiness. Actually going there was – well, rather a trial.'

Not just for you, she thought. 'Has he shown you anywhere else with the same insistence?'

'One other place. But I can't talk about it.'

He spoke calmly, but she knew better than to try to make him: poor man, she thought, he's suffering enough as it is.

'Why do you think he's opened this channel to you – is that the right expression?'

'Yes, it explains it perfectly. I'm not sure, but I'm beginning to suspect he wants me to do something for him.'

'And will you?'

'I'll decide that once I know what it is. But, although I can imagine there might be danger involved – and please don't ask me to explain that, either – I honestly don't believe it would be anything evil. He's just not that sort of a man. He's a good man.'

He spoke with utter certainty.

'But wouldn't an evil man pretend to be good, in order to enlist your help? Surely they have abundant cunning, these spirits.'

'No doubt. It's unreasonable, but I know he's not evil. Anyway, I'll know soon. He's brought me down here, shown me that the places he put into my mind exist in reality – one of them, anyway – and no doubt he'll tell me in due course what I have to do.' He sighed again, sounding very weary. 'Whatever happened that upset him, it happened down here.'

'How do you know?'

He looked at her. 'Because his presence is far, far stronger now. Before, at home, he was always vague, shadowy – I could never really make out his face. Now, I see him as clearly as I see you.'

She swallowed. It would have been easier to keep silent, but she found she couldn't. 'What does he look like?'

'He's tall, broad-shouldered. In the Legion, he was among the biggest. He has dark hair, greying now, and rather deep-set brown eyes. I used to see him in a legionary's uniform – leather breastplate, helmet, skirt with metal strengthening bars and those heavy-soled sandals that the Romans wore as military boots – but, down here, he's dressed in a toga. Usually.' He broke off. 'That's about it.'

She couldn't speak. After a moment he took her hand again. 'Do you think I'm quite mad?'

'Because you're haunted by a Roman who has a mission for you? I ought to, that's for sure.'

'But you don't?' he asked hopefully.

His tone touched her: putting her other hand on top of their fingers clasped together, she said, 'Well, if you're mad, so am I. He frequented the amphitheatre, would you say, and that ghastly place we went to today?' He nodded.

'Then there's no doubt. I've seen him too.'

INTERLUDE

ARLES

AD 175

13

I got used to having Theo around very quickly. Someone had taught him how to make himself useful – taught him well, too; whether it was sweeping the yard or buffing leather, he did the task thoroughly, with no scrimped corners.

Callistus, who deigned to come in to clean, launder and cook for me – when he hadn't anything better to do – was clearly puzzled by the new addition to my household. Reasoning that Theo would only be a temporary guest, I said something vague about him being a distant relation; in retrospect, I wished I'd thought up a better story, since Callistus was a dreadful old gossip and probably spread calumny about me and my new young boy at the first and every subsequent opportunity.

As for Didius – he was the bath servant of a neighbour who also attended a select group of other customers – his eyes lit up at the sight of the boy. '*Lovely* upper torso development,' he remarked as he was massaging my shoulders one night. I knew he wasn't referring to mine – on arrival he'd spotted Theo splitting kindling on the block by the gates.

'Keep your mind on the job,' I told him sternly. 'You're not pummelling hard enough.'

'The youngster'll be ready for my attentions when he's filled your log basket. I'm saving myself.'

Didius was incorrigible. But I'd known him long enough to appreciate that most of it was just talk – he had a kind heart. 'He won't be using the bathhouse just yet,' I said quietly. 'He may take a while to settle down, and I don't want to suggest anything he isn't happy about.'

I realized instantly I'd left the way to misunderstanding wide open. Sure enough, Didius plunged off down it. 'Mmmm,' he sympathized, 'it doesn't do to rush these delicate matters.'

I reached up to remove his hands from my shoulders, sitting up and wrapping the towel round me. Then, for the second time in a week, I reasserted my heterosexual preferences.

Didius was slightly huffy – 'You really can't blame me, sir, for getting the wrong idea' – and I rewarded him with a larger than usual tip.

The glance he gave Theo from under his darkened eyelashes as he left was wistful but resigned.

What I'd said to him about giving Theo time to settle down applied in a wider context than use of the bathhouse. Whisking him away from Arelate had been impulsive, yes, but I'd known what I was doing. I didn't know much about him, it was true, but thirty years' experience of men, in the legions and afterwards, had given me the ability to size people up quickly. I wasn't always right, but this time I was – instinct had told me Theo was a good lad who'd run up against bad luck, and, until he felt like telling me more, that was enough to be getting on with.

For the first week or two I concentrated on feeding him. Gods, how he ate! As the edge came off his extreme hunger, he seemed to remember some table manners, so that sharing a meal with him became more of a pleasure and less of an endurance test. The evening he accepted a small glass of wine, I felt we were getting somewhere.

He'd said he didn't drink, so it was only to be expected that even a small amount of alcohol would loosen his tongue. Soon I realized that my problem wasn't going to be encouraging him to talk, but getting him to stop.

He began with a rather hesitant but quite charming little

speech. I was touched because, very obviously, he'd prepared it in advance.

'You have made me very welcome in your house, even though you knew nothing of me except that I was a thief, and I'm very grateful.' He paused, eyes wide with alarm; I guessed he'd forgotten his words. He gulped, then rushed on: 'I'm strong and willing to work hard, so if you think of any tasks I can do for you, please tell me.'

His face red, he bent his head and went back to his food.

'Thank you, Theo. That's a good suggestion, and I'll think up some things for you to do.' We were approaching sensitive ground: I had to get a few things straight between us. 'Of course, we don't yet know how long you'll be here.'

His head shot up again, and I saw panic in his eyes. 'I'm not going back!'

I had the feeling it had burst out before he'd had time to think. 'There's no question of my making you go back, wherever it is you came from. As far as I'm concerned, you're very welcome here. But I think we should consider some alternatives.'

I hated saying that, especially as it made his open, friendly face close up. 'Like what?' he said sullenly.

'Such as you settling in a new town somewhere and getting a proper job. Such as me making enquiries to see if I can find some reputable farm where you could live and work. That sort of thing.'

He looked brighter. 'I'd like that. I know about farming.'

I would have lit on that as a clue to his past, except that I'd already realized he had a rural background: no town lad chopped wood like Theo did, and when we'd strolled through the fields he'd known wheat from barley, which was more than most people did.

'That's one possibility, then. You'd prefer the country to the town?'

'Yes.' He nodded furiously. 'I didn't like Arelate at all.'

'No, it tends to be over-civilized. Or so its inhabitants

would have you believe. But you couldn't go back to Arelate even if you wanted to, since you're a wanted criminal there.'

Instantly I wished I hadn't said it: he went white, and I knew the spectre of the amphitheatre still haunted him. 'They won't get me here, will they?' he said nervously.

'They won't. Only a few men know I live here, and none of them is likely to come across your fat merchant friend.' Privately I doubted whether Fatso would have pressed charges in any case, given the strong possibility that he'd been trading outside the law, and he was even more unlikely to now that the person he'd have taken action against had gone missing.

He said suddenly, the amphitheatre obviously still dominating his thoughts, 'It's not right, what they do to the animals. Especially the bulls.' He met my eyes. 'I know about bulls, they're my friends.'

Bulls lived out on the delta. Another clue. 'They're fine creatures, those wild bulls, I agree,' I said casually.

'And the horses.' His expression had gone dreamy. 'I could ride before I could walk,' he said proudly. 'They used to let me help break in the ponies, because I was light and I didn't have heavy hands.' He glanced down at his hands, which were square and short-fingered. 'I talk to them, see, that way you make an animal your friend and it's not always trying to hurt you. I talk to all animals.' Abruptly he broke off.

No wonder he didn't like Arelate: the amphitheatre confronted you virtually anywhere you went, and an animal-lover like Theo wouldn't be able to stop his mind running straight to the thought of suffering, bloodshed and slaughter.

I said, careful not to sound too interested, 'I suppose you kept pets.'

He grinned. 'Of course. When I was small I made a pet of everything, but Mother – ' This time the abrupt stop was accompanied by obvious emotion: he closed his eyes, and I saw his throat heave as he swallowed.

I wondered if the emotion was because his mother was dead. That might explain why he had run away. But was he ready for an enquiry?

I sat and watched him struggle with his grief. Then I said, 'You don't have to tell me if you don't want to, but if you do, I'll help you if I can.'

He sat for an instant longer. Then he said, 'I miss her.' He squeezed his eyes more tightly shut, and a tear rolled down his cheek.

'Is she dead?' I asked gently.

'No!' His eyes opened and shot to mine. 'No! She's not!'

'I'm sorry. I thought that might be why you were sad.'

'No.' He took a deep shuddering breath. 'I'm sad because I miss her, and because I'm worried about her. She hasn't got me there any more, and –'

I waited, but he couldn't bring himself to go on.

'Is it out of the question for you to go back?' It was worth a try.

'I can't!' he shouted.

'All right! I promised to help you, remember? *And* that I wouldn't make you do anything you didn't want to.'

'Sorry,' he muttered. Then, straightening up, he said, 'She's a widow. My father was a fisherman, and his boat got lost. There's this *bastard* called Gaius, he owns our house. He likes Mum, and I think she likes him. But I *hate* him, he only pretends to be nice to me when Mum's there and the rest of the time he treats me like shit.'

I'd rarely heard such hatred in a grown man's voice, never mind a child's. I wanted to sympathize, but it would have undermined the courageous face he was struggling to maintain. It was, I guessed, only the fierce emotion that had stopped him breaking down.

'In what way?' I asked calmly. It seemed important that I knew.

'He gives me work to do that I can't do well enough, just so he has an excuse to beat me.'

'He beats you?'

'I just said so! Look, if you don't believe me!' He was up and raising his tunic before I could stop him: across the shoulders and over the thin ribcage were welts, some fresh, some already old scars.

It looked as though this Gaius had been around for a while.

I waited until my own fury had subsided, then reached out and poured more wine into Theo's glass. Gods, he looked as if he needed it.

'So, basically you ran away because Gaius was mistreating you, which solves one problem but raises another, in that you're now concerned about your mother. Is that right?'

He nodded.

There was something else I wanted to know, but asking the question needed delicacy, given his shaky emotional state. 'Did – You said Gaius pretended to be nice to you when your mother was there. Did she never see through his act?'

What I'd wanted to say was, How in Hades could she have let those beatings go on?

Unfortunately he seemed to know: I hadn't been subtle enough.

'Don't you criticize her! She didn't know about Gaius *because I didn't let her*!'

The thought ran through my head that Theo's father must have been a decent man, to have produced a son with the inherent chivalrous desire to keep the more cruel facts of life away from the womenfolk.

'I didn't mean to criticize her,' I said quietly. 'I'm sorry if that's how it sounded.'

He grunted an acknowledgement. I wasn't convinced, but I didn't pursue it.

There was a rather awkward silence. I heard my own words ring out in my head: I promised to help you, didn't I?

Right at that moment, there didn't seem much I could do.

I'd thought things were going quite well – in fact I'd decided on whom to talk to over finding Theo a permanent home and was about to make a first approach – but then he went missing.

It's a truism that you don't miss something till you no longer have it, and this seems to apply equally to a person as to your favourite knife. I'd been calmly making plans to send the boy away – admittedly, not far away – but, when at noon I finally went across to his room to get him out of bed and he wasn't there, for a moment I was hit with a depth of feeling I thought had gone for ever when Marcus died.

Fortunately, I was alone; the sort of search I instantly set off on would have taken some explaining. He'd taken my horse, so I had to hire one; funny that, even when I was forking out a ludicrous amount of money for a sad old relic that didn't look as if it could make it to the end of the street and back, it didn't occur to me that my own horse was gone for good. I'd come to trust Theo: I knew I might be in for a huge disappointment, but I was certain he'd gone off for a good reason and that, in time, he'd come back. Accompanied by my horse.

He'd told me he wouldn't steal again, and I believed him.

Of course, I didn't know where he'd gone. I had an idea and, after circling the village for a while in a fruitless search for tracks, I turned the old nag's head south.

I finally admitted it was hopeless midway through the afternoon. If he had indeed gone where I thought – and it was only a hunch – there were innumerable routes he could have taken. And I didn't even know exactly where he'd have been heading, even if my hunch was right.

Eventually I let the poor old horse do what it had been trying to do all day and turn its head for its stable. Gods, it was the only time I got it up to a grudging canter. I collected my deposit – that crook of a horse dealer tried to make me pay more because I'd got his animal muddy, but I pointed out it was a damned sight cleaner than when I'd picked it up, since I'd banged quite a lot of the caked dirt off it when we stopped for lunch – then I went home.

Theo came in just after midnight. I heard him creeping around in the stable – animal-lover that he was, he rubbed down and watered my horse before seeing to his own needs.

He was filthy, and he looked as if he'd been crying. I think he expected I'd be waiting for him – he came straight up to where I was sitting, in front of a nearly empty jug of wine, and sank down on to the floor. Irrelevantly, I noticed he was sitting on the head of my beautiful mosaic dolphin.

'I'm sorry,' he whispered.

'About what?' I asked gently.

'Stealing your horse. Going off without telling you.' He shrugged, as if he had so much to be sorry for that it was hopeless even to begin.

'You brought the horse back,' I pointed out. I hesitated, then went on, 'As I knew you would.'

He looked up at me. 'How did you?'

'Never mind. I was right, wasn't I?' I grinned at him, and he smiled faintly back. 'Are you going to tell me where you've been?'

There was a long pause. He sat, head bowed, tracing the line of the dolphin's smile with his finger. Then he said, 'I went to see if my mother was all right.'

The hunch had been right. Trying to keep my voice calm, I said, 'And was she?'

'Dunno.' I knew him well enough to realize he always

sounded surly when he was trying to cover emotion.

'Did you speak to her?'

'No. I watched her for a while from the rushes.'

Poor boy. No wonder he'd been crying. 'How did she seem?' It was something you might ask an adult, who would probably understand and answer in the way you wanted. To expect a boy to understand was unrealistic. 'I mean, was she carrying on as normal? Doing what she usually does?'

'S'pose so.' Then: 'She looked sort of hunched. As if she was tired.'

'Ah.'

'Do you think she's anxious about me?'

The light eyes were on mine. He was desperate for me to reassure him, for me to say, great Jove, no! Of course not! But I couldn't. Anxious about him! It was the understatement of the year.

'Theo, she will undoubtedly be worried about you,' I said carefully. 'You said she seems to like this Gaius man?' He shrugged, then nodded. 'Well, even if she does, you're her son, and –' I'd been about to say that she loved him, but I stopped. Some women didn't love their children, not enough to prevent them coming to harm. Not enough to chase after them when they ran away, pleading with them to come back. It would be wrong for me to put some idealistic picture into his mind that wouldn't stand up to the harsh light of day.

I was mentally scratching my head to come up with some way of encouraging him to let it all out when abruptly he began to do just that. 'We had to have somewhere to go when Dad was lost – we'd lived by the sea, at the Saints' Village,' – I nodded, recognizing the local name for the little port – 'but without Dad we couldn't pay the rent, and the only work down there's fishing.' He didn't need to point out that fishing wasn't woman's work – I knew the superstitions about women going to sea as well as he did.

'So me and Mum moved off inland, and she met Gaius, and he offered her a house in exchange for working for him. She can do anything,' he said proudly, 'cook, sew, grow things. He was nice to both of us at first, I really liked him.' His face twisted as if in disgust at the duplicity of men.

'But then he turned nasty.'

'Not towards Mum! I'd have killed him if he'd hurt her.' Somehow I didn't doubt it: he'd have had a damned good try, anyway. 'He treats her like a lady. Brings her stuff, stands up when she comes into the room. Creep!'

I hadn't so much as clapped eyes on this Gaius, but I had to agree with him. My opinion of Theo's mother was falling by the minute – I couldn't understand how she could have been fooled.

'That's why I ran away,' he said wearily. 'He makes her happy, but if she'd found out about – if she'd found out I hate him, she'd have taken me away, then she'd have been sad and worried like she was before. She once said it was great that I could eat as much as I wanted again. After she'd started working for Gaius, I mean.'

I had a stab of sympathy for the wretched woman. I knew how Theo ate, and to have had to watch him scraping up a meagre supper, clearly desperate for more when there was no more, must have hurt even a half-hearted mother.

If she found out, she'd have taken me away, he'd said. Was that just wishful thinking, or was he right? If he was, there could just be a way out of this difficult situation: if she was prepared to abandon a home, security and a man who, to quote Theo, brought her stuff and treated her like a lady because her son wasn't happy, then there was hope. It all depended on how much this Gaius meant to her: I'd known women ignore the needs of their children because they rated their relationship with a man as more important, and Theo's mother might be that type. I said casually, 'What does your mother do when he brings her presents and treats her like a lady? Does she like it?'

'Dunno. I think she does. But she frowns a lot when he fusses round her.'

What did that mean? That she didn't like the attentions, or that the presents weren't grand enough? 'Does she – '

I stopped. Theo was in the middle of an enormous yawn, and it seemed cruel to grill him further. 'Go to bed,' I said. 'You'll fall asleep where you are if you're not careful, and although my dolphin is nice to look at, he'd make a hard couch.'

Stiffly he got to his feet. Through another yawn, he wished me goodnight.

I'd had an idea. After his door had closed, I sat on by myself, working out whether or not it was a good idea.

I'd been into Arelate for several days out of the last week, and there was no work left outstanding on my desk. No reason, from that point of view, why I shouldn't take a couple of days' holiday.

And, I had to admit, my curiosity was so thoroughly roused that I wasn't going to have any peace till I'd at least attempted to answer a few questions. If Theo's mother loved and missed him, and wanted what was best for him, then perhaps there might be some way of getting the two of them back together, of spiriting them away from Gaius. To reunite them was surely the best possible solution, and certainly worth a try. But would the lad be willing to make that try?

At last I got up and headed for bed: I'd decided I'd ask Theo in the morning, and let his reaction decide me.

He was overjoyed at the suggestion. Of course, I didn't say 'Let's go down and spy on your mother and this Gaius bloke and see if there's anything we can do to resolve this mess.' I prettied it up, saying I'd always wanted to get to know the great Rhodanus delta better and, with some leave due and the perfect guide now available, when was I going to get a better chance?

When we'd agreed on what a good plan it was, I added casually, 'We could look in on your mother. *If* we're in the vicinity.'

Equally casually he said, 'Yes, I suppose we could.'

14

After only a few hours on the road, I'd all but forgotten that our expedition had such a serious purpose. Riding out in the clear morning with Theo beside me – we'd hired a better horse for him than the one I'd had the previous day, which I thought was quite likely to have expired in the night – I felt as if years had rolled off me and I too was a boy again. Well, possibly that was an exaggeration. But I did feel incredibly happy.

And, burying the real aim even more deeply, Theo had taken me at my word and was performing his job as my guide most conscientiously. At times, too conscientiously – he would stop every so often and give me a little test, earnest in his anxiety that my ability to tell an egret from a peewit should be foolproof. I've never been much of a one for birds: when he spotted a bittern in the reeds, it was as much as I could do to pretend to share his delight. The damn bird was so well camouflaged and so coy about revealing itself that I wanted to shout, Suit yourself! What's so special about you, anyway?

We made camp for the night on a stretch of sandy ground beside the Great Pond in the middle of the delta. Down there, getting close to the sea, the water was brackish, but we had brought our own supplies of food and drink. The mosquitoes threatened to ruin the pleasure of our night under the stars, until Theo produced an oily liquid which we rubbed on our exposed skin: he said his mother had made it. It smelt foul, but fortunately the mosquitoes thought so too and left us alone.

All my army training came back to me; if I didn't exactly show Theo the ropes (he knew them adequately already), at least I held my own. He was impressed when I told him I could have made us a leather tent, given the skins, and even more so when I told him how, stranded out on patrol one filthy night up on Hadrian's Wall, our lives had been at risk from the blizzard and the icy winds till I'd hit on the idea of killing some sheep and wrapping ourselves in their skins. Their owner hadn't been best pleased, but that's another story; his anger, which in retrospect was entirely justifiable, melted away in the face of a fully armed Roman legion who just couldn't see what he was bellyaching about.

When he'd got over being impressed, Theo remarked bluntly that it had been a bit hard on the sheep.

The romance had faded by morning. I didn't tell Theo, but every one of my bones was aching; my mind might have leapt skittishly back to being eighteen, but clearly my body hadn't been persuaded to go too.

The morning sun soon took the worst of the pain away, and we set off again for another day's nature-spotting. But somehow the spontaneous joy of the previous day had diminished. It had nothing to do with my bones – the cloud was hovering over Theo.

I'd guessed what was coming before his announcement: he'd been acting with increasing wariness, stopping every time we emerged from cover to look right and left before going carefully on. It was quite obvious he was afraid, and I knew exactly what he was afraid of.

Entering the shade of a clump of tamarisks circled by dense reeds, he slid off his horse and led it up to the largest of the tamarisk bushes, where he tethered it. I did the same. Then, grasping my wrist, he led me forward, finger to his lips.

Pulling me down with him, he crawled through the reeds until we were able to push the last of them aside and look out. About thirty yards away was a small house, thatch-roofed, against which huddled a couple of ramshackled outbuildings.

Theo spoke right into my ear. 'That's my home.'

I nodded. 'I guessed.'

We watched and waited. There was no apparent sign of life, but he was right to be cautious – Gaius might have been inside, busy with some task. Asleep, even.

After a very long time, we saw someone coming along the track behind the house. It was a woman, dressed in a clean but shabby gown. Her veil had slipped back and I could see her bright hair, a few shades darker than Theo's. She walked as if she were carrying a heavy load, yet, apart from a wicker basket over one arm, she was empty-handed.

I didn't need his reaction to tell me this was his mother.

She went into the house. There was no sound of voices – either Gaius was ignoring her return, or he wasn't there.

I put my mouth to Theo's ear to ask him what he wanted to do, and saw tears streaming down his cheeks. He had made no sound: I hadn't realized he was crying.

Somehow, I felt it was time I took a decision.

'I'll keep watch,' I whispered. 'If anyone comes, I'll holler and you can race out of the back. There *is* a back way out?'

He nodded, swallowing.

'Go on, then.'

He turned to stare at me. There were questions and doubts in his eyes. Then he looked back at his house, and he knew what to do.

I watched him race across the open ground. Skidding to a stop, he reached the door just as his mother came out to see what the noise was.

I was close enough to see her face; my distance vision has been improving steadily over the years. In turn, she looked overjoyed, angry, tearful, then overjoyed again. I saw her grip his shoulders to shake him, then her arms went round him and she hugged him so tightly to her that I saw him flinch.

Then, looking anxiously all around, she hustled him inside.

I'd said I'd keep watch and I should have kept my word. But curiosity got the better of me: looking in each direction in turn, I hurried over to the house.

I heard their voices as I approached. She said something, he answered, then they were both laughing. She had a musical laugh, as if she were about to burst into song.

I stood in the doorway. They must have noticed the sudden reduction in the light: she spun round, leaping to stand in front of Theo, and I realized she'd mistaken me for someone else.

'It's all right,' I said quickly, 'I'm a friend.'

'It's Sergius,' Theo said at the same time. 'It *is* all right, Mum, he's been looking after me.'

She didn't move from her protective position, so Theo got up and moved in front of her.

'He's been living in my villa north of Arelate,' I explained. 'He . . .' It was going to be difficult to tell her what had happened without sounding self-congratulatory. She might even think I'd come to collect my reward for saving Theo from the lions.

'I got nicked in Arelate,' Theo said. 'This fat storekeeper accused me of thieving and was taking me to the magistrate's office when Sergius rescued me. Then he took me out of the city in case the fat bast– the fat man got the officials to charge me. I'm a wanted man,' he finished with relish.

She said, 'And were you thieving?' Her voice was as musical as her laughter.

'No!' He caught my eye. 'Well, a bit.'

'Theo, you –'

'I needed food! Mum, I didn't take much, and anyway the fat man got his necklaces back!'

'Necklaces? You can't eat beads!'

'I was going to sell them. Except for one, which was for you.' He sounded surly again.

She put her arms round him. 'Theo, Theo, what am I going to do with you?' She closed her eyes, turning her head away. I'd already seen the glint of tears before she wiped them surreptitiously away with the back of her hand.

Then, looking at me, she said, 'He's not normally a thief.'

'I know. Only under dire need, eh, Theo?' I smiled at him.

'Will he go on trial?' Her voice was urgent.

'Not if he doesn't get caught.'

'And will he?' Now the light eyes were fixed to mine, and I felt as if they were boring holes in me.

'If you mean am I going to turn him in, of course not.'

'But you work in the administration! You must, Theo just said you were in the magistrate's office, and –'

'I'm a financial secretary,' I interrupted. 'I have nothing to do with law enforcement.' I felt angry suddenly – why did the silly woman think I was going to all this trouble if I was going to take her son back to Arelate and shop him?

She must have worked that one out for herself. 'I'm sorry,' she said quietly, 'that was a stupid thing to say. But what happens now? Do we –'

It was my fault. I was meant to be look-out. And I was certainly the most experienced of the three of us – it was more of a crime for me to have forgotten all about the need for one.

Heavy footsteps pounded along the track outside from the direction of where we'd left the horses. Before there was time to slip out of the back entrance, he was on us.

'Zillah, there are horses in the tamarisk grove – what's happening?'

He appeared in the doorway, a thickset man with black hair and deeply tanned skin. He was long in the body, with heavily muscled arms that seemed to be too short. He was clad in a leather tunic and leggings, and he looked well fed and prosperous.

It had to be Gaius.

She stood there with her mouth open. Theo tried to stand in front of her while at the same time she was attempting to push him behind her: it would have been comical if it hadn't been so poignant.

The look Gaius shot at Theo before he disguised it behind a smile confirmed that the boy had told the truth. Not that I'd ever doubted it. I wondered if she'd seen, too.

But her head was bent over her son – maybe she hadn't.

I could appreciate his dilemma. He must be furious as a three-headed dog at the sight of the returned runaway, just longing for a chance to take a belt to him, yet, with Theo's mother present, he had to keep up his act of loving tolerance. Unless he had other plans . . .

He breathed deeply a few times, presumably to show us that he was controlling himself with difficulty. Then he said, 'Theodore, you have come back.' Icily, he went on, 'And have you any idea whatsoever of the anguish you have caused your poor mother? And me, what about me? I've been searching high and low for you, I'll have you know.' He was obviously more upset over that than over the woman's grief. And it was probably all pretence, anyway – wherever he'd been, I was prepared to put money on him not having been out hunting for Theo.

Theo said nothing. He didn't even look at Gaius.

'Theodore, I'm speaking to you.' Now the threat was in his voice. 'Have you nothing to say in return?'

But Theo seemed to have frozen solid. So did his mother.

I thought about it carefully – for all of the space of a couple of heartbeats – then spoke. 'The lad is in my custody,' I said grandly. 'In protective custody, in fact,' – I was making it up as I went along – 'since a citizen of A – of the town has made an accusation which the magistrate has serious doubts about. We . . . I . . .'

'Why doesn't the magistrate just dismiss the case, then?' Gaius asked, reasonably enough, I had to admit.

'Because . . .'

'It's an important citizen who's accused me, and the authorities don't want to offend him,' Theo piped up. I silently thanked good old quick-thinking Mercury for coming to our aid.

'That's right,' I agreed. 'These matters are complicated.' I made it sound as if they were outside the understanding of a rural hick like Gaius. It was a mistake.

'Who is this important citizen, then?' he asked nastily. 'I have contacts, I can exert some influence. More important, I can give the magistrate my word that I'll keep the boy here. He won't escape me.' The look he gave Theo made me convinced of that.

'Impossible!' the woman burst out. 'He's the subject of an official inquiry, he has to stay in custody.' She added quickly, 'That man says so.'

'I do, I do.' She was as quick-thinking as her son. But it was time to call a halt before one of us tripped up. 'I'm taking him back now. I wish you both farewell.' I bowed in the best tradition of dignified Arelate officialdom.

I reached out a hand to grasp Theo. He came willingly, almost running out of the house. It would have been better if he'd put on a show of reluctance.

'Just a minute,' Gaius said ominously.

I turned to face him. By my side Theo held his breath.

We stared at each other. I could feel his suspicion, his latent anger at someone ordering him about in his own home. Feel his resentment at being made to appear the weaker man in front of the woman.

I'd met men like him before. I stood there, waiting for him to make a move.

I thought we'd got away with it. I began to turn away, then a hand like an iron clamp fell on my wrist.

'The boy stays here,' he stated. 'Until I see your written authority for taking him away.'

I was trying to estimate his strength and his reaction time and assess them against my own. He was younger than me, broader and probably fitter, yet I'd have the advantage of surprise. Probably.

As I used to tell the smaller of my legionaries: When you're up against a stronger opponent, you've got to make the first blow count. Because you won't get the chance of a second one.

'You can read, then, can you?' As his fury flared at the insult, I punched him on the point of his chin. The shock loosened his grip on my wrist, and I swung the other fist up into his belly.

He slumped to the ground, a gout of blood on his lower lip where a tooth had been driven into the flesh.

'Get going!' the woman hissed. 'Quick, before he comes round!' She didn't have much faith in the long-lasting effects of my punch.

Theo said, 'Mum!', all the anguish racing through him coming out in the one word.

'Go!' she said. She hugged him quickly, fiercely, then pushed us away.

Grabbing his arm, I ran for the horses.

He was all but impossible to deal with over the following days. On the long journey home he'd been too shocked, too upset to do anything but sit dejectedly as his horse paced the miles away. But it was a different matter once we were back.

I was insensitive enough to think he'd be relieved to get back into safety. And I was daft enough to say so.

'No need to sit and tremble, Theo!' I said, trying to sound cheerful. 'You're in no danger here.'

He looked at me as if he hated me. 'You don't know what you've done!' he hissed.

'What? I –'

'You've made him angry!' He got up from crouching in the corner and came right up to me, his pale face upturned and his eyes boring into me just as his mother's had done. 'You shouldn't have made him look small, he's at his most dangerous when he's been bettered!'

'But he can't get at you here, I told you, there's absolutely no possibility that he'll find you!'

'It's not me!' he shouted. 'It's *her*!'

Of course it was. I should have seen it. Seen his deep anxiety, anyway, for I wasn't convinced that she was actually in danger. Wouldn't she be able to talk her way out of it? Gods, she'd probably hit herself in the face and tell him I'd slugged her, too.

'She'll be all right,' I said urgently. He *had* to believe it, or the next thing I'd know, he'd be racing off to save her and we'd be right back where we started, only with Gaius a hundred times more aggrieved. 'Theo, she's no fool, your mother, and she'll convince him she had no choice but to let you go with me. Honestly!' He was beginning to look doubtful, which was a start. 'And you said yourself he was always nice to her – won't that mean he'll be halfway to believing her, anyway?'

He seemed to see the sense of that. 'Yes, but –'

'And why should he imagine she'd connive at letting you go with me, when she so clearly missed you and wanted you back?'

Even as I asked him, I was asking myself: the only answer, which came almost instantly, was that she knew quite well that Gaius was a worse threat to Theo than I was.

He settled down again, superficially at least, and, having blown my attempt at getting him back with his mother, I began to think again about visiting my farmer friend with a view to finding Theo a permanent home with him. But only half-heartedly – the trouble was, I felt protective towards him, and I doubted if I'd have much peace unless I knew he was safe; I was sufficiently arrogant to think he'd only *be* safe under my roof. As well as the fat merchant, after Theo's blood with a century of outraged Arelate officials trailing behind him, my flights of fancy were now haunted by a furious Gaius out for retribution and armed with a leather belt.

A week or so after our return, I was sitting up late over a jug of wine. Unable to sleep, I'd settled myself down on the balcony overlooking the slope behind the house; I'd thought the small night sounds and the vast peace of the darkness might soothe me.

The magic was just beginning to work when a noise from below made me jump. And it wasn't any little foraging rodent, unless the verdant hillside had bred one over five foot tall.

I peered down at the shadowy figure trying to conceal itself behind a pillar.

'Who goes there?' I said sharply. 'Come out and show yourself. I warn you, I'm armed.'

I can be armed as soon as I've gone across to my room and found my sword would have been more accurate, but he wasn't to know.

The figure hadn't moved.

'Come on, I'm losing my patience,' I said angrily. Who did he think he was, lurking around under my balcony?

But it wasn't a he, it was a woman. As she moved into the light and I saw the veil fallen back from her hair, I recognized Theo's mother.

I said feebly, 'You'd better come up. Round to your right, up the steps and in through the gates.'

I went into the courtyard and opened the gates to let her in. Without a word, I led her back out on to the balcony: in the soft light of the oil lamps, I stared at her. She looked quite composed.

First things first: I said, 'How did you find me?'

'I went to the financial secretary's office and asked for you. I said I had a personal matter to discuss with you, and they were most helpful.'

Bastards. I could imagine the tittering and the gossip after she'd gone. Perhaps even before she'd gone.

Then, pushing out the irritation, a chilling thought struck me: if she'd found me, so could Gaius.

'He wasn't with you? Gaius?'

She looked scornful. 'Don't be absurd. And, if you're wondering if he could have gone to your office independently, there wouldn't have been any point since he didn't know your name. Theo told me before he returned, if you remember, and I certainly didn't pass the information on to him.'

'No, you wouldn't,' I muttered.

'What?'

'Nothing.'

Gods, she was a formidable woman, this – what had he called her? Zillah, that was it. A gipsy name, I recalled, meaning wanderer.

'Sit down,' I said, remembering my manners. She sank gracefully on to a bench, smoothing her long skirt. Her veil, I noticed, was demurely back in place. 'Now, what is this personal matter?'

She paused. I thought she was considering her words, but another possibility occurred to me. Afterwards.

'Gaius has made some foul accusations about you,' she said bluntly. 'He points out that certain Roman officials decorate their luxury villas' – she looked around her disdainfully – 'with young boys. In short,' – her eyes swivelled to mine – 'I want to know what is your relationship with my son.'

I met her stare with equanimity. I was innocent of the charge, and she knew it. I wasn't even going to defend myself: if she really believed that of me, then she wasn't the woman I'd taken her for and I was prepared to let her go on thinking it.

After what seemed a very long time, her eyes dropped and she muttered, 'I'm sorry.'

I said slowly, speech coming reluctantly, 'I am extremely fond of your son. There's something about him – I should by rights have turned him in when he was first dragged into my office, but I knew it wouldn't be any sort of justice if I did. I liked him, straight away. And I knew that, whatever he'd done, there was an explanation – even if it wasn't much of a one, he didn't deserve the sort of punishment that would have been imposed on him.'

I was looking at her but seemed to see right through her. To scenes and events that, although they'd happened long ago, still had a fresh charm and a delight that made my heart sore.

I heard my own voice, although I wasn't aware of producing the words. 'I had a son, very like your Theo. He died. I . . . when I saw . . .'

I couldn't explain. Couldn't go on speaking.

I felt her arms go round me, and she was hugging me like she'd hugged Theo. She smelt sweet, and her soft hair brushed my face. There was a deep comfort in her embrace, as if she were the eternal mother comforting one of her children in his sorrow.

She held me close until, beginning to feel awkward, I straightened up and gently disengaged myself. Then, as if she'd thought nothing of it, calmly she went back to her bench.

We sat facing each other. I didn't know what to say – truly, I was so full of mixed emotions I really didn't – and she seemed to be quite content to sit in serene silence.

Then she said, 'I didn't believe you were anything but honourable in your behaviour towards Theo. Gaius is a dirty-minded man, and bound to be suspicious.'

She paused. For the first time, she looked discomfited. Only slightly, but it was there.

Then: 'You have saved Theo twice now, and I could say that I found you in order to thank you.' She was looking down at her hands folded in her lap, but her eyes rose to meet mine. 'That would be true, but it would be misleading.' I heard her draw in her breath. 'I came because I wanted to see you again.'

Put it down to the fact that I've had far more dealings with men than with women. Despite having had a wife and quite a lot of other women of various stations in life, I've hardly scratched the surface of woman's unfathomability: I was probably being very dense, but I hadn't had an inkling.

I sat staring at her, my mind racing, teeming with yet another emotion, this one brand-new.

She was so straightforward, bless her. She'd sat there and told me, just like that, and I knew it was the truth – she had the same shining honesty I saw in her son.

It was time for some honesty of my own. Even if I couldn't say it aloud to her, I could admit it to myself: ever since I'd seen her walking so dejectedly down that track behind her house, I hadn't been able to stop thinking about her.

PART THREE

ARLES

AD 175

15

She told me a great deal, that first night. Mainly about Theo, for he was her prime concern; she looked different when she spoke of him, the lines of care on her face blurring and disappearing. I wasn't particularly interested in the minute details of what he'd been like at six months, but listened because I was so enjoying looking at her.

She told me too about life down there in the salt plains. I already knew her late husband had been a fisherman and that they'd lived at the Saints' Village – Theo told me – but I learned from her that he'd had as deep a love for the land as for the temperamental, dangerous vagaries of Neptune's kingdom. They were a law to themselves, the people of the delta, as anyone the least bit involved in trying to administer them will tell you – in my official capacity, I had inherited numerous headaches to do with unpaid taxes and land ownership, and the impossible task of calculating land yield so as to extract the appropriate dues would have made even Jupiter's hair curl.

Typical of the delta people, both she and her husband, she told me, had come from nomad families. Although many were permanent settlers, there also seemed to be a shifting population who came home at specific times such as the calving of the cows and the branding of the young cattle, disappearing for the rest of the year and returning with traveller's tales to tell round the fireside. And what tales – even in those few hours, she gave me a tantalizing glimpse of a world where strange and unpredictable Eastern deities appeared to grant wishes to the fortunate, where hooded crones crept from the forest to grasp at handsome young men, only to turn magically into beautiful young women when the men did as they were ordered. Where each year's festivals rang with rhythmic songs while the people danced themselves to frenzy round the great fires, where the very animals that were so fundamental a part of delta life were exalted almost to god status.

No wonder we found it difficult to understand them.

Finally she ran out of words. Watching her stifling a yawn, I asked if she would like to sleep. When, after a quick look at me, she nodded, I showed her to the room next to Theo's. Then, walking with deliberately loud footsteps, I retired to my own side of the courtyard.

I had omitted to ask if she wanted Theo to know of her visit, so in the morning I sent him off on an errand before rousing her.

'No! He mustn't know I'm here!' She shot up, pulling the linen sheet around her as if she was about to race away before she'd even dressed.

'It's all right, he's gone down to the village for fresh bread. Stay quietly in here, and when he and I have eaten, I'll send him out to exercise my horse.'

She looked at me gratefully. I didn't ask her why she didn't want him to see her, and she didn't tell me.

After breakfast, the house once more silent – it wasn't one of Callistus's mornings, he was coming in later to cook supper – I went back to her room. I could see she'd been crying; I guessed it was because she'd heard him talking and laughing, and hadn't been able to join in.

'Are you ready?'

She nodded. 'Yes.'

Tight-faced, she stood up. Despite her apparent lack of any personal effects, she'd managed to dress her hair and arrange her veil perfectly. Her robe looked fresh and clean. She was, I thought as I stared at her, a woman any man would be proud to be seen with.

'I'll take you back,' I said. 'I know a quicker way than the road.'

She seemed about to protest, but then gave in and meekly set off beside me.

We hardly spoke on the journey. It was a beautiful morning, the sun not yet so hot as to make walking uncomfortable, and my short cut went down a little-used track that wound along by a stream, shaded by young trees.

When in the early afternoon we found ourselves on the southern outskirts of Arelate, she stopped.

'This is as far as you may go,' she said decisively.

People didn't often tell me where I could and could not go. 'Why can't I take you all the way?'

She sighed. 'Sergius, use your head! The last time you were in my house, you slugged Gaius and made him look inadequate in front of me and my son.'

'I can lay him out again!' I wasn't at all sure I could – he'd be prepared, this time.

She smiled, as if she shared my doubts. 'Perhaps,' she said charitably. 'But I don't want to risk it.'

My mind was full of questions: will you be all right? Have you thought out a watertight excuse for your absence? What if he turns nasty? And – most urgently – when will you come back?

She was looking at me, eyes fixed to mine, and I felt she was aware of all that I was thinking. Moving to stand right in front of me, she stood on tiptoe and briefly kissed me on the lips. 'I wish I could say, give my love to Theo,' she whispered.

'I'll take care of him.' My voice wasn't as firm as it should have been. 'I promise you, I won't let you down.'

Turning to go, she flashed me a smile over her shoulder. She said, 'I know.' Then hurried away.

Back home on my terrace, Theo cross-legged on the floor beside me trying to whittle a piece of wood into a bull and jabbering away about every single thing he'd done since he woke up, I let my attention wander. I could still see her if I closed my eyes, sitting on the bench opposite, small feet crossed, gown gracefully arranged so as to hide anything above the ankle. Lovely ankles, I mused. Slim and shapely. And you could make out the bones in those dainty feet.

I arrested my thoughts.

I'd been more than willing to go on with her to that run-down cabin and face the inevitable showdown with Gaius. In fact, I'd been positively champing at the bit, only deterred by her absolute determination that I shouldn't. Now that I'd had the long trudge home to think about it, I knew why.

She'd implied that, with Theo out of the way and any threat to him thus removed, life with Gaius would be tolerable. Although I wanted to protest that surely a woman such as her should aspire to a life – a partnership – that was better than tolerable, I had let it go. I'd wondered if her remarks about the removal of the threat to Theo meant she'd been more aware than Theo had thought of how things stood, but her obvious remorse and guilt seemed brand-new, as if she'd just discovered the evil that had been lurking under her roof and was only at the start of her penance.

And, I said to her silently, I didn't tell you the half of it.

But there was another, more pressing reason for her decision. If I'd gone with her and by some miracle got the better of the pugnacious and highly motivated Gaius – which did indeed seem unlikely – what then? If I'd been so obviously her champion, there would no longer be any question of her pretending I was her enemy as well as his. No question, afterwards, of her patching up his cuts and bruises – assuming I'd managed to inflict any – and calmly settling down to everyday life again.

If we'd had that showdown, the die would have been

cast. She'd have to have come away with me, and I guessed she wasn't ready for that.

Gods, neither was I!

'You're not listening, Sergius!' Theo said peevishly. 'I just said I was thinking of stealing your horse and going to live with the wild bulls and you said, "Yes, that will be fine!" '

'Sorry.' I made myself smile at him. 'Are you hungry? Shall we eat?'

'Yes please.'

It had been a silly question – he was always hungry. I went into the kitchen to discover that Callistus had left our supper simmering over the hearth, and I poured myself a whole jug of wine to drink with it.

I would, I decided, rather be slightly drunk than go on thinking.

At first I told myself I was imagining it. I had reason enough to be paranoid, gods knew, with all the enemies I seemed to have been making recently, any one of whom could well have been stalking me with evil intent.

There was nothing tangible to begin with, just the sense that I was being watched. I'd think I heard a movement, a footstep, behind me, and when I turned, there would be nothing there. But the feeling would be so strong that I'd believe I saw the air still shimmering with the aftershocks of someone's swift movement through it.

If someone was shadowing me, he was doing it skilfully. And that suggested that he was one of my own, that perhaps, back in Arelate, some aggrieved citizen had employed a professional assassin – some fit and mean-minded ex-legionary, for example – to spy on me, biding his time until the moment was right for whatever it was he'd been commissioned to do.

I didn't have to search my memory very hard to come up with a possible identity for who that citizen might be.

But then I'd remind myself of all the compelling reasons why the fat merchant was far more likely to have dismissed the thought of revenge, and I'd have to think again. I did so much thinking that I made my head spin. Frustrated, I'd tell myself I was worrying about nothing, that Theo and I were perfectly safe and I was spoiling the happy present with my anxieties about a future that wasn't going to happen.

I couldn't convince myself. I remained worried, partly about my own safety.

But, increasingly, much more about Theo's.

I tried to keep a closer watch on him, which wasn't easy. He was used to his freedom, and resented my half-hearted suggestion that he might spend some time sitting with me out on the terrace while I did what I could to improve his education – he could read and write, after a fashion, but he was far from fluent. When, disguising my surprise, I'd asked who had taught him, he'd replied, 'My father,' clamping his mouth shut so that I was sure he didn't want to elaborate. We reached a compromise: he would spend the mornings with me if in return I allowed him to go out on my horse all afternoon. I couldn't help thinking he'd got the better of the bargain.

Amongst all this, I found little time to go into my office. I attended for the minimum hours to prove I was still alive and *compos mentis*, and no one seemed bothered that I was absent more than I was present.

On the way home one day – I'd stayed late, for once occupied with a task that actually needed fairly urgent completion – I got back to the villa as darkness fell. I hadn't been worried about Theo, since I'd arranged for Callistus to stay till I returned, and from the street outside I could hear cheerful voices from the kitchen.

I almost didn't see him. Cloaked, leaning against one of the pillars that supported the terrace so that his silhouette was concealed, it was pure fluke that I happened to be looking right at him when he briefly raised his hand to muffle some soft sound – a cough, or a sneeze.

He hadn't seen me; he had his back to me, looking down the street and not up it. Again, luck was with me – I'd called in to order some more wine and so was approaching the villa from the opposite direction I usually came from. Making use of the advantage, I slipped into the shadow of my neighbour's wall and watched him.

He was good, I'll give him that. He stood for what seemed like hours without one bit of him breaking out from behind the pillar, until I was quite sure he must have melted away when I blinked. I was about to give up and go home to my dinner when suddenly he stepped out from under my terrace and started walking briskly towards me.

He *must* see me, I couldn't possibly hope he wouldn't! I inched back, pressing myself against the wall, sliding along it searching for some better cover: abruptly I all but tripped over as an alcove opened up behind me and I fell into it.

I held my breath as he strode past. This was my chance to see just who it was who had been spying on me, and I wasn't going to waste it.

Nearly bursting my lungs didn't do me any good at all: he was cloaked and hooded, and could have been anyone from the Emperor to the old woman who cleans the public baths.

Disgruntled, I was about to emerge from my hiding place when two more figures came out of a side street and set off after him. These two were bare-headed, and I didn't recognize either of them. They didn't look like the sort of men I'd have chosen as friends, nor even distant acquaintances – strangely alike, they both had flat, vacant-looking faces, a singular lack of anything in the way of a neck, bodies like barrels set on short, thick legs and arms like battering rams.

If they were the hooded man's heavies, I sent up a swift

prayer that I'd always manage to slip into a handy hiding place whenever they passed by.

'I thought we might go out together tomorrow,' I said casually to Theo over dinner; the more time we spent away from prying eyes, the better. 'Hire a second horse, take some food with us and ride up into the hills. Up to Glanum, perhaps.' We could make a short detour so that I could show him the temple where I was a too-infrequent worshipper – I resolved there and then to do better, hoping the god wouldn't be sad because I was only turning to him when I needed his help.

'I'd like that,' Theo said when he had emptied his mouth. 'But not tomorrow, because I'm going fishing with Julius.'

Julius? 'Who's Julius?'

'He lives next to the baker. His mother's the baker's sister – she sometimes gives me a honey cake.'

Theo, I realized, had been making friends. 'Oh. All right then, we'll go the day after.'

He grinned and went back to his stew.

I'd decided that the mastermind behind my silent watchers must be Gaius. I don't know why I was so sure; perhaps it was that the way those heavies moved reminded me of him, although they were twice his size – I didn't fool myself that I could have felled either of them, even with the best-aimed punch I'd ever thrown. *Anyone* had ever thrown.

I spent an anxious day while Theo was off fishing, imagining those men following him, making off with him, even harming him. They wouldn't approach him while Julius is with him, I reasoned, they've been at pains to keep a low profile and they'd undo all the good work if they reveal themselves to Julius.

Nevertheless, as the long hours wore slowly on I became increasingly uneasy. Eventually, any activity being better than none at all, I got up. Feeling absurdly over-dramatic, I went to my room to fetch my short sword, then I went out, closing the gates firmly behind me.

I went down to the pool in the stream where I guessed Theo and Julius would have gone. There they were, lying on their backs in the shade: I heard the faint murmur of their conversation, and once Theo laughed.

No sign of anyone else about. But then, if the spies were watching, they'd make sure they kept out of sight.

I walked on upstream. Behind me the village was drowsing in the afternoon heat; the only things moving were the fat, lazily circling flies.

Then, rounding a bend and emerging from the shelter of a stretch of tall rushes, I tripped over a stout pair of legs and fell against a supine body.

The two heavies were lying side by side, fishing abandoned for the time being, as relaxed and content as Julius and Theo.

'I'm sorry!' I said. 'Did I hurt you? Either of you?'

They both shook their heads. They looked even more vacant at close quarters, the loose mouths now spreading into wet-lipped smiles. They were so alike that they had to be twins, but the special blessings that Mercury confers on twins didn't seem to have included much in the way of intelligence.

'I caught a fish,' said one.

'So did I. I caught two!' replied his brother.

They both giggled, an incongruous sound from two such large men.

I wondered who they were. Distant relatives of some poor soul in the village, who was doing his duty and taking his turn at looking after them? 'Are you staying nearby?' I asked, squatting down beside them.

'We're living with Uncle Claudius,' one confided. 'We have a big bed in the little house where the goats are.'

That accounted for the smell. 'Very nice,' I remarked. Uncle Claudius obviously didn't consider that duty extended to allowing his cumbersome nephews inside his house. More likely – for I knew Claudius – it was his wife Calpurnia who had put her foot down.

One of the twins started humming, and the other joined in. Not only were they simple and smelly, they were also tone-deaf. Wishing them farewell, I got up and left them to it.

Unless the cloaked man was about, waiting for his moment to accost Theo, it didn't seem as if the boy was in any immediate danger. And I might have been wrong about him, too – he might well have had some perfectly innocent reason for hiding under my terrace for hours on end. I was in sore need of some hard exercise, which I always find clears the mind and facilitates sensible thinking, so I branched away from the stream and set off towards the distant hills.

My thoughts were with my god. Having belatedly recognized both my need of him and my failure in regular observance of his rites, I wanted to make immediate amends. It would take too long to go to the temple – I could hardly expect him to rush to help me in my protection of Theo if I was stupid enough to leave the lad alone for all those hours – but I have never considered it necessary to be in the temple to pray.

I thought about him as I walked, of the wonder of his pursuit and capture of the bull, of how the blood from that miraculous slaying gave such gifts to mankind. He had been my guide and friend throughout my days in the Legion, and I didn't imagine he'd desert me now that I was no longer a soldier. He doesn't desert his true followers, I know that.

I found a flat rock which looked quite like the sacrifice stone by my temple. Standing in front of it, using it as an aid to my meditation, I closed my eyes and let my thoughts go to the god.

When I set off back to the villa, I felt much better. For one thing, I'd had a time of calm, of peaceful solitude, and it had helped me put everything in perspective.

Far more important, the cessation of my wild, jumbled thoughts had allowed the god to speak to me. And, typical of him, what he had to say had the virtue of being both practical and providing me with an outlet for my pent-up energy.

He'd suggested I swapped roles with the cloaked man. That, instead of being the hunted, I became the hunter.

My heart full of thanks, I resolved to do exactly that.

I waited until Theo was asleep. Then, securing the villa as best I could, I went out into the night.

I circled the village, gaining a little height so as to afford the best view of any comings and goings. For a long time, nothing happened. In that sleepy, innocent place, everyone was in bed.

Then something moved on the street leading to the villa. Hopping over Claudius's fence – careful not to go anywhere near his goat shed – I cut off a wide corner and jumped down into the road some thirty paces behind the cloaked man.

He heard me. Hardly surprising – I'd meant him to.

He turned and waited for me.

As I approached, I drew my sword. Not the short stabbing *gladius* that is the primary weapon of the legionary, but a heavy, long-bladed, vicious-looking monster, its hilt decorated with grimacing heads, that I'd taken from the hands of a dying Celtic prince.

The cloaked man stood in a beam of light from a torch set in a wall sconce. I got within three paces of him, then I stopped.

Slowly he pushed back his hood, and the torchlight shone on his face. It wasn't a hardened ex-legionary, and it wasn't Gaius – this man wasn't old enough to be either. It was a young face, smooth-skinned, yet it was full of hate.

It was the face of a man I'd last seen more than twenty years ago, in the bone-biting cold of a dawn up on Hadrian's Wall.

A matter of moments before he died.

16

It was back in the days when the Emperor Antoninus Pius was struggling to hold the lowlands north of Hadrian's Wall. In a surge of confidence following the conquest he'd ordered the construction of the northern wall, the one that bears his name, and for a while it had looked as if we were in for an unprecedented spell of peace up in those wild lands.

We should have known better. Certainly, those of us with long experience of the Brigantes shouldn't have expected they'd meekly accept the spread of Roman dominion, not when it involved Brigantian territory. The only excuse for my lot, working on the refortifications at Coriosopitum, is that we were safe in a small corner of Britannia that had long since come to terms with Roman rule, which meant we had no means of detecting the great unrest amongst the tribesmen. Even the most furious and resentful Brigantian chief wouldn't have been foolhardy enough to attack Hadrian's Wall; he might have found quite a few of his own tribesmen defending alongside the Romans. I wasn't the only legionary with a Brigantian wife, and many of the native men had decided we weren't such a bad lot, all things considered, and they preferred to side with us than against us.

But we didn't have to wait for war to come to us: we were ordered out to meet it. In the autumn, I was sent north with a detachment of the Sixth to support the troops fighting in the lowlands.

Don't go thinking that what happened was because

we'd spent so long being builders we'd forgotten how to be soldiers – the Roman army doesn't work like that. It's true that, for a while back then, refitting Coriosopitum fort was a priority; it was right on the road north to the new Antonine Wall, a vital supply base for the campaign. Nevertheless, not a day went by that we didn't engage in some sort of drill, and at regular intervals we were sent out on scouting or foraging parties to keep us sharp and make sure we didn't get too used to the comforts, such as they were, of life within a fort.

No. What happened was the fault of one man.

Our destination was Trimontium, an outpost fort to the south of the new wall. The fighting on the wall had been brutal, the tribesmen as desperate to take it as our legions were to hold on, but in the end our men had been forced to evacuate the wall forts, putting them to the torch as they fled south. Casualties had been heavy, although just how heavy we didn't realize until we saw the number of reinforcements subsequently sent from Germania. All the same, we knew well enough things must have been going badly, otherwise we'd still have been digging latrines back at Coriosopitum.

In sound military tradition, the forces had fallen back to a stronghold, in this case the large fort at Trimontium. We arrived to find a Brigantian onslaught in full swing: three of my men were felled before we'd even reached the south gate.

In the fury of battle there's no time for reaction – you don't even feel the pain of a wound till afterwards. You hear men howling in fear, screaming in agony, you see such damage inflicted on men's bodies that they're scarcely recognizable as human. And these aren't strangers, they're men you've lived and worked beside, perhaps for years, no few of whom you've grown close to. Yet, all the time you're under attack, your emotions are frozen: you become a machine, your brain issuing orders like a centurion which, unthinkingly, your body obeys.

Reaction comes afterwards.

The burial details were kept busy during those dreadful days. There was no time for individual interments, it was just a matter of digging pits and tipping in the dead, along with their damaged armour and their personal possessions. But we did our best for them: whenever there was a lull, the priests would be hauled out from wherever they'd been hiding and made to gabble through the words of dedication. I hope the gods understood that, although we were pressed for time and our priests almost wetting themselves with terror, our prayers for our dead colleagues were nevertheless sincere.

Those bloody Brigantes never let up. We faced wave after wave of them, screaming, half-naked, hair white with lime and sticking up like metal spikes. They were no match for us when we went out to engage them. We advanced in testudo formation, our shields protecting us like the tortoise's shell, and hacked them down with our short swords; their great two-handed weapons were all very well for slashing a man in two in the open, but no use at all for close combat. But, every time we beat one lot off, another rank would come pelting down on us.

It seemed sometimes as if the whole of Britannia was out there, lining up waiting for their turn to have a go at the invader.

The air around the fort soon became unhealthy, to say the least. It was a blessing it was autumn, and too cold for the dead flesh to rot and putrefy as quickly as it would have done in summer; the Brigantes were dutiful to their dead, I'll give them that, and did their best to keep up with disposal. You'll get an idea of just how huge the task was if I tell you that, even working throughout the long hours of the northern darkness, the enemy's burial parties couldn't clear each day's casualties before the sun came up and we went out to chase them away.

So there we were, just about holding out against each day's attack, sufficiently well supplied with food, water and troops to keep going for the foreseeable future. But we began to wonder how long that was to be: we seemed to have killed hundreds, maybe even thousands, yet still they came. Unease spread: supposing they just kept coming? For ever?

That sort of superstitious dread is something a commander must stamp out. It's fatal if it's allowed to take hold – men have been known to crawl away and give up once they start to believe they're up against an invincible foe. Our commander was a practical man: seeing that we were starting to have difficulty with the troops, he gave us all something else to think about. Instead of sitting here waiting for them, he announced, we're going to go out on the offensive. And our aggression was to take two forms: while the enemy's attention was engaged with strongly armed groups of legionaries openly hunting them down, smaller, discreet sorties would creep out to gain what intelligence they could about how many Brigantes there were and where they were lurking.

His tactics were absolutely right, I accept that. It was just a shame that fate decreed I had to lead the first sortie.

I chose a select group of my men, knowing from long experience which were the quietest and the most capable of moving silently. They didn't let me down: we had advanced about three or four miles, and had found ourselves a good vantage point, when our luck ran out.

We were on top of a small wooded knoll, and three of us had managed to climb trees so as to improve our view. The rest of the party were on the ground. Up in the trees, we were getting an excellent picture of Brigantian numbers and dispositions, and I was about to suggest we climbed down and all of us set off back for the fort when a tiny movement at the foot of the knoll caught my eye.

I'd never associated the Brigantes with stealth, probably because my only experience of them had been when they were on the attack, when a more raucous lot would be hard to imagine. I shouldn't have jumped to the conclusion that they didn't know how to be quiet, though, and I accept that my lack of imagination was partly to blame. But, as yet, all wasn't lost: the Brigantes clearly knew we were there, so there was no longer any virtue in not advertising our presence. I ordered my signaller to blow a blast on his trumpet. He stared at me as if I'd gone mad.

'There are Brigantes at the foot of the hill,' I explained. 'If you don't blow soon, they'll be on us and you'll have lost the last chance to summon help.'

He closed his mouth abruptly, instantly lifting his trumpet to his lips. He blew the signal for help as if his life depended on it. It did.

Mars was watching over us. One of our attacking parties was close enough to hear the desperate appeal, and we heard the answer. Those sharp notes that announced help was coming were the best sound I've ever heard.

We heard crashing in the undergrowth below. The Brigantes, breaking cover, set up that appalling screeching they specialize in, interspersing the screams with long ululations that chilled the blood. We grouped together, adopting the tortoise formation, and waited.

They burst out into the open in ones and twos, at first all from the same quarter. Their lack of organization worked against them, as it so often did: acting as one, we advanced and hacked them down. The next group came from behind us: again, overcoming them was a simple matter. They could have had the better of us already, I remember thinking, if they'd only stop being so pig-headed and independent, if they'd learn to discipline themselves under one man's control. If they'd closed in on us in an organized way from all directions at once, we'd all be dead by now.

It was beginning to dawn on even their thick heads that they weren't going to get the better of us by attacking piecemeal. We watched as they dropped back, and, as they put their spiky heads together, we heard them muttering. Further crashings and cursings from below indicated that more of them were approaching: if we waited for them to think it out logically, we'd be lost.

I gave the order to attack.

We had the advantage, at first. We held the higher ground, and our very impetus downhill towards them enabled us to dispatch their front men with no difficulty. They were wild and brutal, but they were untrained, at least in comparison with us: we all knew what to do in answer to most forms of attack, and soon the knoll was heaped with their dead.

But, just like back at Trimontium, they kept on coming. Do you know that story the Greeks like to tell, about their hero Jason facing an endless army that sprang from dragon's teeth sown in a field? That's how it felt for us. We'd kill three, four, ten of them, and immediately another ten would leap up, snarling and waving their swords, to take the place of the fallen.

We were beginning to falter. It takes it out of you, killing; you begin to feel your strength wane after a while. One of my men was taken, dragged away from the outside of the formation. Another went, then another. Those of us left tightened ranks and tried to close our ears to the screams of our colleagues: however the Brigantes were killing them, they weren't doing it quickly.

Over the sounds of their agony and the racket the indefatigable tribesmen were still making rose the sound of a trumpet. It was near at hand. I sent up a prayer of deepest gratitude to my god.

The small group of us left alive were on our knees when the relief column broke out from the trees. The legionaries went instantly on the attack, slaughtering Brigantes with the energy and efficiency of men who'd done nothing more demanding all morning than take a quick trot in the fresh air. Sinking down, exhausted, we pressed together, shields held over us.

Keeping watch, I saw the leader of the group emerge on to the hilltop. I clearly remember thinking, about time! But then I saw who it was.

Quintus Severus and I had been thrown together frequently over the years. I say thrown together because I would never have chosen his company; probably he felt the same about me. We had enlisted in the Legion in the same year, and some of our training had been done side by side. Even then, I didn't trust him, and nothing had happened subsequently to alter that. There was a time on the Southern Wall when he let me down, an occasion at Coriosopitum when I know he lied to get himself out of trouble (and, incidentally, land me in it), and once I saw him administer a severe punishment to a man whose guilt was in doubt, to say the least.

In that dire position on top of the knoll, surrounded by Brigantes, I would rather have had any man in the entire Roman army as my deliverer than Quintus Severus.

He looked very pale, and his face was sweating. He was wiping something from his mouth – I suspected he'd just been sick, and guessed he'd seen what was left of those of my men the Brigantes had taken away.

He stared around the knoll, at his own men efficiently dispatching tribesmen, at my men and me, huddled under our shields. Maybe what he said later was the truth, maybe he really did think at first that we were all dead.

But he can't possibly have gone on thinking that, because I sat up and called out to him.

He spun round and stared at me. Right into my eyes.

I shouted, 'Wait where you are, we'll fight our way across to you and we'll try to . . .'

He turned and ran. As he disappeared into the trees, I heard him order his men to follow. To emphasize the point, he had his signaller blow the retreat. His men were so busy fighting that they may well not have realized there were soldiers left alive on the hilltop: I'm quite prepared to give them the benefit of the doubt, and in any case they'd just received a direct order. Gods, I'd have retreated if I'd have been in their shoes – no man needs much of an excuse to run away from a group of vengeful Brigantes with their decapitating axes in their hands.

We were down to five: the rest of my men had been dragged away. If we stayed, we'd be taken too, so we made a dash for it. It may have been that the Brigantes were at last running out of men, or possibly they were enjoying themselves too much cutting up my men to bother with any more fighting; whatever the reason, all but one of us made it through their diminishing numbers and down the hillside.

We were intent on getting away, and you'd have thought that would have made us blind to everything else. Unfortunately, it didn't. Although at the time I'd have said I only paid scant attention to what lay scattered on the track, I discovered that my brain had recorded every last detail, so thoroughly that I've never been able to forget. The sights I saw that day still have the power to make me sweat with horror, and I pray for the souls of those poor men whenever I feel I have my god's attention.

There were far too many Brigantes milling around below the knoll for such a small group as we now were to attempt to get through, so we hid among the trees till darkness fell. Then, in the silence of grief and shock, we set out for Trimontium.

It took us the rest of the night to cover the few miles that separated us from the fort. We were in no state to fight – one man had lost his sword, another's hand was all but severed – so we lay down in the heather at the least sound. I don't think any of these alarms were actually the enemy – I'm sure the entire Brigantian nation were quite well enough satisfied with their day's work to be back in camp celebrating. We probably wasted long cold hours hiding from owls and hares, but I make no apology.

The lookouts spotted us very quickly. I'd never had occasion to creep up on one of our own forts before, and I was impressed. Fortunately they were keen-sighted and recognized our gear – it would have been ironic if we'd miraculously escaped from the Brigantes only to be cut down by our own men.

As the senior officer of the group, I was taken before the commander as soon as I'd been seen by the medical orderly; he pronounced me unharmed, but, good man that he was, prescribed a hot meal and (far more welcome) a mug of wine to restore me before I made my report.

The commander looked at me for a long time before he spoke. I knew why: my very presence in front of him meant another of his officers had at best been mistaken. At worst . . .

I realized as I stood there that whatever judgement was made on Quintus depended entirely on me.

The commander spoke at last. 'Quintus Severus informed me that there were no men left alive on that hilltop.' Obviously he saw no need to specify Roman men; presumably Brigantes didn't count.

'Sir.' I waited.

'He said he saw many dead, many in the process of being tortured and on the point of death, and a few bodies lying under their shields.' He looked at me as if expecting my confirmation.

'Sir.' I wasn't going to commit myself.

'He said he made the decision to retreat in order to save his own detachment, whose lives he judged to be in danger if he stayed.'

'The lives of his men were certainly in danger.'

The commander nodded impatiently. 'Naturally, Sergius Cornelius. This is war, not a matrons' luncheon.' He leaned across his desk towards me, eyes fixed on my face. 'What I am asking you is whether you consider Quintus Severus had sound grounds for believing you were all dead. If he did, he was right to call the retreat. If not, then his actions constitute desertion of duty, moreover desertion which endangered the lives of his fellow soldiers. The punishment for that you know.'

I knew. If Quintus was pronounced guilty, he'd be executed. Taken out of the fort by the traditional route of the condemned, either to be hanged, garrotted or have his throat cut.

I didn't answer.

I swear the commander knew full well why not. He'd been in office over Quintus for long enough to have made up his own mind about him, after all, so perhaps he knew the truth as well as I did. After a moment he said, 'Would you like some time to consider your response?'

His eyes were on mine. He could have added something about my needing to recover, to get a clear picture in my mind of the relevant events. But he didn't; he merely dismissed me.

I went to my screened-off section at the end of the dormitory and lay down. Closing my eyes, I saw one of my men having his entrails removed and wound round a tribesman's sword. The tribesman was laughing, but my man wasn't. I saw the head of a man I'd got on with particularly well – he'd had a wonderful way with a joke, he could even make you laugh at one you'd heard a hundred times before – but now his head was stuck on the end of a stolen Roman pike, and the expression wasn't that of a man who'd just told a joke. In my ears echoed the sound of screams.

But if I told the truth, Quintus would die too. He

wouldn't die a slow and agonizing death, military executions were as quick and humane as it was possible for a death to be. Nevertheless, he'd die, and hadn't there been enough death already?

What was I to do? Lie, and save Quintus's life? Or tell the truth, and avenge my men's horrible deaths with that of Quintus?

I can't, I thought. Can't betray him.

Yes you can, a voice seemed to say in my head. It is not betrayal. It would be a betrayal of other men if you lied, for your lie would mean Quintus will live to leave other men to die.

The logic was irrefutable.

I got up and requested an audience with the commander.

They executed Quintus Severus at dawn. I hadn't slept all night, and at first light I made my way to a place on the southern wall of the fort from which I'd be able to observe without being seen. Don't think it was the desire to gloat that made me want to watch: it wasn't something that gave me any satisfaction. I just felt I owed it to my men. And, in some strange way, to Quintus.

He was led out through the *porta decumana*, the back gate which, since ancient times, has been the last exit of the condemned. The execution party was already assembled. With swift efficiency he was made to kneel, hands bound behind him. A figure stepped forwards and threw the thin rope round his neck. Another went to stand beside the first, swiftly winding the wooden peg that tightens the rope. There was a faint gagging sound, abruptly cut off. His neck broken, Quintus slumped to the ground.

Turning away, I threw up behind a water butt.

I can't recall what I did for most of that day. No doubt I was kept busy. Towards evening, my duties finished, I went outside the fort and made my way to a place where

I often used to go to watch the sunset. That day, the peace which the sight usually gave me was far away.

Returning, I saw a figure lurking in the shadow of the great walls. It approached me, and I felt a shiver of fear.

It was a native woman, her gaudy robe covered by an enveloping garment which looked like an old army cloak. Even with the heavy folds of the cloak, I could see that she was pregnant; I'd have judged she wasn't far off her time.

No one had spoken up for Quintus, no one had pleaded for his life. No one had mourned him. Until now; for this figure, her hair wild and tangled from where she had been pulling at it in her grief, her face pale, her eyes red and swollen-lidded, was Quintus's woman.

I recognized her, although I hadn't been aware she was with child.

I waited for her to come close enough to speak, for that was what I thought was her intent. I was preparing myself to say he died well, and more to the point quickly, and to tell her where he was to be buried.

But, some five paces off, she stopped. She hadn't come to talk to me after all.

Slowly she raised her right arm. As I watched, horrified into immobility, she spread her fingers into the gesture the Celts use to put on the death curse.

And pointed her hand straight at me.

17

When the first instant of shock faded I realized that it couldn't be Quintus. Of course it couldn't – I'd seen him die. And besides, this young man was in his early twenties at most, several years younger than Quintus had been when they executed him.

But if the child that woman had carried had been male, this could well be Quintus's son.

Questioning him wouldn't have been appropriate – I don't think I could have summoned the wits, even if he hadn't run off as soon as I'd recognized him. It was obvious he knew I had; I felt a sort of numb incredulity spread over my face, which, if his expression of grim satisfaction was anything to go by, he certainly hadn't missed.

Quintus's son here, outside my own villa. Which, far from being in the middle of town, well known and readily pointed out to any stranger enquiring after me, was hidden away in the seclusion of a very small village deep in the country.

If this really was Quintus's son and he'd come looking for me to fulfil his mother's curse, then somebody must have told him where to look.

The thought that I had a vengeful twenty-five-year-old after my blood, moreover with the active support of someone sufficiently well-up in Arelate administration to know me and the address of my private residence, was enough to make me hurry home and reach for the wine jug.

* * *

Theo came out on to the terrace to join me, bringing a plate of supper he'd begged from Callistus before he'd gone home. It was difficult at first to put my anxieties aside and act normally, but fortunately Theo was too excited about what he had to tell me to notice.

He'd been out riding, as usual, and had come across a pen containing a young bull.

'Where was this?' I asked, not really interested.

'On the road to Glanum. Sergius, it was great, I tethered your horse and got in the pen with him, he was so playful and I – '

Playful? Into my mind flashed a picture of those great lyre-shaped horns. 'You could have been hurt,' I said severely.

'No I couldn't! He was only young, I told you.'

'They're *born* with horns,' I pointed out.

'They aren't!' He laughed delightedly at my ignorance. 'They couldn't *be* born if they were! They only have the buds, at birth.'

Technically he had to be right, although I felt he was deliberately evading the point. 'And just what did the farmer think of you teasing his bull-calf?'

Theo looked puzzled. 'That's the funny thing, the bull wasn't on a farm at all. The pen was hidden in among some trees, out in the middle of nowhere. Oh, there was a big house a bit further down the track, but I didn't go up to it.'

At least he seemed to have *some* sense. 'All the same, I don't think you should . . .'

I broke off. A big house down a track leading off the Glanum road. A hidden pen and a young bull. Suddenly I knew where Theo had been today. I knew, too, what that bull was destined for. And if Theo ever found out, he was going to be heartbroken.

'What don't you think?' he prompted.

'Er . . . I shouldn't go there again, Theo.'

'Why not?'

'Bulls are valuable,' I said vaguely. 'Whoever owns that one will be keeping an eye on him, or employing some roughneck to do the job for him. You don't want to get into any more trouble, do you?'

It was mean of me to exploit his guilty past, and I wasn't proud of myself. I was even less so when he said, his face stricken, 'I'm very sorry, Sergius. I won't get into trouble, I promise.' He looked so vulnerable, as if he was afraid I'd chuck him out on the spot.

'Don't look so worried!' I tried to laugh. 'I know you didn't mean any harm. I expect you're used to a far more free and easy attitude to the bulls, down there on your old delta plains. You weren't to know how possessive people up here get about their livestock.'

He stared at me for a moment then, apparently satisfied, nodded and got on with his supper.

When he'd gone to bed I thought about the bull. If I hadn't been so preoccupied, I'd have guessed whose it was the moment Theo had mentioned the Glanum road. The temple of Mithras was at Glanum, and that was where the bull would be taken in little more than a week's time: the pen in the wood, like the big house, belonged to one of the worshippers. And, on that night the week after next, we would celebrate the festival of the god, and our Pater, the father figure of our little group, would slay the young creature in pale imitation of Mithras's miracle.

There was no way I could tell Theo what was to happen, what act I was to participate in – what was a sacred rite to me would, to an animal-lover like him, be simple brutality. And, gods knew, he'd had enough of that in his life.

Perhaps I should advance my plans and get him away to my farmer friend straight away. It would seem abrupt to the boy, yes, but that was better than me having to tell him lies about where I was going next week. He'd be sure to ask, that was certain – any boy with the natural curiosity of youth wouldn't watch a man dress himself in his best and set off into the night carrying a mysterious bag without demanding to know where he was going.

My mind shot back to the young man who'd faced me in the lane outside. I'd all but forgotten about him, but now it occurred to me that if he was indeed stalking me, as seemed increasingly likely, then it would be better for Theo to be safely out of the way when the eventual confrontation came.

Getting up to go to bed, I resolved to take Theo out to the farm as soon as possible.

Two days later, an appropriate occasion cropped up. Although I didn't tell Theo, I was due to go to the temple; Theo, who would be deprived of my horse since I'd be riding him, was demanding something else to do.

'You need hard work,' I told him. 'You're getting soft, idling around here all the time.'

'I don't idle! I work hard, when you can be bothered to think of anything for me to do!'

He was quite right. 'Don't get angry, I was only teasing. You do work hard, I agree. Tell you what – today you can work hard for someone else. Would you like that?'

He looked cagey. 'It depends who it is and what he wants me to do.'

'It's Cassius Marcellinus, my farmer friend.'

'Oh, him.' Theo brightened. 'And what's the job?'

I had no idea, since I'd only just thought up the idea. 'Oh, a bit of this and a bit of that. He'll keep you out of mischief, whatever you're doing.'

'I don't get into mischief,' Theo said piously.

I let that go. 'You'll like Cassius,' I said. 'He's got sons of his own – a daughter, too – although they're grown up now. I expect he's got a few grandchildren.' He was a good sort, Cassius, a sound family man with a warm heart, married to a dumpling of a woman who was the best cook in Provincia, and that was saying something. 'And he keeps all sorts of animals.'

Theo was looking at me, an odd expression on his face. 'He's the man you're going to send me to live with, isn't he?' I didn't answer. 'You said you'd find some farm where I could live and work. Is it his?'

I hadn't meant to break the news so abruptly, but since he'd guessed anyway, there was no point in prevaricating. 'Yes. But I promise you, Theo, we'll only go ahead with the plan if you're happy about it.'

He managed a grin. 'And Cassius is too.'

'Quite. What do you say, then? Shall I take you to meet him?'

After a moment, Theo said, 'All right.'

He and Cassius eyed each other warily as I introduced them. Despite my best intentions, I hadn't got round to having a preliminary word with Cassius, who probably thought I'd produced an illegitimate son whom I was now acknowledging. It would have been impossible to disabuse him of the notion, especially since I couldn't have told him the truth about how I'd come across the boy; in fact it might well have served to make Cassius more disposed to support me if he believed Theo was my son, because, in a moment of drunken melancholy, I'd once told him about Marcus.

'I'd be glad of an extra pair of hands today, I'll tell you,' Cassius said, smiling at Theo. 'Good with animals, you say?' Theo and I nodded simultaneously. 'Even better – you can have a look at my colt. He's too nervous, won't eat, and I've been trying to coax him to feed from my hand. I've had no luck – you might do better, Theo.'

'I'll try,' Theo said eagerly. 'Where is he?'

'In that stall on the end.' Cassius pointed, and, with scarcely a goodbye, Theo dashed off.

'Fine-looking boy,' Cassius commented. With what

I thought was admirable restraint, he didn't ask any questions.

'He's in need of a home,' I said quietly. 'And, although you haven't asked, no, he's not mine.'

Cassius nodded slowly. 'And you're not going to tell me anything more about him, are you?'

'I'm not.'

He was staring towards the stall, into which Theo had disappeared. 'Well, I'll see what I make of him.' He glanced at me. 'Trustworthy, is he?'

I nodded. 'Absolutely.'

'As I say, I'll see.'

'Until later, then.' I mounted my horse.

'Till later.'

All twelve of us were at the temple. We didn't always wear our masks when we met in the daytime, but we were preparing for one of our most solemn rituals, and today we did.

I had dedicated myself to Mithras more than a quarter of a century ago, in a small dark temple on Hadrian's Wall; they told me that Mithras would protect all who pledged their lives to the Roman eagle. My god kept faith with me, and my love for him has grown over the years. The temple where we now worshipped was very different from the place of my initiation, but wherever you were, the rites, the costumes and the prayers were the same: you could go into a strange temple anywhere in the Empire and instantly feel at home.

The temple above Glanum was built into the hillside, the inner sanctum cut out of the living rock. Nearby, a small stream ran off the hill and through a sheltered glade. It was the perfect location: Mithras slayed the Great Bull in a cave, and, even when his temples are in towns or on the plains, they are designed to look like caves. Here, we hadn't had to resort to artifice.

There was a small antechamber which we used as a robing room, and beyond it, down some steps, the sanctum itself. The central aisle was narrow, and flanked by the cushion-covered benches where we lay back to watch the ceremonies. In the end wall, a relief of Mithras slaying the bull was carved into the rock; it was so powerful that it affected me every time I saw it. The temple was kept in darkness until, at a given moment, our Pater lit the torch behind the altar and light streamed out through the ray-like holes in the stone: the dancing golden flame gave the illusion that the god and the bull were moving.

Now, my mind on the ceremony ahead, I stood in the antechamber and put on my mask, arranging my long scarlet cloak round my shoulders. When I came to Provincia I was initiated into a new grade: I became a Lion, and the thunderbolt symbol was tattooed on the backs of my hands. I could never enter the temple without recalling the ordeal of initiation, more harrowing than any I'd undergone before. The grave-like pit where I suffered my temporary 'death' was outside, against the outer wall of the temple, and the sacred fire-shovel they used to pile the live coals on top of my stone coffin was kept hidden in the antechamber. Nevertheless, I remembered. It is meant to be that way – we suffer for our god, and he repays our dedication with his love and his protection.

The other men were robing beside me, the Courier of the Sun with his halo and his bright yellow cloak, the Persian dressed in grey, two more Lions, and a pair each of Ravens, Nymphs and Soldiers. One of the latter was the man who owned the bull-calf: he had recently undergone his initiation, and I guessed that the memory of his trial, buried deep in the earth, was still too fresh for him to relax.

When we were all ready, we filed through the opening in the screen and took up our places in the dark temple. After some moments of utter silence, we heard the slow steps of the Pater as he entered and began to walk up the aisle.

The Courier of the Sun ignited his torch, stepping forward to hand it to the Pater, and the Pater placed it behind the stone altar. The sun's rays seemed to leap into life: an involuntary sigh of awe spread through the temple, and the magic began.

Afterwards, disrobing back in the anteroom, nobody spoke. It was always that way – what we experienced in the temple affected us too deeply for the transition back to normal life to be either quick or easy.

As I was leaving, I felt a hand on my arm. It was one of the Ravens, still masked. He edged closer, then put his mouth right up to my ear. In a whisper so soft that I barely heard the words, he said, 'There is trouble for you.' Then he drew his cloak around him and turned away, huddling into the corner where his Brother Raven was reverently putting his ritual staff into its concealing bag.

I stumbled out into the daylight, my mind reeling. Everyone was leaving, still observing the silence, and it wasn't the moment to start asking questions. I untethered my horse from his place in the shade, tightened the girths and mounted.

Those words echoed in my head as I rode back. There is trouble for you. As if I didn't already know! But to have that well-meaning warning – *was* it well-meaning? I didn't even know that! – from one of my own people made it doubly forceful. Doubly frightening.

I tried to put together all I knew about the two Ravens. One was a relative newcomer, a young man who had come from northern Gaul and whom I couldn't remember having seen without his mask and cloak. The other – I thought he was called Flavius – I understood worked in the Procurator's Office in Arelate, although we were no more than nodding acquaintances. It's like that among the followers of Mithras – we are Brothers when we worship but, although we must never harm one another in our life outside the temple, we are not necessarily close friends.

Trouble. Hunching my shoulders as the temperature dropped with the approach of evening, I tried to dispel my growing apprehension.

Cassius greeted me with the news that Theo had fallen in love with his colt. The animal had taken to him almost straight away, eaten all that Theo had offered and then been a thorough nuisance for the rest of the day because he was suddenly so full of energy.

'Is Theo ready?' I asked. 'We should be setting out, we've got quite a way to go.'

Cassius hesitated. 'I'll fetch him if you wish, but Julia was about to dish up supper. Besides, the lad's worn out – I doubt if he'll manage to keep his eyes open long enough to eat.' You don't know him, I thought. 'He's welcome to stay the night. That way he can get back to my colt first thing tomorrow. We might try him out on the lunge rein.'

I said, 'What are you saying?'

Cassius smiled. 'I like the boy. Whatever you decide about his future, why not let him stay here for a few days? He's enjoyed himself today, and he looks happy. Besides, he's a good worker.'

Why not indeed. 'If you're sure,' I said. 'I warn you, he'll eat you out of house and home.'

'Not my Julia he won't, she's used to lads. Will you come and join us, Sergius?'

'No, thank you. I'll come and see Theo, then I'll be on my way.'

I missed him, riding the last leg home. But he'd been so eager to stay that I hadn't the heart to take him back with me. I'll have to get used to missing him, I told myself, so I might as well start now.

The house was in darkness when I got in. When I'd seen to my horse I went outside again and quietly walked round the walls, but could see no sign of any lurking watcher. Callistus had left a pan of stew on the hearth, and Didius must have been in because the bathhouse furnace was lit. If he'd waited around to give me the usual massage and scrape, he wasn't waiting any longer. Still, I could bathe on my own; I was glad he'd heated the water.

I ate my supper and headed for the bathhouse. I progressed quite rapidly through the *tepidaria*, eager to get into the *caldarium* for the pleasure of lying back in the scalding water; it was every bit as good as I'd anticipated. I was sitting up, rubbing oil into my chest and arms, when I heard the bathhouse door open and close again.

It wasn't the best situation in which to face an intruder, stark naked and with my clothes three rooms away. Making my voice sound deep and threatening, I shouted, 'Who's there?'

She peered round the wall that separated me from the last of the *tepidaria*. 'It's me.'

'Zillah, you're lucky I didn't attack first and ask questions later!'

'You've nothing to attack with,' she pointed out, 'except a linen towel and a bottle of oil. Shall I do your back?'

'You keep your distance!' I shrank back into the corner of the bath, pulling up my knees. I wondered how clear the water was. 'And just how did you get in?'

'Through the gates,' she said innocently. 'Shouldn't I have done?'

I could have sworn I'd shot the bolt across. 'No, it's all right. I'm glad to see you,' I added.

She smiled. 'And I you.'

'Theo isn't here, he's staying on a farm with a good friend of mine and his family. He – Theo – has fallen for a young colt.'

'He's good with horses,' she said absently. Then: 'I know.'

This was getting worse. First she walked in through the gates I'd omitted to bolt, now she knew all about my day's doings. '*How* do you know?'

'I asked your manservant. Callistus, isn't it?' I nodded dumbly. 'Don't worry, he guessed who I was. He's very fond of you, isn't he? Very loyal.' She was unwinding the veil from her head and throat, fanning herself in the steam.

'Not loyal enough to keep my secrets,' I said. I'd have to have words with Callistus.

'He knew it didn't have to be secret from me,' she said sensibly. 'Phew, it's hot in here!'

'It's meant to be, it's a hot room.' I was feeling terribly aware of my nakedness. 'You wouldn't like to turn away while I get out and find my towel, would you?'

'I was just about to anoint your back.' She was rolling up her sleeves as she spoke. 'I'm good at massage – I used to do my husband, when he came in at daybreak all stiff and cold from a night's fishing.'

I felt her strong hands on my shoulders. She was right – she was indeed good.

I frothed up the water, grateful for the clouds of steam which seemed to be obscuring those areas of me under the surface. 'Mmm, this is nice.'

She burst out laughing. 'It can't be! You're about as relaxed as that stone pillar over there. Go on, let yourself go!'

I reached up and took hold of her hands. Lightly – I thought briefly of Gaius, who might well take such a grip on her with a lot more force. After a moment's resistance, she didn't try to pull away. 'I can't let myself go when I'm naked in my bath with a fully clad woman hovering round me.'

'I'm not looking,' she said, the laughter still in her voice. 'Anyway, I'm sure you haven't got anything out of the ordinary – when you've seen one, you've seen them all.'

I twisted round so that I was kneeling up in the bath, face to face with her. Somehow I didn't feel awkward any more. 'You haven't seen *mine*,' I said. Then, my hands on her face so that I could gently pull her towards me, I kissed her.

She kissed me back, there was no doubt about that. Her mouth opened under mine, and she didn't seem to mind that my arms round her were soaking her robe. The kiss grew more intense, and, losing myself in her, I pulled her into the bath.

She broke away from the kiss. Her arms still round my neck, she was half-floating, half-sitting on my lap. I wished she'd sit down more firmly. 'I'm all wet,' she said. 'Look at my clothes!'

'Oh dear. Perhaps you'd better take them off.'

'Perhaps I had.' She stood up in the water, and I watched as she peeled off the dripping gown and underclothes. Her body was rounded and firm, the belly with a slight swell, the breasts heavy. She turned to look down at me, a smile on her face.

'I hope you like what you see.' There wasn't a touch of flirtatiousness in her tone.

'I do.' I reached up for her, and she sank back into the water.

'I've never frolicked in a Roman bath before,' she said. 'Especially not with a Roman in it.'

'Would you rather I got out?' Gallantry seemed to demand that I ask.

'No, I'd rather you stayed.' I loved her forthrightness. 'It's big enough and deep enough to swim in, isn't it? I know how to swim.' She demonstrated the fact, blissfully unaware that the action of her strong legs was lifting her buttocks to the surface.

It seemed unfair to go on enjoying the unexpected sight, so I swam after her. 'So do I. I learned when a tough little sergeant with arms like hawsers threw me in a river.'

'Why did he do that? Weren't you angry?'

'Hopping mad, but there isn't much a new recruit can do by way of protest.'

'You were in the Legions?' She caught on quick, this one. I nodded. 'I thought you were a financial secretary?'

'I am now. They don't let you be a legionary for ever.'

She was running her hands up and down my arms. 'You look more like a soldier than a secretary.'

'I keep myself fit,' I gasped; her hands were now on my chest.

Her eyes held mine. 'I had to come,' she said frankly. 'There's something I have to tell you, but it's only part of why I'm here.'

Whatever it was, it could wait. 'I know.' It might have been presumptuous, but if she was determined to be honest, I had to be too. 'I've been hoping you'd come back ever since you left.'

She looked so happy. 'Have you?'

'Yes.' I kissed her again, very softly. 'You'll stay, won't you?'

'I will. Tonight, at least.' She returned the kiss. Then, smiling, she added, 'I can't very well do anything else, since you've soaked my clothes.'

'Will you sleep with me?' I thought we should get it straight, so as to avoid any misunderstandings.

She put her arms round my neck and snuggled against my wet chest. Her actions were making her answer fairly predictable, but she gave it anyway. Lips nuzzling against my neck, she said, 'Of course.'

18

Beth lay awake for some time after Adam had gone home. The discovery that they had both experienced the same Roman – 'seen' was a word she wasn't prepared to use, not yet, at any rate – had shaken them both. For it to happen to one person could be explained by any number of rationalizations. When it happened to two it was less easy to dismiss.

But as the initial reaction faded, they'd both started to feel elated. 'It's something special,' Adam said, rather inadequately, she thought. 'We have to follow it up, don't we?'

She agreed, unreservedly. They considered various suggestions as to what was the next step – Adam wondered if some authority in the town museum might be able to turn up detailed information on the period, which seemed as good a starting point as any until they realized that they didn't know what period it was. 'Roman Arles covered several hundred years,' Adam said dejectedly. 'And, even given that our Roman was up on Hadrian's Wall, that could have been at any time within a span of more than two centuries.'

'Is there anywhere on the Camargue where we could find out more about that place with the derelict buildings?' Returning there was the last thing she wanted, but if it helped, she was willing.

Fortunately he said, 'No. There's a museum on Camargue life and natural history, but it only makes glancing references to Roman times. And it's nowhere near where we went today.'

They sat in thoughtful silence. She began to feel uneasy: I know what we have to do, she thought, but he's not going to like it.

Eventually he said, 'I'm stumped. What about you? Any bright ideas?'

She took a deep breath. 'Yes.'

'Oh! Why didn't you say?'

'Because I'll be treading on delicate ground.'

He looked amused. 'Do you normally let that stop you?'

No, she wanted to say, but this is different. 'Adam, when you were explaining that the Roman is much more vivid down here, you said he kept showing you that place on the Camargue and another place.' He started to protest, but she ploughed on. 'Yes, I know very well you can't talk about it, you said so. But don't you think you'll have to? Isn't that the only way we can hope to make any progress?'

He didn't answer for a long time. He sat, eyes half-closed, staring out in front of him. Finally, the reluctance obvious in his voice, he said, 'Okay.'

What did that mean? 'Can we find it, do you think?'

He turned to her. 'Beth, I don't know where it is. I don't even know *what* it is. It's just like the derelict buildings – I have a picture in my head, but without some clue to tell me where the place is, I'm completely at a loss.'

'Can you describe it?'

He sighed. 'I see a big rectangle of stone. It's got rocks around it, and some sandy soil. There's a dark place near it, lit by candle flames. There are figures which seem to dance.'

'I see what you mean.' It was incredibly disappointing. 'Can't you think of anything else?'

He hesitated, then said almost brutally, 'The stone's covered with blood.'

'Oh!'

He flashed her a smile. 'Sorry. I did warn you.'

Something was stirring at the back of her mind. Focusing

on it, slowly it became clear. 'When I was telling you earlier about Joe and his discoveries about the Mithraists, you leapt to their defence. And a few days ago, when Joe mentioned them to me, I remember getting a fleeting image of the Roman. You don't think it's possible he – the Roman – is trying to give us a lead?'

'By indicating there's a link with Mithras, you mean?'

'Yes. And he's showing you that rock covered with blood because it was the Mithraists' sacrifice stone.'

'It's possible, I suppose, yes. But, as I told you, they didn't make sacrifices. Only on very special occasions.'

'Couldn't the scene you've been given be a special occasion?'

'No, because –' He stopped. After a pause he said, 'It could.'

'Well, why don't we look at some temples of Mithras?'

'Mithraea,' he said automatically.

'Mithraea, then. Joe said there's one in some place by the sea – Saint Marie, was it?' She got up and fetched the map from Joe's desk. 'Les Saintes-Maries-de-la-Mer. There it is.' She pointed. 'He said there's another one somewhere, but he didn't say where it was. But we could make a start down at Saintes-Maries.'

She wondered why he seemed so very reluctant. 'Adam?'

'All right.' He got to his feet. 'We'll go tomorrow.'

Then, after a brief goodnight, he went home.

Joe wasn't back by the time Adam collected her, even though they didn't leave till mid-afternoon; she'd suggested they might have a lie-in, having been up so late the previous night. She was relieved not to have to confront Joe. She had considered leaving him a note to say where she was and when she expected to be back, then decided not to. If he didn't bother with such courtesies, she wasn't going to either.

They covered the journey down to the coast swiftly. On

the outskirts of Arles they had passed a sign to the village in whose church the girl had experienced her vision of St Theodore: 'Visit Our Lady of the Marshlands!' Beth translated to herself, 'See the tears of Little Saint Theodore!' She watched a convoy of three tourist buses take the turning to the village: Theomania, she reflected, looked as if it was becoming big business.

There was little traffic on their road, and Adam seemed to be driving faster as a result of not talking; perhaps, she thought, the extra concentration makes a difference.

Judging by its outskirts, Les Saintes-Maries-de-la-Mer promised to be a thoroughly modern tourist resort. With growing disappointment, she gazed out on new and raw-looking holiday houses and apartments, between them countless small businesses offering rides across the Camargue; one advertised 'Photographic Safaris'. Bored-looking horses stood tacked up and chewing their bits: trade seemed slack, but then it was the end of the season.

Adam parked the car on the edge of a central square, and they crossed the road to a precinct of shops and cafés. Without exception, the shops offered nothing but souvenirs and postcards.

Then, emerging from an alley between the shops, suddenly they were in an open space, smoothly paved and containing a couple of decorative flowerbeds. And, rising stark above them, a heavily fortified church.

'The church of Les Saintes-Maries,' Adam said. 'Shall we go in?'

It had been expecting far too much to find a perfectly preserved Mithraeum in the middle of aggressive twentieth-century commercialism. And anyway, hadn't Joe said the church had been built over the site of the temple? It looks, she thought, as if we've had a wasted journey. 'We may as well.'

But the church's interior was very far from being a disappointment. There was nobody about: they walked slowly up the aisle with the fine Romanesque walls soaring either side, the stone lit to bright gold by the floodlights concealed behind the pillars; the fortified church had no windows.

At the far end of the aisle, two sets of steps led up to the altar. Between them, there was a narrow stairway leading down to the crypt: walled in rough stone, as if hewn out of the rock, it was lit with hundreds of small candles whose light flickered in the slight draught. The statue of a woman, black-skinned and robed in muslin and lace, seemed to be moving in the dancing light.

Adam was already going down the steps. Hesitating only for an instant, she followed.

'Who is she?' she whispered, going to stand beside Adam in front of the calm-faced figure.

'I don't know. When we leave, we'll see if we can find a guide book in one of those hundreds of shops.'

'I should have brought Joe's book,' she murmured.

Adam had wandered on and was now staring at a slab of stone set into the rocky wall. 'Come and look at this,' he said softly.

'What is it?'

He ran his finger over some very faint lettering. 'It's an altar. I can't read the dedication – too many of the letters have been worn away.'

'An altar?'

'Yes. Not an altar like that one above our heads – this is Roman. Followers of the various gods would put up an altar dedicated to their favourite deity when something good happened, and sometimes on the well-preserved ones you can read the full inscription, so you know the name of the deity, the name and status of the man who put up the altar, and often the year as well.'

'Like the plaques in churches that say "*Merci*" when a saint has healed a child or something?'

'Just like that. The Sixth Legion put up altars on the

bridge they built at Newcastle to thank the gods for their uneventful sea voyage from Germany.'

'So this could once have been a Roman temple? The very Mithraeum we've come to find?' It was such an amazing thought that she wondered why he didn't seem more excited.

He shrugged. 'It's possible, I suppose, although the lay-out would have been different. But it's far more likely that the men who constructed the crypt needed a slab of stone to shore up a weak spot, and used what was handy, stone being in short supply down here.'

'But this stone was originally in a temple?'

'Probably.'

She reached forward to touch it. She half-expected the Roman to materialize in front of her, but nothing happened.

Adam put a hand on her shoulder. 'You never see anything when you're trying to,' he said gently. 'It's the sod's law of the spirit world.'

She smiled. 'I'll stop trying, then. Shall we go and find a guide book?'

'If you've seen enough.'

On the way out she lit a candle and added it to the hundreds already burning. Watching the smoke from the ignited wick twist slowly upwards, she thought of the Roman.

They found a nicely illustrated guide to the town, and sat down on a bench to read it.

'The legend of the Saintes-Maries says they arrived from the Holy Land in AD 40, in an open boat with no sails, oars or rudder,' Adam said. 'The two saints were Mary the sister of the Virgin, and Mary the mother of James and John. Mary Magdalene came with them, with Martha, Lazarus, Maximus and Sidonius, whoever the last two were. Their servant Sarah leapt in at the last moment and came too.'

'Quite a load, for a small boat.'

'It doesn't say it was small, just that it was open.'

'Why did they come here?' She peered over his shoulder.

'Presumably they fled the Holy Land to avoid persecution. There are lots of legends about figures from the Gospels arriving in Europe – think of Joseph of Arimathea planting his staff at Glastonbury.'

'Some people say Jesus himself survived the Crucifixion and escaped to France.'

'They do indeed.'

'Were they evangelists? You'd think they might be tempted to keep quiet about their faith, in case they got persecuted here too.'

He looked down at the book. 'It says the rest of this particular party went off to start spreading the word – Martha went to Tarascon, and Lazarus to Marseilles – but the two Saint Marys were too old and they stayed here, where Sarah took care of them.'

'It's a lovely story,' she said. 'Wouldn't it be nice if it were true?'

'What makes you think it isn't?'

'It's not all that likely, is it?'

'No, but it's possible.'

'I liked that black-faced Sarah.' She thought it would be diplomatic to change the subject, since it was clear they weren't going to agree: she couldn't for a moment see how eight people could miraculously drift from Palestine to Provence in an inadequately equipped boat, especially in view of the fact that most of them were elderly and quite a few in delicate health. Why, Lazarus had been given up for dead at one time, and Martha had exhausted herself on housework, poor thing. Yet there was Adam calmly accepting it as possible.

'She's become wrapped up in gipsy folklore,' he said. 'Although she came from the Holy Land, she's venerated as a gipsy herself – she's their patron saint.'

She was tempted to ask if he was going to include Sarah

in his film, but decided not to as it might be construed as provocative. 'It's all very interesting, but it's not what we came here for. Have you seen anything that looks like the vision?' Silly question, she thought, it's quite obvious he hasn't, first because he'd have told me, second because there's been nothing like what he described.

He smiled. 'No. Afraid not.'

'Well, we'll have to look somewhere else.' She was determined not to be daunted. 'We'll go back and look through Joe's books and find references to Mithraeums, and –'

'Mithraea.'

'To Mithraea, then, and visit all of them. We'll make a list.'

He didn't respond.

'Won't we?'

'If you say so. But not today.'

'Oh. All right, then.'

She thought, I'll do it myself, if you're not keen. I don't have to wait till *you* feel like it!

After a while he reached out for her hand. 'Sorry.'

'For what?' She didn't take her hand away, but stopped short of reciprocating his squeeze.

'For being less than enthusiastic. Right now I'm tired of Romans.'

Is this the attitude you'd expect from a keen young film-maker, a seeker after truth? she wondered, smiling to herself. 'Fair enough. Why don't we go for a stroll along the beach, then come and have an early drink before we go back?'

He stood up. 'Good idea, especially if we make it a short walk and a long drink.'

It turned into a very long drink. They shared a bottle of wine, then, deciding that they shouldn't have any more to drink unless they ate, found an unpretentious restaurant in one of the back streets and ordered fish soup to have with the second bottle. The soup, Adam said, was a Provençal speciality: Beth, having been put off fish soup when given it at an aunt's house as a child, was reluctant, but the dish that arrived wasn't anything like Auntie Madge's offering. This was more a stew than a soup, great chunks of vegetables and delicately flavoured white fish in a herb-scented broth, with croutons of bread to dip into various mustards and sauces before soaking them in the steaming liquid.

'It's not a starter, it's a meal in itself,' she commented, finally giving up on the last few pieces of fish.

'It is. Aren't you going to eat those?'

'No.'

He spooned them up. 'Waste not, want not.'

'And you're far too far away from home to take them back to Barty.'

'You remembered!' He looked pleased. 'Actually, Barty doesn't care for fish, he's a thorough-going carnivore dog.'

She drained the last of her wine. 'I could get addicted to this Vin de Pays des Sables.'

'Me too. I wonder if it travels?'

'Probably not. We'd better drink a lot of it while we're here.'

'No more tonight, though?'

It was nice of him to make it a question rather than a statement. 'No, I've had quite enough.'

They had coffee, then asked for the bill and democratically split it between them. Adam suggested they have a walk round the church square before they left, and, emerging from the restaurant, the night was so beautiful that she agreed.

They strolled across the square and down to the marina, then retraced their steps and went back into the centre of the little town. This is its heart, she mused, looking up at the great walls of the church, this is where you'd feel the spell of the past, if you were going to feel it at all.

They sat down on a bench at the side of the square. There

was no one about; although the night was mild, with the moon shining out of a clear sky, it was late. The last of the diners and drinkers had gone home.

Neither of them spoke – she wondered if, like her, Adam was too full of the afternoon's impressions to want to talk.

She gazed out across the square bathed in the moonbeams. Beyond, she caught a glimpse of the sea. It seemed to be shimmering with silvery light. The low-rise modern buildings faded to mere insignificant shadows: the huge church alone stood out in dark silhouette.

It was an eerie sight, and she suppressed a shiver. It's as if anything belonging to this century – to any century since earliest times – has melted away, she thought. With only a little imagination, I could believe I was looking out on an ancient scene.

Her mind obligingly providing the picture, the church seemed to alter, changing into a smaller building, simpler and far less imposing. The sea seemed to be nearer suddenly, for she could hear gentle waves breaking on the stony shore. The white walls of the little church – *was* it a church? It looked more like a temple – glistened luminous under the moon.

A robed woman was standing outside the temple, veil over her head. It's Sarah, Beth thought sleepily. I'm dreaming, and she's come out of her crypt to enjoy the night. She smiled.

The figure pushed back her veil. It wasn't Sarah – this woman's skin wasn't black, and her hair was fair.

Beth leaned forward to get a better look, and the figure disappeared. The temple reverted to a church, the shops and restaurants came back into their tight formation around the square.

She blinked, then rubbed her eyes. I must be more tired than I thought – I've been asleep!

She hoped Adam hadn't noticed. Not that it mattered. I feel refreshed, she thought, as if I'd had a much longer sleep. I feel . . . She paused, trying to assess exactly how she did feel. I don't know. Eager, I think. Alive, full of energy. As if I'm compelled, being pushed into something.

She glanced at Adam, sitting quietly beside her. If only I can galvanize him into action, she thought wryly, we might actually get somewhere.

'Let's go home,' he said.

'Right.'

He held her hand as they walked back to the car. 'The earlier we get to bed, the sooner we'll feel like starting tomorrow.'

'Starting . . . ? Yes! Okay.'

It looks, she reflected as they drove away, as if the compulsion got through to him, too.

It didn't occur to her till long after he'd dropped her off that there might be something sinister in two near-strangers being affected by the same quiet force.

19

It was nearly eleven when she and Adam said goodnight in the Place de la Redoute. Feeling very tired – she'd fallen asleep in the car – all she wanted to do was drop into bed.

But La Maison Jaune was jumping and bouncing to heavy rock music.

'*Christ*!' she muttered as she banged the front door behind her; the noise had been bad enough out on the steps, and it was deafening inside. '*JOE*!'

Someone had put a portable stereo the size of a suitcase and a stack of tapes in the kitchen. Two couples were standing fondling each other; all four of them looked up at her expressionlessly as she pushed her way between them and turned the sound down.

'Thank you,' she said sarcastically. 'Any idea where Joe is? If he *is* here, that is, and hasn't given you the run of the house while he's off somewhere else!'

'He's in his room,' one of the girls said. 'With Gemma.'

'Ah.' In the double sleeping bag? she wondered. Not sleeping, if they are, not with that racket going on.

She strode out across the hall and along the corridor towards Joe's room. Noticing on the way that the door to her room was ajar, she glanced inside. A couple were in her bed.

She threw Joe's door open with such force that it ricochetted off the wall and almost smacked her in the face. Standing in the doorway, only just resisting the temptation to stride over to the bed and fling the duvet off them, she glared down at Joe and Gemma.

'Well?' she said icily.

Joe frowned. 'You could have knocked!'

'I don't think so. I've come home from a long day, tired out, and not only do I find enough noise coming from my house to keep the whole of Arles awake, in addition there are two people in my bed.' She moved closer. 'What are you going to do about it?'

'Oh. I thought they said they were going.'

'How could you possibly think they'd gone? Didn't you *hear* the music?'

'I meant Nick and Trish. The couple in your room.'

'Perhaps you'd be so kind as to tell them to go now.' She was finding it increasingly difficult to hold on to what remained of her control. 'And you can change the sheets, too.'

The girl – it was the same one who had come for the brandy – gave him a push. 'Go on, then.'

'I can't,' he hissed, 'not with my sister watching.'

'I'm not.' Beth turned her back.

'I'll do the bed,' Gemma said. She sounded perfectly cheerful about being disturbed in the middle of whatever they'd been doing. 'Give us my T-shirt, Joe.'

There were rustling sounds from the bed, and then Joe disappeared into Beth's room. She heard a muttered conversation, quite a lot of cursing in a sleepy male voice, and soon afterwards the sound of the front door banging. The noise from the kitchen seemed to have stopped: she went to see if the quartet were still there, but they'd gone too.

She wandered into Joe's workroom. His desk was exactly as it had been earlier: clearly he hadn't done any work. But then, to be fair, neither have I, she thought.

After a while Gemma came in. 'Your room's ready,' she said.

'Thank you.'

'S'all right.'

Beth looked at her. The long hair looked even more

unkempt, but she had a nice smile. Tonight her T-shirt said 'Levellers', with a logo of a stylized face. 'I'm Beth,' Beth said.

'I know. Look, I'm sorry about this. I'm going back to my place now – I've left your room tidy, and I've told Joe he's got to do the rest of the house.'

Good Lord, she thought, what have they been up to? And fancy this slim leggy girl *telling* Joe to do anything! 'Have you far to go?' she asked, more for something to say than from any great desire to know.

'No, we're in a place just outside the walls.'

'Did you know Joe at home?' I shouldn't be asking her, she thought, I should ask him.

'No!' The girl laughed. 'We met in a caff down on that big road.'

'Ah.' That accounts for him doing what he's told, she thought, he's in the first flush of sexual desire and would probably stand on his head and whistle the National Anthem if she asked him to.

'See you, then,' Gemma said. Then she left.

After a few minutes, Joe came into the room. He went over to his desk and sat down behind it. Beth wondered if he'd placed himself there on purpose – really, she thought, he does seem to be assuming the air of a headmaster about to give out a grade-one bollocking.

But I'm not going to give him the chance.

'This is really a bit much, Joe,' she said firmly.

Instantly he was on the attack. 'I had no idea you were coming back! You didn't bother to leave a note, so how was I to know?'

'You didn't either!'

'I –'

She was determined not to let him beat her down. 'You set the trend for going off without any explanation,' she interrupted, 'so don't you dare lay that one on me. And when *you* came in today, it was to a clean and tidy house, with food in the fridge and fresh bread in the cupboard. *You* didn't walk in on a party, with couples necking in the kitchen and four people already gone to bed. Two of them in mine!'

'You ought to lighten up a bit,' he countered. 'Get a life!'

She'd never heard him use that expression before – he must have picked it up from his new friends. Then the injustice of it struck her. 'That's the exact opposite of what you said the other day! You were acting like a virgin vicar at the thought of me going off with a man I hardly knew!'

'That's different, it's –'

'It's bloody well not different! You've not only gone off with a girl you hardly know, you've quite clearly slept with her!'

There was a pause. Then he said coldly, 'So?'

'So don't be such a hypocrite! You've no right to accuse me of something I haven't even done, especially when you have!'

'It's different for a man.'

She could hardly believe he'd said it. '*What*? And just how does Gemma feel about that particular bit of male propaganda?'

He shrugged. 'It doesn't matter what she thinks. She's not a great thinker, actually.'

'But that doesn't matter since she's a wonderful screw?'

He frowned at her choice of words, but rallied and said, 'That's about it, yes.'

She got up and walked over to him. 'Joe, if you're going to come out of your closet of self-righteous innocence, you'd better know a couple of things. One is that we're no longer living according to Father's rules – women have a say nowadays, they've actually passed a law to give us equal opportunities, although sometimes you wouldn't credit it. The other is that, even if men like you still subscribe to the old attitudes, it's no longer considered correct to admit to it.'

She paused. He was staring up at her, still managing to

look condescending. Before he could say anything and make her even angrier, she said, 'I'm going to bed.'

As she left the room she heard him say, in exactly their father's tone, 'Women!'

She slept deeply until six, when she woke and couldn't get to sleep again. She got up, made herself some tea, and went to sit at Joe's desk. To take her mind off the nastiness of the previous night, she pulled a few of Joe's books towards her and started leafing disconsolately through them.

In the third one was a bookmark. Opening it at the marked place, she found herself looking at a photograph of the church at Les Saintes-Maries. A paragraph beneath the illustration said the church was reputed to have been built over a pagan temple, possibly dedicated to Mithras. A small figure 1 at the end of the paragraph denoted a footnote: at the bottom of the page was a list of the sites of other putative Mithraea.

Running quickly through the list, she only recognized one as definitely being in the immediate area: it was near Glanum. She went through the list again, wishing her knowledge of local geography were better. Then, glancing at Joe's paper bookmark, she saw that under a heading 'Mithraea' he'd written the one word: 'Glanum'.

He should know, she acknowledged. Adam and I were on the lookout for other Mithraea to visit – Glanum it is, then.

She looked at her watch. It was still only just after seven, ages till she might expect Adam to collect her; he'd said he'd try to get along soon after nine, but that it was highly likely he'd sleep through his alarm. Anyway, she thought, I've got at least two hours – I'll shower and dress, then fill in the time by reading up on this Glanum place.

Even a quick look in the index of the first book gave a promising number of entries for Glanum: she began to wonder if she'd have long enough to do the job thoroughly.

* * *

Nine o'clock passed. So did ten o'clock, but she was so absorbed she scarcely noticed. She'd gleaned the basic details about Glanum quite quickly – it had developed into a large and prosperous place, by the standards of Roman times, because of its location on the conjunction of two major routes and because of the beauty of its situation, in a sheltered valley in the foothills of the Alpilles.

She read of the public buildings and the temples, of the busy forum and the sacred well, of the private houses and the great curving theatre on the hillside behind the town. In a rapid trip through two hundred years of Glanum's history she read of the worship of Jupiter and Mercury, Mars and Aphrodite; of Mithras, the god of soldiers and merchants; of the coming of Christianity, which, intolerant of rivals, swept away all that had gone before so that temples were defaced and razed to the ground, the sacred places used as the sites for the new Christian churches.

All the time she was reading, some small chord of memory was sounding. She pressed on, thinking that whatever it was would become clear; with any luck, she'd come across some reference which would bring it to the forefront of her mind.

Suddenly she remembered that it had been something she'd read, but that it hadn't been in a book. What else could it have been? In a notebook – that's it, in one of Joe's notebooks!

His main notebook was alongside the books. She opened it, raced through the pages and found the place, the memory rapidly becoming crystal-clear: no wonder Glanum rang a bell, she thought, it was where Joe's Little Saint Theodore was killed.

She read swiftly through Joe's précis of the ancient writings of Lucius Sextus, refreshing herself on the details. The child found tied to the altar, his throat cut, the body left exposed yet miraculously untouched by wild beasts. The subsequent judgement of the magistrate at Fréjus, who had apparently condemned some Christians to the lions because they insisted on elevating little Theodore to the status of saint.

Whereas, if it was true he'd offended Roman sensibilities by refusing to participate in sacrifices to the state gods, then in official eyes he was nothing but a nuisance, guilty of a criminal act and so, despite his youth, best dealt with by permanent removal.

She closed the notebook, slowly putting it and the text-books back in their places.

She felt that she was on the edge of a momentous discovery. If it's true, if the hunch is right, she thought, then surely it means –

No. She made herself stop. I don't know yet. And I'm not going to jump to any conclusions, no matter how seductive they may be, until I've got more in the way of proof. It won't be much, not to a sceptic, anyway – she smiled ruefully – but it'll be the best we can do.

She went out on the balcony so that she could look out for Adam.

But the next arrival wasn't Adam, it was Gemma. She let herself in, called out a greeting to Beth, who had gone into the hall to see who it was, then strolled into the kitchen.

'I've brought the stuff for the wash,' she announced, spilling the contents of three bulging Monoprix bags on to the floor: her dirty washing all seemed to be the colour of old tennis socks.

'But –' Beth began.

'It's okay, I'll do your things too,' Gemma said.

'No!' She'd just seen a shirt with a filthy black rim round the collar go in, its sleeves lovingly wrapped round a grey-ish pair of underpants – Joe's? – and there was an increasing aroma of stale sweat. 'Don't worry, I'll do mine later.'

She felt very awkward; it must be perfectly plain to Gemma that she didn't want their things to share a machine, and surely Gemma's feelings would be hurt.

Then she thought, damn Gemma's feelings! She may have a nice smile and been decent about making up my bed last night, but that doesn't give her the right to come pushing into my kitchen with three bags of laundry!

'Doesn't your place have washing facilities?' she asked. God, I sound like some prissy old spinster!

'Yes, but the spin-dryer's bust.' Gemma was trying to get a pair of jeans into the already crowded drum.

It's now or never, Beth thought. If I don't say something, she'll be asking next if I can do her surplus in with my load. 'I'm sorry, Gemma,' she said firmly. 'I don't know what Joe has said, and you can do the load you've just put in. But I'm afraid that's the last, I really can't –'

'There isn't any more.' Gemma had forced the second leg of the jeans inside and was leaning on the door to close it. 'That's everything – I needn't do another wash till next month!'

Despite her annoyance, Beth almost laughed. I must take after my mother after all, she thought, to be so amazed at the thought of someone only washing their clothes once a month, and even then, presumably, only if they can borrow someone else's machine.

And, thank God, I shall no longer be here when Gemma next does her laundry.

'I'll go in with Joe while it's doing,' Gemma said, reaching for the kettle. 'Want a coffee?'

'No thanks, I'm going out any minute.'

'With your fella?' Gemma winked. 'Nice bloke.'

'*I* think so.' But he's not actually my fella, she added silently. Although I must say I wouldn't mind if he were.

Joe emerged from his room, and paused to look in through the open door of the study. Coming into the kitchen he leaned against the worktop scratching his chest. 'Morning, Gemma. Is that coffee for me? Hello, Beth.' She wondered why he was frowning at her.

'It's mine,' Gemma said. 'Kettle's just boiled, you can make your own.'

Good for you, Beth thought.

Joe glared at her again. 'What's the matter with you?' she asked.

'Have you been at my notes?'

His choice of words threw her on the defensive; before it occurred to her to reply that of course she had, wasn't that what she was there for? She found herself saying apologetically, 'Yes. Sorry, have I muddled up your papers?'

'Some of them are – private.'

'*Private*? What are you talking about?'

He seemed ill at ease. 'It's – they're – I'm working on something new. Someone – I'm going to look at the church of Our Lady of the Marshlands.'

She didn't understand. 'Where the girl had her vision? Fine, so what's private about that? Half of Arles will probably be there too.'

He hesitated. 'She's had another vision.'

'Is that so?' She couldn't help the cynicism showing. 'More tears and drops of blood? You'd think –'

Then something struck her. 'Who told you?'

'Nobody,' he answered defensively, 'I – er, I heard it on the radio.'

She glanced across at the radio on the worktop, which to the best of her knowledge hadn't been switched on since they'd arrived. It wasn't even plugged in.

'On the radio,' she repeated.

Joe took a step towards her. 'I don't like your attitude,' he said angrily. 'You and that friend of yours,' – he placed an unpleasant emphasis on 'friend' – 'you're cynical, destructive. You have no belief, he asks too many questions. He was giving me the third degree the very first time we met, when he was trying to find out what I was researching and you so eagerly told him!'

'Nonsense!' Her own anger flaring, she was aware of

Gemma watching avidly. Sod Gemma, she thought. 'He merely asked what anyone might have asked! I couldn't see then what was so secret about it, and I'm damned if I can now!' She pushed her face up to his. 'What the hell's got into you, Joe?'

'I – ' For a moment she thought he was going to answer. Then, a disgusted expression on his face, he turned away. 'Mind your own business,' he muttered.

She leaned back against the worktop. Gemma flashed her a sympathetic smile.

'What time are the others coming?' Joe asked.

'What others?' Beth said warily.

'I wasn't talking to you,' he said coldly. 'Gemma and I are doing pasta for Nick and Trish later.'

'But . . .' She stopped.

Is there any use in protesting? she wondered. Joe's so used to getting his own way, and I'm outnumbered. I suppose, she thought fairly, there's no reason why he shouldn't entertain his friends here, since he's paying half the rent. Just as long as they supply their own food.

The thought of coming back later and finding them all there again, music thumping, couples virtually making love in the kitchen, suddenly made her feel very weary. Without speaking, she went into her room and put her overnight things back in her shoulder bag. I don't know where I want to be, she thought dejectedly, I just know I don't want to be *here*. There must be plenty of reasonable hotels in the town, and they're not likely to be full at this time of year. I'll book into one – I can afford it.

The thought of the new job she'd be going to when she went home fizzed brightly across her mind like an exploding rocket: she hadn't thought about it for some time, and the delight felt brand-new.

She felt like cheering.

When Adam arrived a short time later, she went out to meet him with that particular joy still making her glow. In addition, she thought as she ran down the steps, I've found a purpose for our travels today, and a head-full of things to tell him about Glanum. Not to mention a theory to test out.

Getting into the car, she dismissed the surprisingly attractive thought that Adam might well have a spare room she could borrow.

20

Adam had a map, and as they set off into the mid-morning traffic Beth opened it and started to look for Glanum. She found a mountain range marked the Alpilles, but Glanum didn't seem to be there.

'What are you searching for?' he asked. He looked refreshed – sleeping on, she'd decided, had done him good. And he'd already apologized for being late.

'I've been reading through some of Joe's books and I found out there's a Mithraeum at a place called Glanum. I thought we should go there, but I can't find it on the map.'

He was changing lanes, indicating right. 'No need – I know where it is.' He smiled. 'In the opposite direction from the one we were taking, so it's just as well you said. Look for a place called St-Rémy-de-Provence – it's near there. It's probably not marked because it's an archaeological site, not a modern town.'

Of course. She felt silly for having expected to see it. 'St-Rémy?' Then, after a few moments, 'Got it!'

It wasn't far; the journey took under half an hour, and they hadn't been hurrying. Adam parked on a dusty patch of ground that did duty as a car park. Although it was still not yet noon, the day was getting hot, the sun casting dense black shadows from a majestic tower and triumphal arch in the field next to the car park.

The ancient town of Glanum lay in the fold between two low hills. Pausing to look at the informative notices placed by the path, she read that it had lain buried for centuries, under silt washed down the valley by the watercourse flowing from the mountains.

There were few people about. They went through the entrance hall, where some of the statuary unearthed on the site was displayed, then emerged again into the morning sun. And there, stretching away up the peaceful valley, were the very ruins she'd just been reading about.

Soon she noticed that she and Adam had become separated; he was some way behind her, gazing down at a fragment of mosaic floor. Deciding she'd like to look down on the whole site from above, she walked quickly up the track until she was well past the highest of the remains.

The view down the valley was magnificent, and gave a better impression of the town's layout. Standing there, enjoying the absence of voices or traffic noise, she realized that the only sound, other than birdsong, was running water. Beside the track was a stream; she followed it back down into the valley, where, level with the first of the ancient buildings, it disappeared.

It's gone underground, she thought; maybe it emerges again to feed the well I read about. Listening for the sound of the water, she crossed the site until she came to a partially covered construction with steps leading down: at the bottom of the steps was a large stone-lined cistern.

She could almost see robe-clad women bearing water jars, stooping to fill them from the sacred water to take them off to the temple.

She sat down on the steps, letting the atmosphere of the well work its spell. When Adam eventually came to find her, she almost felt she was entranced.

'This place is magic,' she murmured as he sat down beside her.

'It's a healing well,' he said. 'The waters were said to cure a range of ailments.'

'Including severe mental fatigue brought on by arguing with one's brother, it seems.'

'Oh dear.' He hesitated. 'Something you want to talk about?'

She sighed. 'Not really. Not at the moment, anyway – I'd rather enjoy the peace.'

'Fine.'

They sat in companionable silence for some time, until they were disturbed by an insensitively loud group of sightseers. Then, vacating the steps, they strolled off back towards the entrance.

'Where's the Mithraeum?' she said suddenly: the site had been so seductive, so absorbing, that she'd almost forgotten what they'd gone there for. 'Did we miss it?'

'No. While you were daydreaming by the well, I went to ask that rather supercilious woman who sold us our tickets, and she said it's not here. It's down the road, back towards Arles – you have to take a little road that goes steeply up into the hills. Madame says there's a signpost. We shouldn't have any trouble finding it.' He sounded as if that were a matter for regret.

'Come on,' she said encouragingly. 'Let's go for it.' She put out of her mind thoughts of the last time they'd been looking for somewhere. This is quite different, she told herself. There's nothing to be afraid of!

But Adam's set expression belied her determined optimism.

And, at the very worst moment, she heard in her head what he'd said about that other vision he'd been shown. A dark place lit by flame. Eerie dancing figures. A stone covered in blood. Involuntarily, she shuddered. Still, she reminded herself, there's absolutely no reason to suspect this is the place – even if what the Roman has been showing Adam so persistently really is a Mithraeum, which I admit is only a hunch based on the slimmest of evidence, then it's one hell of a long shot to suggest it has to be *this* one.

They returned to the car, and Adam drove off down the

road. They found the turning, off which another, narrower, track led on up into the hills. The terrain became increasingly rocky, and eventually Adam pulled into a grassy space beside it.

'We'd better walk from here,' he said. He sounded as reluctant as if he were being marched to the scaffold.

She wanted to ask him what was the matter, but she thought she already knew.

A flat slab of stone, from which the blood dripped: she could almost see the vision herself.

She reached for his hand. Side by side, they set off up the track.

It was further than she'd imagined. Or, she acknowledged, trying not to pant too obviously, it might just seem a long way because the going's so rough.

At first the path had wound its way between stands of juniper, pine and cypress trees, and the spiky grass underfoot had been springy with decades of pine needles. But as they'd climbed higher and the ground had grown sandier and rockier, the trees had thinned to nothing. What remained of the grass seemed to be struggling for existence in the dry soil. She felt they'd wandered off into a wilderness, that they were encroaching on a place where nature ruled alone, where mankind was not welcome.

Don't be fanciful, she told herself. There was a sign, back down there in the trees where the path forked. It said *Temple de Mithras*, and clearly pointed this way.

Still . . .

Adam was obviously fitter than she was, and unaffected by the steep ascent. He would wait for her at regular intervals to let her catch up and regain her breath, and she was just thinking how considerate he was being when it struck her that there might be another reason, nothing to do with her: he might just be dreading the moment when they found the temple.

He might even be making sure he didn't reach the place alone.

The path had all but disappeared now; not enough footsteps pass along it, she thought, to keep it well trodden.

A shudder ran through her, so violent that Adam must surely have noticed. They were resting again, perched uncomfortably on the sharp backbone of a great flattish slab of rock that lay across what remained of the track.

A big rectangle of stone . . .

Stop it!

She got up. 'I'm ready for the final assault now,' she said, 'so, as soon as the sherpas have packed up . . .'

It hadn't been much of a joke anyway, and she wasn't really surprised that Adam took no notice. He strode on ahead, and she hurried to catch up. Then abruptly he stopped, waited for her, and took her hand.

'The track opens out enough for us to walk side by side,' he said. Then, almost apologetically: 'Do you mind?' He held up their joined hands.

'Of course not. I'm feeling a bit –' She broke off. 'Good idea.'

The comfort of a warm hand holding hers was surprisingly strong: she hadn't realized how the place was affecting her, how strangely lonely and isolated she'd been feeling, until the reassuring contact had taken her fears away.

Some of them.

It was very quiet. As they strode up the last hundred yards to what seemed to be the summit, the only sound was Beth's harsh panting.

It seemed to echo against the rocks, giving the strange illusion that other people – other creatures – were hidden there, their breath coming fast in their apprehension.

It's only the echo, she told herself. To test it out, momentarily she held her breath.

The sounds from the rocks continued unaffected.

'We're nearly there.' Adam sounded strained. Nevertheless, a human voice was a welcome distraction. 'This must be the top,' – they stopped, looking around, and it seemed that the track petered out against a sheer rock face – 'so where's the temple?'

He removed his hand from hers and began a slow prowl around the open space of the hilltop, repeatedly pausing to crouch down and examine the ground. Being left on her own with nothing to occupy her mind allowed too many disturbing thoughts; she said nervously, 'What exactly are you looking for? Can I help?'

He was brushing earth away from an outcrop of stone. 'I don't really know. Anything that might suggest a man-made structure, I suppose – the remains of a wall, or something.'

She started to do the same, beginning on the opposite side of the hilltop. It wasn't very wide – she was only about ten paces away from him – but she felt increasingly frightened as the distance between them widened.

He was standing in front of an outcrop of rock that jutted out from a cliff face at the back of the clearing, swishing at the thorny, densely growing undergrowth with a stick. Breaking the silence, making her jump out of her skin, suddenly he shouted, '*Beth*! Come here!'

'Don't *do* that!' She hurried across to him. 'You –'

She stopped. He was holding back the dry shrubbery with his stick, and behind its dusty leaves and rope-like stems she saw what had made him shout. It was a column, standing on a flat slab of smooth stone – marble? – and supporting what looked like the end of a lintel.

She waited till her heart wasn't beating quite so wildly. 'It's well hidden,' she said. 'You wouldn't find it unless you were determined – most of the people who come up here must turn away disappointed.'

Her words seemed to be absorbed by the silence, leaving no resonance on the still air.

'No one can have looked at this for ages.' He sounded hushed. 'This bush is as dense and tangled as the forest round the Sleeping Beauty's castle.'

She was surprised at his choice of simile, but it was accurate. 'Can we get inside? Assuming it's the temple, and *has* an inside.'

'I think it is.' He was pushing at the undergrowth around the pillar. 'There's an opening – look – but it doesn't seem to be too safe. There's been a rock fall – several, probably – and bits of dressed stone are all mixed up with chunks that have fallen off the hillside.'

She peered over his shoulder. She could see another pillar, which presumably had held up the other side of the lintel to form an entrance. Now it lay at an angle against the other pillar, as if someone had put a barrier across the threshold.

'Could it have been deliberately destroyed?' she asked.

He shrugged. 'It could. Lots of Mithraea were desecrated and ransacked by the Christians. They could have come up here and had a go at this one.'

'Let's go in.'

He turned and stared at her. 'You're sure you want to?'

'Yes! It looks as if it's been like this for centuries, it won't fall down on us if we're careful.'

'I wish I shared your confidence. But that wasn't exactly what I meant.'

She caught her breath. Then said anxiously, 'What *did* you mean?'

He smiled briefly. 'Never mind.'

He means can I brave the atmosphere, she thought. But it's all right, it's not as oppressive in here under the cliff as it was out in the open. I wonder if that means –

'Come on, then.'

He shouldered aside a thick clump of greenery – judging from the way he winced, at least one thorn must have stuck into his skin – and bent down to get beneath the fallen pillar.

She followed. Stepping carefully round sloping heaps of sandy earth and large chunks of rock, they found themselves peering into what looked like a cave.

'Do we go on?' he whispered.

'I don't know.' She waited for her eyes to adjust to the darkness. 'It doesn't look very deep. I wish we'd brought a torch!'

He made an exasperated sound, reaching in his jeans pocket. He held up an object that rattled.

'Matches! You hero!'

'I don't usually carry them – I used them this morning to light the gas ring and for some reason put them in my pocket instead of back on the shelf. Fate, do you think?'

He said it lightly, but she wasn't so sure he hadn't got it spot-on. Equally lightly she replied, 'No doubt.'

The noise of the match striking the side of the box was surprisingly loud. Then, leaning forward, simultaneously they moved further into the cave.

The rear wall looked as if it had once been carved. Although centuries of damp and erosion had eaten into the rock, and although it was half-obscured by ancient tangled roots and streaks of moisture, still a vague outline was visible. Stepping carefully towards it, Adam reached out a hand and ran his finger around it.

'What is it?' she whispered, moving up beside him.

'Can't you see?'

'No!'

He was still tracing. 'I could be wrong – it's possible I'm seeing what I want to see – but to me it looks like a bull.'

She followed his finger as he traced the faint outline again. 'Head, thrown back – shoulders – backbone – tail. Can you see it now?'

She frowned in concentration. 'Only just. I must say, I think your imagination is working overtime.'

'Quite possibly. What do *you* make of it?'

The match had burned down, and he struck another.

The bright light after the temporary darkness shone on the relief, and for a moment she thought it moved. 'There's a man on the bull's back!' she cried. Then he was gone. 'No, sorry, I was wrong. It must have been a trick of the light.'

He said softly, 'I saw it, too.'

'How did it happen? Why should a sudden light make us see a moving figure? And why didn't we see it the first time?'

'I have no idea.'

They stood staring at the wall, striking several more matches. But the illusion of the moving figure didn't come back.

Eventually she said softly, 'This is it, isn't it? The Mithraeum?'

'No doubt about it. I've never seen a bull-slaying relief outside a museum. Maybe they left this one where it was because it'd be virtually impossible to remove it – it wouldn't be worth the effort, especially as it's in such poor condition.'

She stroked her hand across the raised areas in the stone, feeling almost protective. 'I think it's marvellous. Its condition isn't important – even worn almost away, it's still full of power.'

'It is, isn't it?' he agreed. 'And you know something else? It's not threatening – or at least I don't find it so.'

'Nor do I. You'd think we'd have been scared silly, in here in the dark with that carving leaping out at us, but we weren't. Awestruck, yes. But not frightened.'

'There's no need to fear power if it's beneficial,' he said. 'And, as you pointed out yesterday, I've always been a fan of the Mithraists.'

She smiled. 'If the atmosphere in here is anything to go by, I'm beginning to see why.'

'I'm nearly out of matches. Shall we go while I can still light our way out?'

Reluctantly she said, 'Okay.'

There's nothing else to see, she thought as they edged their way out again, whatever else there once was in this secret place is buried under tons of soil and rock. We'd find nothing, unless we came back with shovels, and that would probably be contravening some French ancient monuments regulation.

They emerged into the daylight, and Adam pushed the thorny undergrowth back in place against the rocks.

'Why are you doing that?'

He looked slightly sheepish. 'I don't know. Because I don't want anyone else to go in there, I suppose. Selfish, isn't it?'

'Maybe.' She went to help him. Then, as they stepped back to look at the effect, 'Is this it, Adam? Is it the place you were shown?'

She'd had to ask, was quite unable to hold back her curiosity any longer. 'I'm sorry,' she added, 'perhaps I shouldn't have asked.'

'It's all right.' He perched on a humped rock, and she sat on the grass beside him. 'It could be – the rocky backdrop and the sandy soil are just right, and I did have a sense of recognition when I saw that figure on the bull move. But . . .'

He was quiet for some time. 'But?' she said softly.

'That isn't the crucial part of the vision,' he said. 'Sorry, I'm not explaining very well – I see a dark interior, which could be that one, with candlelight and figures moving. That's the good bit.' He hesitated. 'It's as if whoever is showing the scene to me is preparing me for what comes next – setting the scene, if you like.' He drew in a breath. 'Then I'm taken somewhere else – although I get the feeling it's very close – and I see the rest.'

He didn't seem to want to describe the rest, up there, and she could well understand why. 'So you don't think this is the place the Roman was showing you?'

'I don't know. No.'

She said, aware she might be pushing on when he'd rather stop, 'Should we look around some more? I mean, it's very small inside the Mithraeum – you could hardly sacrifice a rat in there, never mind a bull. Do you think they did the slaughtering somewhere else, and that's what you're being summoned to find?'

She wished she'd phrased it more diplomatically; the concept of being *summoned* was uncomfortable. Even to me, she thought, and I'm not the one who's been shown the rock and the gore.

He was gazing around the hilltop. 'There's nothing else to look around *at*,' he said. 'We've circled it, and there are no slabs of stone.'

She was looking at the steep, rocky cliff rising above the outcrop. 'There's the suggestion of a gap there. Yes, it's overgrown and doesn't look much now, but there could be a way through. Do you see where I mean?'

He turned his head. 'Yes.' Then, without saying more, he got up.

She went with him. He picked up his stick again, and once more hacked at the thorns. With them pushed out of the way, a narrow passage opened up between two shoulders of rock.

Adam walked through it: it was wide enough for him not to have to turn sideways. It would have to be, she thought, hard on his heels, if they once led sacrificial animals through it.

The passage ran on for several yards, then the right-hand spur of rock abruptly ended, affording a sudden view down the hillside; beyond, the first range of the Alpilles soared into the blue sky.

Jutting out from the left-hand wall, looking almost like a table that had been set up there, was a thick slab of stone. Some fifteen feet across, its depth ranged from roughly three feet to five.

She found herself wondering whether it was entirely natural, or whether man's hand had shaped it.

Then she heard Adam. It wasn't a shout or a cry, it was more a groan.

Spinning round, she saw he'd slumped to the ground. He was pointing, saying something again and again.

'What is it?' she demanded anxiously. 'What's wrong?'

He said, audibly now, 'Blood. Covered in blood.'

She turned back to the rock. 'Blood? I can't see any blood! I can't see anything!'

Then suddenly she could. Not blood, but a man. A boy. He was screaming. Or was it a bull making the noise? There was a bull there, held by a grim-faced man in a dark cloak.

The screaming got louder. She realized it was her.

'Come on,' – she caught hold of Adam's arm, dragging him to his feet – 'we've got to get away from here, they –'

She looked for the figures. They weren't there. But now she could see what Adam was seeing: a broad slick of blood flowed lazily across the slab of stone.

Feeling the retching begin, she pulled Adam back along the passage.

They got no further than the hilltop. She was sick twice, Adam looked as if he'd pass out if she tried to make him go any further. When, some time later, they began to feel better, she said, 'This is the place. Isn't it?'

He nodded. He still looked very pale. She felt a surge of compassion for him, and reached out to take his cold hand. Poor Adam, she thought, if *that's* what he knew we were going to endure, no wonder he was so reluctant to face it.

'Did you see him?' she asked gently. 'The Roman?'

'No. But I know he's here, or was once. I can sense him, very strongly. What about you?'

'I saw a man, but it wasn't him. There was a boy, too.'

She'd wondered if that would be enough. If Adam would

make the connection, too, and come up with the same hunch.

He didn't.

'Adam, did you hear what I said? I saw a boy. I also saw a bull.'

'That thing down the rock passage is a sacrifice stone,' he said quietly. 'You probably saw a fleeting glimpse of the rites.'

'I don't think so. If I did, they weren't rites connected with the temple we've just been in – they felt wrong.' She wasn't ready to elaborate. 'A boy, a bull, a man. Remember I told you about Joe and his boy saint, whom he's decided got himself killed for refusing to pay homage to the Roman gods?'

'You said Joe thinks the officer was a Mithraist.'

He didn't continue. He must surely have realized, she thought desperately. It's crystal-clear, it must be!

'*Adam*! Are you doing this on purpose?'

He fixed her eyes with his. 'It's your theory, *you* say it!' His voice was harsh, and he was almost shouting.

'All right, I will!' Angry, upset, she pulled away from him and began pacing to and fro across the hilltop.

It was strange, but having geared herself up to speak, she felt almost that the words were catching in her throat. As if they shouldn't come out.

'Listen to this,' she said, with an effort. 'Joe's Little Saint Theodore – that's his name, Theodore – becomes a Christian. He's got to be a new convert, or perhaps a first-generation one – they're always the most zealous. He's meant to be involved in sacrificing to one of the Roman gods – let's say Joe's right and it's Mithras – and he refuses. Says his God is the Christian God, the Father of Jesus, who, far from wanting his followers to sacrifice to him, would hate the idea and virtually forbids it. The Roman in charge tells Theodore he's got to sacrifice or else he'll be killed, because if the people stop keeping the gods happy, then the whole Roman Empire will suffer. The boy still refuses, so the Roman brings him up here with a bull and a priest and says, "This is your last chance."'

'The boy won't do it, so the Roman sacrifices him instead,' Adam said distantly. 'Back there, where the blood is.'

'Yes!' She was aware of feeling cold; a chill wind seemed to have blown up. From the rocky heights came a sound like an animal moaning in fear. Ignoring it, she ploughed on. 'But what if the Roman –'

She got no further. The sudden wind howled and whirled to a tornado, and she and Adam were thrown to the ground. Cowering, arms over their heads for protection, they felt a hard rain of dust, pebbles, leaves and twigs.

The wind ceased. In the silence, their eardrums still reverberating, they sensed it about to begin again.

But this time it sounded like words, spoken in their own tongue. A voice roared like a hurricane, the sound bouncing off the rocks and echoing down through the valley and out across the plain.

She thought it shouted, '*It's not true*!'

PART FOUR

ARLES

AD 175

21

I hadn't wanted her to return to that desolate house on the marshes the first time she came to me. The second time, it was all I could do to let her go.

But she was a determined woman. As well as a resourceful and courageous one: when, after the incredible joy of our night together, she calmly got up, washed, dressed and said she would set off for home straight away, before it was fully light, I thought she must be joking.

But she wasn't.

'Why do you have to go?' Why *now*, I could have added, when any reservations you might have had before about committing yourself to me must surely no longer apply? Unless –

'Unless' was not to be contemplated. And, for all that she had come to me and made no secret of why she'd come, I was absolutely sure that what had happened between us had meant as much to her as it had to me.

She must have understood what I was feeling. She came to sit on the edge of the bed, reaching out her hand to touch my cheek. 'Don't think I want to go,' she said. 'The temptation to get back into bed with you, then later get up, eat, walk, talk, go together to fetch Theo,' – her voice almost broke over that, but she recovered herself – 'is all but swamping me.'

'Then why –'

'Because I have to get back to Gaius.'

'You –'

'Stop interrupting! I don't mean it like that, as well you

know.' She looked exasperated, but she was smiling too. 'Let me tell you about Gaius. When Theo and I were homeless and virtually penniless, he offered us somewhere to live in exchange for the sort of work that, even if it was repetitive and sometimes demanding, certainly was no worse than the daily lot of many people. We didn't complain.'

In my head I heard Theo's angry voice. 'He gives me work to do that I can't do well enough, just so he has an excuse to beat me.' Before I could think what I was saying, the protest burst out. 'But Theo –'

He hadn't wanted her to know. I clamped my mouth shut.

'But Theo what?' Her eyes were on mine, her expression wary.

'Nothing. Go on.'

After a moment, during which she went on eyeing me, she did. 'Seems he took a fancy to me,' she said bluntly. 'Gaius, I mean. He began bringing me little presents. At first it was delicacies to eat, sometimes a jug of wine – I was pleased enough with them, I can tell you, especially the food. I tried to make Theo eat it all, only he wouldn't have that – said we had to share.' She laughed briefly. 'Mind you, a hungry boy with his head down over his dinner doesn't bother getting out the weighing scales to make sure two plates contain exactly the same amount.'

'You must have been happy to see him enjoying himself.'

'Of course. If it had just been food and drink, it would have been all right. I didn't realize what Gaius was up to till he started bringing things that were obviously meant just for me – he even said once that he hadn't been going to all that expense just for Theo to pig most of the stuff, but when I tackled him over it, he pretended to laugh it off.'

'So he brought you more personal gifts.'

'Yes. A length of cloth, flowers, amber beads.' She had

been gazing across the room, but now her eyes shot back to mine. 'I gave the beads back. It puts you under an obligation, accepting a gift as valuable as that.'

That explained why Theo had tried to steal an amber necklace from the fat merchant. But I was quite sure I didn't need to point it out.

'How did Gaius react to that?'

'Seemed to think I was playing hard to get and redoubled his efforts. I felt sorry for him, to tell the truth – you always do, don't you, when someone clearly shows that they fancy you and you don't feel the same?'

I nodded, not that it had happened to me all that often. 'You do.'

'Well, pitying him didn't last long. Only till the day he said if I didn't start acting more grateful, if you understand me,' – I did, although I wished I didn't – 'and being a bit friendlier, he had plenty of willing women who would be more than ready to take my place.'

'He was threatening to chuck you out of your job and your house if you didn't . . .' I couldn't bring myself to say it.

'If I didn't become his mistress,' she supplied for me. 'Yes.'

There was a long silence. Then she said: 'I'm sorry, Sergius. I wish I could say I refused, told him to go stick himself, but I can't.'

I thought she might have said more. Offered excuses for having slept with a man she didn't love, such as, I had to think of Theo. We needed security, food, a roof over our heads. They would have been reasonable excuses, more than reasonable, and anyway, gods knew, I had no right to sit in judgement of her. Wouldn't any woman have done the same, in her place?

But she didn't say another word.

Suddenly I was overwhelmed with admiration for her: it was as if she were saying, this is what I did, relating merely the facts with no attendant explanation to soften them.

What a woman.

I thought of various things to say, dismissed them all, and eventually pronounced feebly, 'Sometimes we all have to do things we don't like ourselves for doing.'

She raised her head. 'You understand, then?'

I took her hand in both of mine. I could have said 'Yes, of course,' or, 'It doesn't matter if I do or not, you're not answerable to me.' But I just said, 'Yes.'

She nodded then, disengaging her hand, stood up. 'Time to go.'

I said, 'You haven't told me why you have to return.'

She sat down again. 'No, I suppose I haven't.' She sighed. 'It's just that he's still angry and suspicious, and if I disappear now, he'll try to find me. And, since I shall want to reclaim my son, that'll mean he'll also find Theo. I need to get back to normal with him – if I can lull him into believing I've accepted that Theo's gone, then, when I finally leave, he may well think I've simply drowned in a ditch, or been taken by the gipsies, or murdered by some ruffian. I'll think of a way to encourage him to believe something of the sort.' I didn't doubt it – as I said, she was a resourceful woman. 'In the meantime, I'll tell him I've been to Arelate and found out that Theo's in prison and there's nothing I can do to get him out. Then, after I've sobbed and wailed for a while, I'll have to persuade him I'm happier with just the two of us.'

I snorted in disbelief. 'You'll never make him believe that! Not unless he's amazingly stupid or outstandingly arrogant!'

She smiled briefly. 'He's both. And I'll make him believe it, don't you worry.'

Although I tried to prevent it, a vivid memory of our recent lovemaking flooded my mind. And my body. The thought of the means she might employ to make that sod

Gaius believe she enjoyed being with him, so much that she no longer missed her own son, filled me with such furious jealousy that I had to turn away.

I felt her hand on my arm. 'There are ways other than in bed,' she said quietly. 'Did you never hear the old saying that the way to a man's heart is through his belly? And Gaius, since his initial enthusiasm cooled, hasn't been much of a one for billing and cooing.'

She might have been saying it purely to calm me, but I chose to think she was telling the truth: her eager response the previous night suggested it might have been some time since she'd made love.

Reading my mind – which can hardly have been very difficult – she said, 'I might have slept with him, but I wasn't truly a participant. I've been dead, that way, since Theo's father was lost.'

I rolled over and put my arms round her. 'You didn't have to tell me that,' I mumbled against her comforting breast, 'it's no business of mine.'

'No, it isn't,' she agreed calmly. 'But I wanted you to know.'

I raised my head and, pulling her down towards me, kissed her.

Later, when once more she was straightening her clothes, I asked her how long she was expecting to take over convincing Gaius she'd adjusted to Theo's absence, and was settling to life alone with him.

'Not long.' She smiled grimly. 'He never enjoyed Theo being around, so he's already halfway to being convinced – he hasn't the imagination to realize that others might see things differently from him.'

'*He* certainly won't miss Theo,' I said. I was hurrying to get dressed which, although not an excuse for saying what I said next, is an explanation of how I came to be so careless. 'Well, only as someone on whom to vent his anger.'

There was an awful silence. Then she said, 'What do you mean?'

I tried to cover up. 'Oh, nothing – just that I expect he used to find Theo irritating, so he probably shouted at him. Maybe clipped him round the ear sometimes.'

She stood quite still in the middle of the room. She wasn't looking at me. 'Did Theo tell you that?'

'Theo? Gods, no, I'm just conjecturing. It's what most men would do, isn't it, with a boy they didn't like?'

'What makes you say Gaius didn't like him?'

'I . . . Theo . . .' I trailed to a halt. It's not that I was a poor liar, just that I couldn't lie to her.

'Come on,' I said with hollow heartiness, 'if we don't get going soon, it'll be fully light, everyone will see us, and the village will start gossiping and your good name will be irrevocably ruined.'

I caught a glimpse of her face before she arranged her veil and turned away. If she'd had her suspicions before, I had now made her life hell by as good as confirming them.

Just like before, I took her as far as the southern outskirts of Arelate. Again, I watched her walk away until she was a small dot on the horizon, then I went home.

But, this time, I didn't know how I was going to bear being without her.

When I got back, the villa seemed more lonely than it had ever done before. Typical, I thought, full of hurt and quite unjustified resentment, there I was, living a peaceful bachelor existence, and first Theo then his wretched mother come crashing into my life, filling these empty rooms with non-stop chatter, only to flit away again and leave me –

I made myself stop. The maudlin self-pity was threatening to make me sick.

Callistus arrived in the afternoon and, humming cheerfully to himself, began preparing an elaborate meal for my supper. 'Just you, is it, sir?' he asked innocently. 'The lad's still over at the farm?'

'Yes!' I snapped.

Callistus looked quite hurt. Then, rallying, 'Nice woman, his mother. She –'

'Go and find Didius,' I ordered. The last thing I wanted to do was stand assessing Zillah's good and bad points – she didn't have any bad points that I'd detected – with Callistus while he peeled garlic and chopped onions. 'I want a massage.'

Callistus muttered something about evil-tempered employers who needed a good pummelling to stop them picking on hapless servants, but he did as I asked. And, not very long afterwards, I was lying on my stomach feeling as if Claudius's elephants were dancing on my back: it hurt, but it stopped me pining for Zillah. Temporarily.

Before I went to bed, I prowled round the house checking that the shutters were secured across the windows. Then I went out to inspect the outside, but there was no sign that anyone was about. No one hiding under the terrace, no suspicious cache of wooden poles or piles of stones to facilitate a climb over the walls.

I had walked all the way round and was coming up to the gates, the key in my hand ready to lock them behind me, when he struck. I say he, but it could have been she, I suppose – I didn't see. Whoever it was must have slipped silently out of whatever shadows he'd been hiding in and crept up behind me on wings, light-footed as a cobweb.

But there was nothing light about the way he hit me. I heard the swish of something whistling swiftly through the air and, as I began to turn, the blow fell just above my left ear. There was an instant of sheer agony, my head seemed to fill with brilliant orange, then it burst open. Or it seemed like it. I felt myself falling, then nothing more.

I don't know how long I was out, except that I hadn't

noticed the moon earlier and, when I came round, it was high in the sky. As I tried to raise myself to elbows and knees – even without trying, I was sure that any idea of standing was over-optimistic – I felt something in my hand.

Unclenching my fist, I looked down. It was a small fragment of parchment, the cheapest sort made of sheep's skin, and it was a scrap taken from a used piece – I knew because it was the sort of thing we used in the office for rough drafts.

Someone had written on it before they'd hit me and pushed it into my hand. I tried to make out the words in the dim moonlight and through a pounding headache.

They said, 'Your time is running out.'

In the morning I debated whether I was well enough to get out of bed. The self-pitying part of me moaned that, with a lump the size of an egg above my ear and the sort of headache I hadn't had since my wild drunken nights as a young legionary on leave, I owed it to myself to take it easy. Doze away the morning, summon Callistus to make me a delicate invalid's lunch and get Didius to pamper me for a couple of hours in the afternoon.

But I had given my word I'd be at the temple today.

Our great festival to celebrate Mihr's day was close now, and we were preparing to welcome the beginning of winter in his honour. Whilst no one expected a sick man to crawl from his bed in order to attend, there was an unspoken obligation not to absent ourselves unless we were virtually dying.

'I *am* dying,' I groaned, my head pounding with renewed viciousness as I sat up.

Then – perhaps the god put the thought into my mind – I remembered lying in that stone cistern as the live coals were piled on top of the lid, remembered fighting increasing pain and panic. The god had given me strength to endure, and he had rewarded me with such a forceful awareness of his presence that sometimes I felt he was still right there beside me. I bore my time in my coffin, I thought, I can bear a headache. And, if I am strong, my god will be with me.

Concentrating my thoughts on him, I got up.

I took my time over washing and dressing, then saddled my horse and set off for the temple. As I rode, I confessed to the god that, as well as worshipping him, today I was also intending to glean what information I could about those two Ravens. 'There is trouble for you', one of them had said. And now I'd had a second warning.

Written on a piece of parchment of the sort we used in the Procurator's Office.

A voice inside my head told me to beware of jumping to conclusions: anyone else knowing that one of the Ravens worked in the Procurator's Office could easily have used that parchment in order to throw suspicion on him. And, unless the plot against me was particularly cruel and complex, why should Flavius be warning me of my peril one moment and viciously attacking me the next?

Trying to reason it out was making me feel ill. Massaging my forehead, keeping in the shade as much as possible to help the pain behind my eyes, I reached the meagre conclusion that the best I could do was keep my eyes and ears open and see what I could find out.

I had no chance to investigate either of the Ravens, because they weren't there. Since apologies for absence need be made only to the Pater, I didn't know what reasons they had given.

In a way, I was relieved: not having to puzzle over them meant I could devote myself wholeheartedly to the ceremony. And, as always, I felt greatly uplifted – as I left, I felt more confident than I had for a long time.

And my headache had gone.

On the way back I called in at the farm. Theo was cavorting with the colt, but abandoned him for long enough to come over and give me a warm welcome. He looked well: I could have sworn he'd put on weight, and his face was glowing with health. He appeared to have grown, although that might have been my imagination.

Cassius came out to join us, putting an affectionate arm round Theo's shoulders. 'Good lad, this one,' he said. 'He put up a post and rail fence all by himself yesterday. Look!'

I did. Theo's fence wasn't as straight as a purist might have wished, but it looked solid enough. 'Well done,' I said. 'I'll go home and knock down the rickety old hurdles round my new vegetable patch, you can build me a fence too.'

'Today?' Theo said.

It was tempting. But I had a strong feeling he was safer here. 'Not today. Far be it from me to tear you away from your colt. But soon, maybe.'

'All right.'

'Go on, he's waiting for you.' The colt was whinnying plaintively. Theo grinned at me, then rushed off, vaulting his new fence with ease.

'You want us to keep him a while longer?' Cassius asked quietly.

'Yes. Do you mind?'

'Not at all! I've plenty more jobs he can do.' He hesitated, then said, 'Everything all right?'

'I think so.' I smiled. 'I hope so!'

'Ask me no questions and I'll tell you no lies, is that it?'

I patted his arm. 'Something like that.'

Nothing happened for several days. No night-time visit from Zillah to tell me Gaius was on his way, no threatening anonymous notes, no mysterious strangers lying in wait. The anticipation was almost worse than an outright attack.

Just when I was thinking that I really ought to put in an appearance at the office, somebody there decided to check up on me. I was finishing my breakfast when Callistus announced I had a visitor.

'Who is it?' I almost added, Is it Zillah? but managed not to – anyway, Callistus would surely have said so if it was.

'He didn't give his name,' Callistus said, his tone eloquently expressing his opinion of such poor manners. 'He says he's from the office. In Arelate.'

I suppressed a smile: for all that I didn't go to my office very often, I hadn't forgotten where it was. 'Show him in, please.'

I recognized the young man he ushered in. He was familiar on two counts: I'd seen him going in and out of the Procurator's Office, and I knew him from the anteroom of the temple.

It was Flavius.

It was not our way to greet our Brothers openly in public, but surreptitiously I held out the back of my hand, briefly displaying my thunderbolt symbol. He reciprocated: the caduceus on the back of his hand, symbolizing the Raven's function as messenger of the god, was well executed. It didn't look like the work of our own tattooist – the style was quite different. Wherever he'd been initiated, it hadn't been with us.

'What can I do for you?' I asked, indicating that he should sit down. 'May I offer you refreshment?'

He shook his head. 'No. This is not a social call, Sergius Cornelius.'

He didn't go on, merely sat there staring at me. There was something like contempt in his eyes.

Suddenly I was irritated. 'Speak your business,' I ordered.

He looked momentarily taken aback at my brusqueness – which I'd fully intended him to – then rallied. 'I come as a friend,' he said, his voice low, 'out of duty to a Brother.'

Warnings were sounding in my head. Although I

couldn't have said why, the implication that he was out to do me a favour rang false.

'Go on.'

'There is a boy,' he murmured. 'A boy who you are shielding.'

'No,' I said instantly. 'Where is he? Do you see him?'

He shook his head impatiently. 'It makes no difference whether or not he is actually under your roof. You took him out of the town, and now you are hiding him from justice.' He leaned towards me, the dark eyes slightly hooded by heavy lids. 'It is unwise. I must warn you that if you do not give the boy up, you will suffer the consequences.' He paused, then added coldly, 'As will he.'

An image of the arena shimmered before my eyes. Banishing it, I stood up.

'Don't threaten me,' I said, my hand closing on the neck of his tunic. I twisted the cloth, and he tried to jerk away. I tightened my grip. 'On whose authority do you speak?'

He said with some effort, 'No-one's. I told you, I've come to warn you out of loyalty.'

Not with that expression in your eyes, I thought. Whoever had given him his instructions hadn't said anything about trying to look like the friend he claimed to be.

'I hear your warning,' I said sarcastically. 'Now get out of my house.' I let him go, and he fell backwards, almost slipping off the bench.

Getting to his feet, he edged to the doorway, walking backwards so that he still faced me.

I laughed. 'Don't worry, I won't hurt you.'

He waited till he'd reached the relative safety of the yard, then said, 'You will be sorry you didn't listen to me.'

While I was thinking up a suitably crushing reply, he hurried across the courtyard and out through the gates.

I'd already decided it was high time I went into Arelate, although I admit the young man's visit would have made me go anyway. Whatever the truth of it, it would do no harm to make a few enquiries myself.

Everything was much as normal. There were a few minor matters awaiting my attention, which I saw to in under an hour. Lucullus and Ulpius both sauntered in to have a chat – in Ulpius's case, nothing more than a long moan about his workload, his wife and his piles – and I saw the Procurator in the distance, although not near enough to greet.

In the afternoon, when the October sun was making people lazy and more inclined to gossip than to work, I strolled along the corridor to pass the time of day with anyone else who happened to be about. I found my friend Maximus, and, after chatting for a while about the price of corn and the Emperor's campaign on the Danuvius – Marcus Aurelius had decided to deal with the troublesome Sarmatians by the drastic but effective method of wiping them out – I asked how his new man was shaping up.

'Avidius Valerius?'

'Er – yes,' I said. I could have been wrong about the young man being called Flavius. Or – much more likely – he was going under an assumed name for some devious purpose of his own.

'He's doing well,' Maximus was saying. 'Want to come and meet him?'

Why not? 'Thank you, yes.'

I followed Maximus out of his room and along to another, bigger chamber where several young men sat labouring at their desks. I cast an eye over them – there were about eight or nine of them.

I couldn't see the young man who'd come to see me that morning.

'This is Avidius Valerius,' Maximus said, stopping beside a thin, earnest-looking youth with a fine crop of spots. 'Avidius, this is Sergius Cornelius.'

The youth stood up, managing to knock both stylus and wax board to the floor. 'Good afternoon, sir,' he whispered.

'Good afternoon. Please, don't let me disturb you.'

He dropped to his knees, located his board and stylus, and, sitting down hurriedly, bent his head over his work as if hiding his face made him invisible. Feeling sorry for him in his extreme nervousness, I caught Maximus's sleeve and indicated we should return to the corridor.

'Er –' I began. 'Have you any other new recruits?'

'Employees,' he corrected, smiling. 'You're not in the army now. No, nobody else has joined us recently.'

'What do you mean by recently?'

He paused, obviously thinking. 'Last new man we took on was over a year ago. Well over,' he added, 'it was before my daughter had her baby, and he's –'

Before he could launch into the sort of family update he was notorious for, I said, 'And was that man also a youngster, like your Avidius?'

'No, more your sort of chap – used to be in the Legions. The Twentieth, I seem to recall – want me to check?'

'No, thank you – no need.'

Belatedly, his curiosity stirred. 'What's this all about, Sergius?'

I wondered how slim an explanation I could get away with. 'Oh, someone mentioned a young man he thought worked here. It seems he was wrong.'

'Ah.' Maximus was satisfied, apparently. Curiosity had never been his strong point. 'Oh, I know what I meant to tell you! Remember that merchant who came in, accusing some street urchin of trying to rob him?'

It was so unexpected that it was all I could do to answer calmly, 'Yes. What about him?'

Maximus was laughing. 'Didn't we have some fun with him! First the boy disappears, leaving him with no one to pin his accusations on, then we get our lads to go and have a look in his warehouse.'

'And?'

'He's now in prison for tax evasion.'

I laughed dutifully with him – they have a funny sense of humour in the tax collectors' department. 'And the boy?' I said, trying to sound casual. 'Did he ever turn up?'

'No. He probably slipped back into whatever part of the town's underworld he came from.'

We exchanged a few more pleasantries, then I took my leave. Walking back to my own office, I was trying to rid myself of the superstitious dread engendered by his choice of words.

Even in fun, I didn't like the thought of Theo being in the underworld.

When I deemed I'd done enough to give the illusion I'd completed a day's work, I tidied up and got ready to go home. On my way out, Lucullus caught up with me.

'Don't forget about tomorrow!' he called.

'What about tomorrow?'

He tutted. 'You *are* out of touch! It just goes to show what you can miss if you don't keep yourself informed! Tomorrow's the games!'

Gods. 'Thanks,' I said.

He must have detected my lack of enthusiasm. 'It wouldn't be a bad idea to show your face,' he said, edging closer and lowering his voice. 'You know the First Secretary's a devotee, and he likes his staff to support him.'

He was right, and it was decent of him to remind me. Especially in view of my somewhat haphazard attendance in the office just recently. 'I'll be there,' I said. I turned to go, but Lucullus hadn't finished.

'It should be a good show,' he said. 'They've been having trouble with the Christians – there's a group living up in the hills who've been refusing to sacrifice to the gods. They defaced an altar to the Imperial Cult!' His eyes were wide with pleasurable horror.

'Have they been brought in?'

'Arrested, tried, condemned,' he said with satisfaction. 'They'll face the beasts tomorrow.'

And I've virtually been ordered to attend, I thought. Gods save us. 'Will it be a long show?'

'There are gladiator bouts first,' Lucullus said. 'It's rumoured that The Hook's going to fight!'

'Can't wait,' I muttered, not loud enough for him to hear. The Hook was an ex-slave who had clawed his way to the upper branches of the gladiatorial tree. His real name was lost in the past; they called him The Hook because his favourite weapon, used to devastating efficiency, was a heavily barbed trident.

I set out for home wishing I was still in the Legion, with nothing worse to face the next day than a few hundred shrieking tribesmen to dispatch.

And my headache was back.

22

If I'm honest, I have to admit that I used to be as keen on the games as the next man. In the Legion, you went along without thinking, and once inside the arena, the atmosphere got to you. I don't like the picture of myself yelling and bawling with the best of them, but nevertheless it's an accurate one.

We had an amphitheatre in Eboracum, and there was a small wooden one at one of the forts up on the wall. They got some good acts for us in Eboracum, knowing full well that legionaries back at the base fort after a spell on the wall required top-quality entertainment. (They also knew that if they didn't supply it, the men were quite capable of brawling in the streets and providing their own fun.) We didn't have any Christians to chuck in the ring there, and exotic beasts were in pretty short supply; this resulted in the development of a particularly ferocious school of gladiators. There was a chap from Syria, a great hulk of a man with skin like seasoned wood; he used to anoint himself with oil so that he gleamed, and, although he maintained it was to prevent his opponents getting a grip on him, we all reckoned it was to make his muscles look good for the women. Women, incidentally, could be as wild in their appreciation of a good fight as men. Carmandua came to a show with me in Eboracum once, and waved her arms so enthusiastically that she blacked my eye. I told her the fighting was meant to be confined to the arena, but she didn't care.

I'd gone off the games long before I left Britannia. It was

largely to do with my trouble; the loss of so many of my men, by such barbarous methods, took away what was left of my taste for witnessing people suffer and die. I was still a soldier, so I had no choice but to fight when I was ordered to. But I didn't have to mix with death in my leisure time.

When I came to Arelate, I realized very quickly that the people supported every single show put on in their magnificent amphitheatre; most events were a sell-out, and there was a thriving black market in tickets. And the games here weren't restricted to two men slugging it out, each with a chance of winning; here they also had beasts versus beasts, beasts versus armed men, and beasts versus unarmed victims, often bound so that they couldn't even raise a hand to defend themselves.

The Procurator, who amongst other commodities procured fighters, beasts and human animal-fodder, regarded it as a handy and highly economic means of execution to throw criminals into the arena. For one thing, he didn't have to pay for gladiators to fight the animals; for another, he could pocket a good slice of the box-office receipts since he was providing the passive half of the competition. Don't think this made him a particularly callous man: it was common practice throughout the Empire.

The only problem was that bound, prison-weakened criminals – among whom were the hapless Christians – didn't put up much of a fight; sometimes the crowd threatened to become bored. Then they'd send on a pair of gladiators, or a gladiator and a beast – we had bulls, lions, bears, even crocodiles once, although the arena had to be flooded for them and the crowd were disappointed since the hot sun made the crocodiles too soporific to offer more than token resistance.

I awoke on the day of the games feeling depressed. I didn't want to go, and I was going to have to: enough to make anyone depressed.

I got into town in the late morning, and already the amphitheatre was packed. People liked to make a day of it, and take the whole family along; they'd settle in their seats hours before the first event, often taking a large picnic lunch and plenty of wine. There was an atmosphere of cheerful holiday, the women showing off new gowns or elaborately dressed hair, the men in their best togas. The brilliant light sparkled off the jewellery of the rich; it was hot today, and there'd probably be the usual quota of heat-stroke patients in the cheap seats in the full sun. Still, the majority of cases wouldn't prove fatal.

I made my way to the seats reserved for the Procurator's staff. The high-ups had a special canopy over their little area – sheer exhibitionism, since they were in the shade anyway – and the rest of us sat on cushions supplied by the office. Slaves circulated regularly with trays of refreshments. I spotted Lucullus, who waved and beckoned: 'We've saved you a place,' he mouthed. Well, he was probably speaking aloud, but there was so much noise from the several thousands already amassed that I didn't hear.

The entertainment started with a blast on the trumpet and a suitably rousing piece on flutes, pipes and percussion. The band contained a quartet of bucina players – the bucina was the sort of trumpet we used in the Legion, and it curves round the player's body as if it's a snake about to hug him to death – and they played a marching tune. It was one we'd put colourful words to in the army – there must have been a lot of old soldiers in the crowd, because I heard the words echoing from several sections of the arena.

Then the master of ceremonies strode into the centre of the arena and, to a mixture of cheers and shouts of 'Get off and let's see some fighting!' announced the first item. They were kicking off in style – it was a bout between two renowned gladiators who fought with the sword.

They were good, both of them, and fairly evenly matched. The predictable roar went up at the first drawing of blood, but the wounded man rallied and fought back. The crowd was behind both men, with neither one the obvious favourite; for some time they slogged it out, and eventually, when it became clear that neither was getting the upper hand, the President called a halt and asked the crowd to vote on whether the fight should continue to the death or the men be spared to fight another day. With few exceptions, we lifted our fists with the thumb enclosed in the palm: to tumultuous applause, the two gladiators left the ring.

We had a dozen or so more gladiator bouts – no sign of The Hook, much to Lucullus's disappointment – and then they brought on the beasts. For a couple of hours we watched a variety of creatures attack, defeat and slaughter one another; there was a preponderance of bulls, which suggested there hadn't been a shipment of anything more exotic recently, and a rather weary bear which I was sure I recognized from an earlier games day.

Towards the end of the afternoon, the great gates that led down to the waiting pens below were opened again. A party of armed and heavily armoured guards appeared. As they broke ranks and dispersed, we saw that they had been escorting prisoners into the arena. Duty done, the guards stepped hastily back through the gates and up the steps to safety. Down in the dusty, blood-spattered arena, the six prisoners blinked in the sunshine.

There were four men, a woman and a youth of about sixteen. Their clothing, although dirty and ragged, looked as if it had once been good quality. They didn't look like condemned criminals: they had to be the Christians from the hills.

Lucullus nudged me. 'The Christians!' he said eagerly. 'Now we'll see some fun!'

For some time nothing happened. The prisoners stood huddled together against the enclosing wall; it may have given them a fleeting illusion of safety to have something firm at their backs, although it was so high that they must have known there was no hope of scaling it. Not that there would have been anything more than a brief respite if they had, since the crowd would have thrown them straight back into the arena.

Then the gates opened again and a pair of lions came in, a third trailing them. The leading pair were both female, and looked mean and hungry. One had enlarged teats: she'd no doubt been selected because being a nursing mother would increase her hunger and her ferocity.

A moan rose from the woman in the arena. With pathetic gallantry, the four men and the youth closed round her. I saw her catch hold of the youth, trying to pull him close to her, but he shrugged her off. I guessed he was her son, and that her desire to protect him was equalled by his to defend her.

Piercingly, I was reminded of Theo and Zillah fighting to shield each other from Gaius.

The lions had noticed the cowering people, but made no move towards them. The crowd howled their disappointment, and the master of ceremonies hurriedly sent in a group of guards to ginger up the beasts, prodding at them with long spears, waving swords at them; soon the lions began to look angry. The guards got round behind the prisoners, thrusting them towards the lions. Then, job done, they raced out of the ring.

Once the attack was launched, the end came very quickly. Maybe the men had been coached, maybe they knew that it was better to hasten the inevitable by racing at the lions, screaming and punching at them so that they fought the harder. Or perhaps they had some vain hope that, if they put up a brave show, the crowd would vote to spare them.

Didn't they know that never happened?

One man was down, then two more. Once blood was spilt – a great deal of it, the mother lioness was an efficient killer and went straight for the throat, which she tore out with a couple of bites – more lions were sent in, a pair of males.

The youth went as he stood with his thin arms round his mother. She was the last: for a few moments she stood alone, her own arms wrapped round herself where her son's had been. Then the lioness pawed at her, the force of the blow knocking her to her knees. Her eyes were closed, whether in prayer or a faint I didn't know. I thought I saw her lips move, so it was probably prayer.

The lioness, apparently realizing that the other lions had noticed there was only one victim left, suddenly pounced. The woman screamed, cried out something – perhaps the name of her god – then she was down. There was a confused image of many lions with their jaws working on her, blood spurting on the dirty gown and the scuffed sand, then a stillness. The lions, satisfied, languidly made their way to the shady side of the arena and lay down, licking the blood from their muzzles, to digest their meal.

The roaring of the crowd trailed off. Other than the occasional desultory shout of derision, the vast amphitheatre was utterly quiet.

Guards sheltering behind heavy shields rounded up the now-docile lions, shepherding them out of the ring. The master of ceremonies sent the band in again, and the crowd rallied to the brassy music. While the musicians circled around in the centre of the ring, teams of attendants slipped in to clear the debris. The human remains were shovelled up, then the sand was raked smooth, a new layer strewn across the most heavily bloodstained areas.

When everything was once more ready, the master of ceremonies announced the last item: The Hook versus as many opponents as he could dispatch before the close of the day.

I didn't wait to watch The Hook. Although Lucullus was highly disappointed in me – 'You'll miss the best bit! This is what we've all come for!' – I'd seen more than enough.

I pushed my way along to the end of the row, but could get no further because of the throng of people clustering round the bookmakers. The Hook was the odds-on favourite, but one or two of the gladiators lined up to fight him had at least a chance of winging him; you could bet on things like who drew the first blood and who lopped off the first limb as well as who was the outright winner.

Unable for the moment to get out, unwilling to watch what was going on in the arena, I leaned back against the stone wall behind me and let my eyes roam around the packed tiers soaring up above me. Some move in the arena roused the crowd to scream their approval, and automatically I looked to see what was happening. I must have missed whatever it was: The Hook was standing lazily swinging his trident, his opponent circling him, his expression wary and his body tense. His barrel-chested body was clad in a leather tunic, and his short arms and legs were heavily muscled.

The way he watched The Hook, sizing him up, looking for the moment to pounce, reminded me of someone I'd seen recently. Someone who'd been doing the same thing to me.

He reminded me of Gaius.

As the realization hit, I thought with cold certainty: Gaius used to be a gladiator.

I don't know why I was so convinced, but I was absolutely sure. It was as if I'd remembered a piece of information I'd long been aware of.

My eyes going back to the rows of spectators, suddenly I saw him: in among a bunch of men who all looked strangely like him sat Gaius. He was staring straight at me, and I had the uncomfortable feeling that he had been watching me all day.

I sensed his antipathy, even from across the arena. I'd damaged him – there was still a dark bruise on his jaw –

and wounded his pride. His eyes still fixed on me seemed to be rays of hatred.

You don't scare me, I told him silently, staring steadily back. I felled you once; it's I who won the howl of applause for drawing first blood.

He broke the hold. I liked to think it was because he had yielded, but it was far more likely he was responding to his neighbour digging him in the ribs to point out The Hook swinging into the offensive.

The way out was still blocked with optimistic punters desperate to be parted from their money. There was no option but to stay where I was till they cleared.

In the event, I didn't leave until the day's entertainment was over. While I was patiently waiting to get out, The Hook's opponent got in a lucky blow and knocked the champion out. I don't imagine he was seriously hurt, but he wasn't in any condition to go on fighting. The master of ceremonies hastily announced there would now be bouts between the gladiators who'd been waiting their turn against The Hook, but he was the star, he was what the crowd had come to see, and most people weren't interested in any lesser amusements.

The gaggle of punters dispersed and I pushed my way towards the exit, along with what seemed like most of Arelate. It always took a long time to get out if you waited till it was all over, which was another reason why I usually left early.

There was no point in trying to hurry, but that hadn't stopped the group behind me from trying: I'd been aware of pressure at my back, and was about to turn round and say something sarcastic like, 'Why don't you go first if you're in such a hurry?' when I felt a new, sharper pressure.

It felt as if someone was holding a dagger to the small of my back.

With a sharp blade very close to your skin, the one thing

you don't do is make a sudden movement. Very carefully I turned my head, letting my shoulders follow the turn, until I saw a muscled arm and the sleeve of a leather tunic.

'Gaius!' I said, trying to sound as if I'd been hoping all day I'd bump into him. 'Did you enjoy the games?'

'Some of them,' he said. He, too, sounded friendly. More friendly, anyway, than you'd expect from someone holding a knife to your back. 'Not much sport with the Christians, but some of the gladiators were worth watching. One or two of them fought skilfully.'

'And you're qualified to judge,' I said softly.

There was a pause, as if he was weighing up whether or not to admit. Then, bravado clearly winning over discretion, he said, 'What if I am? I was good, I tell you, I wasn't beaten in fifty fights!'

Surely he had to be exaggerating. I know I should have resisted the temptation – I could still feel the dagger point – but I said, 'You must have lost your touch, then.'

The sharp point penetrated the cloth of my tunic and pierced my flesh. He hissed, 'That wasn't clever, citizen Sergius Cornelius.'

I was thrashing round for a witty riposte that would deter him from pushing his dagger further into my back when suddenly I realized. He'd called me by my name.

He knew who I was; it was only a short step to knowing where I lived.

I sent up a violent prayer of thanks to my god for his suggestion that I leave Theo with Cassius.

'Since even you wouldn't be so foolish as to kill me with about thirty thousand witnesses,' I said coolly, 'why don't you stop toying with your knife and put it away?'

He laughed hoarsely. 'Hurting, am I?' He twisted the dagger point, agonizingly, then I felt it withdraw. 'It's nothing to what you're going to suffer.'

Freed from his knife, I turned to face him. 'You don't frighten me. Your threats are –'

He wasn't listening. 'See those Christians, did you?'

I nodded.

'See the lad? Plucky little sod, wasn't he?'

I didn't answer. I had a dreadful feeling that I knew what he was going to say.

'Makes you think, doesn't it?' He paused, as if for maximum effect, then said: 'Makes you aware of what can happen to kids who won't do as they're told. Who run away, make a nuisance of themselves. Get hidden away by Roman citizens who ought to know better.'

The threat was crystal-clear. There was no point in evasion – better to accept that war had been declared, battle begun.

'You won't get him,' I said. 'There's no way on earth you'll find him, let alone bring him back and get him thrown in there.' I jerked my head back towards the arena.

He laughed again, that same harsh laugh. 'Oh no?'

Then he swaggered away.

Empty threats, I assured myself as I went down the long flight of shallow steps descending from the amphitheatre. He couldn't have said No, you're right and I'll give up, he'd have lost too much face. Bluster was the only option, and –

I caught sight of him then. He'd vanished in the heaving crowd, but it had momentarily cleared, and there he was.

He was talking to someone, a young man. And the young man was familiar: it was Flavius. Who had come to see me the previous morning, to warn me I had to give Theo up or suffer the consequences.

And there he was, talking earnestly to Gaius.

It's not as bad as it looks, I tried to reassure myself. It's not as if the young man works in the Procurator's Office, I proved that yesterday. If he did, we might have a problem, because it would mean Gaius had a direct link to the very man who gathers victims for the arena, and it'd be child's play to push Theo in among the criminals, the Christians and the condemned.

But as it is . . .

My optimistic thought faltered and died. I'd just seen the Procurator himself, strolling majestically down the steps, nodding to acquaintances, acknowledging congratulations for a good day's sport.

I watched as the Procurator approached Flavius. Gaius, after exchanging a brief greeting with him, had slipped back into the crowd: my Brother the Raven stood alone.

He might not work for the Procurator, but clearly they were on the most intimate of terms. The Procurator slapped him on the back, linked Flavius's arm through his own and said cheerfully, 'There you are! We must hurry up, now, my slaves will have prepared supper and the bathhouse will be ready.' He glanced over his shoulder, beckoning to the rest of his party. 'Come along, everyone!'

As the young Raven was swept away, he looked back. Straight at me.

And I didn't like the way he was smiling one bit.

23

I hardly noticed my journey home. I was so preoccupied with trying to see through the fog of mystery swirling all round me that I was blind to anything else. It was just as well my old horse knew the way without any guidance.

That young Raven had now issued me with three warnings, assuming it was he who had knocked me out and put the piece of parchment in my hand. Why? Because, out of loyalty to a Brother in Mithras, he couldn't see me land myself in trouble without at least trying to help? And what a way to help, slugging me on the head!

And, although I'd got the idea he worked in the Procurator's Office, I now knew he didn't. But he *did* know the Procurator – very well, apparently. The vast, intricate edifice of Roman public life was constructed around who you knew, and the better you knew them, the greater the benefits they might put your way.

My Brother Raven was close enough to the Procurator to be lavishly entertained at his residence. Close enough that he felt free to pop into the Procurator's Office whenever he was passing, for I knew he did, I'd seen him. His presence in the vicinity had crystallized the vague idea I'd had that he worked there.

Who had put that idea in my head in the first place?

Racking my brains, I tried to remember. Then – for a forgotten fragment is more likely to come back when you're not thinking about it – deliberately I made my mind turn to the prospect of supper and a hot bath.

In my memory I heard the voice of my Brother Soldier,

the one whose young bull Theo had played with. 'The Raven's going to have a new Brother,' he'd said a few months back. 'A fellow from Gaul's joining us, another Raven. Perhaps having a Brother his own age will stop him spending all his time lurking around the Procurator's Office and get him out in the fresh air – he ought to be following pursuits more suited to his youth!'

At the time, I'd thought my Brother Soldier, a real out-of-doors type himself, was merely expressing his usual disdain for those who worked in administration and rarely saw the good, clean light of day. Now, analysing his words, I realized he hadn't actually said Flavius worked for the Procurator. Merely that he lurked around the office.

I had jumped to a conclusion, but it had been a false one.

In view of the fact that the Raven knew Gaius, the truth – that the Raven was not an employee of the Procurator but an intimate friend – was far more sinister.

Gaius, my Brother Raven, the Procurator. Gaius had as good as said, not an hour before, that if he found Theo, he'd make sure the boy ended up in the amphitheatre.

And I didn't understand that, either. Oh, I could appreciate that Theo's intense – and well-deserved – dislike of Gaius had made Gaius loathe his guts. But in that case wouldn't Gaius have been overjoyed to see the back of the lad? More likely to slip me a backhander for having taken him away than to threaten me because I wouldn't give him back?

Gods, it was beyond me.

But, even if Gaius's mental processes were unfathomable, I was left with the unpleasant fact that he was after Theo's blood. Literally.

There *had* to be something else. Gaius was an ex-gladiator, strong on muscle, weak on brains. My experience of him, admittedly limited, nevertheless had given me a strong picture of a man who was none too bright. And who, surely, would redress a grievance by murder in a back alley rather than by the elaborate device of arranging for his enemy to be thrown to the wild beasts.

And anyway wasn't it I who was his enemy? He might have detested Theo when the lad was under his roof, but was that hatred strong enough for him to continue the pursuit long after Theo had left? Bearing in mind what I'd done to him, wasn't it far more likely that he'd come after me?

As I rode into my courtyard, I was haunted by the unpleasant knowledge that I was still very far from knowing the whole story.

Callistus served me my dinner, but I didn't pay it the attention it deserved. Eager to hear about the games, he took his time over clearing away each course and presenting the next, interspersing his actions with questions. Finally accepting I wasn't going to provide the lurid details he wanted to hear, he whipped away the platter of cheese before I'd had a chance to make up my mind if I wanted a second helping, banging down the fruit bowl and stomping off back to the kitchen with an injured sniff.

Some time later I heard him set off for home. The gates were too heavy to slam, but he did his best.

I went across to the bathhouse, but I can't say I enjoyed my ablutions much. I don't need to tell you why, do I? It wasn't the same, without her. And, besides, the wound Gaius's dagger had made in the small of my back burned like a flame in the hot water.

I dressed myself in a comfortable old robe I kept for relaxing in and, my mind too alert to promise easy sleep, went out on to the terrace.

I'd been sitting out there for some time, gazing out across the dark landscape, when what I'd been seeing finally penetrated. Put it down to anxiety, fatigue – I was both anxious and tired, certainly – but I swear I didn't realize what I was watching until it was almost too late.

I said he was good, didn't I? Right at the start, when I first suspected I was being watched, I was aware that whoever it was knew his stuff. Well, I was right.

As soon as I'd tumbled to it, I was amazed I hadn't spotted it before. The night was reasonably clear, but there were clouds dotted around the sky which periodically crossed the moon, making the darkness more profound. On the slope that dropped away below the terrace were clumps of young trees, little more than saplings, too slender to allow a man to hide behind.

Which was probably why I hadn't been keeping more than a cursory eye on them.

With each renewal of the brightness as the next cloud moved away from the moon's face, one of the saplings was suddenly thicker: every time it went dark, he was moving to a different one.

And his progress was in one way only – straight towards me.

The god's presence stirred in my consciousness. I remembered what he had said: let the hunted become the hunter.

I still had my military uniform. Largely for sentimental reasons, I kept the plates of my cuirass greased against rust, the leather straps supple with oil; I stored my tunic in a moth-proof chest. My shield was polished, my sword was always sharp: my dagger was in its sheath on my belt.

Within a few minutes I was as ready to go on the offensive as I'd ever been in the Legion. I took my helmet down from its place of honour on the shelf above my clothes chest and, its weight on my head and the back of my neck as reassuring as it had always been, set out to look for him.

You might have thought I had the advantage in that I knew the lie of the land better than he did, but I don't think that was so. He'd doubtless spent so many nights skulking around down there that the reverse was more likely to be true – I wasn't in the habit of spending time crawling up and down the slope in front of my house.

The only advantage I did have was that he didn't know I was stalking him.

Bearing that in mind, I moved as silently as a ghost, my shield arm held across my chest to prevent any sound from the metal plates of my armour. Broader than him, I couldn't hope that my silhouette would be concealed by any sapling if he happened to turn round; I just had to pray he'd go on being so intent on staring up at the house that he forgot to watch his back.

For what seemed an eternity I shadowed him up that slope. Sometimes I lost sight of him – I guessed he must have been crawling through the grass – then, when I spotted him again, I'd have to hurry to close up.

I think that was where I gave myself away: I'm fairly fit, but speeding up a steep slope in heavy armour whose burden I'd grown unused to was a challenge, I admit. My legs began to hurt, and, despite my best efforts, occasionally I had to gasp for breath.

I thought I'd lost him for good – I'd been crouching behind a bush, waiting for him to make himself visible again, for so long that my breathing was right back to normal. I was just about to stand up and begin inching forwards, checking every possible place of concealment between me and the base of the walls, when a tiny sound behind me made me stiffen.

I knew he was there, even before I turned my head. For all I knew, he might be poised to attack the moment I moved, but that didn't stop me: I had to see him.

Twisting round to face him and standing up in the same movement, I stared at him.

He was arrayed in much the same way I was; at first in that faint light I thought he was wearing legionary armour. He looked more like his father than ever.

Then, the initial impression fading, I realized his cuirass was a cheap imitation, his weapons inferior. Reason returning, I reminded myself he wouldn't have had access to Roman army uniform since he wasn't a legionary; his father's equipment would have been returned to stores after his execution.

For some moments neither of us spoke. Then, his tone giving nothing away, he said, 'You would have looked as you do now the morning they killed my father.'

I hadn't needed the confirmation, but it was interesting that his opening remark should have provided it: clearly, there was to be no more hiding in the shadows.

'I was not on duty that morning,' I replied in the same bland tone: we could have been discussing some minor occurrence on which we wanted to compare notes.

'But age has taken away your fitness,' he continued, as if I hadn't spoken. 'You no longer scale hills like a soldier, Roman, for all that you dress like one.'

He was quite right; it galled, that my panting breath had given me away. Not that there was anything I could have done about it.

He had gained the offensive, both tactically – for his drawn sword was poised too close for comfort – and psychologically; I was old and past it, he was implying, infirm age against strong youth.

We'd have to put him right, on both counts.

My left arm bore my shield; I pressed my right hand against my side, wincing. Instantly his sword point was against my throat.

'Keep still!'

I lifted my head so that I could meet his eyes. 'I'm in such pain!' I gasped. 'My side – it's as if there's a knife sticking between my ribs.'

He snorted in disgust. 'You've only got a stitch! You shouldn't go running up hills, at your age.' He had marginally lowered his sword: I was in with a chance. 'Go on, old man, nurse your pain,' – the disdain was poisonous – 'I can see you're –'

When I think about it now I go cold. But, in the heat of the moment, it didn't seem all that risky. Swiftly I moved my right hand from my side to my sword hilt, drawing my blade and swinging it up and to the right. Although I felt the fierce jarring go right up my arm and through my shoulder, it worked: his sword fell out of his hand and, with the nail-studded toe of my military sandal, I kicked it away down the hillside.

Lunging uselessly after his weapon put him off balance. I pushed the boss of my shield against his chest and he fell; before he could get up again I put my foot across his stomach. It was my turn to rest my sword point against his throat, and the moment was sweet.

The headiness of triumph didn't last long. I was going to have to decide what to do with him.

Probably I should have killed him: with the benefit of hindsight, it would have been the best thing. But I didn't. Perhaps I was too weak, perhaps my years as a civilian had taken away the fighting instinct. But I'm not even sure I'd have killed him when I was still a soldier – it takes the adrenalin of battle to dispatch a man who lies disarmed at your feet, and we hadn't been engaged in battle.

Putting down my shield, I unfastened my belt, slipping off the scabbard that held my dagger. It wasn't easy with one hand, and I was out of practice, but in the end I managed it. I ordered him to sit up, then fastened his hands behind his back with the belt. It was made of thick leather: I reckoned it would secure him.

Then I took hold of his arm and, getting him to his feet, marched him up to the house.

I took him on to the terrace, where I rebuckled the belt round one of the stout pillars that held up the balustrade. Then, pulling up a bench and sitting down in front of him,

I said, 'Quintus Severus's son. You're a long way from home.'

Momentarily his head drooped, as if he were suffering a sudden stab of longing for that northern land. For friends, family. If he had any. Then, looking up, his eyes fixed on to mine. I noticed his were blue; in that aspect he wasn't like his father, whom I remembered as being dark-eyed. Presumably this young man had inherited his light eyes from his Brigantian mother. Although it was the last thing I wanted to dwell on just then, I saw her in my imagination, long hair dirty and tangled, face puffy with weeping. Body swollen under the cast-off military cloak which, other than the child she carried, was possibly the only thing Quintus had left her.

I shook my head. Here I was facing a man who apparently was out to kill me, and I was dangerously close to feeling sorry for him.

'What do you want with me?' I asked harshly. 'I'm aware how long you've been after me, I – '

'You are?' His voice was bitter with sarcasm. 'And just how long would that be, Roman? Since you saw me walking away from your house that night?' So much for my fond belief that he hadn't spotted me. 'You have no idea, have you?' He strained towards me, face a rictus of hatred, but the belt held him firm against the pillar.

'You'd better start – '

'I've been *after you*' – he mimicked my words with a viciousness I hadn't employed – 'ever since I was old enough to understand what you did to us. My mother had to live out the rest of her life in mourning for her man. She had offers, you'd better believe she did – she was a handsome woman, skilled in ways you can't begin to imagine, and, even though most were in awe of her, some brave men asked for her hand. But oh, no! She was loyal, she'd given her heart to her man and she didn't want any pale imitation taking his place.'

I was finding it hard to credit this image of an attractive woman spurning suitors. It didn't tally with the wild harpy I remembered, but then she hadn't been at her best that night. 'It can't have been easy for her,' I said neutrally. 'Or for you.'

'*Easy*? I didn't want it to be easy! I was glad she didn't take another man, no one could have lived up to my father! He was the best.' He shut his mouth in a hard line.

'But surely – ' I stopped. For some reason he wanted me to think he'd known Quintus, loved him. Presumably he wasn't aware that I knew it wasn't possible. He was clever, this one – it showed in his eyes. I sensed a sharp intellect questing after mine: I decided on a different tack. 'Have you considered the possibility that you only have one side of the story?' I said reasonably. 'Quintus and I were fellow soldiers. Do you think I'd have let him go to his death if there had been any other way?'

'You were the only one who testified against him!' he shouted. 'It was your word against his!'

'But he was lying!' I shouted back. 'The very fact that I'm alive now proves that. If he was right, and everyone on that hilltop was dead, how do you explain my presence? I'm no ghost, I assure you!'

He wrestled against the belt again, and I heard the leather creak. 'He didn't see you! You were hiding under your shield!'

'So would you have been, if you'd had fifty screaming tribesmen hacking at you. And he did see me.' I wasn't going to emphasize the point, to promise, to swear by the gods: it was the truth, and it stood alone.

'He didn't! He can't have done!'

Because if he did, he couldn't have been the brave father you want him to be? *Need* him to be? I didn't speak the thought – there was no point. I said instead, 'What's your name?'

'Varus Severus.'

A Roman name. I was surprised – it meant his mother must have had citizenship, for Quintus would not have been allowed to legalize his liaison with her, and so make their offspring Romans, until he retired from the Legion. I was about to comment to that effect when I came to my senses.

Of course she wasn't a Roman citizen! How could she have been? Some of her tribesmen acquired citizenship as freed slaves, but that couldn't have applied to her, she'd have had to serve in some plush Roman household for years to win such a gift. She hadn't been anyone's slave, that one.

So his name had to be an assumed one. Making his way from the north of Britannia, through Gaul and on down to Provincia, life would certainly have been easier if he'd passed himself off as a citizen. And language wouldn't have been a problem: he'd proved in the last fifteen minutes that he was fluent in the everyday speech of the Empire.

Varus Severus. Severus was the family name – Quintus had been Quintus Severus. And Varus – yes, that was more likely to be an assumed name, since not many fond parents actually chose it for their sons: presumably Quintus's son didn't know that Varus had been one of the most unfortunate of Augustus's generals, suffering the loss of three legions under his command in the haunted depths of a forest in Germania. Not a happy association with which to bless a child.

I wondered what his real name was. Not that I was ever going to find out.

But I wasn't going to let him get away with thinking he'd fooled me.

'You're not a Roman citizen,' I said calmly.

'I am!' Again, the leather creaked: he looked as furious as if I'd hurled at him the worst of insults.

'How can you be? The only way you could have acquired citizenship is to have served in the Legions, or as an auxiliary, and you're not old enough to have put in the required number of years.'

'I'm the son of a Roman.' He sat up as straight as his bound wrists allowed.

'There's no disputing that, not for anyone who's seen you both. But unfortunately the biological fact of being someone's son doesn't automatically confer citizenship, as well you know, and your father wasn't married to your mother, not in Roman eyes, he –'

He died before he had the chance, I'd almost said.

And whose fault was that?

The blue eyes were blazing, his violent frenzy projecting out at me with such power I swear I could feel it. Superstitiously I recalled his mother's hand in that death curse. Heard again his recent words: she was skilled in ways you can't begin to imagine.

Oh yes, I could.

I'd seen her, or at least I'd seen women just like her. One winter night I'd been out on patrol along the wall, and we'd been delayed because one of my men got himself stuck in a marsh. We only just got him out, and we were all feeling shaken; quicksand exerts such a pressure on the last part of the body to go under – usually the head, unfortunately – that the blood vessels swell and bulge, and to see someone's face distort as they scream out for help, feeling that foul stuff creep up their throat, over their chin, into their gaping mouth, is enough to shake the sternest character.

Anyway, we saved him. But, as I said, we were late – those tribeswomen, that coven in their black robes crouched round their foul-smelling fire, wouldn't have expected a party of legionaries to march by. We worked according to set routines, and it was understandable they'd think us long retired inside our barracks.

We were moving fast, in the lee of the wall between it and the Vallum to the south (the wind invariably seemed to blow from either the north or, even worse, the north-east). We smelt them before we saw them: they had lit their fire in a dell on the other side of the wall, and we probably would have missed them if it hadn't been for the smoke blowing our way.

We clambered up on top of the wall and there they were. Three of them, chanting, putting gods knew what into the small pot they'd suspended over the fire. I said we were shaken, and it's possible that, another time, we might have descended on them, kicked over the pot, stamped out the fire, and, their curses notwithstanding, sent them about their business. We might. Although such was the terror I felt at the sight of them that I don't know for sure – somehow, I doubt it.

And, that night, we'd had enough: we slunk back to the sheltered side of the wall and left them to it.

And, without a doubt, Quintus's woman – this young man's mother – had been one such as those. Didn't they say such powers are inherited?

'You killed my father,' Varus said into the silence. 'And my mother put a death curse on you.'

'Which you are having to fulfil, since she failed.' One way to diminish your fear of curses was to remind yourself that they didn't always work.

'She didn't fail! A curse can employ whatever instruments come to hand.'

'Her own son?'

'Who better?'

'So I was right. You're going to kill me.' Somehow I felt better for having spoken it aloud.

He was watching me, a slight smile on his face. He looked unbelievably evil, and a shiver of fear ran up my spine. 'Kill you? Perhaps.'

'What do you mean, perhaps?' I shouted. 'Come on, explain yourself!'

He relaxed against the pillar; quite obviously he was

enjoying the moment. 'You killed my father. You robbed me of someone I loved.' Again I wanted to protest, to say he couldn't have loved his father because he hadn't known him. Again, I kept silent. 'It would not be a reciprocal blow, would it, for me to kill you?'

I knew before he said it. Knew what he was going to do. As he spoke the words, the whole terrible picture fell into place.

'Better, don't you agree, that *I* kill someone *you* love. You killed my father, I kill your adopted son.'

I tried to swallow, my mouth gone suddenly dry. 'Theo is out of your reach.'

'Oh, no.' He was almost laughing. 'And, since you inflicted on my father a public death, the boy must have the same.'

The amphitheatre. 'It's not possible! You can't arrange it, you're a stranger, not even a citizen, you've no power to carry out what you threaten!'

'No power?' He laughed again. He'd planned it, he must have done, must have been sitting there working away at his bounds waiting for the right moment; as he spoke he wrenched his arms violently forward, the belt creaked again and finally gave way.

I had my sword halfway out of its scabbard when he fell on me. I'd have got it all the way out in my prime, but I was out of practice. He threw his arms round me, momentarily preventing movement, and the respite gave him the chance to draw from somewhere under his cuirass a dagger I hadn't even suspected he had. I should have searched him: gods, I was out of practice in every way.

'I could kill you now,' he said in my ear. 'I've a mind to.' I felt the blade cut into my throat, felt my own blood wet on my skin. 'But I shall stick to my original plan. It will prove more painful to you.'

'You bastard,' I said.

'Bastard? Yes.' I hadn't meant it that way, but he was

right. 'Now, where were you hit before?' His fingers went over my head. 'Ah, here.'

I didn't know what he hit me with. I discovered later it had been a bronze figurine of Mars, which I suppose was appropriate.

When I recovered consciousness, dawn was lighting the sky. There was, predictably, no sign of him. Crawling over to the edge of the terrace to be sick, I noticed the belt, still wrapped around the pillar.

So much for relying on old equipment. My care had preserved the leather well enough – it was still supple and strong.

But, under the extreme pressure exerted by a vengeful and violent man, the thirty-year-old stitching had given way.

I made my way over to my couch, pulled a warm rug over myself and lay there waiting till I felt sufficiently recovered to start working out what to do next.

24

I dozed on and off till mid-morning. Although I wasn't sick again I still felt very queasy, and my head felt as if Varus's dagger was sticking in it, just above my left ear. It wasn't one of Callistus's days for coming in early, and I didn't know if I was glad or sorry: on the one hand he'd have tutted and nagged, telling me (quite rightly) that I was too old for such carryings-on, and now look what had happened. On the other hand, he could have made me one of his herbal pain-killing drinks – the chief ingredient was willow bark, of all things – and he had the gentlest of touches with wound-dressing.

I now had three injuries: a stab wound in my back, quite a deep cut in the skin of my throat, and a very tender lump on the side of my head; he'd broken the skin – I guessed with the point of Mars's helmet, which was bloodstained – and it took me quite a while to clean the drying blood from the tiles of the terrace.

Callistus could have done that, too.

All things considered, it wasn't surprising that it took me till mid-afternoon to realize that I was meant to be going to the temple that evening: it was the night of our long-anticipated ceremony, our great sacrificial rite to greet the start of the winter.

Bad enough that I forgot that. Far worse – for there was still plenty of time to get to the temple – was that it didn't occur to me until then that I should check up on Theo.

He's safe, I reassured myself as I bathed, no one knows where he is. Cassius's farm is so far off the beaten track that even people who've been visiting him for years sometimes get lost! It took all my willpower not to rush my ablutions: you might be forgiven for thinking I should have set off for the farm straight away, but the correct preparation is an integral part of our ceremonies, and I didn't want to skimp on it on such an important occasion.

Washed, dressed in a clean white shift under my usual tunic, I checked that I had my scarlet robe and my lion mask. Tonight my hands would be anointed with honey before I lit the sacred incense; I folded the crisp white cloth that my hands would be wiped with and put it on top of the mask.

Then, breathing deeply to keep myself calm, I saddled my horse and rode out of the courtyard.

The resolution to travel unhurriedly – to enable me to meditate on the coming ritual as I rode – didn't last. Perversely, my old horse was for once restless, crabbing and pulling at the reins in his eagerness to move faster than I wanted him to. In the end his impatience ignited mine: I let him have his head, and he broke into a gallop as if he were the impetuous and spirited young creature he was when I first had him.

The shadows were lengthening by the time I got to the farm. Theo's colt was kicking his heels in the meadow, and the post and rail fence now reached right up to the barn: the boy had been working hard. I dismounted and tethered my horse, then glanced into the outbuildings to see who was about. There was no sign of anyone, so, guessing they were sitting down to eat – they kept irregular mealtimes in that household, working on the very sensible principle that the best time for food was when everyone was hungry – I went across to the house.

Cassius and Julia were seated either end of the long table, with sundry children and grandchildren making the sort of racket you get in a big happy family.

'Sergius! Come and join us!' Cassius got up to greet me, and Julia reached for another bowl.

'Thank you, but no – I'm on my way somewhere else. I – er, I was wondering how Theo's getting on.'

I'd looked at every face round that table. He wasn't there.

And there was no vacant place laid ready for a latecomer still washing his hands.

'He's doing very well,' Cassius said, 'he's made a grand job of the fence. Want to have a look?'

'I saw it,' I said, trying to restrain my anxiety and reply politely. 'Is he here?'

'No, of course not!' Julia, a worried look appearing on her cheerful face, got up and went to stand beside her husband. 'We sent him off with your messenger, like you said.'

Oh, Mithras!

'My messenger,' I repeated. I swallowed. 'And when did this happen?'

'Noon,' Cassius said, his expression puzzled. 'Just after we'd eaten.'

'Yes, I remember I said it was just as well Theo'd had a good meal, since he was going to have to walk all the way home.' Julia, trying to be helpful, nodded her head as if to confirm the accuracy of her words.

'They were walking?'

'The man had a horse. But Theo was walking – at least he was when they left here.'

'And they set off towards my house?'

Cassius and Julia exchanged a glance. Then Cassius said, 'We don't know. Nobody actually watched them out of sight – we all got back to work once they'd gone.'

Julia said, 'Oh, Sergius, I'm so sorry! Did we do wrong? The young man sounded so convincing, he –'

'What did he look like?'

'Medium build, medium height. Wore a cloak,' Cassius said. Then he smiled briefly. 'Sorry. That could apply to almost anyone.'

'Dark eyes,' Julia said. 'I know now's a fine time to say so, but I didn't care for his eyes.'

'Describe them.' I realized it had come out like an order. She must have thought so, too, judging by the way she flinched. 'I beg your pardon, Julia. Can you tell me why you didn't like his eyes?'

'They were heavy-lidded. Dark, very dark, and with these round, heavy lids, sort of like a snake.'

'Snakes don't have eyelids,' piped up a young voice from the fascinated audience sitting round the table. 'They have –'

'Shut up,' Julia said. 'Like a lizard, then – the sort of lid that comes down like a shutter and covers the eye so well you can't imagine it's there at all.'

It was a perfect description – I knew exactly what she was trying to say.

I also knew who the messenger had been. I'd noticed those dark hooded eyes, too.

'You've been more help than you can know,' I said to Julia. 'Bless you for your observation.'

'Sergius, what's the matter?' Cassius said urgently. 'Was it a false message, what he said?'

'What *did* he say?'

Cassius screwed up his face. '"Sergius Cornelius bids you greetings and requests that you release the boy Theo to my care so that I may escort him away, for Sergius has planned an event tonight at which the boy's attendance is required."' He paused to draw breath. 'That's more or less what he said, I think.'

Escort him away, not take him home. They could have gone anywhere. And, even if Flavius had said they were going home, it could have been a lie.

An event planned tonight. My only plan for tonight was the ceremony at the temple. Did he mean that? Did he *know* about it?

My head was aching so fiercely that it took me a moment

before I realized. *Of course* the messenger knew – Flavius was a Raven, he would be there too.

Then what in the name of Jupiter was he proposing to do with Theo?

I turned and strode towards the door. I wasn't going to find out any more here.

Cassius came with me, trotting to keep pace as I hurried across to my horse. 'We didn't know, Sergius! Obviously we shouldn't have let the lad go, I can see that now, but you didn't tell us! Oh, we guessed there was trouble, but –'

I turned to look into his kindly face. He was biting his lip, his remorse evident. 'It's my fault,' I said. 'You're right, I didn't tell you. I thought he'd be safe here, I didn't think I need warn you.'

'I'll never forgive myself if something's happened to him.' Cassius looked as if he was about to burst into tears. 'Such a grand lad, we've become truly fond of him, he's –'

'I know,' I said. I didn't want to be unkind, but this was wasting time. 'Cassius, don't worry. I think I may know where they've gone.'

'You can find him?'

'I hope so.'

As I swung up into the saddle he said, 'Let us know what happens?'

'I promise.'

This was no time for a leisurely meditative ride: hoping he still felt as energetic as he had done earlier, I kicked my surprised horse into a gallop and we shot out of Cassius's yard as if the Furies were flapping at our heels.

The dilemma was whether to trust that Flavius would be at the temple – even if he didn't have Theo with him, I could question him – or follow the thought that said the temple was only a blind, he was far more likely to have headed back into town and given the lad to Gaius. If not straight into the hands of the Procurator.

I'd have to make up my mind soon. We were nearly at the end of the track that led from the farm; in a few minutes I'd have to turn right for the temple or left for Arelate.

What would he do, my Brother Raven? He'd told Cassius he was taking Theo to meet me, since Theo was involved in some plan I'd made. *Surely* that was a lie, a convincing tale to lull any suspicions Cassius might have so that he would let Theo go!

I just couldn't make myself believe that Flavius would take Theo to the temple. Why, there'd be ten other men up there, witnesses to any foul play! What would be the point in arranging for a confrontation there?

But Flavius *had* to be at the temple. Tonight was so vitally important to us, he just couldn't afford to miss the sacrifice.

Nor could I, although in that moment I knew my god would understand and, I hoped, forgive my absence. Even if the Pater didn't.

Arelate or the temple? Follow my logic and go to Arelate, where by now Theo could be locked in some dark dungeon? Or do what every instinct was screaming at me to do and go to the temple? Flavius would be there, I knew it in my bones – he must have detailed someone else to take Theo to Arelate, if that's where Theo had been taken: he, I was certain, was at the temple.

Could I bear to leave Theo imprisoned? Could I get him out, even assuming that's where he was?

I didn't know what to do.

Nearing the crossroads, I reined in my horse to a slow walk and tried to think.

Suddenly, powerfully, I felt the presence of the god. Deliberately I emptied my mind so that I could listen to him.

When I was a mile or so along the road to the temple I noticed fresh tracks ahead of me. A man's, walking alone.

Cautiously I rode on. The track was fairly straight; I saw him when I was still a good distance behind him.

He was clearly anxious not to be seen, although his actions suggested he was more afraid of unexpectedly catching up with someone than of being surprised from behind. In all the time I watched him, he only looked over his shoulder twice, and I was well concealed.

I was close enough to recognize him. With ease: away from the centre of town, there weren't many around like him.

As I led my horse off the track and into the scrubby undergrowth so that I could overtake him unobserved, I wondered what Gaius was doing on the road to the temple.

Our rites began with a ceremony of praise, which ended with the formal dedication of the coming sacrifice to the god. We then prayed that he would look kindly on our offering and give us his blessing. The sacrifice itself came later, and was not performed in the temple: at midnight we would convene around the great slab of rock that lay hidden behind the temple glade, where the young bull would be dispatched by the Pater's knife in his throat.

There was stabling at the foot of the incline, where the path up to the temple began. I rubbed down and watered my horse, then, my bag on my shoulder, set off up the slope.

There had been several other horses already tethered, so I knew I wasn't the first to arrive. But there was no sign of anyone on the path. As I neared the summit I thought I heard fast breathing, as if some frightened creature was hidden among the brush-choked rocks.

I told myself it was my imagination.

I don't think I really expected to see Theo, and I didn't. It was strange, but, catching up with another Lion and then a couple of Nymphs just before we all reached the glade, part of me seemed to have forgotten that anything was amiss. It must have been the peace that proximity to the temple always engendered.

Nevertheless, something *was* amiss. And I had to try to put it right.

We stood round in groups of two or three, speaking quietly, greeting one another. When all eleven of us were there – the Pater wouldn't join us till we were inside and ready to begin – we went into the antechamber to put on our robes and masks. All but two of us; the Ravens had arrived fully costumed.

As we stood in the temple waiting for the Pater I stared at the Ravens. I couldn't tell which one was the dark-eyed Flavius; although I'd seen him, studied him, spoken to him even, he could have been either of the two figures in the dark cloaks and heavy-beaked black Raven masks. Their build was similar, and they were roughly the same height.

I have a score to settle with one of you, I thought. Even if I have to tear those masks off you, I shall find out which it is. And I swear by Mithras, here in his own sacred place, you will tell me what I have to know. You will tell me where Theo is, and, with the god's help, I shall get him back.

A low chanting began from behind us. At the signal we took our places on the benches either side of the central aisle and watched as the Pater slowly walked up to the altar.

It was a long ceremony, and sometimes I had to fight a restlessness that would have had me jumping up and rushing out to look for Theo, had I not sternly ordered myself to be still. The god had promised to help me, I knew it – the least I could do was show my gratitude and my faith in his support by concentrating on his rituals.

It was easier when the time came for me to play my part. The more senior of the two Soldiers – not the one whose bull we would sacrifice later, the other one – took his place at the altar and called me in the prescribed way: '*Melichristus*! *Melichristus*!'

Honey-anointed.

I stepped forwards and held my hands out over the sacred vessel, my sleeves pushed back to the elbow. The Soldier settled the kitbag on his shoulder – it symbolized his willing bearing of his burden, and I knew how heavy it was – then slowly and deliberately began to pour the thick golden honey over my upturned palms.

As a Lion, my element is fire: not only was this why I had to be cleansed with honey, water being hostile to fire, it also meant it fell to me to burn the incense. When the Soldier had wiped the honey from my hands, he went back to his bench and I stepped forward alone to the special pillar where the incense had been placed in its stone bowl.

Chanting the prayers, I reached behind me to where I knew the Courier of the Sun would be waiting with his lighted spill. I felt him put it into my hand. Without turning, I thanked him. Then, while the flame still burned high, I touched it to the black cones of incense.

It was a crucial moment. If they lit, the god was with us. If they didn't . . .

I turned my mind from that prospect. I knew the god was with us – this was no time for doubt.

From the tips of the cones rose tiny flames. Watching, waiting until I felt they had taken hold, slowly I leaned forwards and, very gently, blew.

The flames went out.

But the tips of the cones went on burning, spots of bright orange in the darkness.

And a thankful sigh went up from my Brothers as the sweet-sharp smell of sandalwood filled the temple.

We were another hour in the temple. As the clouds of incense floated down the aisle and over the Brothers on their cushioned benches, the Pater spoke his dedicatory prayers. Our eyes closed, we followed the sound of his voice as he put us under the god's spell, leading us down mystical pathways and telling us of wondrous things we could only strive to understand.

When it was over, it took us even longer than usual to descend from the heights. Not that we were required to, totally, for the sacrifice was still to come. As the spirit slowly receded from us, one by one we got up from the benches and went quietly back to the antechamber. There was little point in disrobing yet; most of us merely paused to remove our masks before going out into the night air.

The Soldier went off to collect his bull. One of the Brothers offered to go with him – it was the Persian – but the Soldier said he was better alone, a stranger might make the young creature nervous. He was a considerate man, clearly keen to give his bull as easy a time as possible: if the animal didn't realize until the very last minute what was in store for him, he would suffer less anticipatory fear.

Which would, of course, also make it easier for his handlers.

I stood at the edge of the glade and watched my Brothers. The Pater and the Courier of the Sun were still inside the temple – they would pray in there until the moment of the sacrifice. My Brother Lions were talking to the two Nymphs, the Persian was helping the other Soldier rearrange the weights in his kitbag. The Ravens had seated themselves on an outcrop of stone, heads together in conversation. They were the only Brothers still masked.

There was under an hour to go before the midnight sacrifice. Hardly the best moment to make my move – I stood and debated with myself for a long time before I made up my mind. Then, moving across to their rock as unobtrusively as I could, I went and stood in front of them.

The two masked faces stared up at me. Through the

eye-holes I saw two pairs of eyes. Neither pair were friendly.

It was dark in the glade, the brilliance of the almost-full moon blocked by trees and overhanging rocks; the only light came from a torch flaming over the temple entrance. I stared at the eyes, but they shone so brightly in the reflected torchlight that it was hard to see their colour: it looked as if one pair were darker.

Was this Flavius?

I said to him, 'Why don't you take off your mask, Brother Raven? It's allowed, and it's refreshing to breathe freely while we may.'

Slowly he raised his hand, unfastening the restraining strap and removing the mask. The hooded eyes were expressionless as he said, 'Well met, Brother Lion.'

I wanted to kick him for his nerve. 'You have never told me your name,' I hissed, bending towards him, 'but you know mine. You know much else about me, too, and I resent your interference.'

'Interference?' He laughed shortly. 'Is that what it is?'

'You are taking payment from another to act against me,' I said deliberately – I was only guessing, but he wasn't to know that. And wasn't it the only explanation, that he'd kidnapped Theo on Gaius's behalf? There was no reason, other than a financial one, why he should want to deal me the immeasurable hurt of arranging for Theo to be thrown to the beasts.

'And just who, do you imagine' – his tone was silky with sarcasm – 'is paying me?'

'Gaius.'

He burst out laughing, quickly suppressing the inappropriate sound as several of the Brothers turned to stare. 'Gaius!' he whispered. 'You think he has the sort of money I would charge for such a service? Think again!'

'The Procurator, then.' He had me on the run and I didn't like it. 'Gaius has told the Procurator he can provide him with a young boy he wants to be rid of, and your good friend the Procurator has detailed you to bring him in. I tell you, it won't work, you –'

'Fool.' The single word was alive with contempt. 'You have no idea, have you? Too worn-out to put two and two together, as well as too old to guard a prisoner.'

'Theo was never my prisoner! He –'

The furious words choked in my throat.

Too old to guard a prisoner. Wasn't that one of the many things I'd berated myself for last night, that I'd let Varus Severus escape because I was past my prime?

Mithras help me, but finally I saw what I should have seen all along.

The clues were all there, only I'd been too stupid to pick them up. Varus repeatedly referring to his love for his father. 'No one could have lived up to my father. He was the best.' 'You robbed me of someone I loved.' In my smug certainty I'd made up my mind that, for some reason best known to himself, he was deceiving me. I'd overlooked the obvious answer.

And he'd said, before he slugged me with my own Mars statuette, 'Where were you hit before?' He'd known about that, then. And there was only one way he could have found out.

My Brother Soldier, all those months ago, had been right, far more so than he could have guessed. 'Perhaps having a Brother his own age will stop him lurking round the Procurator's Office,' he'd said of Flavius when the new Raven from Gaul had come to join us.

The one whose face I'd never seen.

Not till he'd stood in the road outside my house one night and pushed back his hood.

I tore my gaze from the unmasked Raven and stared down at his Brother. Who, as if he knew as well as I did there was no more need for pretence, began to take off his mask.

The bright blue eyes were full of malicious amusement as Varus Severus smiled up at me.

And, very softly, Flavius said, 'I believe you have met my elder brother?'

25

I'd speculated over Flavius, worried about him being so pally with the Procurator. Gods, I'd been convinced he had to be behind the threats to Theo and me, for all that I'd never managed to work out what he had against us.

But he wasn't the only Raven: there were two of them. Both of them plotting against me, and I hadn't made the connection. It was all my own fault, for taking it for granted Quintus had only had one son.

Flavius was the child born posthumously, the baby who had swelled his mother's belly when I'd seen her after the execution. Varus was his elder brother – no wonder he'd spoken with love of his father, he hadn't been deceiving me, he'd truly known him. And, apparently, grown to love him.

I could only conclude that Quintus had been a better father than he'd been a soldier.

I stood there staring down at them, my mouth open. I must have looked as stupid as I felt. They sat on their rock, totally relaxed, supercilious smiles on their faces. Now that I saw the pair of them together, I could make out a faint resemblance. But it was only slight: nowhere near as strong as that between Varus and their father. I remember thinking it was a shame the younger brother hadn't inherited Quintus's looks too, because if he had I'd have noticed the likeness straight away. And I wouldn't now be in this mess.

On the other hand, if they'd been so alike as to be unmistakably brothers, they'd have concocted a different plot.

When they'd enjoyed the moment long enough, the

dark-eyed one said, 'I am Flavius Severus. It is good that we are formally introduced at last, Sergius Cornelius.'

That was a matter of opinion. Flavius, I thought. If Varus had unwittingly gone down-market in selecting for himself the name of a disgraced general, his brother had chosen something far more grand: his famous namesake had given rise to one of our better imperial dynasties.

The shock was receding: a far more vital preoccupation rushed into the vacuum.

'You took Theo,' I said urgently to Flavius. 'Where is he? What have you done with him?'

That smile spread over his face again. 'He is in safe hands.' He appeared to consider. 'Or do I mean *secure* hands?'

Varus laughed softly. 'You do,' he said.

He looked up at me. I remembered the tracks I'd followed. Remembered watching that stocky figure as he made his cautious way along the Glanum road. 'Gaius,' I whispered.

Oh, Mithras.

They'd brought Theo here, or rather Flavius had. And Gaius had turned up, primed and ready, to take care of the lad while we got on with our praying.

For a moment the soldier in me protested. I should have been out here, fighting for Theo's life, I thought wildly, what good did I do him, lighting incense in the temple?

The god spoke in my head, calmly reminding me Theo wasn't dead yet.

I sent him a quick word of gratitude for the reassurance. And for his presence, which I felt as powerfully as if he stood beside me, Phrygian cap on his head, flowing cloak brushing the ground. Loving smile on the serene face.

No. Whatever had been going on outside, I'd been in the right place.

'Where are they?' My calm voice surprised me. It seemed

to surprise them, too – Varus gave me a look of grudging admiration.

'They are close,' Flavius said. 'Gaius awaits our signal.'

For what?, I wondered. But I wasn't going to fall into their trap and ask. 'I'd imagined you would have him locked in an Arelate dungeon by now,' I said conversationally. 'Delivered to the Procurator all ready for the next games. Wasn't that the plan?'

He laughed shortly. 'It was the plan we allowed Gaius to believe.' His scathing tone indicated with admirable clarity just what he thought of Gaius. 'It was, we decided, the best way of ensuring his loyalty. He didn't make a good stepfather, our Gaius – the woman might have fawned round him, but the boy made no attempt to hide his hatred. Gaius used to beat him, but never enough to vent all his anger. Then the boy ran away. Gaius has been itching for another chance to get at him ever since.'

I hardly heard his last words. Stepfather, he'd said. As if Zillah and Gaius had been legally married. And, he'd said, she used to fawn around him. I felt sick, betrayed.

The foolish gullibility left me almost as quickly as it had come. They hadn't been married. And she wasn't a woman to fawn on anyone, especially a stupid, brutal ex-gladiator like Gaius.

Either Flavius had been trying to poison me against her – which was unlikely as I could see no way he could have been aware that I knew her, certainly not of the depth of our relationship – or else he was simply repeating what Gaius had told him. On reflection, that was far the more credible alternative.

'You have a different plan, then.' It was too early for relief – not that I'd have shown it, anyway – since the alternative might be worse. If anything *could* be worse than death in the amphitheatre.

'We have.' It was Varus who spoke this time. 'A further refinement – Theo was not in our original scheme, which was simply to kill you. Discovering your . . .' he paused, as if taking care to select the right word, '*attachment* to the boy allowed us to devise a further twist. And certain facts which we have discovered have led to the final version. More appropriate, under the circumstances, as I am sure you will agree.'

There was a heavy pause. 'Well?' I said eventually.

They glanced at one another. Almost imperceptibly, Varus nodded. The gesture seemed to indicate that he was the dominant brother; he was the elder, after all.

Flavius said, 'Have you discussed religion with Theo?'

For the life of me, I couldn't see the relevance. 'No,' I said shortly. 'It never occurred to me,' – I couldn't help the sarcasm – 'he's hardly the sort of boy you associate with any degree of spiritual fervour.'

'The outdoor type,' Flavius agreed. 'Nevertheless, it may surprise you to know he is a Christian. Nominally, anyway, for I don't suppose he is a regular worshipper.' He paused. 'However, his mother is.'

Zillah a Christian? A regular worshipper?

The concept took a while to sink in. This time, though, somehow I knew he was telling the truth. Gods, it had been even more courageous of her to come to me, given how we were persecuting the Christians.

Amid all the anxiety, I had a moment's joy that, knowing all that divided her people from mine, she'd overlooked the differences and seen only herself and me. Two individuals who needed each other. Who had something to offer each other.

I pulled myself back to the present. 'What relevance has all this?' I said sternly. 'Had you still been pursuing your absurd plan to throw Theo to the beasts, then the fact of his being a Christian might have been significant. As it is . . .'

'It's of the utmost significance,' Varus interrupted. 'As you're soon to find out.'

Whether or not he would have told me then, I don't know: at that moment the quiet of the night was shattered by the angry lowing of a bull-calf. The Soldier was on his way up the hill, and, from the nearness of the sound, he'd almost reached the glade.

Several things happened at once, or so it seemed in the heat of the moment. Varus leapt to his feet and, surely before anyone but I could have noticed, disappeared behind the great rock on which the two of them had been sitting; immediately afterwards, there was a sound like the screeching peep of a little owl, swiftly answered from some unseen point close at hand. I heard a cry, quickly curtailed – all my senses told me it was Theo, but in truth there was no way of knowing, it could have been anyone.

Flavius was still sitting on the rock, innocently staring out across the glade, when his and everyone else's eyes turned to watch the Soldier lead his bull into the clearing.

If the screech had been Varus's signal, immediately answered by the waiting Gaius, then they must have rehearsed what happened next till it was faultless. There came a crashing from the undergrowth below the glade as if someone were hurrying towards us, then, from a slightly different direction, a great shout.

It might have been Gaius's voice – who else *could* it have been? – but people's voices are notoriously difficult to identify when they're shouting.

Whoever it was wanted to make quite sure we heard, because the words were repeated: he cried, 'They're coming! They're coming! The Christians from Glanum have come to destroy the temple!' Almost immediately came the repeat, almost like an echo, 'Destroy the temple!'

It only occurred to me afterwards that, given all the rocks, caves and deep gullies in the vicinity, it was probable he actually was making use of an accidentally discovered echo.

My Brothers stood irresolute, shocked into immobility.

Then, as if they'd been prodded, as one they all took off, racing down the hillside, their thundering progress sending up a great racket of breaking branches and dislodged rocks. Gods knew what they had in mind – the charitable interpretation was that they'd gone on the offensive in defence of their sanctuary and their god, although, since none of them was armed with anything more weighty than an ornamental lance or a tin sickle, it was much more likely they were simply panicking.

The Pater and the Courier of the Sun had not emerged from the temple: the shouting must have been audible, even in there, so I guessed they were too deep in the trance-like rapture that preceded the sacrifice for it to have penetrated.

I spun round to face Flavius. The Raven mask was still lying on the rock beside his brother's, but he had gone.

The Soldier was standing on the edge of the glade. His young bull, bored, was idly pulling at the sparse grass, trying to get a decent mouthful.

The Soldier said helplessly, 'What do we do now?'

He wasn't going to be much use for anything, even if he tethered his bull and offered to help; he looked totally bemused.

'Stay with your bull,' I said. 'The most useful thing you can do is keep him calm. We'll soon send those Glanum Christians packing – this is only a temporary interruption in our proceedings, I'm quite sure.'

I wasn't sure at all, but fortunately he was innocent enough to be convinced by my confident tone.

Leaving him standing dejectedly beside his bull – I half-expected him to start cropping grass as well – I removed my scarlet cloak and hid it behind a rock, then set off down the hillside after the others.

Some time later, when I'd searched every track I could find and found precisely nothing, I realized we'd played right into the brothers' hands. For some reason they'd wanted to disrupt our ceremony, an aim they'd achieved with total success; that loud and unexpected cry, 'The Christians are coming to destroy the temple!' had made my fellow worshippers run like hares. Even if they came sheepishly back, the mood was broken – it might be better to abandon the whole thing and perform our sacrifice another night.

Trudging back up the hillside, I almost hoped I'd find that everyone had gone home.

Then I remembered that tonight was special: it'd be no good sacrificing the Soldier's bull tomorrow or the next night – tonight was the beginning of winter, and tonight was when the ceremony must happen.

But wasn't the sacrifice the very thing the brothers had been trying to prevent?

I didn't know.

Belatedly it occurred to me that I ought to be on the lookout for them, as well as hunting for my fellow worshippers; moving as quietly as I could, keeping to the shadows wherever possible, I crept up to the glade.

There was nobody there.

Swiftly crossing it, I peered inside the temple. That, too, was deserted.

Where was everyone?

Had the Pater and the Courier of the Sun discovered the absence of their followers and gone to look for them? Had the Soldier got sick of waiting and taken his bull home?

Perhaps I should go home, too.

A voice in my head said, stay. Stay and watch.

He was still with me.

It was no good watching from the glade – it was too well sheltered, both by tangled undergrowth and by the great rock that rose up above the temple, to provide a lookout in any direction. I set off down the track again, following it until, almost at the bottom, I found a hiding place from which I could see both the track up to the temple, the road back to Arelate and the one to Glanum.

I climbed the bank and crept in under the deep shadow of an overhanging rock. I tried to make myself comfortable: I fully expected to be in for a long wait.

Deep silence covered the hillside: the land was fast asleep. There was no sound from Glanum, just up the valley, although the breeze that blew from that direction bent the conifers so that their long shadows wavered against the moonlit ground beneath them.

It was as if I was seeing a scene I'd watched before: one minute I was looking at the waving shadow of a juniper tree, the next, part of the shadow detached itself and moved on to another tree. One nearer to me.

It was exactly what he'd done before, on the slope before my house.

Pushing myself right to the back of the cramped space – he wasn't going to spot me, not this time – I waited.

I noticed almost immediately that he wasn't alone – another shadow was following him, moving to each patch of shadow as he vacated it and moved on. Behind them came another man, but, progressing less carefully, it was easy to make him out.

Mind you, he *was* leading a bull.

They came closer, and I was able to identify them: Varus in the lead, followed by Flavius. Gaius had drawn the short straw and was walking beside the bull.

He was less fit than the brothers – I could hear him panting. He didn't have the Soldier's kindly touch with animals; some emotion in him – anxiety? fear? – had communicated itself to the bull, who was rolling his eyes and sweating. Someone – probably the Soldier – had recently put a ring in his nose, and the poor creature was torn between pulling away, which hurt, or walking beside Gaius, which made him afraid.

What had become of the Soldier? I tried to dismiss the picture of him lying injured – or worse – somewhere, but it was difficult. He probably went back to his villa, I told myself, penned his bull for the night and went to bed. He'll be horrified in the morning when he finds the animal gone.

I prayed for that to be the truth. I knew in my bones that, if he'd stood in the way of the brothers and refused to let them take the bull, he'd have been in for a bad time.

Why had they wanted the bull?

Before I could start trying to puzzle out what on earth they were up to, I suddenly thought agonizingly of Theo. Wherever it was they'd stowed him, he must be still there – I was glad, for an instant, that he wasn't having to witness the bull's suffering.

Only for you, I said silently to my god, can I endorse what we would have done to that creature tonight.

I shall have to get that bull back, I thought dejectedly. I'll get going as soon as they've gone, try to find the others – perhaps it won't be too late for the sacrifice, assuming we can overcome those three and –

I didn't get any further with my over-optimistic planning. At that moment I caught sight of another figure following the others. This one was smaller, a slim, slight shadow that at times I lost completely.

But I knew who it was. A sudden fury took hold of me – how *can* he be here, putting himself right back into peril when surely he must just have escaped? – and for a moment I didn't know what I should do.

Go on, said that familiar voice. Go after them.

Taking care to make no sound, I climbed stiffly down from my hiding place and, once more, set off up the track.

I stood on the edge of the clearing, concealed in the undergrowth. The moon had shifted in its course since I'd last been up there: now it shone right into the glade, making it as bright as day. Gaius was standing in front of the temple, the bull giving regular bellows of fear. As I watched, Varus and Flavius emerged from the temple, blinking as their eyes adjusted to the bright light.

Varus had in his hands the Pater's sacrificial knife.

I couldn't believe it. They were going ahead with the sacrifice, just the two of them and Gaius, and they had the nerve to steal the sacred knife, which only the Pater was allowed to touch!

Why?

In the name of the god, *why*?

I had my answer, even as the silent protests rang out in my head. As if he could no longer bear the sounds of the bull's terror, Theo leapt down into the glade.

'Let go of him!' he shouted, pummelling his fists against Gaius's sturdy back. 'You're hurting him!'

Gaius pushed him easily away. I heard him laugh. 'He's going to be hurt a lot more before the night's much older,' he said. 'And he's not the only –'

'Gaius,' Varus said warningly. Gaius shut his mouth.

It seemed that Theo had been so intent on the bull that he hadn't noticed the brothers, standing silently side by side, until Varus spoke.

'I'm not going back with you,' he burst out, glaring up at Flavius, 'you lied to me, you said you were bringing me to meet Sergius, and you didn't!'

It was all I could do not to rush out to him there and then. But I made myself wait: there was still so much I didn't know.

'You will do as you're told,' Flavius said coldly.

'I won't!' Swift as a lizard, Theo turned, darting off in the direction of the track. But Flavius caught the hem of his tunic and hauled him back.

'You will not escape us again,' Varus said. He glanced at Gaius, contempt in his face. 'You will be entrusted to a better guard, this time.'

'It wasn't my fault the little beggar escaped!' Gaius

protested. 'He kicked me, I'll show you the bruise, then when I was down he –'

Flavius waved his free hand. 'We do not wish to hear your excuses,' he said crushingly. 'Not that your carelessness disturbed us unduly,' – he gave Theo a shake – 'since we knew full well this young man would not go far.'

'What do you mean?' Theo shouted. The bull gave a frightened snort, and Theo, edging forward, put a comforting hand on its neck as if in apology.

'You would not be able to leave your friend here,' – Varus nodded towards the bull – 'knowing he was in trouble.' He raised the great knife, testing the keenness of the blade with his thumb. His gesture could have only one interpretation.

'*No*!' Theo leapt forward, but Flavius caught him, this time wrapping both arms round the wiry body.

'Yes,' Varus said quietly. 'We needed you to be here. When this fool admitted he had let you escape, we knew you would not be able to stop yourself following us back to the temple.'

Cat and mouse games again, just as his brother had played with me. Pretending to be solicitous and friendly, just to make the inevitable blow hit the harder.

Were they so perverted that they wanted the poor boy actually to *watch* the bull die?

They were moving off, Flavius carrying the wriggling Theo, Varus bearing the knife, Gaius dragging the sweating, moaning bull.

As soon as they had all disappeared along the rock tunnel that led to the sacrifice stone, I followed.

But they acted fast, too fast for me – I was still negotiating the passage when the awful sounds began. The bull sent up a bellow of protest that rang against the rocks – I guessed they were tethering it, tying it to the slab of stone – and the bellow grew to a squeal, a single piercing note of pure hysteria.

It stopped.

Was it done, then? Had Varus plunged in the knife and found its heart?

But then the scream began again. Only now it was human.

And I knew what they were doing. Pretending right up to the last moment that they were going to sacrifice the bull, all along they'd planned the substitution. Hadn't they told me that justice would be done on me by my losing someone I loved? That his method of death would be 'appropriate', even more so than the amphitheatre?

Yes. I'd brought about their father's death by execution. Three men had taken him out in the half-light, and I'd watched as they had executed him. Now three men had plotted another killing, only instead of an execution it was to be a sacrifice.

I couldn't stand by and watch this time.

My dagger in my hand, I burst out of the rock tunnel. It was as if one glance took in a tableau, frozen round the sacrifice stone: the bull-calf was cowering against the cliff, shaking with fear; Flavius held Theo's head, tipped back to expose his throat; Varus had the knife in his right hand.

Gaius, abruptly leaping out of immobility, rushed towards me. He raised his fist and caught me on the point of the jaw, exactly where I'd hit him.

All my teeth seemed to jar against each other, and at first I didn't realize that he wasn't capitalizing on the moment by hitting me again. Then, as he grasped my arms and his weight began to topple me over backwards, I tried to raise my hands to push him off.

My right hand, holding my dagger, wouldn't respond.

Looking down, I saw that it was embedded deep in Gaius's chest. I hadn't been aware of lunging at him: he must have impaled himself as he rushed at me.

He was falling, and, clinging on to me, taking me with him.

As the back of my head crashed against the rock, I heard Theo scream again.

26

The violent wind dropped as abruptly as it had sprung up. In the sudden quiet, Beth seemed to hear those words echo off the rocks, again and again, before they, too, faded and died.

It's not true.

She said under her breath, 'I know.'

She had the brief sensation that someone was gently stroking her hair. And a calm voice – quite different from the one which had shouted out that desperate cry – said inside her head, *Help him. Do not fail him now.*

Sitting up, she brushed the leaves and twigs from her clothes, flicking her hands against her jeans to remove some of the dust. It had got into her eyes and her mouth: her eyes were smarting, and she could feel grit between her teeth.

In the stillness, she realized that she could hear the faint sound of running water.

She smiled. Hadn't someone – Joe – said, aeons ago, that Mithraea were always sited near running water? Well, this was a Mithraeum. Where once water had found a way, the chances were it still might be flowing.

Even after nearly two thousand years.

She got up, tiptoed past Adam – still sitting with his head in his hands – and followed the sound. Beyond the outcrop of rock that concealed the temple, through thorn-covered bushes that scratched at her jeans, down a steep bank. And there, rushing fast out of the hillside and off down through a deep gully, was a narrow stream of clear water.

She knelt down as close to it as she could get, dipping her hands into the water – which was surprisingly cold – then splashing handfuls over her face, washing the dust and the grit from her eyes and mouth. Standing up, she felt suddenly invigorated, as if the water had bestowed a greater blessing than merely making her clean.

Thoughtfully, she went back to Adam to tell him.

Later, when he too had washed in the stream, they sat side by side in the glade; there was so much she wanted to say – she guessed it was the same for him – but couldn't think where to begin.

After a while he took her hand. 'I think,' he said slowly, 'we just cleaned up in what used to be a sacred spring.'

'It still is,' she said without thinking. Then: 'Oh! I mean . . .' She trailed off. She didn't know what she'd meant.

He smiled. 'If so, I can't think that the god would mind, since the reason we needed to wash seems to be very much to do with him. Or one of his worshippers, anyway.'

'He didn't do it,' she said urgently. 'Your Roman. He's innocent, it's impossible to think he could have – '

'You're preaching to the converted,' Adam said calmly. 'I know what you were trying to say, before that wind came. You were about to explain how he's brought me – us – here because he wants someone to know he's not guilty, he didn't do what they say he did.'

'He didn't sacrifice the child,' she said.

'No. And being wrongly accused still matters enough to him – wherever and whatever he is – that he had to go to these lengths to prove his innocence.'

She sat thinking for some time, then said, 'Why now? Why, after lying quiet for the best part of two thousand years, is he suddenly so concerned that the truth is known? And is it going to be enough that *we* know?'

'Why shouldn't it be?'

She realized he hadn't understood what she was trying to say. 'Look, the Christian church has kept alive an enduring legend concerning what happened up here. They've made a saint of the child who died! Little Saint Theodore has a statue in a church down in Arles – in any number of churches, for all I know – which people still pray to when they get a sore throat, and probably when they're suffering from a hundred other ailments and problems, too. And the legend's sufficiently well known for my brother to have come across it in the library of a provincial university in England; it seems to feature in the standard book of martyrs and it says, quite unequivocally, that a Roman officer brutally slaughtered a Christian child because he wouldn't worship the gods of Rome.'

'Yes, I'm aware of all that. Only – '

But she didn't hear him. Taught to think logically, to move step by step through the stages of an argument, suddenly she knew the answer to her own question. 'When did you first see him? The Roman, I mean. How long ago was it when he appeared at your spiritualist gathering?'

'A few months back.'

'Be more exact!' She hadn't meant to sound so dictatorial, and smiled briefly in apology.

'Let me see . . . Once he'd come through, the pace hotted up very fast. We're only talking of a matter of weeks . . .' He was frowning, and fleetingly she was sorry to make him work so hard after all he'd just been through. Only, she thought, curbing her impatience, it's so *important*.

'It was July,' he said decisively. 'The middle of July.' He turned to her, a triumphant look on his face. 'I remember because Wimbledon had just finished.'

The juxtaposition of a Roman apparition and Wimbledon fortnight was so absurd she almost laughed. But the matter in hand was too pressing for distractions. 'The middle of July,' she repeated.

'Is that significant?'

'Oh, yes. Because it was in the middle of July that the girl had her original vision.'

The slowness of his mental processes was, she thought charitably, only because they'd just had such an extraordinary experience. Then his face cleared. 'The little girl who saw the statue cry tears!'

'St Theodore's statue. Yes.'

'What happened to her – '

'What she *says* happened to her,' Beth interrupted.

' – has focused attention on an ancient legend that everyone had forgotten about.' He stared into her eyes. 'No wonder our Roman's upset. The whole sordid tale has been put back under the spotlight.'

'The wrong tale. They've got all the facts upside down.' She took hold of his hands. 'We *know*, now.'

He stretched out on the grass, smiling. 'Yes. The truth is out – the Roman's been vindicated.'

He looked so satisfied that she was stung to protest. 'It's not enough!' she cried impatiently. 'It can't possibly be – don't you see? You and I have a gut feeling that your Roman is a decent guy who has been blackened down through the centuries – we've been *told* he's innocent, very forcefully, and we're convinced. But – '

'But we have to convince others,' he finished for her. 'Yes. I see what you mean.' He looked dejected suddenly. 'And just how are we going to do that?'

'We'll tell people! Describe what happened here, explain about the great wind and the voice, and . . .' Even as she spoke, she realized what she was saying. God, she thought, no wonder he's dejected.

'And get patted on the head and told we've had too much wine and sunshine? Think again, Beth!'

'It's not enough, is it?' she said after a while. 'We have to find proof.'

He didn't bother to put his opinion of *that* idea into words, merely going 'Ha!'

She heard again that quiet voice. *Do not fail him now.*

She got up, staring down at him. 'We must go back to Arles,' she said firmly. 'If there is any proof, that's where it'll be. He's Saint Theodore of Arles, isn't he? If he was canonized by that name, there must be records.'

'It was two thousand years ago!'

'We've got to try!' she shouted. Then, more calmly: 'Let's treat this as a scientific experiment. We have a hypothesis – that the story's wrong and the Roman's innocent – and now we have to find supporting evidence. We'll start with the church records.'

Reluctantly he stood up, looking at her resignedly. As they set off back down to the car, he said, 'Can we have a beer before we start?'

On the way back she said, after quite a long time spent wrestling with her conscience, 'I've had an idea.'

'Oh, yes?'

'It's a very mean idea, and I'm ashamed of myself.'

Looking over at him, she saw him smile. 'I can't wait to hear it.'

She took a deep breath. 'Why don't we go home to La Maison Jaune and both get on with what I'm meant to be doing down here anyway?'

'Helping Joe?'

'Exactly. Joe has made masses of notes on his St Theodore, he'll have all the references and he's photocopied heaps of relevant extracts from musty old tomes that aren't allowed out of the library.'

'But surely he's looking for material to prove the story's true, not question its very foundation?'

'It doesn't matter! If he's got hold of the earliest sources, we can use them just as well to *dis*prove as he can to prove!'

He laughed briefly. 'No wonder you were ashamed of yourself! How sly can you get?'

'Truth must out,' she said sanctimoniously. Then added: 'It'll serve him right for being so smug!'

La Maison Jaune was quiet when they got back in the middle of the afternoon, and there was a lingering aroma of garlic and onions – belatedly she realized they hadn't had any lunch. They found Joe in his study, writing up notes. Several books were stacked on the desk, most of them marked with pieces of paper.

She went to stand beside him, putting a hand on his shoulder: if we're going to get him to co-operate, she thought, better to be friendly.

'Hi,' he said, eyes on the screen of his laptop.

'Hello. Adam's come back with me.'

Joe looked up briefly. 'So I see.'

'How was the pasta lunch?'

He shrugged. 'Okay.'

She got the impression the occasion hadn't been a roaring success. 'The others have gone?'

He was typing again, hammering the keys rather hard. 'They've gone off to the beach. At some place on the Camargue.'

'You didn't want to go too?'

'*I've* got to work.' He managed to make it sound as if he was the only person who ever did any. Among that particular group, she thought, he probably is.

'We've come to help,' she said, and was surprised when he looked up and gave her a genuinely grateful smile.

'Have you? It's more than bloody Gemma was prepared to do.'

'We'll be better assistants than Gemma,' she said. 'Where shall we start?' Before he could answer, she went on, 'This morning I was going over your Lucius Sextus notes about what happened after Theodore's death. Adam and I'll get on with that.'

'Okay.' Joe had gone back to his books, picking out one from halfway down a huge pile. 'I found another reference,'

– she felt her heart leap – 'it's in that book on the floor. The place is marked.'

'Right.' She tried to sound casual. 'I'll make some notes while Adam reads the Lucius Sextus. Can I have your notebook?'

For a moment he didn't answer. Remembering his earlier hostility, the protective way he'd virtually ordered her off his papers, she thought he was going to refuse. But then, surprisingly, he smiled. 'Help yourself,' he said. 'To anything – it doesn't matter any more.'

The smile had become a smirk, with more than an element of triumph in it. Apprehensive suddenly, although she didn't know why, she said, 'What doesn't matter?'

Joe was clearly enjoying himself. 'I've guessed what you're up to,' he said, glaring at Adam. 'All your talk of gipsies is just a blind. You're down here because of St Theodore.'

He knows, Beth thought. She fought the despair: let's at least wait to see *what* he knows!

'What makes you think that?' Adam said calmly.

'It's exactly what I'd expect.' Joe managed to put a sneer in his voice. 'You've been commissioned by some over-sophisticated, Doubting-Thomas film company to come down here and disprove what's happening at Our Lady of the Marshlands. That's what you've been doing these past few days, and my turncoat sister has been helping you.'

The relief was enormous. He's on the right track, Beth thought, but he's missed the vital ingredient. She didn't let the relief show; instead she said mildly, 'I'm hardly a turncoat. I never said I believed the story of your little saint, if you recall, and I certainly don't go along with this child's visions. I –'

Joe was nodding, infuriatingly. 'You don't? And that applies to you, too?' He shot a look at Adam.

'It does.'

'Wonderful! Well, I'd like to invite the pair of you to stand beside me in the Church of Our Lady of the Marshlands, the day after tomorrow.'

'Why?' Beth asked. She had an idea what the answer would be.

Joe was beating an intricate tattoo on the desk with his pencil. 'I could say, "Wait and see",' – he glanced up, grinning, and Beth could have hit him – 'but I think I'll tell you. Remember those phone calls, Beth?'

'Of course,' she snapped.

'They were from my Arles contact.' He was smiling smugly. 'My man on the spot. You may have heard of the Reverend Derek?'

Beth and Adam shook their heads.

'You don't read the right magazines,' Joe commented. 'Derek Hill has been reporting regularly on Chantal Bordanado. And not only her visions – he's interviewed her extensively, met her family, talked to everyone who knows her. I wrote to him back in July, when I read his article on the first vision, and we've been in contact ever since.'

Wanting to laugh, Beth thought, I've been maligning him. When he was muttering on the phone to late-night callers and disappearing for hours on end, I thought he was planning his assault on Gemma's double sleeping bag. And all the time he was hanging on every last syllable of the Reverend Derek.

'And what is this chap's conclusion?' Adam was asking. 'Clearly he believes she's genuine, but –'

'Of course she's genuine.' Joe was more condescending than indignant, as if he had nothing but pity for poor mortals who hadn't seen the light. 'As I said, come with me to the church, and see for yourselves.'

Beth said, 'What's going to happen, the day after tomorrow?'

'Chantal has had warning that she's going to see another vision.'

'What sort of warning?' Beth could hardly believe he was taking it seriously.

'In a dream. She's been told to be there, in front of the statue of St Theodore, at sunset.'

'And she's told the Reverend Derek, who has told you, and probably the world's press too?' Adam, too, sounded sceptical.

'Derek wouldn't do that,' Joe said. 'He's only told a few select *sympathetic* journalists' – the look he gave Adam suggested he didn't consider Adam could possibly have been one of them – 'and he has their word that they won't leak the story before the event.'

Adam muttered, 'He has an over-optimistic view of the press.'

But Beth was struck with the enormity of what Joe was saying. In two days' time, the world was going to watch as a child had a vision, and the legend of St Theodore of Arles would be the subject of a thousand headlines, news reports, articles.

Do not fail him now.

Dully she said, 'Let's have your notebook, Joe. We may as well get on.'

He looked at her, and beneath the triumph she thought she saw pity. Don't! she wanted to shout. Don't remind me what you are to me, when I'm trying my darnedest to upset all that you believe in!

He held out his notebook, and she took it. Then he returned to his work.

She held the notebook for a moment, summoning strength. Then, finding the place where Joe had copied out the Lucius Sextus references, she gave it to Adam. Dropping down to kneel on the floor, she picked up the book Joe had pointed to.

It was entitled *The Canonization of the Early Christian Saints*. She opened it at the marked place, and was confronted with an illustration of the simpering saint from the little church behind the Place de la Redoute. Realizing she'd been holding her breath, she let it out and began to read.

> In the last quarter of the second century AD, the authorities in Roman Provincia were forced to take a hard line with Christians, especially an enclave of the new faith who had settled near the ancient town of Glanum. In 173 or 174, a group comprising two families and their friends, preferring to live according to the dictates of their own faith, established a commune in the hills behind the town.
>
> Although at first the authorities left them alone, their continuously defiant attitude eventually left the Fréjus magistrate no choice. Not only were the Christians refusing to make sacrifices to the Imperial Cult and the other Roman gods, they were actively interfering with the religious observances of others: an attempt was made to tear down and deface the Jupiter statue in Glanum, and a Temple of Mithras was attacked.
>
> In 175, six of the group were arrested, tried and condemned and thrown to the lions in the amphitheatre at Arles in October of that year. The official records show that a capacity crowd attended.
>
> A retributive attack by the Christians on the Temple of Mithras near Glanum was mounted, although it appears that the Christians, possibly demoralized by the deaths of their friends and family, lacked sufficient force to be effective. They were overcome, and a young boy in their number was killed when he held out against pressure to make sacrifice to the god.
>
> There seems to have been some doubt over the boy's identity. The records of the magistrate imply that the Glanum Christians may have claimed the boy as a member of their community in order to win

for themselves the kudos of having their own martyr: the magistrate comments that this is contrary to what he was led to believe, which was that the child, whose name was Theodore, came from Arles.

The Christians' persistence in associating themselves with Theodore served only to hasten their inevitable fate. The remaining Glanum Christians perished in the Arles amphitheatre in 176.

Later Medieval tradition embellished the story of Theodore, borrowing elements from other 'miracle' tales. Theodore, it was said, went on breathing after his throat was cut, moreover he was killed on his way home from choir practice, and his dead body went on singing Ave Marias. There is a suggestion that his pure and holy singing kept the body safe from the depredations of wild beasts as he lay out on the hillside.

The Christian church canonized Theodore in 1156, in response to continual pressure from the people of Arles, who claimed he had effected countless cures over many centuries, primarily of ailments connected with the throat. In commemorative images and statues he is represented as a small child, usually indicating his slit throat.

Beth went on staring at the page for some time after she had finished reading. Gradually it dawned on her that, despite her initial excited response, in fact the extract had told her little she didn't already know. And the mention of the Fréjus magistrate was distinctly familiar – his doubts over the origins of St Theodore of Arles sounded very similar to what good old Lucius Sextus had said.

Depressingly, it looked as if the writer of *The Canonization of the Early Christian Saints* had done no more than write out his own account of what Joe had copied from Lucius Sextus's original text.

She glanced up at Adam, but, engrossed in Joe's notebook, he didn't notice.

I'll wait till he's finished, she thought. Maybe he'll spot something I've missed. And it'd be a pity to dash his hopes until I have to.

Idly she turned the pages of the thick book. Theodore the Studite, Theodore of Canterbury, Theodosius the Cenobiarch. Flipping back, she came to Thais, Thaddaeus, Teresa. A couple of Teresas. And a Teodoro, from some place in Italy – he seemed to have been a forerunner of St Francis, being similarly associated with a simple rural life . . .

She skipped the next few sentences. Then, moving on to what the book went on to say, she stiffened. Leaning forward, feeling her heart beat faster, she read the paragraph again.

No. It's just coincidence, another example of – how did the author describe it? – later Medieval additions embellishing the story.

It *can* only be that! Otherwise –

No, she told herself firmly. I'm not even going to think about 'otherwise', it'll be too disappointing when, inevitably, I find I was wrong.

She read the whole entry again.

And found that it was increasingly difficult to convince herself that coincidence was the only explanation.

27

Despite her eagerness, growing almost uncontrollable, there was no chance to show Adam what she'd found out: just as he was closing Joe's notebook and reaching out to take *The Canonization of the Early Christian Saints* from her, there was a loud banging at the door and a voice shouted, 'Joe? We've come to disturb you, you've worked enough for one day!'

She noticed the irritation on Adam's face. Then, glancing at Joe, saw that his response was similar.

'Shall I send them packing?' she suggested hopefully.

Joe sighed. 'No. I said they could come back, provided they cooked supper.'

'But you're getting on so well!' It was an assumption, since he hadn't actually said he was; she was only going by the fact that he hadn't said a word nor stopped typing since she and Adam had settled down to reading.

Joe grinned. 'I'll tell them to cook quietly, then we can work till the meal's ready.' He got up and went to answer the renewed poundings on the front door. 'I'm coming!' he shouted.

Adam was staring at her. 'Have you found anything useful?' he asked.

'I think –' No. Don't tell him what *I* think, let him look for himself and see if he comes to the same conclusion. 'I'll show you later.' She got up. 'I'm going to see if Joe's got a map of the Mediterranean. There's something I want to look at.'

'Okay,' he said absently, going back to Joe's notebook.

She smiled – she didn't think he'd heard her last remark. Now, she thought, searching on Joe's desk for his road atlas, I just have to wait.

It took all her control not to shout out her discovery there and then.

It turned out that Joe's friends were celebrating their last night in Arles; they'd packed up their van and were moving on in the morning, and, as Nick engagingly explained, had wanted to do a special supper for Joe in exchange for his having let them 'crash' in his house.

Beth was resigned to having to wait to talk to Adam; he seemed to have thrown himself into enjoying the evening, and there was nothing she could do but copy him. It wasn't difficult to have fun in that company; now that she knew she was highly unlikely to meet any of them again after that night, Beth found she could tolerate them much more readily. Even like them – she warmed to Trish, who had been training as a nurse back home in Nottingham, but given it up as a bad job when she found that her earnings from a sixty-three-hour week, once she'd paid out for necessities such as accommodation and food, weren't even enough to keep her in tights.

When Beth asked her how she was funding her travels, Trish said Gemma was paying.

'Very decent of her,' Beth commented.

'She's my sister.'

Beth found herself warming to Gemma, too.

They ate out on the terrace, and over the prolonged meal – the girls and Nick had cooked a succession of Chinese dishes and a vast tub of rice – she listened to the lively conversation of Joe's new friends. Soon to be former friends, she thought, unless they're planning to meet up back home. Even that wouldn't be happening for a while: Gemma, Trish and Nick were heading next for Turkey, with the loose plan of going on to India, 'if it's not a hassle'.

Beth found it hard to imagine how going to India in a converted ambulance could be anything but a hassle.

'Aren't you tempted to go with them?' Adam asked Joe. Beth, who happened to be looking at Gemma when he spoke, decided he might have been, only he hadn't been invited. She was on the point of feeling sorry for him when he said, 'Not in the least. I have unfinished business to see to –' he glanced at Beth – 'some of us haven't the time for six-month holidays.'

Gemma banged her glass down on the table. '*Some* of us left school at fifteen and have been grafting ever since,' she said sarcastically. '*Some* of us were putting aside the money for our travels when others were swanning it at college.'

'University,' Joe muttered.

Adam, clearly realizing he'd inadvertently put his foot in it, tried to make amends. 'How did you come by your van?' he asked Nick. 'Did you fit it out yourself? I've always wondered what –'

'It's mine,' Gemma said neutrally. Then, turning to Beth, she added conversationally, 'Have you noticed how people always assume it's the bloke who owns the vehicle?'

Beth smiled. 'Indeed I have. *And* how they also assume he's the breadwinner.'

'Makes you sick, doesn't it?'

'It does.' What on earth, she wondered, would Gemma make of Father? She suppressed a laugh: the prospect of Gemma putting Father right on a few matters made it almost worth hoping the relationship with Joe would survive Gemma's absence along the India trail.

But Joe had just pointed out caustically that Gemma would in any case be lost without Nick to keep the van on the road, and Gemma had retaliated by saying she'd done motor mechanics at evening classes. Then she'd called him a misogynist pig.

It didn't really look as if there was much chance of the relationship even surviving the night.

Adam stood up and stacked a few of the dirty plates. 'Shall we start washing up, Beth, since the others cooked?'

'Good idea.' She reached for the almost-empty rice bowl. 'We'll put the coffee on while we're out there.'

In the kitchen he said quietly, 'Sorry to land us with the dishes, only I thought a diplomatic withdrawal was in order.'

'Quite. *I* thought she was going to hit him.'

He was running water into the bowl, rinsing the plates before immersing them. Efficient in the kitchen, she thought absently. 'I suppose they haven't really got anything much in common,' he said.

'Except sex.' She'd said it without thinking. *Damn.* 'I mean, they obviously fancy each other, or they did, and . . .'

'I'm sure you're right,' he said as she trailed to a stop.

There was a slightly awkward pause. She dried a few dishes then, having caught him up, went to get out mugs for coffee.

He said suddenly, 'Do you think we have much in common?'

She spun round, but he had his back to her.

What's he saying?

It's a straightforward enough question, she told herself. So give him a straightforward answer.

'Professionally, almost nothing. As regards our interests, I'd say quite a lot – it hasn't been any hardship for you, has it, all that we've been doing these past days?' She saw him shake his head. 'Nor for me. But surely . . .' She stopped.

'Go on.' He'd turned away from the sink and, leaning against it, was watching her.

'We have your Roman in common. We've both felt him, both seen him. For his own good reasons he's appealed to the two of us. Somehow it makes me feel . . .'

No, I can't, she thought. Can't say it makes me feel as if some man who lived nearly two thousand years ago seems to want us to work together. To *be* together. Or why else would he have involved me, too?

'Do you think he reckoned we'd do better as a team than on our own?' Adam said softly.

'Something like that.'

He stepped forward, putting his hands on her shoulders. 'And do you agree?'

She stared up into his eyes. I liked the look of you, she thought, right from the first, when you made me jump out of my skin in the Alyscamps. And, all this time we've been so preoccupied with your old Roman, part of me has been aware I've been enjoying *you*.

Until this moment, I wasn't sure you felt the same.

She whispered, 'Who am I to question the judgement of a Roman ghost?'

His arms went round her. She stood on tiptoe as he bent to kiss her.

After some time he said, 'Do you think they'd mind getting their own coffee?'

Belatedly she noticed that the voices from the terrace had got louder and more acrimonious.

'I don't really care. What were you going to suggest we did instead?'

He kissed the top of her head. 'I'd like to stroll with you round the amphitheatre, then look at the gardens in the moonlight. I'd like to find a quiet bar where we can drink to finding an answer to our mystery, then –' he kissed her again – 'I'd like to take you back with me.'

'But I –'

'Only to make sure you get a good night's sleep!' he said hastily. 'I don't hold out any hope for you at all here, if that lot are going to be arguing into the small hours. But please, don't think I was suggesting anything else.'

Standing wrapped in his arms, she thought that was rather a pity.

Then she started to laugh.

'What's the matter?'

'This morning – God, doesn't it seem a long time ago? – I realized I didn't want to be here any more. For pretty much the reasons you've just mentioned – too much of other people's pushy presence. I thought I'd either find a hotel, or . . .' She hesitated, then decided that, since he'd already made the offer, it was all right to admit to what she'd hoped might happen. 'Or I'd ask you if you had a spare room I could use.'

'I have,' he murmured, hugging her to him. 'And, funnily enough, it's all ready for you.'

'For me? But you didn't know I was going to need it!' She pulled away, looking into his face.

Slightly sheepishly he said, 'A man can always hope.'

She left a note for Joe propped against the kettle, on the assumption that sooner or later he'd notice the coffee hadn't arrived and would go out to make it himself.

She'd hesitated over writing 'I'll be staying with Adam': there was no way to say in a brief note 'but don't go assuming we'll be sleeping together because I'm having the spare room'.

In the end, deciding it was absolutely none of Joe's business *what* she did, she just said, 'Adam will put me up for the night.'

Joe, she concluded, can think what he bloody well likes.

A long time later, they collected Adam's car from the Place de la Redoute and he drove her the short distance across the town to where he was staying.

It's such an atmospheric place, Arles, she thought as they went slowly through the now-empty streets. Even without your own Roman standing at your shoulder. He had left them alone tonight: she'd been surprised, then grateful, when no urgent presence manifested itself outside the arena.

Is it because you don't need to tug at our sleeves any more? she asked him silently. Because you're aware we're quite determined to put it right for you, if we possibly can?

She remembered what she'd been longing to tell Adam before dinner. It'll keep a little longer, she thought. Although, bearing in mind we only have until the day after tomorrow, not *much* longer. And even this is such a faint hope, I'm probably making far too much out of nothing . . .

Adam was parking the car outside a small apartment block. 'Not as lovely as your Maison Jaune,' he said, 'but it's low maintenance. And there's no garden.' They went into the hall and he led the way to the stairs. 'I don't usually bother with the lift – it's only two floors up.'

It must, she decided, have been a very early example of an apartment block – it reminded her of a turn-of-the-century hotel she'd once stayed in on the Boulevard Haussmann in Paris, which had been complete with grey-clad concierge and a lift like a cage. There was a faint aroma of garlic and Gauloises, and from somewhere she heard the yapping of a dog.

'They don't have a "no pets" rule,' she observed.

'That's Madame Perrichet's Pekingese. Bloody thing bit my ankle last summer.'

'Didn't you complain to the management?'

'She *is* the management.'

Last summer. He comes here regularly, then. 'Is it your own flat?'

They'd reached the second-floor landing, and he was opening his front door. 'It was what my father called his southern retreat. He left it to me when he died because he said I was the only one of his children who'd use it.'

He reached to switch on a light, then stood back for her to precede him inside. She had an impression of cream walls, old dark-wood furniture, white floaty curtains at the long windows blowing in the breeze.

He went to close the shutters. 'To keep the mosquitoes out,' he said.

She sat down on a dark red leather-covered sofa. 'It's delightful. Every bit as lovely as the Maison Jaune.' And, she nearly added, it has the great advantage of belonging to you.

He came to sit beside her. 'Would you like coffee? A drink?'

She looked at him. I know what I'd really like, she thought, but I'm far too tired.

And – she was quite shocked at herself – I don't know him *nearly* well enough!

Yet.

She took his hand. 'I would absolutely love a bath. And then I'd like to go to bed.'

He stood up. 'I'm not surprised, it's been a long day. Bathroom's the door at the end of the hall – there's plenty of hot water, take as much as you want – and the spare room's next to it. Come on.'

Still holding her hand, he showed her. The white-painted spare room had twin beds with cream covers. Other than a vibrant painting of a Camargue scene on one wall, it was bare of decoration.

'I don't use it much,' he said; she thought he sounded slightly apologetic.

'It's fine. I'm so grateful for a bed I wouldn't mind a nun's cell.'

'You've very nearly got one.'

She put her arm round him. 'Nuns don't get lovely paintings of the Camargue, it might put unseemly ideas of wide-open spaces into their heads.'

'I'm glad you like it. I'll fetch you a towel and see if I can find you a bathrobe.'

He turned on the taps for her, then left her to it. She lay

soaking in the hot water for some time, then, in danger of drifting off to sleep, she made herself get out.

In bed, warm in the bathrobe (which smelt faintly of lavender), she heard him splashing in the bath. She wondered if he'd look in on his way to his own room: he didn't say goodnight earlier, she thought, so he probably will. At which point he will without doubt get more than he's bargained for.

She was reviewing the facts she'd gleaned from *The Canonization of the Early Christian Saints* when she heard him come out of the bathroom. Then there was a gentle tap on her door.

'Come in.'

'I didn't knock loudly,' he said, coming over to sit on the edge of her bed, 'in case you were asleep.'

'I almost went to sleep in the bath.' Although I don't know how, she thought, in view of all that's on my mind.

He reached out to touch her hair. 'Your hair's wet.'

'It'll soon dry.'

The sudden intimacy of having him sitting on her bed, both of them fresh from the bath and naked but for towelling robes, was disconcerting. But not disconcerting enough that she wanted him to leave.

'Do you think they've noticed yet that we've gone?' she asked.

'Joe and the others? I shouldn't imagine so. They'll either be still shouting at each other or else have fallen into a drunken stupor on Joe's study floor.'

'Joe's study being where the booze is kept?'

'Exactly.'

She was glad all over again not to be there, having to put up with them. 'Thank you for letting me stay.'

'You're welcome.'

Out of nowhere came the sudden desire to speak up for Joe. 'He's not always like this – he seems to have been taken over by this vision business. He's usually hard-working and responsible, and when he goes home he'll hand in the most thorough and convincing thesis you ever came across, including a first-hand account of Chantal Bordanado's third vision.'

'So I gathered – you implied the night we met Gemma that he was acting somewhat out of character.'

'I liked Gemma.' It seemed rather soon to be speaking of her in the past tense, but she didn't correct herself.

'She'd have been good for Joe, don't you think?'

'I do.' She remembered her earlier thought. 'She'd have been *very* good for my father.'

After a moment he said, 'Can I ask you something?'

Slightly apprehensive, she said, 'Of course.'

'That night we were just talking about, when Gemma burst in, you'd started to tell me about your work. We'd got as far as you getting your degree, then we were interrupted. There doesn't seem to have been a chance to ask you till now, but what were you about to say?'

'You *are* nice,' she said impulsively. 'People are never interested, and it's so important to me.'

'I know,' he said softly.

'I'm going to be Dr Amery's deputy – she's my boss, remember?' He nodded. 'She'll train me as intensively as she can, and, if I'm good enough, next year we'll think about a further qualification.'

'You'll be good enough. I've never seen such determination.'

'It's a far cry from journalism and film-making.' She didn't at first see why the thought should be so depressing.

'We've already admitted we have nothing in common professionally,' he said gently. 'Although, come to think about it, both our spheres require an enquiring mind.' Then abruptly, 'Where do you live?'

'North London. Finchley.' She smiled ruefully. 'Quite a long way from Northumberland.'

He touched her hand. 'Yes, but as I think I told you, I'm

away as much as I'm there. And much of my time away I spend in London.'

She said lightly, 'Have you got a flat there too?'

'No, just a bedsit.'

Good grief, she thought, is that all?

He said after quite a long silence, 'I know you're tired and longing to get to sleep, but there's something else we need to talk about.'

'The Roman. Yes, I know. I've been waiting all evening to talk about him.'

'You said just now that Joe will complete an outstanding thesis which, together with all this publicity for the visions, will reinforce the old legend of St Theodore in flashing lights.'

'He's not writing it specifically for that reason – it's not only about Theodore.'

'Yes, but the rest doesn't concern us. What we have to do is present the counter-argument. We've made a start, and –'

'More than a start.' I wish I'd brought Joe's book with me, she thought: I'm not sure I can remember enough of the details. 'Adam, I think I know where we might find the proof we need.'

He looked amazed; as well he might, she thought – apart from anything else, he's probably wondering why I didn't mention it earlier.

But there have been one or two other important things to consider.

He was gazing at her, his expression tender. 'Are you thinking what I'm thinking?' she asked.

'I imagine so. Two-thousand-year-old grievances have lost their total hold on me, this evening. But will you tell me now?'

Concentrating – with an effort – she did. Once started, some of the thrill of the initial discovery returned; judging from his face, he seemed to pick it up.

'What do you think?' she prompted when, having finished explaining, he didn't speak. 'It's probably not in the least relevant, and I've put two and two together and made ninety-eight, and –'

'And you're not being in the least scientific or empirical? No, you're not. But on the other hand, you seem to have had a hunch – what's more, a very strong one.'

'Hunches aren't scientific.'

'No. But under some circumstances they ought to be trusted, at least as much as laboratory-verified test results.'

'Under what sort of circumstances?'

'Well, for a start the sort when you've got an impatient Roman employing you as his agent in the tangible world.'

She digested that. 'You mean *he* was prompting me? Making me have the hunch?'

And he said calmly, 'Why not?'

After a while she said, 'So what are we going to do?' In under two days, she might have added, only it was too depressing.

'Where did you say this place was?'

She told him.

'Too far to drive there and back in two days,' he muttered, 'if we were to have any time at all for research.'

She wanted to be sure what he was thinking. 'You're suggesting we *go* there?'

He looked surprised at the question. 'Yes.'

'You *do* believe in my hunch, don't you?' she said softly.

He looked at her affectionately. 'I do, but I have to say I've travelled further on slimmer evidence.'

She was still trying to absorb the fact that she and Adam were going to set off for Italy some time in the immediate future. 'We'll have to fly,' she said, hoping she sounded blasé, as if she was used to setting out across Europe at the drop of a hat.

'No problem. We'll get down to Marseilles early

tomorrow and be in Rome by lunchtime. We'll hire a car – I've got a contact in the hire-car place at the airport. A few hours' drive and we'll be there.'

She looked at him, her mind full of conflicting emotions. I'm thrilled at what we're going to do, I'm overjoyed that you believe in me, I'm so glad we've found something positive we can do.

But, over and above all that, I wish you would take me in your arms and kiss me again.

It wasn't the moment, and she knew it. No doubt he did, too. Before either of them could let desire override common sense, she said, 'I suppose we should get some sleep, in view of our early start tomorrow.'

Instantly he stood up. 'Yes, you're right. I'll call you around six. All right?'

'All right.'

She turned her attention to locating the switch on the bedside light so that she would not have to watch him walk away.

28

I was hallucinating.

I thought I saw Zillah, rising up, arms held aloft, lamenting her agony as wildly as Ceres mourning for the lost Proserpine. I felt a powerful guilt; my failure had wrought in my mind this picture of the mother of the poor child I had been unable to save.

As if my will became her deed, I saw her sweep her son up in her arms, crush him to her breast. Saw her strong right arm lift high above her head, saw a flash of moonlight strike on something she held in her hand. Heard, yet again, that dreadful scream.

The vision faded.

I regained consciousness, instantly aware of such pain that I almost closed my eyes again and gave up.

There was a heavy weight on my chest, making it hard to breathe. The clammy, rapidly cooling body of Gaius lay across me.

I pushed him off. His blood had soaked my tunic; the force of his fall had driven my dagger further into him, and it took almost more effort than I could summon up to wrench it out. As the long blade finally came free, a gout of dark, half-congealed blood came with it.

I lay back against the rock, waiting until the nausea subsided and the strange floating feeling in my head went away.

Then, steeling myself, I looked up at the sacrifice stone.

The moon had set, but the sky was starting to pale with

the early dawn. A thin mist swirled just above the ground, breathed out from the awakening earth.

The stone was shadow-black. On it lay a body, and from the body a denser shade spread out.

On hands and knees I crawled forward. He lay on his back, arms flung out, wrists bound to the corners of the great slab. His head was tilted back, exposing the throat.

I couldn't make myself go right up to him. From a distance I stared at him. His face made a pattern of black and white, of dark and light. Where the waxing dawn caught forehead, cheeks, chin, the young skin shone bright, unblemished. But the eyes were dark hollows, and under his chin gaped a sickle-moon of black.

I failed you, I said to him. Gods, but I'm sorry.

I bent my head, sending after his flown soul the prayers that would protect him, speed him on his way. Then, on my knees, I went closer, close enough to reach up and grope till I touched one of the upturned hands, still half-curled into a desperate fist.

He was cold.

I took his hand in mine, just as I'd done in life when I'd hauled him up some steep bank, or shown him how to hold a sword.

His hand was too big. This wasn't Theo's hand, it was the hand of a grown man.

I grabbed hold of the stone slab, pulling myself up so that I stood over him.

It wasn't Theo. It was Varus.

I know full well I should have got away from that place the moment I realized, but I didn't. I wasn't in any state to get away – the nausea had increased, and the pain in my head was making me have moments when I felt myself going under again. I crawled as far as I could away from the bodies and the stench of the blood, then lay down and closed my eyes. I had some idea that a brief rest, a sleep even, would make me feel better. Yes, I know I was acting stupidly, but no one's at their best when they're suffering the after-effects of concussion.

It can't have been long afterwards that I woke again. Or rather was woken; there was a crashing from the glade, then heavy footsteps along the rock passage. Two, three, four of them, the last two sounding as if they were wearing military footwear.

Dazed, half of me still in the troubled dream I'd just been wrenched from, I looked up. Flavius stood over me, and he'd brought with him men from the Procurator's Office. Two of them were guards.

He said over his shoulder to the man standing behind him, whose face was expressionless as he stared at the two dead bodies and then down at me, 'That's him. That's the murderer.'

The man said something to the guards, but I didn't catch what it was.

'He killed my friend Gaius,' Flavius said. 'That's the one lying at the mouth of the passage, you just stepped over him.'

One of the guards bent down, putting his fingers to Gaius's throat. 'Dead,' he said.

'Gaius was trying to save the life of that poor young man on the slab – he's a Christian, he was Gaius's stepson. Oh, how are we to tell the boy's mother?' I swear Flavius's voice cracked on the words – he should have been on the stage, that one.

The other guard was leaning over the body on the stone. 'This one's had it as well.' Men of few words, those guards. And imperturbable, even in the face of violent death. They were probably ex-legionaries.

Flavius was staring at me, his face unreadable. 'I don't know who he is,' he said to the man behind him. 'But I can guess – he's one of those Mithraists. They were holding one of their ceremonies tonight, and Gaius's boy here probably tried to stop them – they slaughter bulls, you know, and the lad was fond of animals.' Again that catch in his voice.

The man from the Procurator's Office addressed him for the first time. 'I'm aware of what goes on in the Mithraeum,' he muttered.

'Well, you'll agree with me, then, that it's perfectly clear what happened?' The man didn't respond to Flavius's eager tone except with a non-committal grunt. Flavius plunged on. 'The Mithraists were about to make their sacrifice, the boy rushes in to stop them, and they tell him he can either join in the sacrifice or else he'll be put to death himself. Gaius, who must have followed him here because he feared this very outcome, rushes in to try to save the lad, and our Mithraist down there –' he kicked me, quite hard – 'kills him, then slits the poor young boy's throat.'

'You can't possibly –' I began. Somebody had to speak up in my defence, and it didn't look as if anyone else was going to.

But the man from the Procurator's Office was no longer standing still and silent while Flavius railed at him. Straightening, squaring his shoulders, he looked quite different. And, for all that he was now well past middle age and liked nothing better than to drone on for hours about the latest achievements of his grandchildren, fleetingly Maximus was as tall and proud as the young man he'd once been.

'I greet you, Sergius Cornelius,' he said gravely. I breathed a sigh of relief; from his silence I'd feared either that he didn't recognize me – increasingly unlikely as the daylight grew stronger – or, to save himself the embarrassment of arresting a friend, that he knew full well who I was but wasn't going to admit it.

As I stared at him I saw him smile faintly. Then he said to Flavius, 'What would you have me do?'

'Get your guards to haul him away!' Flavius cried. 'I've

just told you, he's a murderer! A double murderer, and there are his victims, scarcely cold!'

The frown on Maximus's brow deepened; I could almost hear him thinking. Poor man, this wasn't the sort of thing he was usually confronted with.

The silence extended. Suddenly the strangeness of it all struck me: there was Flavius, his elder brother lying dead not five yards behind him, but where was the grief? Gods, far from lamenting Varus's death, he was standing there with all the aplomb in the world, claiming that Varus was Theo and trying to lay the blame for his death on me!

Why?

Thinking made my head hurt even more. I gazed up at Maximus, waiting for him to speak.

'I would like', he pronounced slowly, 'to hear Sergius Cornelius's version of events.' He looked at me, eyebrows raised questioningly.

I didn't know what to say. Unless I thought it all through – which as I've just explained I was in no condition to do – there was a danger that telling the truth might make matters worse. If, for example, I blurted out that it wasn't any stepson of Gaius's on the slab but Flavius's own brother, then I'd lose the undoubted benefit of having everyone think the dead youth was Theo.

If they all thought Theo was dead, no one would go looking for him any more.

'Sergius?' Maximus prompted.

I made up my mind. 'I am wounded,' I said weakly. 'My head was banged against the wall – I can't recall how, it was when Gaius launched himself on me.' It wouldn't do any harm to sow the idea of self-defence in Maximus's mind. 'As for the lad on the stone – I can tell you nothing about him, other than that I didn't kill him.'

'Liar!' shouted Flavius. 'It's just what you Mithraists would do, you order people to make sacrifices to your god and when they won't, you kill them!'

The calm voice of Maximus spoke. 'I have heard tell of no cases where Mithraists have acted as you say. And – '

'*This* one has!'

Maximus turned to stare at him. It was Maximus's finest moment – his expression seemed to imply that Flavius was something nasty he'd just stepped in. 'Kindly do not interrupt. As I was saying, if indeed Sergius enforced the death penalty on one who refused to worship the state gods of Rome, then he was acting within his rights as an official of the administration.' He paused. '*If* he did what you accuse him of,' – Maximus's entire demeanour said he didn't believe it for one moment – 'then there is no case to answer.'

'But he killed Gaius! I mean, he must have done, he . . .' Flavius trailed off. Unless he admitted to having witnessed it, he could hardly say with certainty that I'd done the killing.

The same thought must have run through Maximus's mind. He said, 'And just what were you doing up here?'

'I didn't get here till it was too late! I heard the screams, from below. I . . . I . . .'

I hadn't seen Flavius cornered before. It was an enjoyable spectacle.

'You happened to be passing?' Maximus suggested.

'Yes, that's right. I – ' Flavius shut his mouth on whatever wild excuse he'd been about to give. It seemed wise, all things considered.

'I do not propose to continue this investigation standing on a rock-face with two dead bodies littering the scene,' Maximus said decisively. He turned to his guards. 'One of you – yes, you – stay with the dead. I'll send assistance – we'll have to bring them down. You' – he turned to the other guard who, as if impressed by this new authoritative Maximus, jumped to attention – 'help Sergius Cornelius to his feet. We shall take both him and this young man' – he glared at Flavius – 'into my office in Arelate, where a proper investigation will be carried out.'

Flavius looked as if that was the last thing he wanted. 'But I . . .' he began. Then stopped. 'Very well,' he said, his tone far too compliant for my liking.

The guard had helped me up. Apart from a pounding in my head like someone knocking in six-inch nails and the brief sensation that someone was repeatedly drawing a black veil across my eyes, I felt all right. Maximus took my arm, dismissing the guard, who bent to pick up my bloodstained dagger. 'I'll look after Sergius,' he announced. 'You take the youth.'

The man who was to stay on guard over the corpses was gazing down at Varus's body. As we left, I saw him pull a fold of the black cloak over the face and the ghastly wound in the throat, and he made some sign with his right hand.

I had to brush against him to pass on the narrow path. The top button of his tunic was undone: against the hairy chest he wore on a thin chain the Chi-Rho symbol.

I hadn't realized we were employing Christians in the guard force.

We took our time going down the hillside. I pretended I was having trouble walking – not that I had to pretend very hard – to give me the chance to look around.

Apart from my panic-stricken Brothers, none of whom had shown their faces since they'd all rushed off, there was someone else missing.

It wasn't Theo lying dead on the sacrifice stone, thanks be to Mithras. But if he wasn't up there, where was he?

There was no sign of anyone, man or boy, the length of that path.

There were horses tethered at the foot of the hill, mine and three others. Maximus and his guard helped me to mount, and the four of us set off down the road to Arelate.

I knew right from that moment up by the stone – when Flavius had agreed to go with Maximus – that he had no intention of allowing himself to be taken in to face an investigation. For his own good reasons he'd disassociated himself from his dead brother; there was no way in the world he was going to let anyone find out his – their – real identity.

And that made sense, when I thought about it. They'd both been masquerading as Roman citizens, had wormed their way into Roman institutions; Flavius was a welcome guest in the household of the Procurator himself. As soon as Flavius was called on to prove his identity, which would probably happen the moment we all arrived in Maximus's office, he'd be in trouble.

The truth was that the two of them had come to Arelate for one reason only: to fulfil their mother's curse on me. Too subtle to simply kill me, they'd decided to kill Theo.

The biggest question of all, however, I was still too sick to tackle: I couldn't even begin to wonder who had rescued the boy.

Who had slit Varus's throat.

I was riding along in a painful haze, which was probably why I didn't notice at first that Flavius had come up to ride beside me.

Maximus was saying something to his guard; it would have been the perfect moment for me to come out with some witticism on the lines of, 'Ha! Thought you'd dropped me in it up there, didn't you?', only I couldn't summon the energy.

But Flavius had no such handicap. Leaning close, speaking softly, he said, 'Don't imagine you're in the clear. They may let you off one murder, but there's no doubt you killed Gaius. They've got your dagger, and it's covered in blood. They'll match the blade up with that great gash in Gaius's chest, you mark my words!'

I said wearily, 'It was self-defence.'

'You'll never prove it!'

I turned to him. Feeling like I was, it was difficult to get as much out of it as I might have done, but I did my best. 'You seem to have overlooked the fact that Maximus is my friend,' I began, 'and in fact –'

'Friend! That won't do you any good, not on a murder charge.'

'I think it will.' Haven't I kept saying that, in Roman public life, everything depended on who your friends were? Flavius must have known that as well as I did, but his problem was that he wasn't aware quite how well I knew Maximus.

I tutted gently. 'You haven't been very observant, have you?'

He stiffened. 'What do you mean?'

'I suppose you haven't been with us all that long,' I went on, 'certainly, nowhere near as long as Maximus and I have worshipped together.'

He knew, then. There was no need to tell him, but I did anyway. It made me feel better.

'If you'd taken a really good look at dear old Maximus,' I whispered, 'you'd have seen he was familiar. Perhaps more familiar in a grey cloak: he's the Courier of the Sun. And he and I have been fellow Mithraists for as long as I've been in Arelate.'

He made no move until we were only a couple of miles from Arelate. I imagine he had so much to think about, so many options to consider – none of them all that hopeful – that it took him that long to decide what to do.

He launched himself on the guard first. That made good sense; the guard was the strongest and the fittest, so it was best to utilize the element of surprise – which would be lost after his initial move – to get him out of the way. Flavius attacked him from behind, leaping on to his horse, getting one arm round his throat while the other hand stuck a knife in between his ribs before the poor man had time even to shout out.

Maximus, hearing the thud as his guard landed in the dust, spun round. Flavius was right behind him, knife still in his hand.

I shouted, *'No!'*, at the same time kicking my horse and lunging towards Flavius. I was too slow: although my action succeeded in nudging him and spoiling his aim, somehow he must have caught Maximus with a glancing blow – maybe with his elbow, I don't know. Anyway, poor old Maximus fell off his horse, and I heard him groaning as he lay on the ground.

Flavius wheeled his horse round, facing me.

He stared at me, dark eyes more threatening than any man's I've ever seen. He said, 'I'll get you.'

Then he kicked his horse and galloped away.

It was callous to leave Maximus where he'd fallen, and I'm not proud of it. Especially when he'd supported me so loyally. But I had Theo to think about, and anyway Maximus wasn't badly hurt.

He seemed to understand. I took his cloak out of the bag hanging on his saddle and made a cushion for his head, and he thanked me in a faint little voice.

'I have to go,' I said. 'You'll be all right – this is the main road into the town, someone's bound to come by before too long.'

'Don't worry about me,' he whispered. 'I'm fine. He didn't stab me, although I fear my nose may be broken.'

I looked at it. It was bleeding quite badly – he might have been right. 'I'm sorry,' I said.

'Go.' He pushed me feebly away. I stood up, and was getting ready to remount when he said something else. I thought he said something about the boy – Flavius, I imagined he meant – but when I turned back to ask, he had his eyes closed so I didn't bother.

I'd already decided where I had to go. Theo might have

run to Cassius's farm, or back to my villa. But I knew he hadn't.

That quiet voice inside my head had been telling me, ever since we left the hillside, that he'd run home.

29

I kept to the tracks and the little-known paths across the marshes. There were never all that many travellers crossing the delta, especially first thing in the morning, and those who were about probably desired secrecy as much as I did: a place with a reputation for nefarious goings-on, the delta.

But few of even the shadiest characters went around with their tunics soaked in other men's blood.

As the sun grew stronger I stopped by a pond to refresh myself. My horse had a drink, I had a drink, then I took off my tunic and held the soiled part under the water, rubbing at it until the worst of the blood had come out. I squeezed it out and put it back on again. It felt horribly chilly against my flesh, but clean water was preferable to Gaius's blood, even if it was a great deal colder.

At first as I rode off again, I thought it was the wet tunic making me feel shivery. But when I started to feel dizzy as well, I realized it was probably something more serious. I wished I had my old military cloak, but last night I'd only taken with me the scarlet cloak of my Lion costume. And that I'd left stashed away on the temple hillside. Not that wearing a bright-red cloak would have helped my desire to be inconspicuous.

I began to worry that I wouldn't remember the way to Theo's house. I'd only been there once, after all, and, with all the circling round Theo and I had done on that trip, we'd probably approached the place from a different direction.

Concentrating hard – which was becoming increasingly

difficult – I ticked off various landmarks until, many hours and several wrong turns later, at last I found it.

But the shutters were up and the door closed; it looked as if nobody was there.

I felt like giving up. All that way, all that effort, and they weren't there! I'd have to start back for the villa, for the farm, and hope it wouldn't be too late, that I'd find him before Flavius did.

I'll sit here a while and rest, I thought, sliding out of the saddle. As my feet touched the ground my legs gave way. The dark earth smelled good under my face. I closed my eyes.

In a dream I saw Zillah, bare-headed, hair escaped from its knot and blowing round her face. She looked very beautiful. My hands went up to pull her closer to me, and I kissed her.

The pain of being shaken, dragged into a sitting position, made me cry out.

'Shh!' someone said. 'Hold the horse still, Theo, he'll have to ride to the house. He's far too heavy to carry.'

More pain. Standing up made my head swim, and I thought I was going to be sick.

The horse's pace was considerately gentle. He was probably as worn out as I was. We were both far too old for this sort of fun and games.

Theo and Zillah supported me as we crept inside. Theo said something about seeing to my horse – 'Hide him well!', his mother ordered – and she helped me to a narrow bed, where, thankfully, I lay down.

I felt her hands on my head. She found all three lumps, gasping with growing alarm as she discovered each one. Then I felt something cool being rubbed on, something that stung at first then soothed. My head started to feel numb, which was a great improvement.

'Drink this.' She held a cup to my lips. 'You must sleep.'

'We have to get away,' I said drowsily.

'Oh yes? And where were you thinking of going, when it took two of us to get you across the fifty yards from where you'd collapsed to the house?'

She was right. 'Zillah?'

'Yes?'

'Give me a hug.'

She made a sound that was half-laugh, half-sob. Then she put her arms round me and held me to her luxurious chest. Whatever she gave me in that drink took effect quickly: I fell asleep still in her arms.

When I woke up the sun was pouring in through a window on the other side of the house; I must have slept away the rest of the day and all the night. I realized straight away that I felt better.

Zillah and Theo were sitting on a bench beside my bed. It looked as if they'd been waiting for me to wake up.

'Hello,' I said.

Both faces broke into smiles. 'How are you feeling?' Zillah asked, at the same moment as Theo said, 'Are you all right, Sergius? You look dreadful.'

'I'm feeling fine,' I said, trying to sound hearty.

'Are you hungry?'

'Zillah, I'm starving.'

Instantly she got up and disappeared into the next room, returning with a tray she must have prepared for my awakening. There was bread, goat's cheese, some pieces of dried meat, some fruit. She made Theo hold in his impatience till I'd finished everything, then said, 'All right. Now we can talk.'

I glared at him. 'You played right into their hands when you followed them back up the hillside. You should have run as fast as you could back to Cassius's farm once you'd escaped from Gaius! I was so angry when I saw you that

I'd have given you a good thrashing if I'd caught you.'

He grinned. 'No you wouldn't. And I *had* to go after them – they were going to kill the bull!'

'That's what they wanted you to think. The bull wasn't in any danger.' Or he wasn't once Flavius had disrupted our ceremony, I could have added.

'I know that *now*,' he said quietly.

I put out my hand to take his. 'All right. It wasn't your fault – they were cunning, those two.'

'What's happened to the other one?' Zillah asked.

'He got away. That's why we have to go –' I swung my feet to the floor, preparing to get up – 'he may find his way here. And he's after both of us now, Theo.'

'He's –' Theo began.

His mother shushed him. She watched me for a moment, then said, 'He's after all three of us.'

I stared at her. She turned to Theo. 'Go and get it,' she said.

He slipped into the next room, returning with something in his hands.

He held it out.

It was the Pater's sacrificial knife.

I said as the shock subsided, 'Theo, you shouldn't have stolen it.'

'But –'

'It's all right,' Zillah said softly. 'He said we could. He said we should be armed.'

I wasn't following them at all. 'Who did?' Then, as the implication of what she'd just said sank in, '*We*?'

They glanced at each other. Then Zillah said, 'I think I'd better start at the beginning.'

'I wish you would,' I muttered.

'You were so busy trailing Gaius without letting him see you that you didn't look behind you to see if anyone was trailing *you*,' she said.

'And presumably someone was.'

'Yes. Me.'

I smiled. 'I guessed that much.' She'd done it well, I had to give her that. 'May I ask why?'

'You once said Gaius must be outstandingly stupid, and I said you were right. Remember?' I nodded. 'He was stupid enough to drop hints about where he was going last night. He thought he was being subtle – far too subtle for a mere woman to understand what he meant – but naturally he wasn't. He didn't reveal the entire plan, but I picked up enough to know Theo was in danger.'

'So of course you had to follow him.'

'Of course.'

I'd been about to make some sarcastic comment about her needlessly putting herself in danger when others were perfectly capable of looking after Theo, but I didn't. Bearing in mind what had happened to me, it wouldn't have carried much weight. 'So you were up at the sacrifice stone,' I said.

'Yes.'

I saw you, I thought. What I took for hallucination was actually happening.

She had gone quite pale. I wasn't surprised.

'I heard you scream,' I said to Theo. 'As I fell back against the rock, I heard you. And –'

I didn't want to recall that moment of hopelessness.

Zillah put her hand over mine. 'You couldn't help it,' she said quietly.

'What happened?' I hated having to ask.

'Two men in cloaks came along the passage,' she said. 'It was weird – they had masks on, and one had a great staff in his hand – it was almost as if they were figures out of a dream. They were very angry – they said one of the young men had stolen a sacred knife. They saw what was happening . . .' she paused, then went on. 'They were like some terrible avenging force, they had swords and they overcame those men as if they had some supernatural power working through them.'

I could see it. The Pater and the Courier of the Sun, acting partly as the senior Mithraists they were, partly as upholders of Rome and her laws. In neither capacity would they have tolerated the killing of an innocent boy on their sacrifice stone.

And, as Zillah had perceived, the full power of Mithras was with them.

'They released Theo, then tied the man who'd stolen their knife to the stone,' she whispered. 'I was terrified that the other one would launch himself on them – he was years younger, he looked as if he could have fought the pair of them, under normal circumstances.'

She was staring in front of her, wide-eyed. I guessed she was seeing the scene all over again.

'But he didn't?' I prompted softly.

'No. He ran away.' There was contempt in her voice, as well there might be. I felt more than contempt. But then I knew that Flavius and Varus had been brothers.

'And then?'

'Then – then – I hadn't realized they knew I was there. But they called me. Said, "Come forward."' Briefly she covered her face with her hands. Then, sitting up straight, went on: 'Theo came running to me, and I was torn between wanting to comfort him and wanting to kill that man who'd been about to . . .' She couldn't say it.

'I understand,' I said.

She looked at me, and I had the impression she was making up her mind about something. Then: 'They did too, those masked men. They offered me their knife.'

I saw again that savage wound in Varus's throat. Inflicted by the terrible hand of the mother whose son he'd been about to slaughter.

She'd accepted the offer, I knew. I didn't even bother to ask.

'I had to tell you,' she muttered. 'It's only fair.'

I didn't know what to say. I would have killed Varus,

had I not been rendered incapable. Varus had deserved to die. I squeezed her hand. 'Yes.'

Her eyes shot to mine. 'You don't mind?'

I almost laughed. 'It's not up to me to mind, he's your son.' I glanced at him; he was sitting on the edge of his bench as if my reaction mattered as much to him as it did to her. 'Your mother's a wild woman,' I said lightly. I looked back at her. 'As well as a brave one.'

She slipped to her knees and buried her face in the blankets still tangled round me. I stroked the back of her head.

There was something else I had to know. It was unfair to wonder, perhaps, in view of everything else that had been going on, but, although I tried to stop myself, in the end I had to ask.

'Zillah?'

'Hmm?'

'Did you see me, up there?'

I felt the movement of her head against my thighs as she nodded.

'And you . . . didn't you . . .'

She raised her face and looked at me. 'Didn't I try to help you?' she supplied.

'I have no right to ask,' I said hurriedly, 'when –'

'You have every right.' She dropped her eyes. 'I tended you, of course I did – I was terrified that you'd been killed too, and I thanked God with all my strength when I felt your heart still beating. They – the men with the masks – looked at you as well, and one of them said it was a miracle you had such a thick skull.' I sent an ironic thank you to whichever of my Brothers had made that reassuring observation. 'They said you were best left, that you'd come round in your own good time.'

'And you agreed?' I couldn't prevent the self-pitying tone.

She hung her head. 'Yes.'

'Why didn't you . . .'

Her eyes returned to mine. 'I was afraid. Afraid you'd see what I'd done, and that you wouldn't approve.'

'But now you've admitted it of your own accord.'

She smiled slightly. 'I've had time to adjust. And as you said yourself, Theo's my son.'

Indeed he was. I didn't have any argument with his mother dispatching the man who'd just been about to kill him.

And I understood now why she'd left me lying there.

She had dropped her head into my lap once more, and I resumed my stroking of her hair.

I didn't see that there was anything more to say.

'We have to get away,' I said some time later.

'Yes.' She stood up, began looking around the sparsely furnished room as if deciding what to pack.

'Flavius will be after us.' It was quite possible that there would be repercussions from the Arelate administration, too; double murders weren't common, and Gaius had certain connections. Maximus, Mithras bless him, would do his best for me, I had no doubt. But would Gaius have friends who would argue the opposite case and insist on my arrest?

I don't know if I was really concerned about those dangers. What I do remember is a sudden weariness, an urgent need to leave it all behind me. To start again.

With Zillah and Theo.

'Where shall we go?' Theo asked eagerly. He was bright-eyed, full of the excitement of setting out.

Several possibilities flashed through my mind. None of them were any good. I realized with a sinking of the heart that I didn't have an answer.

She had gone to stand beside Theo. Both of them waiting for me to tell them what to do, and I didn't have a clue. Wherever we went someone would notice us – a man, a woman and a boy stood out more than a solitary traveller. Whichever way we went we had several hundred miles of Roman Empire to cross before we would escape into anyone else's territory. Not that I'd have suggested we went towards the wild lands beyond the Rhenus – even Flavius would have been better than warring tribesmen.

Could we get hold of a gipsy caravan and join the migrant people of the delta? No, we'd be spotted in no time. Someone would betray us, sooner or later – there would be a price on our heads, before long.

'Shall we go to Cassius's farm?' Theo said.

'No.' I looked at him, aware that I was dashing his hopes. 'If anyone came after us and found us there, Cassius would get into trouble for harbouring us.'

'Oh.'

I'd never realized how much sadness could be expressed in one short word.

Despair spread through the little room like a bad smell. I tried a few more possibilities, seeing us on the road, hiding, searching for food, shelter. I saw a troop of soldiers hunting for us, sweeping down across the delta until we had our backs to the sea and there was nowhere else to run.

It wasn't a good picture.

Theo said suddenly, 'Why don't we take a boat? Father's boat is still tied up at the Saints' Village.'

'And just where would we go?' I regretted my tone, but somehow I couldn't help it.

'The two Marys came from over the great sea!' he cried, his hopeless idea taking firm hold. 'They came in a boat with no sails and no rudder, all that way, and they landed here! We can sail off somewhere too!'

I said patiently, 'Theo, do you know how to navigate?'

'No, but –'

'Neither do I, beyond working out which way's north. And where would we be navigating *to*, anyway?'

'*I* don't know!' His tone seemed to suggest he'd had the

brainwave, the details were up to me. 'You could take us somewhere safe.'

I hated to do it, but I had to squash his bright optimism. Before it really got a hold on him, and he started resenting me for not adopting his plan. I loved him and his mother far too dearly to risk taking them off out to sea in some dubious craft that had been neglected for gods knew how many years and probably leaked like an old bucket. It would be better to stay here and somehow face whatever was coming to us.

He was still going on about the Marys, how they'd trusted to their god and he'd protected them.

'Theo, it's just a legend,' I said gently. 'Things like that just don't happen in real life.'

But I heard his words in my head, over and over again. They trusted to their god and he protected them.

Theo and Zillah had a god. He was different from mine, but apparently they trusted in him.

I trusted in my god, too. He'd been guiding my steps for a long time now. He'd guided dear old Maximus, too, and the Pater. Deliberately I emptied my mind to let him speak.

I saw again the image of the three of us, Theo, Zillah and me, on the shore. A circle of guards was closing on us. A man with a sword was coming up to me.

Flavius stood laughing in the background.

Then I saw a small boat, its patched sails filling with the offshore breeze as it curved in a wide arc away from the land.

I said to Theo, 'Just how long do you think it'd take us to get to this old boat, then?'

We left at dusk. I let my horse go free: patting his neck one last time, I said a silent prayer for his safety. There was plenty of grazing on the delta – plenty of other horses, too. Perhaps he'd summon the energy to add something of himself to the stock.

Zillah had prepared two large packs, clothing and food wrapped inside blankets. They weren't very heavy; she didn't have much. Outside one of the outbuildings I found a water butt which I sawed in half; we'd need to catch every drop of water to supplement what we could take on board.

Nobody was about. We had an uneventful journey, and Theo led us straight to his father's boat.

We untied and cast off before anyone had a chance to spot us. Before any of us had a chance to think, too: it seemed best.

As the land fell away to our stern, I felt the god beside me.

I could see him in my mind's eye. He seemed to be smiling.

30

Beth's lasting impressions of the Gargano peninsula were that it was as rich in saints and holy legends as most places of a similar quiet nature are in corner shops and postboxes, and that it had little sleepy towns where the roads were so narrow that the traffic jammed up; she and Adam had to wait an impatient twenty minutes in their hire car when a huge load of tomatoes was spilt from a lorry negotiating a tight corner.

Like everyone else in the immediate vicinity, they'd got out of the car and helped themselves to a kilo or two. In later years, when something happened to remind her of those hectic two days, she would taste plump, sweet tomatoes.

A new side of Adam revealed itself as she watched him slip into working mode. In a way she regretted the loss of the man she was just beginning to love; a more sensible part of her recognized that this efficiency – which seemed to allow little time for anything but pursuit of the Roman's trail – was the only option.

They'd caught an early flight, arriving in Rome in time to collect the car before everything shut down for lunch. She had navigated, somehow managing to guide Adam out of the city and on to the Naples *autostrada*. That was the hard bit – she wondered if the Roman had been lending her a helping hand. After that, it was simply a matter of telling Adam when to turn off at the junctions which, along successive motorways and minor roads, finally got them to Gargano.

Again and again, she wished she'd brought *The Canonization of the Early Christian Saints* with her. But, she consoled herself, I've remembered the most important fact.

The name of the town where a saint called Teodoro had lived.

The priest of the Church of St Teodoro had not only answered all their questions, but also found them lodgings for the night in his sister's small hotel. Adam had introduced Beth and himself to the priest, giving their full names, Adam Gilbert and Beth Leighton. This had naturally meant the priest's sister had put them in separate rooms.

Beth, who had been so worn out that she'd fallen asleep the moment she'd lain down, reflected in the morning that to have pretended they were married and asked for a double would have been a complete waste of time.

On the flight back to Marseilles, they put together what they had found out. It had been easy: in the small port whose name she'd remembered from Joe's book, not only the priest but everyone else had known about St Teodoro – he was as popular as St Spiridon was in Corfu, and, judging by the number of times they heard people calling out the name, there were as many local Teodoros as there were Corfiot Spiros.

'Listen to this and see if I've left anything out,' Adam said.

'Go on, then.' She closed her eyes, partly as an aid to concentration, partly because she enjoyed listening to his voice without any visual distractions.

Adam read from his notes.

'"Legend has it that, on a dark night with a howling storm battering the coast, a small boat was cast up on the shore of the Gargano peninsula, on the only safe spot beneath a cliff face. In the boat were three passengers, a middle-aged couple and a young boy. All were far gone in exhaustion, suffering terribly from exposure and dehydration; their rescuers had all but given them up for dead when the boy spoke, saying that God had guided them."'

'You didn't say about the little chapel that was built on the spot where they landed, the one which we saw.'

'It's not relevant.'

That shuts *me* up, she thought, smiling to herself. 'Carry on.'

'"The people were tended by the villagers, and slowly they recovered. The boy, whose name was Teodoro, claimed they had come from what is now Provence but was then the Roman Provincia; they were, he claimed, fleeing from persecution." Okay?'

'Mm.'

Taking that for assent, he continued. '"Little more is recorded of the man and the woman. Once Teodoro had grown to manhood, they seem to have slipped quietly into the background. The young Teodoro was a great animal-lover, and –"'

'Wasn't it great when we found that animals' corner in the church by the market and the priest told us about Teodoro blessing the creatures in his preaching?' she interrupted.

'Yes. It was another bit of evidence, wasn't it?'

'Circumstantial, a policeman would say.'

'What a good job we're not policemen. Shall I go on?'

'Please do.'

'"Teodoro acquired a reputation as a healer and protector of all life. In his case there is evidence for the reputation being justified and not, as with St Francis of Assisi, a subsequent sentimental addition."'

'The Establishment won't like that,' she remarked.

'They won't like any of this. Isn't that the whole point?'

She thought of Joe and his certainty. Of the Reverend Derek, to whom she'd taken a dislike before even having met him. 'It is.'

'"In maturity Teodoro became a champion of the

oppressed, a protector of the persecuted. And, unusual in his day, he showed remarkable tolerance of other faiths; a devout Christian, nevertheless he had the width of vision to accept that other gods were as deeply loved by their followers as was his own."'

'Are you going to put in what we thought, that it could be because he'd lived with and grown to love the Roman, who wasn't a Christian but a Mithraist?'

'I could add a footnote.' He did so. '"In old age he – Teodoro – became an advocate of the doctrine – many called it a heresy – that all gods were ultimately united in the one Godhead. He died peacefully around the year AD 255, at an advanced age, a loved and honoured figure. He was canonized in 284, and has been commemorated and revered ever since."'

'Great,' she said. 'That says it all.'

'It says enough to make us believe St Teodoro of Gargano and St Theodore of Arles are the same person. Whether or not we'll be able to convince anyone else remains to be seen.'

'Let's assemble our argument.' The steward had just gone by, and Beth and Adam had ordered gins and tonics. 'The accepted story of Little Saint Theodore says he was murdered by a Roman officer.' She poured tonic on what looked like a huge gin, taking a large sip. 'The child's body was found by the local Christian community, who broadcast the details of the boy's slaughter far and wide, holding it up as an example of brutal Roman persecution of the young Christian faith. Roman tolerance finally ran out when the Christians began to attack the sites sacred to the Roman gods, at which the Romans rounded up the Christians, put them on trial and executed them.'

'The Gospel according to Joe,' Adam said. 'So, how do we make a convincing case for showing it's all wrong?'

'That's where Teodoro and Gargano come in. If the Roman didn't kill Theodore, either the Christians made up the story of finding the body or else the body was that of someone else. But the Roman was the killer – he'd killed *someone* – that was fundamental to their tale.'

'So if the Roman was innocent and being framed, what was more logical than that he'd try to get both the boy and himself away, considering he'd gone to the trouble of saving the boy from being a sacrifice?'

'The woman went too, whoever she was. Perhaps she was the Roman's wife.'

'Hold on a minute.' Adam sounded worried. 'This is a Roman we're speaking of, a Roman in a Roman province. Why should he have been on the run from a group of Christians, when they were in the minority then and already the subject of persecution?'

'Damn,' she muttered. Then, rallying, 'Maybe he was afraid some sort of Christian resistance movement would get him.'

'That's possible. Or maybe he was worried that his own people would think he was just too much trouble, and quietly dispose of him.'

She was silent for some time. Eventually he said, 'What are you thinking?'

'You're going to think it sounds sentimental and silly.'

'Don't mind me.'

'Well, I was just picturing him. Imagining him caring for the boy he'd saved. Perhaps he ran away with him because he loved him.'

'There speaks the scientist,' Adam remarked.

She said loftily, 'The best scientists have imagination.'

'Perhaps you've just experienced another prompted hunch.'

Although he said it with a laugh, she didn't think he was so far from the truth.

She finished her gin. 'All that's left is the Saintes-Maries connection.'

'That has to be pure speculation,' he objected.

'So what's new? We ought to think about it – it's fuel to our argument.'

'Only just!'

'If those people could get from the Holy Land to Provence in an open boat, then Theodore and co. could get from Provence to Gargano. The whole bloody Mediterranean was probably constantly criss-crossed with bands of people helplessly drifting about in open boats.' She wondered if the gin was going to her head.

Adam took her empty glass from her so that he could hold her hand. She thought he might be suffering from the gin, too, because he flopped against her lovingly and said, 'My darling, you're pissed.'

It was late afternoon by the time they'd collected Adam's car at Marseilles and driven back to Arles. The priest's sister's hotel hadn't had very luxurious washing arrangements; Beth was longing for a shower and a change of clothes.

'Back to my place?' Adam suggested as they were held up for the umpteenth time by heavier than usual Arles traffic.

'Yes please. We must have at least a couple of hours before sunset – that ought to be long enough to freshen up and get out to Our Lady of the Marshlands. Provided this traffic lets up, that is.'

'I've only seen it as bad as this on bullfight days. Perhaps there's one today, and . . . Oh, hell.'

'What is it?'

Silently he pointed, and she looked where he was indicating. It didn't make any demands on her French to translate the huge banner strung across the road: *Come to Our Lady of the Marshlands! Witness the miracle for yourselves!*

Now that they were alerted, they could see that the whole town was stirred up. Newspaper headlines screeched of Little Saint Theodore and Little Chantal Bordanado, stalls which had suddenly sprung up where they hadn't been before were groaning under the weight of plaster effigies of the saint, plastic rosaries, postcards and bundles of carrier bags with Theodore's sickly face crudely copied on them.

The whole of Arles was dressed in its best, women in national costume and starched headdresses, men in dark suits, girls in their first communion dresses, whiter than white, as if proud mothers had hoped that a daughter in pristine, virginal white might be rewarded, like Chantal, with a vision.

Adam said, 'So much for the trusty sympathetic journalists. One of them's let the cat out of the bag.' He turned to Beth, grinning. 'Ready for the fray?'

She replied firmly, 'You bet!'

The traffic was so thick on the road to the Church of Our Lady of the Marshlands that they abandoned the car and walked the last mile. As they entered the village, deep in a throng of elated people and already over-excited children, the sun was just touching the distant horizon.

Although the road was full of shuffling people, a vehicle of some sort was trying to get through, from the direction of Arles. Incongruously, a public address system somewhere was blasting out 'All Things Bright and Beautiful'. Turning, Adam said, 'You're not going to believe this.'

She turned too. Through the crowds an ancient Renault truck was gently nosing, its open back festooned with white ribbons and flowers. Among the sombre-clad clergy, clutching on to its rail and vainly trying to maintain a vestige of dignity, stood Joe.

Beside him was a short tubby man wearing a sleeveless pullover over his dark shirt and clerical collar. He was joining in with 'All Things Bright and Beautiful' with a strong Birmingham accent, encouraging the bemused French faithful to sing along.

Beth wanted to laugh. 'The Reverend Derek, do you think?'

'Without a doubt. He –'

Joe had spotted them. Beth saw him lean across to say something to the Reverend Derek, who nodded.

'Beth! Adam! Over here!'

The Renault paused while they made their way across to it. Helping hands dragged them up on to its back, then they were off again.

'I said I wanted you standing beside me, didn't I?' Joe was looking very smug. 'I thought I'd missed you in the crush.' Then, flinging out his arms, he bellowed, 'It's a miracle!'

Beth caught Adam's eye. 'We'll see about that,' he murmured.

Joe was making introductions. The Reverend Derek gave them each a sweaty handshake. 'The little girl is already in the church,' he explained, 'with her escort of priests. Roman Catholic priests –' he lowered his voice, glancing over his shoulder at the French clergymen behind him – 'which I suppose is only right and proper. Although on an occasion of such import as this will surely be, one might be forgiven for wishing for a greater spirit of ecumenicalism, mightn't one?'

Beth had lost the thread of his argument, but Adam agreed that one might.

'As representatives of the Church of England, we've been allotted seats inside the church,' Joe said. He was having to shout now to compete against the hymn-singing; the French had given up on 'All Things Bright and Beautiful' and had begun on something of their own. The Reverend Derek's expression suggested he considered this typically traitorous of them.

'Drop us off outside, then,' Beth shouted back, 'we'll –'

Joe's eyes had an unaccustomed brilliance. 'You're coming in,' he said. 'Didn't I just say? When Chantal Bordanado has her vision, you'll be right beside me.'

For the first time, Beth felt a tremor of fear.

Adam helped her down off the truck. They fell into step behind the French clergymen, the Reverend Derek and Joe; the Frenchmen's robes commanded respect even if the Reverend Derek's sleeveless pullover did not, and the crowd fell back for them, leaving a clear way up to the church.

Inside, every pew was crammed full, every chair taken, with as many people again standing around the areas without seating. There was a smell of sweat and garlic. What air there was felt unpleasantly damp; the humidity was building up, as if rain were on the way.

The priests went forward up the aisle, pausing to take holy water from the stoup and cross themselves. Joe and the Reverend Derek ostentatiously refrained. Beth felt embarrassed.

They sat down on a bench a few feet in front of the altar steps, on the right-hand side; Beth was crushed between Joe on her left and Adam on her right. There was only just room for them all in the small amount of space remaining; it looked as if everyone else in religious orders in the Arles area was already there.

In a wooden chair immediately in front of Beth, under a statue of St Theodore remarkably similar to the one in the Arles church, sat a little girl, dressed in a frilled and starched white dress. Her hair was in two plaits tied with huge white ribbons, and on her head, concealing her face, she wore a net veil held in place with a coronet of white flowers.

Beth studied Chantal Bordanado.

At first sight, the girl's small size suggested she was about eight or nine. But then, almost as if she felt Beth's curious eyes on her, she made a gesture of shaking back her plaits which momentarily moved aside her veil.

The face wore make-up, giving the impression of a painted doll. The eyes, beneath the crude blue eyeshadow and the mascara, held the last expression Beth would have expected to see on a devout child who genuinely believed she was about to witness a miracle.

Chantal, who was clearly nearer fourteen than eight, didn't look awestruck, nervous, or even plain scared.

She looked bored.

Then she lifted a hand whose nails were painted bright pink and gracefully drew her veil back into place.

Beth looked at the rows and rows of people. With the exception of herself and Adam, everyone else appeared to be praying.

She put her mouth right up to Adam's ear and whispered, 'Did you see what I saw?'

He nodded. He whispered back, 'The saintly child looks, as my old mum would say, like a right little madam.'

She murmured, 'Is it all just a great big con?'

'Can't be. Everyone else is fervent enough, you can feel it in the air.'

Beth shifted her weight on the narrow bench and waited to see what would happen.

Perhaps, she thought, as the minutes went by and nothing did happen, it's because nobody really knows what's meant by 'at sunset'. We've arrived too early – Chantal's dream messenger ought to have been more specific.

One of the French priests detached himself from an enclave of his colleagues and walked up to the altar; he knelt down on the steps, crossed himself and spent a few moments in silent prayer. Having thus commanded the rapt attention of the entire congregation, who stopped their muttering and shuffling, he turned to them and began a long address. He spoke too fast for Beth to understand exactly what he was saying, but he seemed to be reciting the details of Little Saint Theodore's martyrdom.

He was a fine preacher; the force of his conviction flowed from him out over the awestruck congregation. Beth found it didn't matter that she couldn't manage to catch every word – she was with him, prepared to believe him . . .

As he reached the core of the tale, the priest raised his arms out wide in an expansive gesture to match the power of his voice. But the words that spoke of the slaughter, of the brutal Roman hand that cut the throat of an innocent Christian child, were drowned by a sudden appalling sound.

It could have been the first clap of thunder that heralded one of those swiftly burgeoning Mediterranean storms which beset the Midi in late summer.

To Beth, it sounded like the bellow of an angry bull.

Clutching on to Adam, she felt her own fear mirrored in the hundreds of people in the church. The priest felt it, too; instead of repeating the lost words, he turned back to face the altar, and once more knelt in prayer.

Beth was watching Chantal. As the priest returned to his bench, the girl, almost as if she were responding to a cue, slowly got to her feet.

Moving as if in a dream, she approached the altar, where she sank to her knees. The congregation was utterly still.

Then, as if obeying a silent command, suddenly she stiffened, stood up, and strode over to the statue of St Theodore. For some moments she stood beneath it, then, throwing back her veil, she gave a great cry.

Her words rang out in the hushed church. '*Il pleure! Regardez, regardez lui, il pleure!*'

The congregation responded with a collective gasp, and Beth felt an enormous pressure build up behind her as people strained forwards, desperate not to miss the miracle.

The cry was taken up by a reedy, cracked voice: '*Il pleure!*' An elderly nun in the row behind Beth was on her feet, thin body swaying, ecstasy on the face. The rheumy old eyes were swimming, as if she were weeping in sympathy with the little saint.

And another voice joined in. An English voice, male: Beth felt a violent, surging movement beside her as Joe leapt up and shouted, 'He's crying!'

For several minutes the whole congregation, which was rapidly rising to its feet, was loud with a buzzing of joyful reaction.

But then it faded. There were no more shouts; no one else claimed to see the saint's tears.

With an effort, Beth had turned her attention from the bland pink face of St Theodore, unmarked by any suggestion of a tear, to the figure of Chantal, now on her knees before the statue. Close enough to see what almost everyone else would have missed, she saw the child glance over her shoulder towards the priest who had addressed the congregation.

It was conceivable that Chantal might have sought guidance as to what she should do next, even if she had just witnessed a vision, although Beth felt that such an experience would surely have rendered most children incapable of anything but a shocked numbness.

What surprised Beth was the angry scowl on Chantal's face; it was as if she were saying, I've done my best, now get me out of here!

'Adam,' she whispered, nudging him.

He had his eyes on Chantal. Without turning round, he nodded.

As the girl had done earlier, the priest, too, now took up his cue; striding once more to the altar steps, he exhorted the congregation to pray in thankfulness for being present at such an event. The Reverend Derek got up to join in, but Joe, who seemed to be quite overcome, clutched him round the knees as if he were tackling him and refused to let go; the Reverend Derek, not to be denied his moment of glory, merely began to belt out a prayer where he stood.

But priest, parson and faithful people were all silenced by another great blast from the darkening sky above; as the echoes of the furious sound died away, the rain started to hammer down on the roof.

It sounded like galloping hooves.

The last light of the sun must have been obscured by clouds, for it was very dark now inside the church. Whispers of panic crept from the corners; a child's frightened cry was abruptly hushed, an elderly man's querulous voice broke on a nervous sob.

One of the priests pushed past Beth, grabbed a handful of the tall votive candles from the box beneath St Theodore's plinth, lit them and stuck them in the holders before the statue.

Behind the little saint, a shadow seemed to leap across the stone wall of the church. The young bull's strong muscles bunched as he ran, the cloak of the figure on its back flew out behind him. And the face of the god was kind, full of love . . .

Beth blinked, shook her head; the god and the bull were gone.

Other candles had been lit – the storm must have blown the electric lights – and the growing panic had disappeared with the coming of the light. People were leaving, calmly, contentedly, as if they had forgotten what they had been there for and were setting off for home after some ordinary, pleasantly everyday gathering.

Adam stood up, grabbing her hand. 'Come on – let's mingle with the crowd, see if we can pick up any reaction.'

'But what about Joe?' She turned to look at him; the Reverend Derek had sat him down on the bench and was fanning him with his prayer book.

'He'll be all right.'

Adam was shouldering a way through the massed ranks of clergy towards the central aisle, and, her hand held too firmly for her to wriggle it free, she went with him.

Outside, their inhibitions removed once they were no longer in the church, people were chatting, relating what they had seen. Or hadn't seen: there were shrugs, smiles, remarks to the effect that whatever had been revealed to Chantal Bordanado had remained hidden from everyone else. The elderly nun, it was suggested, was probably almost blind, and the young man who had shouted – my brother! Beth thought, struck with the familiar mixture of affection and irritation – had probably had too much sun.

'"*On voit ce qu'on veut voire*": you see what you want to see,' Adam said. 'That's the judgement.'

Beth said softly, 'Did you see the shadow on the wall? Like we saw up at the Mithraeum?'

He hesitated, then said, 'Yes.'

'Did anyone else?'

He looked down at her. 'Don't ask me.' He smiled wryly. 'I doubt it. I imagine we only did because we'd seen something so similar before.'

'Yet it calmed them. Didn't it?'

'Something did. More likely it was the sudden light shining out in the darkness.'

They were gradually moving away from the church. Conversations around them were now showing a degree of scepticism: a woman remarked that she'd heard the Bordanado girl had a history of attention-seeking, and her companion replied she didn't see what all the fuss was about. A man said he'd have been better off at home watching the football than listening to some priest spouting ancient legends that no one believed in any more.

By the time they'd got back to the car, they'd heard enough; public opinion, it seemed, was that the evening had been an interesting diversion, ultimately unconvincing.

The practical men and women of Arles, Beth decided, all looked slightly embarrassed.

They went back to The Yellow House where, some time later, Joe joined them.

He was alone: when Beth asked what had happened to the Reverend Derek, he merely shrugged.

She and Adam watched from the doorway of the study while Joe started to pack up his books and his papers.

I've got to ask him, she thought.

'Joe?'

'Hm?'

'Did you really see the saint crying?'

He didn't answer. She glanced at Adam, who silently shook his head.

'Er – we're going out for a drink,' she said. 'D'you want to come?'

Without looking up he said, 'No thanks.'

Outside, Adam said, 'I have a feeling his paper may not now have the conviction it once might have had.'

A part of her wanted to cry. 'No.'

'Beth?'

'I'm all right!'

They walked on in silence. Then Adam said, 'Where are we going? Do you really want a drink?'

'No.' Suddenly she knew exactly what she did want. 'Let's go to the amphitheatre.'

What had once been the heart of Roman Arles was as full of strolling, chatting people as it would have been after an afternoon's entertainment in the arena. The bars and restaurants were full, and there was singing from one of the pavement cafés. Beth and Adam were not the only ones to be drawn to the amphitheatre; several groups had settled on the curved rows of seats, and occasional bursts of laughter rose into the clear night air.

The storm had passed as if it had never been.

Beth led the way, going in through the arched entrance and setting off around the shadowy colonnade. Without comment, Adam walked beside her.

It's gone, she thought. Whatever it was I was picking up – despair, grief, hopelessness – is no longer here. Not for me, anyway. It's just an old ruined building.

She didn't know if she felt sad or relieved.

She walked on, to the point where she'd first seen the Roman. The dark passage ahead remained empty.

'It was here, wasn't it?' Adam said softly.

'Yes. How did you know?'

'I – Something told me, that day we all came here together, when Joe and I were arguing about the Christians. I felt as if I wanted to come and help you, yet I couldn't. In retrospect, I suppose you had to experience him for yourself.'

'I did that, all right.'

They slowed to a stop, and stood side by side.

'He's not here,' she said.

'He doesn't need to be.'

'Have we done what he wanted, do you think?' She looked up at him, hardly able to make out his features in the dim light.

'We must have done.'

'I'm not sure what we did do. We proved to our own satisfaction that the legend was wrong, we went along to that fiasco at Our Lady of the Marshlands, and nothing happened. How is that doing what the Roman wanted of us? We didn't do anything!'

'That's what I thought too, at first.' He hesitated. 'But now, I'm not so sure. I think – oh, I don't know how to put it into words! I feel that somehow, because we knew what really happened, perhaps also because we'd discovered that Mithras relief up in the hills and seen it move, he – the Roman – was able to use us as a catalyst. To move through us, through our faith in him, so that his power – the power of his god, perhaps – was able to spread out over the congregation.'

'It was when the candles were lit,' she whispered. 'They'd been starting to panic, those hundreds of people, then suddenly there was calm.'

She sensed Adam move towards her, and felt his arms go around her. He said quietly, 'Mithras was a god of light.'

After a while they strolled out from the colonnade and in among the stone seats overlooking the arena, finding a place to sit down a little apart from any of the other groups.

'Shall we go back to my flat?' Adam said presently.

She turned to smile at him. It was what she wanted, more than anything. 'Soon,' she said. He leaned towards her to kiss her, slowly, gently. She knew what was ahead for them, and she welcomed it with all her heart.

She looked down into the arena, empty now, its golden sand pale grey in the moonlight. She said suddenly, 'Are you in a hurry to do your gipsy film?'

'Why do you ask?' She heard amusement in his voice, as if he knew very well the reason for her question.

'I was just thinking what wonderful material we've discovered. What a story we – you – could tell. And how thoroughly you could put the record straight if you decided to go ahead.'

He laughed softly. 'I guess the gipsies could wait a year or two.'

She nodded in satisfaction. 'Right. Let's go home.'

As they stood up, she noticed someone standing in the shadows where once wild animals and doomed human beings had been pushed out into the sunshine. He was dressed in some white garment, and she could see him quite clearly.

Just before she turned away, she thought she saw him raise his right arm, the hand clenched into the fist of the Roman salute.

Glossary of Roman Place-Names

Aesis	Iesi
Arelate	Arles
Britannia	Britain
Coriosopitum	Corbridge
Danuvius	Danube
Eboracum	York
Gallia Narbonensis	Provence and Languedoc
Gaul	France
Glanum	ancient site with no modern equivalent; close to St Rémy-de-Provence
Germania	Germany
Italia	Italy
Mare Suebicum	Baltic Sea
Nilus (Fluvius)	River Nile
Rhenus (Fluvius)	River Rhine
Rhodanus (Fluvius)	River Rhône
Trimontium	Newstead